The Golden Gate
IS Empty

The Golden Gate *is* Empty

Eric Del Carlo

and Victor Del Carlo

White Cat Publications

The Golden Gate Is Empty is published by White Cat Publications, LLC.
Copyright © 2015 Eric Del Carlo and Victor Del Carlo

Cover art by Zagladko Sergei Ptetrovich
Cover & Interior design by Vasha Lewkowicz
Edited by Charles P. Zaglanis

FIRST EDITION
Published in February 2015

White Cat Publications, LLC.
33080 Industrial Road, Suite 101
Livonia, MI 48150
www.whitecatpublications.com

We dedicate this volume to our wives

Patricia Del Carlo (1931-2012)
The love goes on forever....

and

Samala Ray
co-conspirator, true believer, loved and loving mate

ONE.

---∞---

WARD: Nate Arrives

I BEGAN TO DIE THE DAY MY SON WAS BORN.

"Mr. Pentecost?" asked the young nurse.

I had the lights out in the waiting room. The half pint I brought with me was empty and hidden at the bottom of the waste container in the hall. My battered leather jacket was thrown over my shoulders, and I'd been sound asleep on the couch. My breath was heavy with the diesel odor of cheap vodka. I rolled over into a sitting position and my feet dropped to the floor. The last memories of a dream fragmented, leaving me to wonder who was that beautiful, Oriental girl my sleeping mind conjured, and would she be back.

"Mr. Pentecost, you're a father."

So much for the world of dreams.

"Is my wife all right?" I believe that was the first question you were supposed to ask.

"She's fine, and you have a beautiful son."

I got to my feet. They were steady. The slight limp to my step was an old friend, a souvenir from an early childhood bout with polio, which I lost, and which convinced my parents that I could never go near the water again, where they were sure I'd contracted it. With the specially built half boot I was wearing my walk was near normal. I'd contracted the acute viral infectious disease after its 1952 peak. Mine was considered an almost anomalous U.S. case. Wasn't I special.

My left leg was one inch shorter than my right. With years of exercise, however, the other devastated muscles grew back into normal functioning members of my body.

The nurse led me into Margot's room. She was holding a small, prune-faced bundle, and her face was aglow as I'd never seen it before.

"Mrs. Pentecost," said the nurse, "your husband is here."

"Come closer, so you can really see him," said Margot. Her eyes merely swept across my face, returning instantly to the small bundle that claimed all her attention.

I approached the bed. The infant gave forth a scent reminiscent of mornings, and milk and cereal.

I smiled. "He's beautiful," I said. My breath wafted towards them, and Margot's nose wrinkled slightly.

Yes, I said silently. I've been drinking again. *Still* would be more accurate. However, the sleep helped and I was sober. I leaned across the bed. My lips brushed Margot's and planted a healthy kiss on the infant's forehead. His reaction was to frown and then burrow deeper into the blanket.

"Did you call anybody yet?" asked Margot.

"I was asleep," I said. "Besides, it's four o'clock in the morning."

Margot looked at the bedside phone. "I'll make the calls, Ward," she said.

I sat down on the edge of the bed. "How long will you and Nathaniel be here?"

We had agreed on the name.

"The doctor said two days."

"And you'll be staying with your mother for a few more?"

"We agreed that would be best. The baby will be pretty demanding at first." She looked at me and then at the nurse. The young, uniformed woman got the message and quietly left the room.

Here it comes, I thought.

Margot hugged the baby closer. "After I get out of here we have to talk," she said.

"About my drinking," I said.

"Yes, mainly that, but that's not all."

My stomach dropped. I didn't say anything, but I knew that my life had suddenly and quietly and profoundly changed.

I stayed until Margot fell asleep again. The nurse came and took the baby away. I followed her out to the nursery and watched as he was quietly laid in one of the transparent cradles. He fell asleep almost immediately, giving no sign that he even knew I was there, in spite of my wavings and cooings.

I made my way out of the hospital.

It took me three separate buses to get home across town. Paying for the taxi that brought us to the hospital made a substantial dent in the family exchequer. Thankfully, that's one thing about San Francisco; it has mostly dependable public transportation.

Usually I carry a paperback science fiction book with me to use up the time when traveling by bus and streetcar. Last night I think I left it at home.

I tortured myself with thoughts of what she wanted to talk about, besides my drinking, which I was determined had come to an end last night.

I stepped off the third bus and walked one block to the apartment we'd been renting, which now would be too small for the three of us. I amended that thought. *If* there was to be an *us*.

When I got inside I immediately went to the small kitchen,

opened one of the cabinets, and took out the remaining bottle of vodka. It hadn't been opened. I remedied that, removed the screw top, and, with a mighty inward effort, poured the contents down the sink.

As it gurgled I wondered if it was too late, for my marriage, for my sobriety.

No burning bush appeared on the table, and I was reasonably certain the waters of San Francisco Bay hadn't parted. But I felt better. Somewhere, deep inside, something had changed. I think I knew what it was. Nobody was watching. This wasn't a performance. It wasn't another one of my many, meaningless dramatic gestures. I really meant it. It was for me alone. Suddenly, for this measurable present moment at least, I didn't want to drink anymore.

It had been a phase in my life, which may have just quietly ended here in this kitchen, perhaps in time and perhaps too late. Maybe I wasn't an alcoholic. Perhaps I'd just been a drunken kid, who had grown up, in this one way only, at the ripe old age of thirty-three years.

I allowed myself to preen a little, and anticipate really impressing Margot. I was certain that she would understand the importance of that gesture of upending the bottle of vodka.

I wasn't due back at my job in the mail room of City Hall for three more days, and that was Friday, and easy to get out of. The short sleep I'd had in the hospital waiting room hadn't really refreshed me, so I planned to lie down for a few hours before calling my father and mother.

The bed was still rumpled from our hurried exodus last night, but I didn't care. Throwing off my jacket, and sliding out of my zippered half boots, I dropped like a rock.

Sometime during my sleep of exhaustion, the alcoholic convulsion hit me. I lay there for two days, missing the phone calls to be made, failing to answer mine, and leaving Margot and the baby to be picked up by her parents.

I woke up without any time sense at all. It could have been any day of the week, any month of the year, or any year. The electric clock in the kitchen told me it was eleven o'clock. The sun streaking through the back window told me it was day time.

Using the bathroom and splashing water on my face did nothing to relieve this sense of temporal isolation. My legs were very weak. I realized that I'd probably had the D.T.'s. There were some foggy memories of dreams of giant ants.

I made myself a peanut butter and jelly sandwich. Instant coffee was just up to my ability level, and I made a strong black cup. When I finished ingesting those things, I felt almost able to call Margot at her parents' house, but I was not looking forward to it.

"Where have you been?" asked Margot as soon as we were connected.

"Marge, I stopped drinking," I blurted.

"I don't believe it," she said. "I believed you the first hundred times, but I'm not biting anymore."

From the cadences of her voice I realized that she was grandstanding for her parents.

"They're pretty mad?" I asked.

"Do you know what you've put my parents through?"

"No," I said. "I do not know what I put your parents through. I know I have *really* quit drinking, and you don't believe me. I've been unconscious since I got back from the hospital. Something has happened in my head. Hell, I don't even know what day it is. So, I guess I just don't care what your parents think they've gone through!"

"This conversation is ended," she said and hung up the phone.

I'd call her later, hopefully when her parents weren't hanging on every word. In a few days we were bound to be back together.

But, a few days later, we were not back together, nor ten days later, nor a few weeks later. I tried to talk to Margot by telephone. All my calls ended up with Phyllis Morton, Margot's mother, and the chill coming off the handset was strictly Antarctic.

The second week I took a bus to the outer Sunset district and tried in person. Harry Morton was in charge of handling in-person visits. We ended up swearing at each other on the front stairs, giving the neighbors quite a show, as well as possibly enlarging their vocabularies.

Fortunately it did not become violent. That would have been very bad indeed.

I didn't even think of drinking. I went to work each day. I cleaned up the apartment, washing all the dishes and silverware, scouring the pots and frying pans, and even scrubbing the floor in all three rooms. It had never looked that good when she was in charge. Of course, I didn't have to spend any time mollifying an amorous and sometimes violent drunk.

At last I'd done everything I could do. I went to bed early and tossed restlessly all night.

The following day was Saturday. I had calendars in each room of the apartment and made sure my wristwatch was accurate.

⚶

I called and talked to my father and mother briefly, explaining that Margot needed more time to recover from the childbirth, and otherwise lied about it.

My father scarcely took notice, but my mother was growing anxious to see her grandson, and was soon going to take matters in her own hand and visit the Mortons.

It was a confusing time, and while I *knew* that sooner or later we would get back together, I had misgivings about the quality of life we would have. I strongly suspected that, although I'd stopped drinking, it would be just as bad and just as painful—for me.

What happened during those months of estrangement before we resumed the marriage were privately unpleasant and unimportant matters. But I had one of the great common experiences of men, in particular, men who have had their wives leave them and then come back. The wife who came back was a stranger. She looked the same, talked the same, and in the most intimate and important ways was completely different.

I learned to wear a suit of armor over my emotions. It wasn't that uncomfortable, and the slight chafing of my soul it caused was more than offset by the lessening of my chronic emotional pain.

Six months later on a Saturday morning I went out to the big house on Santiago. Both of my parents were out and I let myself in with my own key. This time I hadn't come to raid Drake's liquor supply. I really didn't know why I was there—until I saw the dining room table. The lovingly polished mahogany surface gleamed just as I remembered it, exactly as it was the day I angered my father and frightened my mother.

Without thinking, I removed the vase of flowers and the tablecloth. Then I took a seat at the far end facing the kitchen.

"What am I doing?" I asked myself out loud. "I'm thirty-three years old, not a prepubescent kid."

They say in most stories on the subject that the gift leaves you after puberty, and they were dead wrong.

I placed my hands on the polished tabletop at arm's length. Then quietly, without strain, I drew my hands towards my body. It was effortless.

The very solid, very heavy mahogany table behaved now the same way it had when I'd startled my parents.

Quietly and gracefully it rose two feet from the floor.

TWO.

⎯⎯◈⎯⎯

NATHANAEL: The Gap

FATHER'S GRAVE WAS A SPECTACULAR ABSENCE.

There are candy-colored shuttles that will buzz one straight from the airport to the Bridge site, but I rented my own wheels instead—one of those anonymous fiberglass crafts—and driven Highway 101 in spotty traffic.

I did the city by Braille, swinging off and taking Geary, then grabbing Park Presidio going north. I was feeling my way by memory, mostly from memories of when I was too young to drive, getting around the city on a public transportation system I remembered as being a cattle car experience, full of cramming bodies, unpleasant jostling and obnoxious kids playing their obscenity-laced music. Even as a kid myself, they were *kids* (read: "hooligans") to me. I didn't like the crowding, didn't like the general rowdiness. Already what was normalcy to most people was a hostile environment to me. What did that portend?

I concentrated on the road, trying not to interview myself. I drive a lot in New York, though not so much in the city itself, which is about as fruitless an urban exercise as one can imagine. Mostly, lately, over the past eight months, I'd been making trips back and forth to Rhode Island, to a particular house with yellow shingles and a Cantonese character painted on the front door and those goddamned bolted-down toilet seats ...

Coast-hugging State Highway 1 had been rerouted, naturally, to go around the Bay to the east; but this road had been it once. I entered the Presidio, a bygone military preserve full of woods and swept by the ocean winds. I was holding the wheel tightly, watching the center stripe with exaggerated caution. Was I expecting something untoward and dramatic to happen now, just before I reached my destination? A blowout, a cracked axle—something that would spin me helplessly into the guard rail?

Shut up. For the love of God, shut up. Stop turning every moment of your life into literature that no one is interested in reading.

I deliberately dropped a hand from the wheel, snapped on the radio. Again I worked off of memory, tuning in semi-familiar frequencies. I am a native San Franciscan, and though that fact didn't fill me with any especial pride, I wasn't about to be a timid tourist in my home town. I knew where things were, damnit. I didn't need to ask anyone for help.

Some stations seemed to have retained the music formats I remembered. Some hadn't. But by now it didn't matter. I was at the Bridge site. Time to find parking.

There had been a great hue and cry—of a particular San Franciscan tenor—when they tried to make this an entrance-fee attraction. I'd seen the protests on the national news back East, heard the local politicos doing their grandstanding best to get in a catchy sound bite for the cameras. The Bridge Highway and Transportation District had some claim to the disposition of the land in question, but in the end the site was left in the public domain.

Even so, here I was parking in a crowded, steeply priced lot. If they don't get you one way, they'll find another.

My thumb was buzzing as I got out, taking along my jacket. October is usually warm here, but the inescapable Pacific winds sawed at me. I glanced down. I'd turned my pager back on after getting off the plane. It was past business hours back in New York, but "business hours" is a term mired in obsolescence, since, at age twenty-seven, I belong to the Plugged-In Generation ... and so it will remain until technology installs the inevitable service outlet in the cerebral cortex. Probably you'll be able to get night-light plug-ins in many festive colors for when you're not electronically mainlining.

Digits crawled around the outside of the band I wore below the knuckle of my left thumb. I shut off the buzzer and checked the area codes. 212 and 401. Of course. The New York office, probably Terry or April. *Nathanael, where's your copy on* Gap Through Her Heart? I'd read the book on the flight out here. That wasn't any sort of disaster. 401, however, was Rhode Island, and that meant the Purple Witch. Attitudes, moods, hysteria, delirium, fury. So wide a range that the only way to determine what she wanted was to answer the page.

I wasn't up to it. Not now. Not just this moment.

It was the weekend, and the site was busy. Lots of tourists, but this place had always drawn them. Japanese, Europeans, Australians. Also a lot of out-of-state license plates in the parking lot. Washington, Colorado, Georgia, Rhode Island. Hey, maybe that was one of the Witch's neighbors. And here were the jellybean-shaped and colored shuttles I'd seen at the airport, disgorging or devouring their gawking tour groups. They all bore logos that were variations on the basic label of GOLDEN GATE TOURS.

I am a native of San Francisco, born and bred, an increasing rarity, soon to be a veritable curiosity. Like all locals did, I imagined, I was looking ahead and up for the towers as I crossed the lot. There was a mild hummock of land, and then the toll plaza opened up before me. My breath actually caught as I stepped out onto the preserved roadway, where 1 and 101, coming from the south and east respectively, funneled in toward the toll booths.

The lanes were empty of traffic, but you could see the darker stripes of oil and exhaust that left their marks on the asphalt. A fantastic amount of vehicular traffic passed this way in this road's time. Some mind-boggling tonnage of people and cars and trucks and buses.

And here, now, me ... crossing the lanes on foot. Merely a man, without the comforting armor of a car. My steps were soft, as if I were feeling guilty about committing this outrageous act of jaywalking.

I was still looking for the towers.

New Yorkers, now nearly a decade and a half after the fact of their disappearance, still use the World Trade Center's Twin Towers as a psychic reference point in the landscape of their city—and rightly so. The Golden Gate Bridge serves the same function on this far brink of the continent, though its disappearance is a *true* disappearance and so carries an extra magnitude in the minds of San Franciscans. Still, it's not being here is equivalent, in all its resonance, with the Twin Towers being gone.

In fact, when the Bridge vanished, it set off a nearly nostalgic wave of terrorism panic. The words "secret weapon" got punted about by some very respected newscasters. Wacko theorists had their day in the sun, and that hoary durable, conspiracy theory legend about the *U.S.S. Eldridge* being flung instantaneously from Philadelphia to Norfolk, Virginia, was exhumed and autopsied for everyone's benefit.

Eventually it passed. Even with hard, undeniable evidence of metaphysical forces beyond our ken, life eventually returned to more familiar rhythms in the city, in the nation, in the world. The phenomenon, if not casually accepted and dismissed, was at least universally acknowledged as having actually occurred. And with that acknowledgment, people had been able to return to normal patterns of living, without the terror that the event evoked.

But a supernatural uneasiness lingered. And certainly, so did curiosity.

I came to the far edge of the roadway and entered the grassy common that lay to the right of the rank of toll booths. On the other side of the lanes were the Bridge District's administrative offices and utility buildings—props now, really, for the tour groups. A fire truck was parked over there, occupying the same ready berth it had when the Bridge was a functioning entity.

As with all American cities that think they have a special claim to history, San Francisco had taken great pains to preserve this important site. It didn't matter that now it was just a tip of land offering a view of the Pacific's waters where they washed in and out of the Bay through a bottleneck of land, one boundary of which was Marin County, the other being San Francisco. What lies between is called the Golden Gate. Once upon a time, dear listeners, this interval of ocean was spanned by a mighty feat of construction and engineering. Can you guess what it was called?

The gawkers were thick here. But where there had been a picnic-like or carnival-going atmosphere back in the parking lot, as people unloaded coolers from trunks and switched on their camcorders, here the ambience was different. I felt it. Surprisingly, so did the others, even the clump of college-age meatheads, obviously beer-drunk, who'd brought along a beach ball.

Voices were subdued. It was library-quiet, church-quiet, though we were outdoors with late afternoon clouds and passing aircraft overhead, with the Bay sprinkled with boats to the east. Walking tour groups were organizing at various points around the common. There was an information kiosk at the center. But you couldn't buy an ice cream sandwich there or a Pepsi or a tacky little plastic model of the Bridge. This site had, I admitted, been preserved with at least some measure of dignity.

Plaques told the story of the Bridge's construction from 1933-37. These were being examined rather somberly by the tourists. Cameras whirred. Shutters clicked. A man with a thick Eastern European accent was talking, in hushed tones, about having driven across the Bridge twenty-two years ago, as if the event were of vast significance. He talked about the severity of the wind and how it buffeted the car. Others were solemnly eavesdropping.

I crossed to the northward edge of the green. To my left were the toll lanes that extended beyond the booths. This area was cordoned off. National Guardsmen kept watch, faces as imperturbable as the sentries outside of Buckingham Palace. Still, from where I stood, one could see the straight line where the road ended. Simply ended. As utter and definite a drop-off as any in the world. Beyond this point, the line said, there is *nothing*.

Just that spectacular absence ...

There were more than sightseers, and tour guides, and soldiers in evidence. This site drew the curious in many forms. Some were more official than others. As I stood watching, a member of the Scientific Investigation Team came into view. He wore one of those powder blue jumpsuits with the shoulder emblems, like you see on television. He had dark hair, a purposeful air. The Guardsmen passed him through, and he went out to the drop, as if he had every right to be there. He halted six feet or so from the lip. He had an aluminum clipboard in hand. He looked out across the Golden Gate, made a notation, then turned back. I met his eyes across some distance, but he gave me nothing more than the briefest glance. The whole thing seemed both businesslike and ritualistic.

The Scientific Investigation Team, the federal government's visible ongoing probe into the phenomenon of the disappearance, is based inside Fort Point, which lies on the San Francisco side of the Golden Gate, at sea level, just about in the vanished shadow of the Bridge. It was an actual military fort in the days of cannonballs and ramrods; then, a museum; now, a scientific analysis headquarters. If the SIT has figured out where the Bridge went, they're not saying.

My breath was still catching in my throat. I felt a weakness in my knees and a general lowering of my blood pressure. Yet it was all physiological. I didn't know what emotions went along with these physical symptoms. Despite knowing well in advance that I was going to visit here, I had not preprogrammed my feelings. That was deliberate. I wanted to expose myself to the sight of the empty Golden Gate, which I'd not seen in six years, and see how I would respond. Nakedly, spontaneously. Without false sentiment or sugary melodrama.

So, what was I feeling?

I'd read *The Gap Through Her Heart* during my flight. It was a first-time novel by a woman named something Tucker. It was doggerel. It was an overblown story of a woman living in Sausalito who becomes estranged from her lover, a married man living in San Francisco, when the Bridge vanishes. Cloying, amateurish, literarily vulgar. Right down to that license-taking *Through* in the title instead of the grammatically honest *In*. It was much like in the late 1980s when the market was flooded by appalling AIDS-themed novels that got a free pass from editors and the reading public purely because they addressed an important sensitive issue.

Tucker, said the bio, had a relative on the Bridge when it went.

It wouldn't even matter if it was a third cousin twice removed. Lost somebody on the span that day? Nephew, wife, boyfriend, broker, the guy that unstuck your gutters? Well, hell, here's a fat contract. Write us a book about it. Add to the pile of worthless opportunistic literature.

Like matter to a black hole, the books—fiction, true accounts, every possible printable venture on the matter—had been coming for the seven years since the Bridge vanished. Such books were called "Bridge lit." I read others. Now I'd read *Gap Through Her Heart*.

And ... despite the overwrought prose, despite the Danielle Steel-clunky characterizations, despite the shameless heartstring pulling about the many hundreds of people who'd disappeared along with the Golden Gate Bridge that day ... despite everything, the goddamned book had gotten to me. I was affected. And now, facing the gaping poignant void, I found I wasn't experiencing whatever actual emotions I might have felt. I was, instead, feeling cheap sympathetic sentiment for the two star-crossed characters in that trashy, awful, insipid novel.

It was grotesque.

I turned away and saw the Memorial. It hadn't been up when I'd left the city six years ago. A great deal of controversy surrounded the Memorial, and I'd stayed abreast of the proceedings. I was away at college, I was immersing myself in ambitions that had nothing to do with the city of my birth, and yet the debates and the hemming and hawing, the objections and criticisms, the whole contentious circus of the Memorial captivated me.

Designers were commissioned and their designs rejected. Contests were held and no winners announced. It must be a local artist. No, it must be an artist who lost someone in the disappearance. No, *no*, just choose the most qualified, the most talented. No no no ...

San Franciscans know how to raise a tempest in a teapot like no other breed of people.

I was moving toward it now, my steps as soft as before. It had quite a crowd around it. But there was no jostling, no raised voices. Here it was graveyard-quiet.

At first it was going to be all black, like the Vietnam Memorial, which had similarly turbulent beginnings. But that renowned San Franciscan hue and cry was heard once more, and the artist—whose name I couldn't recall—relented, and here it stood now, painted that distinctive orange-red of the original Bridge.

It was proper, I judged. It *should* be this color.

The Golden Gate Memorial was a platform raised three steps off the ground. You could enter from either end. It was held up by pylons below. The two towers and the accompanying suspension cables were suggestions rather than representations.

I went around to one end, respectfully waited a few minutes while others shuffled ahead. Then I went up onto the span.

The names were underfoot. The surface was coated, of course, and it probably got swabbed twice a day, but people made an automatic effort to step around the imprinted names.

Everybody was here. Right where they'd been when the Bridge simply, impossibly—but manifestly—ceased to exist in our world on November 7, 2010. It was a Sunday. The conscientious weekend carpoolers were grouped together in their little bundles. Here was the place where the busload of Novato schoolchildren had been, returning late from a field trip into the city. Along the eastward edge was the railed walkway that had been open to pedestrians and bicyclists; the westward side had been closed for routine maintenance six days earlier. Here were business people, nurses, carpenters, musicians, clerks, people with hopes, with expectations, with sorrows and secrets. And they were all gone.

I read some of the names. But I didn't want to loiter, even though I knew that here, in this strangely preserved zone of old world manners and decorum, no one would tell me to move on.

The Memorial was about thirty feet, end to end. I paused three-quarters across. From here I discovered I had an even better view than from the edge of the common. Here the ocean entryway to the San Francisco Bay yawned sensationally wide, a fantastic display of emptiness. Of absence. Of missing-ness.

Because right there, right *there*, was where the Golden Gate Bridge belonged.

I could even see the corresponding stub of roadway on the far side. Somehow, that site—though objectively just as worthy—didn't have the same impact as this side of the disappeared Bridge. Poor Marin County.

Now the tears did come, streaming, though without any accompanying sobs or wracking weeping. Still, if I'd wanted to flaunt my grief, I don't think anyone would have interrupted me. No doubt some among the other viewers, noticing my tears, were wondering if I was just a sentimental slob or if, perhaps, one of my own had been on the span that day.

I was looking down now, at the name imprinted on the Memorial's surface just beyond the toe of my left shoe. It was in the middle southbound lane, heading into the city, almost past the southward tower of the Bridge.

WARD PENTECOST.

He'd been my father, and now he was gone. And behind himself he left an absence like no other.

THREE.

WARD: Domestic Chores

AFTER WE GOT BACK TOGETHER, it was a short time until we moved from the apartment, across town, to a flat on 25th Street between Diamond and Castro Streets, in the area known as Noe Valley. To me everything east of Twin Peaks was the Mission.

Margot was immediately at home. The fog she had grown up with in the outer Sunset stopped two blocks above our flat, even on those days when it sailed across Twin Peaks with wind-blown speed. She exulted in the newfound, daily warmth. Each morning she had little Nate dressed, blanketed, and fastened safely into his stroller, and off they went on whatever mysterious rounds young mothers structure their time with.

I went to work each day.

I came home each day.

I went to work each day.

It was monotonous, but not actively unpleasant. I was fascinated watching Nate use those dark eyes he presumably inherited from me. There wasn't a thing that didn't interest him, from floor tiles to dirty dishes. He looked carefully at them all, seeing more than I ever did, making liquid sounds of approval or disapproval. Like most first-time parents I found him fascinating and absolutely special.

Both Margot and I were still young, she being twenty-five to my thirty-three, so, while sex changed greatly, there was plenty of it. Nature had done a good job that way. It persevered in spite of the personalities, knowing that it had a much more important job to do than did our little, fragile egos. I read just enough of Freud, Adler and Jung to be mistakenly well-informed. But even through that filter of academic double-talk, it was obvious that things were working out better than either of us hoped.

It didn't change all at once. That already occurred with her alarming character change after Nate's birth, and I adjusted.

The instinct-driven squirmings and squirtings of youth gradually subsided. There was never any overt rejection, and we certainly did not give up sex entirely, but the frequency lessened, and the joy left. It became physical only, and I anticipated with dread the day when either of us needed the other's cooperation to make it work.

Throughout the year this took place, our lives settled down to a bearable and not unpleasant routine. Nate thrived, either oblivious to our emotional problems, or too happily alive to be bothered. His dark eyes sparkled all the time now. His curiosity could not be quenched, and his picture books became a budgetary expense.

Margot did not work at this time, as we both thought that in these early years it would better for him to be raised at home than warehoused in some preschool dumping ground.

I learned how to do a weekly shopping, with Nate huddled in his stroller amidst the grocery bags, enjoying it all. The mysteries of doing a family washing in our own building's washing machine were revealed. I even ironed clothes.

My job at the City Hall mail room was undemanding, and I showed up for work five days a week now, after several years during my drinking period of pioneering the four day work week.

I'd even begun to think of replacing my old, manual typewriter with one of those new personal computers, if we could somehow manage the money.

⚬⚭⚬

"I've been thinking about a computer," I said to Margot.

She was folding some clothes on the kitchen table. She stopped. "Do you know anything about them?" she asked.

"I think the word processor function would be great for my writing." I'd been trying since age sixteen to write commercially without success. While I could use language better than most, I didn't have the foggiest notion of what a story really was. If you asked me about a plot skeleton, I would have thought of an autopsy room.

The promise of eventually succeeding at a literary profession had been a factor in the attraction I held for the young Margot Morton. I had been unable to keep that promise.

"Let's see," said Margot. "You want to buy a computer? That's how you get them, you know. We don't have the money in our budget, and have you thought that it wouldn't be much good without a printer, and God knows how much they cost." She continued, turning it into a litany. "Then there's the printer ribbons, probably cost more than typewriter ribbons, perforated paper by the ream. Have I left anything out?"

"It was just a thought," I said.

She resumed folding the clothes, not ignoring me, but I certainly felt dismissed.

Welcome to reality, the country of unfulfilled dreams, budgets that don't stretch far enough, and problems enough for a lifetime.

I felt very sorry for myself.

I did what I always did when I was faced with the obstacles of the real world. I changed my attitude. That sounds very grown-up, but it wasn't. As a child I salved my wounds of unrequited wants by retreating into the world of books— picture books, coloring books, comic books, pulp magazines, adventure novels, and, most lovingly, science fiction and fantasy novels.

The magic still worked.

For most of the rest of that Saturday I buried myself in the pages of George R. Stewart's old novel, *Earth Abides*. There's nothing like a good post-Armageddon novel to cheer me up. I'd read the book several times in the past, but I found myself once again entranced to live in a world— never mind *its* problems—without jobs, money, or so damn many people.

It's a common fantasy for a young man facing the marketplace moralities and realities of working for a living to imagine himself in a different world. I always wondered why they called it working for a living, since it seemed more like slavery to me. *Wage slave* is one of the more accurate labels we as a people have coined.

I closed the pages of the book, temporarily abandoning Ish and Em to their far more desirable problems of living in a catastrophically depopulated United States.

Much of the day, into the late afternoon, passed during my reading. I closed the book and placed it back in the crowded bookcase, right next to my old, worn books on sleight of hand, legerdemain, and AMUSE YOUR FRIENDS WITH MAGIC TRICKS. Much of the bookcase was a time trip into the past of a physically limited boy.

I looked back at myself at that age and felt a more honest self-pity than the earlier one.

The odds had certainly been stacked against me. The polio at the age of five, the ensuing treatment and the final, devastating, inescapable fact that I was going to be crippled for the rest of my life, fixed the boundaries of my reality.

Added to that was the never concealed disappointment from my father over his less than normal, male offspring.

There was also the fact that I would never participate in sports. After all, who wants a base runner who can't run? Hobbling around the bases doesn't score much.

I will say this for Drake, my father, though: he didn't give a damn about sports, probably because he ran away from home at age fourteen. No, it was the presence of any kind of infirmity that put him off. The fact was that my left leg was an inch shorter than the right. To my father's generation, I was a crippled offspring. It wasn't a personal judgment on his part. It was the way things were.

It didn't matter that I was very bright. Not a genius to be sure, but pushing close to it. Nobody took notice. School was very hard for me, because all the way along the line, in the parochial schools, which my mother had insisted I attend *for the better education*, nobody bothered to notice that they hadn't taught me *how* to learn.

If I were to ask myself today, "What did you learn in school?" I would have to answer, "Nothing." That applies to grammar school and high school.

I acquired my education by cutting classes in high school, and spending my days at the main library in downtown San Francisco. I read my way through fiction and nonfiction, history and historical romances, philosophy and psychology, physics, chemistry and so many others, practical and esoteric. I read through the equivalent of grammar school, high school and college—and further. Nobody observed it or acknowledged it. But I was a lot smarter than before. I was a lot smarter than my peers. And a lot dumber.

I was good looking. Most young people are. I measured my appearance against the artificially perfect people in the movies, or the equally fake perfection of characters in popular novels. As a result of this thinking, I never found myself attractive. So, I attended the few social functions I deigned to honor with my presence as a beggar for attention.

Because I missed sports, I also missed the camaraderie that goes with such participation, the easy acceptance of my masculinity, the confidence that goes with it and, most importantly, the male tribal wisdom that is transmitted from one generation to another in locker room confidences.

The dumbest jock knew more about girls than I learned in all the books I'd read.

I learned how to dance by a combination of books and records. I actually became good at it. My built-up footwear made it possible for me to perform all the requisite movements, and I did them well.

But I danced with strangers who frightened me.

"Poor little fellow," I said aloud, concluding my indulgence in negative reflection.

Margot entered the room. "Did something happen to Nate?" she asked anxiously.

Our son was in a corner of the room, happily perusing, for the hundredth time, his collection of picture books.

"I was talking about myself," I said.

She looked at me in that not-hostile but awaiting-disapproval expression, on which women seem to own the copyright. "And what happened to you?" she asked.

"Life."

It was a very short conversation.

"Are you going to cook tonight?" she asked. I'd promised to make my Italian sauce and cook spaghetti to go with it.

"It's a little late for the sauce ..." I began, and noticing the incipient disapproval on Margot's face continued, "... but I'll take a few short cuts."

She smiled. "He *loves* spaghetti."

"But not too much," I said, remembering Nate's marathon vomiting after his last overindulgence in spaghetti. Thankfully it was a commercial sauce that time, although the eruptions were caused by the quantity and not the quality, I am sure.

There is a marvelous medley of aromas in any kitchen that plays host to informed Italian cooking. I think the keyword is *cooking*. My Italian grandmother, on my mother's side, taught me many of the secret recipes and methods of old country cooking. It was one of the better times in my life. My shortened left leg posed no problem to learning how to cook. I could walk—or hobble—from table to stove, and the recipes didn't care at all. My grandmother was always caring and kind, although she did raise her voice when I proved a less than bright student the first time she called upon me to separate egg whites. But I did learn. I always learned what I wanted to learn. It took me a long time to understand *that*.

Margot set the table, while I managed the simmering sauce and boiling spaghetti. Eventually it appeared on the table, together with Parmesan cheese, French bread, and butter.

Margot had two modest helpings of the spaghetti and none of the French bread and butter.

Nate ate his fill, after his serving cooled down.

I ate too much. But it was delicious.

FOUR.

NATHANAEL: Jiggety-Jig

I CAME TO REST IN THE PARK. The daylight was starting to wane. I checked my watch. At this time a week or so from now, when daylight-savings time ended, it would be dark already.

Growing up a bicycle ride away, on Santiago Street, made Golden Gate Park my neighborhood playground. My most curious years were probably spent in here. That singular time of life, when you have all the necessary motor skills to get about on your own, when you're never tired, when virtually every facet of your environment gives off a glow of sheer enticement, begging to be explored. All this is, of course, before the first queasy misapprehended thoughts about sex ever enter your head.

Here, I definitely knew my way around. But I was in a car now—a big grown-up car—not peddling a Huffy on jogging trails and over grass. I pulled to the curb and killed the engine.

A triumvirate of joggers went past in a bustle of pink spandex, but the symbolic nine-year-old on his two-wheeler must have missed his cue because he didn't come whizzing by, reminding me wistfully of my own lost childhood. Granted, that would have been flirting dangerously with schmaltz.

I pulled my briefcase off the backseat, flipped it open next to me. There was *Gap Through Her Heart*. Minnie F. Tucker was the author's full name, I now saw. Even the cover irritated me, a cheesy Photoshop picture of the Bridge's towers poking up through a dense ghostly fog bank. I batted it aside.

Underneath, I had several back issues of *Diamond*, which contained reviews I'd written. *Diamond* is the unclaimed magazine love child of *The New Yorker* and *Details*, and its attention-deficit book reviews all conclude with academic-like grades. As in C+ or D or the occasional A-. That's how I hand in my copy. I thumbnail-sketch a novel, then I award it a grammar school grade. Classy, idd'nit?

These were to show to Mom. Last thing she knew I was still interning at the publishing house. That gig, of course, cratered. But I'd wanted to bring along actual proof that I was doing something, working an adult job. The fact was, I'd been steadily employed by *Diamond* for over a year and a half now. And—presuming one was gracious with the definition—I was working in the field of writing.

I picked my phone from the briefcase's inside flap. I checked my left thumb again and found the 212 area code still circling the band of my pager. The Purple Witch's Rhode Island number was still there too, but the thought of talking to her right now still made my innards twist coldly.

I speed-dialed New York. My phone is a relic. But I don't care for the new breed of phone, microtech artifacts which are the size and shape of what a stick of chewing gum looked like when I was a kid.

Navigating through the secretarial obstacle course to the editorial offices, I was eventually greeted with: "Where's your copy, Nathanael?"

Which was what I'd been expecting.

It was April's voice. "I read the thing," I said. "It's excrement covered with confectionery sugar."

"That's lovely," April said. Office sounds in the background. "Put five hundred words after that and send it in. Soonish. More like, nowish. Are you far away, Nathanael? You've got that I've-left-the-city vibe happening."

"I'm in San Francisco."

"Well, I'd recommend a restaurant, but I've never been there. Too busy being the responsible editor collecting overdue copy."

"I'm not overdue," I said.

"That's true. But you're three thousand miles away from the nest, in a city no one in this office sent you to. I can't help but wonder. You won't let us down, will you, Nathanael? You won't betray our confidence in you?"

"Not in my wildest dreams, April."

"That's what we like to hear. Send me that copy. Love you. Mean it." She clicked off.

April Gregoire was ten years my senior and used completely unself-conscious, obsolete youthful slang. It was her privilege, I supposed.

I rubbed my eyes. I'd cried quite a lot at the Bridge site. But once I'd stepped down from the Memorial and put my back to the water, the tears evaporated totally.

The second number I dialed wasn't programmed into my phone. Still, I knew it. The house originally belonged to Father's father and mother, and these seven digits connected to there for a long, long time. The longevity of the telephone number struck me with a profundity that, when I paused to examine it, signified nothing. So this phone number existed for fifty-whatever years. So what?

A lone jogger was coming back along the sidewalk, dappled sunlight through the branches flashing across her toned figure. She had dark tufted hair, a yellow terry cloth sweatband across her forehead. My windshield, facing west, was probably just glare, but I gave her a steady look as she passed.

"Hello?"

It rung six times, far past the point when an answering machine would have taken over just about anywhere else. Instead, she made her way, at her own pace, from wherever she was and whatever she was doing around the house and picked up the telephone and said ...

"Hello?"

The second one was as polite as the first. Mom didn't rush to snatch up the phone; didn't snap at her callers when they failed to speak right away.

"Hi," I said. "Hi, it's me." All at once my mouth was dry. The triteness of that bothered me, but it couldn't be helped.

"Nathan," Mom said. No hesitation in it. Not a question. I could have rung at five in the morning and gotten this same response. "Oh my. How are you?"

"Fine." I swallowed, hard. "Hey, I'm here in the city. On ... business. Fact, I'm in the neighborhood ..."

"You're here?"

"In the Park."

"Well, come to the house, Nathan." Her voice was amiable, gentle, but not old-ladyish. She sounded very happy to be hearing from me. "Is ... Janeane with you?" The pause was Mom deliberately arranging the syllables of my wife's name. In the past she slipped and said "Janice" or "Jean Ann." I certainly didn't fault her. She never met Janeane. And now probably wouldn't, ever.

"No, Mom. I'm here on a business trip."

"Well, come to the house," she said again.

"I will. I will. I'll be there in a few minutes. Okay?"

"Oh, I'm looking forward to seeing you."

"Me too. I'll be right there. Okay? Bye."

I hadn't seen my mother since she'd come out to New York for my college graduation. She'd worn an antique choker of pearls and a black dress and carried the look impeccably. She was proud of me that day and told me so.

I turned the key in the ignition.

I cut out of the Park and took 19th Avenue. Streets are easy to find in the Sunset district. You need only know the alphabet. It goes Anza, Balboa, Cabrillo and so on, a legacy of the region's bygone Spanish proprietorship. (They're lucky they got out when they did; the escalating rents during the dotcom boom in the 1990s would have wiped them out.) So it was that I found Santiago between Rivera and Taraval, right where it belonged. And, finding Santiago Street, I found the house where I'd lived from the age of five.

Maybe I should have come here before phoning Mom, so to sit in the car and just look at the place awhile. Studying it wouldn't have yielded much; it looked precisely as I remembered it. But the place radiated so much memory it was almost physical, and I would have liked to have mustered up my strength before slogging against it to the front door.

I found a parking spot across the street. I grabbed my briefcase and left the rest of my luggage in the back. I was wearing slacks, a black turtleneck and my dressy-casual jacket. Clean-shaven, neat short hair. I looked like a grown-up. An awful lot like one.

Evening was settling in. I crossed toward the big house. Climbed the three stone steps. Reached the front door. Once again my mouth was tritely dry. I swallowed and put my finger to the doorbell.

I was surprised when that funereal bong-*boong* imprinted in my brain from childhood didn't sound from inside the house. Instead, a buzzer *zzzzzzzzt*'ed somewhere beyond the front door. It had three small pebbled panes at about eye-level, and I saw movement behind them.

Then a lock was undone, and Margot Pentecost opened the door to her only offspring.

"What happened to the doorbell?"

It jumped out of me with all the inane force of someone blurting an awkward compliment on a first date.

"It broke. I replaced it. Oh, Nathan, it's so good to see you!" She didn't even break verbal stride, as though it were all one sentence, one thought. Impressive. Such poise.

"Good seeing you too." My voice was pitched wrong. Now I was exaggerating a casual tone. Memory radiation continued to pour out of the house. With the door open it was even more intense, streaming from the foyer, from the rooms beyond, from the upstairs.

Mom stepped forward to hug me. I lifted my arms, banged my briefcase on the jamb, managed to get my body into some sort of an embrace, my balance slightly off so that I was tipping and couldn't hold it long enough for a good squeeze. She let me go.

"How long are you in the city for?" She was stepping back, holding the door open. Inviting me inside.

How long? That stumped me for a beat, which I wasted rebuking myself for not having given my cover story even that much forethought. Blurting once more, I said, "Two weeks." *Two weeks?* Who takes two week business trips?

Mom was still waiting for me to step past the threshold. "That's wonderful. I hope we'll have plenty of time to catch up. Nathan?"

She looked terrific. She really did. Mom was from a pre-obese America, and age hadn't added any pounds to her.

She'd always been on the wiry side, never shying from a long hike to the grocery or a taxing household chore. Her years were in her face, in the mild seams that held the parts of it in place, but even here she retained a durable vitality. Her gray eyes were clear. She'd gone redhead, and it suited her. It was a cheerfully fake sort of red, with nice highlights, as if in sporting a counterfeit color she was dealing honestly and openly with her encroaching gray.

"Nathan?"

"Yes ..." Was I answering a question? No. I focused myself.

Mom regarded me a moment, the smile she'd worn when she opened the door now settling a bit. Somewhat formally—but without reproach or irony—she asked, "Would you like to come in?"

For that instant I realized she actually was giving me the choice. Come in. Or don't. You don't have to if you don't want to. That was generous of her.

But the thing to do was to laugh off the awkward moment and say I was feeling my jet lag and go on in, and I did all these things. I waded into the current of memories, planting my feet, leaning into it. The flood broke across my chest. Mom closed the door behind me.

The foyer's wallpaper was different—something floral now—but the furnishings were exactly what and where they'd been when I last saw this place. Here were the stairs going up. Here was the front room off to the other side. Beige carpet on the floor in there, dust covers on the arms of the couch, blue and white striped shade over the lamp on the end table. Through that front room, through the sliding doors that were standing wide, I could see the dining room from where I stood. The mahogany table was in there. The white lace tablecloth didn't hide it from me.

There you are, you big old bastard.

"Come into the kitchen," Mom said. "I'll make us some

coffee, and we'll sit. Are you hungry?"

I followed my mother toward the kitchen, the dining room table in the periphery of my vision all the way.

FIVE.

WARD: Young Love

THOUGH MY SON IN HIS SULLEN TEEN YEARS probably never would have credited it, there was a time before his birth, a time when there was just Margot and myself ...

She actually liked me.

For the first time, I regretted not having a car. We'd gone to a show, and, although I love movies, I think I scarcely saw a scene. My whole body tingled. The images upon the screen were some distant message. My whole concentration was on my companion. I felt gloriously adolescent. I was thirty-one.

Margot Jean Morton sat beside me, her eyes intent upon the movie I elected to ignore, not because it was bad, but because she was so much more appealing to me than any of the characters upon the screen.

She wore a cotton print blue dress, cinched neatly at the waist by a matching belt. Her white cardigan sweater lay bunched on the seat beside her.

When the movie ended and the credits rolled—I always watch the credits—we rose. She draped the sweater casually across her shoulders and took my hand. The shock was high voltage electric. Her touch sent blood hammering to *all* my extremities. If the roof of the theater caved in at that moment I would not have noticed, even if it hit me.

We allowed ourselves to be carried out of the theater, by the tide of exiting patrons, and down the block to a coffeehouse and short-order restaurant that catered to the young crowd. Tonight I was very young.

In the relatively harsh light of the booth I examined her more closely. She was about five feet five inches tall with lustrous hair, which was one of those variants of brown that I never seem able to name. Her eyes were slate gray and very intelligent, and her attention was upon me.

My usual facility with words fled and I found myself making the most inane remarks about movies, books, and myself, which she found, judging from her attention, fascinating.

I felt like leaping upon the table and strutting, preening myself like a rooster. For the first time in my life I was thoroughly comfortable in the presence of a woman, feeling no compulsion to prove myself.

It was a new experience, which I devoutly hoped wasn't the last of its kind. I thanked the powers that be for arranging this marvelous evening, which was so completely different from all my other experiences.

Of course, I forced myself to have the usual rite of passage, as a younger man, out drinking with his fellow employees. It was a coldly commercial consummation, conducted in an overpriced, ugly hotel room, with a disinterested prostitute, and my drunken coworkers cheering me on, sloppy, embarrassing, and as far from satisfying as anything can get. I even considered the priesthood for a few days afterward.

There were a few other occasions, but all of them left me not really wanting more. I never understood why young men strutted and took such airs upon themselves, all because they achieved erection and fulfillment. How did this make them more manly, better looking, important?

Tonight I understood—from a touch.

Instinct was not logical, or rather it followed a far more practical logic than all the syllogisms I read. I agreed. If instinct told me tonight to strut, jump, shout, and run around in circles, that was what I would do. If it promised to make me feel like this forever, I would obey it forever.

A thought nagged at the edge of my mind. Wasn't this the same as my reaction to my first drunk, the night all the fears and doubts left me, and I felt *good* for the first time? I remember the night, the liquor I was drinking, and even the book I was reading while I sipped and wondered at the marvels, as the book came alive. I saw pages in vivid color. I heard voices and background sounds in stereo, with Dolby, and distantly but clearly, I heard myself say, *This is what I want to do with the rest of my life.*

Now was it happening again?

Was it love or addiction?

Was there a difference?

I decided to postpone the question and answer session with myself, and enjoy the real-life woman sitting across from me, her beautiful face immune to the harsh, commercial lighting.

We ordered hamburgers and milkshakes. Nothing ever tasted so good.

Margot, *Marge*, as she preferred to be called by her *friends*, was eight years younger than me. She worked as a clerk and general secretary for an insurance office, which was managed by an old curmudgeon, well past his prime, which relieved me greatly, to my surprise.

She'd gone through grammar and high school in the parochial system, but, where I'd been severely traumatized by the experience, she emerged with both feet on the ground, well-educated and clearheaded.

Marge was intelligent. The only reason she'd not pursued her education further was that her father suffered an on-the-job injury at a crucial time, and she'd taken the position she now occupied. While her father had since fully recovered, and was back at work as a warehouseman, the family finances had not rebounded quite as well, and it looked like she would be working in her present job for an indefinite time. Her mother did not work, finding the care of the family home more than enough for her limited personal resources.

Both of her parents were devout Catholics, unlike my parents, who were lip-service-only Romans and faithfully showed up at church on Easter and Christmas.

Marge, I am sure, was equally as devout as her parents. But in her I saw it as enriching, rather than limiting, although I certainly could not share in her devotion.

Wisely, I talked of other things.

Her two sisters, Ruth the oldest, was married to a San Francisco policeman, and Sarah was wed to a stockbroker and "put on airs," according to the mother.

The whole family, I learned, attended church with all the faithfulness of the mother's full-blooded, Irish ancestry. So far as I had seen, it hadn't harmed Marge. The mild religious mania—as I thought of it—seemed to form an anchor for her personality. I was leaping far ahead in my thoughts, anticipating one of many probable futures. It was an old habit.

"I have to see you again," I said. The suspense was agonizing as she received this tidbit and mulled it over.

Finally she reached across the table and took one of my hands in both of hers. She squeezed gently. I didn't dare breathe. "I wouldn't have it any other way," she said.

To get to her house, where, like myself, she still lived with her parents—make that one parent for me, as my mother and father were currently in their third separation—I don't recall if we took the N streetcar, walked, or flew on a magic carpet. I was simply delirious with happiness.

I wasn't invited inside the simple one story house on 43rd Avenue, but that didn't matter to me. We lingered long enough on the front steps to pass the time until midnight, when she excused herself and went inside, but only after kissing me and arranging another date for the weekend.

It's a long walk from 43rd and Judah street to my family's house on upper Santiago. I could have taken two different Muni buses, but I got there strictly on foot, wearing down my built-up half boot in the process, and luxuriating in wondrous thoughts.

I didn't take a drink that night, but lay awake for many happy hours before sleep took its gentle hold of me.

When I picked up Marge at her home on Saturday evening, I was invited in to meet her parents. As Phyllis' nostrils flared, ever so ladylike, when my alcohol-laced breath wafted her way, I regretted having taken a drink for courage before leaving home.

Harry Morton did not seem offended. He took my hand in a strong grip and shook it vigorously. He had a solid, compact body, hair that was just starting to turn gray, and strong features he had given to his daughter.

Phyllis was more frail, with those same slate gray eyes that so attracted me to her daughter, but they seemed turned more inward than outward, as if she were constantly checking everything against some interior balance sheet. She did not like me, and managed to convey that dislike with courtesy and graciousness. Evidently, confrontation was not to her liking.

I made some points with Harry when I told him that I'd been consistently employed by the San Francisco Civil Service for six years.

I lost the same number of points with Phyllis when I admitted that I held the same position, that of a lowly clerk, for all of those years.

I didn't explain that I *liked* being a clerk, that I counted myself lucky to have escaped from the infinitely expanding trap of ambition. Of course, it did help that I still lived with my mother, information I did not volunteer either.

Eventually the inquisition was over. Harry walked us to the door. I glimpsed, from the corner of my eyes, a curtain pulled back ever so discreetly, and although I could not see them I could feel Phyllis' slate gray eyes. They were not approving.

We made our way across to my side of the Avenues by bus, got an L streetcar, and rode up Taraval Street to a marvelous Mexican restaurant that Marge heard of from some of her friends. Her friends had good taste.

We were seated in a dark wooden booth. Serapes, sombreros, and other south of the border artifacts adorned the walls. The background music was Latin and festive, but not intrusive.

We took our time reading the extensive menu. I ordered a bottle of wine and, before we had been served the first course of our dinner, was on a second bottle.

The food was marvelous, fiery with spices and thermally hot. No microwave food here. We lingered over it. Marge lingered over the post-dinner coffee. I lingered over the wine until I consumed it all.

When we finally left, it was too late for the movie we planned on seeing, and I escorted a mildly irritated date back to her residence.

The goodnight kiss I received was mostly perfunctory. I was not invited inside, and my request to see her tomorrow was answered with a maybe. I was still coasting on the effects of the wine, but I was enough of a veteran of chemical happiness to recognize the fact.

Very humbly, for it was how I felt, I made my goodbye, holding onto her hand to the last possible second, trying to draw from it the strength I so sadly failed to manifest that evening.

For the second time that week I made the trek, on foot, across the Avenues to my mother's house. It took longer than last time, when I practically skipped in joy, and never mind what the onlookers might think. I didn't exactly walk this time. I *trudged*, with each step seeming heavier than the preceding one, and my heart weighing more than either of my feet.

I allowed myself more self-honesty than is usual with me. As they say, I lost the power to control my drinking.

No doubt about it. No cutesy remarks. I was in trouble. I also might lose the girl I loved. There, I'd said it!

So, in spite of a disastrous second date, in spite of the less than glorious impression I left with her family, and mostly in spite of the questions that must be buzzing through her head, I felt good again.

So good that I finished the walk home and celebrated with a few drinks.

SIX.

NATHANAEL: The Spelling of the Name

IT TOOK MY UTTERING THE WORD "MOTEL" for Mom to insist I stay at the house while I was in the city.

"It won't affect whatever business you have to do here? No? Fine. Not another word about it, then. Here, I've got some raisin scones. You used to like them. I'll put some on a plate."

After a while I went out to the car for my bags. A motel? No, I'd never once thought I'd be staying in a rented room while I was in San Francisco. I had known I'd come to this house and be welcomed here. It hadn't even occurred to me that that might not happen.

I put my luggage at the foot of the stairs when I came back inside. I wouldn't go so far as to assume my old room was waiting for me up there. It might be Mom's sitting room now. It might be piled full of Father's effects.

I went back into the kitchen. We'd been talking almost an hour, drinking coffee and enjoying cookies and pastry-type nibbles. Food had always been that for me when I was a boy: just food. Not a substitute for anything. To be appreciated in the moment but not obsessed over. Like Mom, I tended toward the slim. It was Father who paid an unseemly amount of attention to meals.

But the snacks wiped out whatever pangs for a (by my internal Eastern clock) late dinner I might have had. Maybe I'd get hungry later. Whatever, I was sure my mother wouldn't let me starve.

An hour of chitchat and I'd managed not to tell her I was no longer an intern at the publishing house, a gig I'd picked up right out of school. I'd been so juiced about it at the time. The publisher was a big one, a household name—at least in *this* house, where traditionally a lot of books got read. I thought my tiny toehold there meant ... meant—well, much more than it turned out to mean.

My departure from that servile, subservient, lick-my-boots-boy internship had been less than amicable but ardently agreed upon by both parties.

Now it was time to tell Mom I wasn't climbing the rungs of the publishing world's ladder.

"Mom, about my job at that publishers ..."

A gentle smile spread its way across her lips as I told the condensed, expletive-free version of the story. Finally she patted my hand as I segued into a long pent-up apology for keeping her in the dark. She didn't let me finish.

"There, Nathan. I didn't guess you were still a trainee. Or—what was it? An intern. No. Not after all this time. Not when you never told me about getting promoted."

Gently said, but the implication was that I would have phoned to brag about making junior associate editor—or even slush pile reader. However, she knew this wasn't the only significant event in my life I neglected to inform her about when it was happening.

"Well"—I laid my briefcase on the kitchen table and opened it—"I *have* been working."

She was still smiling. "I guessed that too. You hadn't asked for money, and New York's not cheap."

Neither was San Francisco, but Mom didn't have to worry about money. Father's life insurance paid handsomely, once that Presidential directive unilaterally ordered all the hedging insurance companies to pay on the policies of anybody who'd been on the Bridge when it disappeared. I've never voted in my life, and I certainly didn't think much of that chimpanzee who occupied the White House at that time, nor the chimp that followed, but I'll tell you ... that was one very decent gesture on his part.

I started pulling copies of *Diamond* out of my briefcase, like some salesman from the last century affably conning some hapless spinster, laying out my samples, smooth-talking her, manipulating her into buying something she didn't need.

But Mom's eyes lit brightly, and she cooed happily.

"Oh, Nathan, it's marvelous!"

And for a minute or two there, while I was showing her some of the reviews I'd written, it did feel, if not *marvelous*, then at least not painfully mediocre. Not like I'd botched my primary effort and been forced to settle for something far from what I so wanted to be doing.

She put on a pair of reading glasses and looked with great pride upon the words her son had gotten into print in a nationally circulated magazine. She was looking at the first review I'd written. My first paid professional words.

It was for a book called *People Who Visit People in Hospitals*, another first-time novel. I awarded it a D+. I could remember referring to the book's dénouement as "that moment when the magician holds up the Ace of Clubs and smugly says `Is that your card?'—only you'd picked the Four of Hearts." My, I'd thought that was clever, despite the fact that I intensely dislike card tricks. Robert Hammer had been the name of the author. He'd never written anything else.

I watched Mom reading my words. The familiarity of that suddenly raised gooseflesh on my arms. I'd written many, many truly appalling short stories as a teenager, and she'd read every one I showed her. Some stayed tucked away in my files, those that had the word "fuck" in them or those that *very* clumsily made use of sexuality. She'd been a biased reader, to be sure; but she always found one particular thing that she liked—some adolescently overwrought turn of phrase or some surprisingly insightful image—and pointed it out to me. She'd been very kind.

In contrast, Janeane, my wife, read three of my unfinished novels (I stopped showing her my work after that) and offered a comment on exactly one sentence contained in one of those books. The sentence read: "There was a tract in Vincent's memories of his first schoolboy crush where mental insecticide guaranteed nothing would ever grow again." Janeane's comment was this: "I like that." Nothing else was ever said by her about my fiction. Not another word.

Mom was making that chuckling-squealing sound that I remembered from when she would find that special something she liked in one of my incompetent stabs at a short story.

I thought it would be the line in the review about the magician, but she was instead tickled by my unsolicited advice to the author that he should write as if someone other than himself and his undergraduate pals were going to read his book.

"A bit catty, isn't it?" she observed, amused.

"It is." And I wondered what Robert Hammer thought, reading that; wondered if he'd felt a prickling of humiliation; wondered if he'd ever shown his own mother this review.

"It's wonderful, Nathan." She gave my hand another pat. Then she was squinting closer at the page. "Is this a ... typo?"

I leaned over. A flush tried to climb out of my turtleneck.

"No," I said. "That's—that's just the way I spell it for the magazine."

"Oh, that's interesting," she said sincerely.

I had been christened Nathaniel. When I was ten or so, Mom told me I'd been named after Nathaniel Hawthorne, something she and Father agreed upon. That had thrilled me; it was like I was guaranteed my destiny of becoming a writer. I got a hold of a copy of *The House of the Seven Gables* and tried trudging my way through.

Two years ago I legally changed the spelling to Nathanael. Why? Was that delectably Old English "ae" too irresistible? Did I think Nathan*ae*l Pentecost would look tremendously better than Nathan*ie*l Pentecost on a book jacket? Was I trying to rewrite my present so that it less resembled my past? Yes. Yes. And yes.

This was something else I hadn't informed my mother about.

"I'd like to read more of these," she was saying, thumbing the other issues of the magazine I'd brought along. Then she removed her reading glasses and regarded me. "But you probably want to get settled, don't you? Here I've been holding you prisoner ..."

"Hardly that, Mom." I smiled.

"Well, come on upstairs. I want to change out of these glad rags anyway. Do you remember where everything is?"

I said I did, and I collected my bags and followed her up.

She'd never had a particularly unhappy nature. I'd never consciously seen her depressed, not even when things were at their emotionally sketchiest here in the house, when I was younger. She weathered things, remaining upbeat, sometimes verging on chipper. At least, in my presence, and to my perceptions. During the long sulk that was my adolescence, I thought her unrealistic, myopic even, for not seeing how things were. Deeper, though, I'd envied her. She knew a kind of casual happiness that neither Father nor I had ever had the knack for.

Now, however, Mom seemed, above all else, relaxed. She was comfortable here—in this house, in this phase of her life. There had to be a loneliness that went with Father's absence, but she wasn't suffering to an unduly or unseemly degree. I felt this firmly.

Earlier, I'd wondered if my old bedroom would be waiting or if it had been turned into Mom's den or piled with Father's belongings. Actually all three turned out to be true.

My bed was where I'd left it when I went off to school. There was a television set in here now and an overstuffed chair. I'd noticed the set was gone from the front room downstairs. Mom explained she didn't like having a tv in her own bedroom, but sometimes she watched it so late she fell asleep in front of it in the chair. Easier, she said, just to cross the hall to get into bed than to climb the stairs.

Also, in this room where I'd grown up, were quite a few cardboard boxes. They weren't neatly stacked or taped up. They simply lay willy-nilly around the room. Father's items. Things Mom had no use for but which she'd not gotten rid of.

"Go through them if you want something," she said. "Your father wouldn't mind."

It was the first mention either of us made aloud of Ward Pentecost since I'd arrived at the house.

Mom left me alone in the room.

I did some cursory unpacking. I packed for a lengthy stay, it looked like. Or at least for more than an overnight visit. How long *did* I plan to stay? Two weeks, I'd told Mom. Naturally it didn't mean I was committed to that.

Back East, it was late by now, but the Purple Witch was still awake. I felt it in my bone marrow. But I still wasn't ready to talk to her. Neither did I have the mental and emotional energy to tell Mom about her just yet, about the project I was involved in; about the drastic turn my life had taken eight months ago.

I left my shoes under the bed, swapped my turtleneck for a comfortably shabby sweatshirt. San Francisco is generally chilly. The mercury hovers at an annoying 55° about ten months out of the year, with gusts and fog and widespread grayness. This was a large old house, and the heat didn't always distribute evenly. In the winter months it could be a little nippy indoors here.

New York has more honest weather, to say nothing of the fact that it is visited by actual seasons. Blizzards in the wintertime, summers hot and humid enough to boil the cockroaches. San Francisco offers fog in the summertime. October, however, can almost always be relied on for an Indian summer of near-balmy temperatures and a rare chance to leave the house without a coat, scarf and ...

October. October. It was late October. Oh, Christ.

The anniversary of the Bridge's disappearance was ... what? ... a little over a week away. November 7th would mark seven years since it had gone wherever it had gone. If anywhere. If indeed it hadn't simply been erased.

And I just happened to be visiting San Francisco.

From downstairs, owing to the acoustics of the house, I clearly heard my mother's distinctive chuckling as she evidently found some other bon mot in one of my reviews.

I looked around the familiar room. The boxes were everywhere, their flaps loose, offering glimpses of their contents. Father's things. Father's personal things. Which Mom said I could go through.

I actually backed out of the room, then pulled the door shut behind me.

SEVEN.

---●○●---

WARD: Rules of Engagement

THE RULES OF MY ENGAGEMENT WERE THREE.

From Harry and Phyllis Morton: "Don't drink."

From my father and mother: "Don't drink."

From Marge: "Please, don't drink."

I'd been dating Marge some while now, and I'd been drinking. She had been tolerating it, which I took as a measure of her growing affection for and seriousness about me. But I'd shown up at the Morton house too inebriated one or two or three times too many, and her parents cut me off.

For a month I was not allowed to see Marge, nor did the house on 43rd Avenue receive any phone calls from me. If not for the occasional, surreptitious call Marge would make from a friend's house, we were effectively incommunicado.

I passed the time in a variety of ways. My old electric typewriter was hauled out and was used to compose eight stories, all of which were doomed to failure before they were submitted. At bedtime I read myself to sleep, tearing through my collection of doomsday science fiction.

Best of all, almost every night, I enjoyed the wildest, most colorful, most erotic dreams I ever experienced, necessitating frequent changes of pajamas.

While my intake of alcohol had been steady, it was not of a sufficient quantity to cause severe withdrawal symptoms, and I suffered little physical discomfort.

At no time did I feel sufficiently grown-up to protest any of these conditions or restrictions. I don't know how Marge responded to the same circumstances. Do all adult children living at home continue to be children?

During that long calendar month, I am sure there were at least eight weeks.

But at last they ended. After an examination from Harry and Phyllis, involving the not so surreptitious sniffing of every centimeter of air escaping from my mouth and nose, I was given a reluctant okay, and Marge and I went forth.

We decided to visit the same restaurant on Taraval Street where we'd previously tried that disastrous dinner experiment. The booths were the same, the sombreros and serapes and other artifacts on the walls were the same, and the food was still delicious, actually more delicious, now that I could taste it. I don't know how the wine was. I drank six cups of coffee.

It was not easy.

In back of every taste was the echo of years' worth of drinking, telling me how everything could be so much better, if only I would have a sip, just a sip. I never had "just a sip" in my life, and now would definitely not be the time to try it.

We completed the evening by making up for the movie my drinking caused us to miss on that previous date of ours, catching it at a second run theater.

Marge was beautiful.

I wanted the night to go on forever, but we agreed to get her home by midnight, and the time was not that far away. We sat on the front stairs of her house. It was hard not to imagine Phyllis' eyes peering out at us—If it was imagination.

Marge sat next to me with her head cradled against my shoulder and my arm around her.

"Ward," she asked, "why don't you drive?"

It was a fair question and I had been expecting it, not necessarily tonight, but it was bound to come up. I considered a number of possible replies, from the truly outlandish and wildly inventive to the simple truth.

In the end, it was my respect for her that decided my answer.

"They gave me a choice," I said. "If I want to live in my parents' house I can't drink and drive."

"Do you have to live there?"

"The price is right," I said, pausing to kiss her.

She returned the kiss passionately, but still brushed aside my exploring right hand.

"We can't live with them," she said.

My breath stopped. "I know," I said.

The slight movement of the curtain caught my eye. I ordered my right hand to behave and nudged Marge. "If you look at the window, you'll see someone watching us," I said.

It was five minutes after midnight. We rose and I received a kiss and an unreserved embrace.

She slid into the house.

We? I played with the word all the way home. It was the most beautiful word I had ever heard, the stuff of mighty poetry. I was on the verge of being very silly, and I didn't care!

I took a bus across one of the outer Avenues, transferred to the Taraval streetcar, and was home in less than forty-five minutes.

My mind raced like the motor of the car I didn't have. If it had come up, if she had broached the subject—and even if she hadn't—I had been ready to answer the next question: "Why do you drink?" But it hadn't come up.

The answer was that I liked the world a lot better when I viewed it through the bottom of a glass. What did that say about my affection for Marge? That was a question I was certainly not prepared to answer. But I *was* certain of my love.

Maybe it was the only thing in this whole damn universe that I was certain of.

My mother was waiting for me in the kitchen when I got home. A cup of cocoa was on the table before her, and steam wafted from it.

"You're home early," she said.

"It seemed like a good idea." I smiled. "Besides, Mrs. Morton was at the window."

She did not respond to the humor.

"What's wrong?" I asked.

"Your father and I have decided to make it final this time."

I felt the familiar lurch in my stomach, the same one I felt when my parents were first separated and I was eleven years old. It felt every bit as bad, although it was probably the best thing that could happen for Mom. But her world was going to change, almost as much as my reality had been shattered that first time.

"Will you be all right?" I asked. I stood beside her and hugged her.

She smiled and loosened up a little at that. "Well, the house is paid for, and the monthly settlement will be more than enough. It's just …"

The tears came. My mother returned my embrace and cried like a baby.

I actually understood, in a very adult way. My father could continue his relentless pursuit of booze and broads, and close us off like a chapter in a book he decided to stop reading. Regardless of the circumstances, rejection hurts.

The real trouble was that he was not all bad. Where I was a child—not nice to admit, but pretty obvious—Drake E. Pentecost would be a selfish adolescent for all his life. He was a successful sensualist. He had been a wife-beater and a child-beater. He had outgrown both of those pursuits.

In finding himself, he replaced a chronic uncertainty, which was dramatized by an unreasoning rage, with the certainty that he wanted nothing more than to sleep with as many women as possible, and it had a calming effect. The beatings, the violence stopped overnight, and they didn't ever resume. He even apologized to us.

The first separation followed within weeks and lasted eight months. Shortly after the second separation I turned sixteen and started drinking. He never reproached me for it, just, in collaboration with my mother, made the rule about driving and several other restrictions designed to protect me from myself.

I didn't resent it, knowing all the time that someday my spree would have to end.

Upon closer examination, my mother's plight wasn't that awful. She was feeling bad at this moment, but that would pass, and she would be able to settle into the life of a divorced wife and mother quite easily, I thought. After all, the country was full of them.

"I'm sure it will work out, Mom," I said, knowing that in the very near future it was quite possible I would also be deserting her.

She shuddered in my arms and stopped crying. Two weeks later I proposed marriage to Marge, and she accepted.

⌘

I continued to see Marge, and I drank nothing that had been forbidden to me. Marge was wearing her parents down, exhibiting an uncustomary stubbornness. She loved me and would accept no future that did not include me. The one month isolation we had just gone through was a final, last ditch effort, on their part to be rid of me.

I was very happy, very content, and very unconscious. I did not know where we would live, certainly not in her house, and I knew she didn't want to live here, which meant I would have to give up my comfortable cocoon. I was ready to enter a world where Marge was my constant companion. God knows, I had been fantasizing about nothing else for months. But was I also ready to enter the adult world I so far successfully evaded?

You can't have one without the other.

The lyrics from that old song played a few *bars* in my head. What a choice of words.

Marge found the apartment, eight blocks away from her parents' house. It was reasonably new and spotlessly clean. I wondered if we could keep it like that, and when I learned about cleaning deposits, I was certain we would.

So, with our marriage only one month off, we began to move our things into the apartment. My mother picked out and paid for a substantial portion of our brand new furniture. By mutual agreement, we did not move in together in advance of the nuptials. This, I am certain, relieved her folks, and kept me at home just a little longer. My mother seemed to be taking it very well; that is, she was not losing a son so much as she was gaining a daughter, and reconciled to the former and really seemed to like the latter.

⌘

Two weeks before the impending wedding, my father took us all to dinner. It was his way of doing something helpful.

The sun had not yet set when we found a parking place on the Embarcadero, far along the waterfront where the line of piers veered to the west and gradually gave way to the shops and restaurants of Pier 39.

The seafood restaurant my father selected was new, expensive, and crowded. The food was great.

Sandwiched in between other early evening diners, we manipulated our utensils with arms held closer to our sides than was usual. But, except for that minor inconvenience, caused by the greed of the restaurant owners, the meal was a success.

My father refrained from any of his usual antics when surrounded by three reasonably attractive women, representing two different generations, and was the soul of discretion and humor.

I ate lighter than was usual and declined all offers of drinks, aperitifs, and refreshments, even if "One won't hurt you." Both Marge and I were quieter than usual. We each independently realized that how well our parents got along together would have an effect on our future lives.

As I dawdled over the excellent *sole petrale*, not quite savoring but still enjoying the stuffing of mushrooms and minced shellfish in a butter sauce, Marge called my attention to the view.

From where we both sat, on the same side of the table, we could see all the way out to the Golden Gate. The sun had not quite set, and the fog was rolling in from the Pacific. As I watched, its encroaching fingers bleached the international orange color from the bridge, turning it a silver gray. The last rays of the sun contributed to the picture that was forming. The prismatic effect twisted my perception of the cables of the bridge, and what I saw, hanging across the Golden Gate, was not a bridge, but a gigantic spider web.

EIGHT.

———❧———

NATHANAEL: The Examined Life

CLICHÉ MET DÉJÀ VU AS I WOKE AS AN ADULT IN MY CHILDHOOD BED, swung my feet over the side and stood. Banal or not, doubtlessly I should have some insight just at that moment. Here I was, twenty-seven, climbing out of the same bed I'd slept in at seventeen and seven, in a room crowded with my vanished father's effects, and I couldn't muster up some serviceable observation about the human condition? About the gentle cosmic irony of growing up and older. About the inability to return home even when you *were* home. Nothing?

Jesus Christ. I sure wasn't leading the unexamined life Plato warned us about. But was this life of mine actually worth examining?

I brushed my teeth, showered. My personal hygiene products made a beachhead in the bathroom. I was settling in here.

It was a few minutes after nine when I went downstairs. Mom, an early riser, had coffee on. She herself was in the backyard, in dirty-kneed jeans, doing something to a furrowed row of dark soil. The big plum tree was still there in the center of the plot, not especially bigger than I recalled it being.

"How did you sleep?" She shaded her eyes against the morning light with a large yellow work glove. Her smile was easy. She was already used to having me at the house, I realized.

We chatted a bit while I drank my coffee. I sat on the back steps. I remembered the wood being spongy, rotting. The stairs had been rebuilt since.

I had some memories of the apartment on 25th Street on the other side of Twin Peaks, where I'd spent the first years of my life. But those memories there centered mostly on objects and people—objects and people that had been transported here when we'd moved. It was this house, though, here on Santiago that I called my childhood home. Its memories were much more vibrant, much more powerful. This morning I was no longer being buffeted by memory radiation, but those memories were all here, all alive. And I was among them once more.

"Well"—I drained my cup and stood—"I've got some business to do. I'll be back in a bit."

"Wait." Mom rose, without any of the jerkiness of old joints, and led me into the house. She pulled open a drawer in the kitchen. "Here."

I took the offered key. I smiled, perhaps a bit more moved than the moment warranted, told her again I'd be back, and exited the house.

I took Santiago west, meaning only to go a few blocks and then pull over. Instead, probably from reluctance to get down to business, I went further, across Sunset Boulevard and all the way out to the dunes. The beach. The ocean.

Too cold to ever really swim in, this was one of the places I'd come to during my high school years, on those few fluke occasions when I was invited along on nighttime social outings. I parked across from the Great Highway and went on foot through one of the pedestrian tunnels—smelling urine and crunching beer bottle shards underfoot—until I reached the sand.

Today, October's usual clement weather was in full effect. Even with the wind off the waves it was very warm, maybe in the high 70s. Dogs were running around along the long beach. One, a white husky bitch with penetrating blue eyes, came near me. I put out my hand for her to sniff, but her owner called her off.

I remembered sitting around a driftwood campfire out here one night. I was a gangly teenager who read too much and got too good grades, who didn't keep up on the ebbs and flows of pop culture sufficiently to really fit in with his popular peers. Nonetheless, that night I'd made out—for one of the first times in my life—with a pixie-faced girl named Rachel. It was a wonderful experience. It was as near to being a perfect night as one could reasonably hope for. Probably, for sheer fun and enjoyment, I'd never duplicated it.

That was okay, I told myself. I hadn't signed on in this life for fun and enjoyment. Or happiness. My purposes ran deeper.

I went back to the car. I took up my phone. I breathed awhile, steadily.

There was no saying with any certainty what hours the Purple Witch kept. I'd seen her pass out—literally—at one in the afternoon. I'd received phone calls from her at four AM, where she would speak in passionate but mechanically precise sentences for a solid hour, describing whole passages of our book or delineating its characters so thoroughly that, by the end, I knew which were the first teeth those characters cut as infants. Of course, as often as not, she would throw out all this material. Or even not remember recounting it to me.

I certainly wasn't going to phone from the house. For one thing, I wasn't going to put a call to Rhode Island on Mom's bill. For another, I'd be damned if the Purple Witch was going to get ahold of *that* number and be ringing at any and all hours. Neither did I want to make this call on my phone from the house; I didn't want Mom to inadvertently overhear any part of the conversation.

I listened to the rings. In the middle of the third the line engaged. Even that sound had a curtness to it, a kind of impatient, unpleasant, frenzy.

"Fairy? That's you?"I heard the fast puff-blow of her taking a hit off the cigarette grafted to her hand. "Where the hell are you?"

"San Francisco."

"What the hell're you doing *there?*"

"I ..."

Actually I had no words to follow that "I"—not because I didn't have reasons for being here in the city (I did) and not because I wouldn't get to have my say eventually (I would). First, however, the Purple Witch would cut me off and snap and snarl and not want to hear my *excuses.*

"I don't want to hear your bullshit!" she shrieked from the far end of the continent.

I closed my eyes, slouched back behind the wheel.

She frothed awhile. I listened to the shallow angry breaths she drew. What came between them was a lot of invective, most of it nonsensical. She was blaming me for things I hadn't done, for things I didn't even know about. Possibly for things that never happened anywhere outside the confines of her mind.

Eventually, when she was starting to lose momentum, I cut in on her—something I wouldn't have dared to do when we'd met, over eight months ago; but eight months is a long time to listen to someone's rantings.

"*You* sent me out here, Irene," I said, stepping bluntly on her lines.

"Oh, bullshit, fairy!"

My eyes were open now. I watched a woman—young, maybe just out of high school, long blond hair—come out of a house across the street, a dog pulling on a red leather leash. They both headed off for the beach.

"You sent me out here," I repeated, not argumentatively. Arguing with the Purple Witch wasn't profitable. "You sent me to find George Starks."

I imagined the invocation of that name would shut her up for a moment; and it did. I found myself enjoying the silence so much, though, that I didn't rush in to fill it.

"Georgie?" she asked finally, and it was the voice of a totally different person. Gone were the histrionics and the indiscriminate fury. She spoke now as a little girl. Bruised and innocent. "Oh, Georgie ..."

I could not connect this voice with what I knew her to look like, what I knew her to *be*. She had no tenderness in her. Yet I heard her adolescently intense longing. George Starks obviously occupied a place in her life that probably nobody else visited in the past thirty years—certainly not since Irene I. Isis became a recognizable name in literary circles.

It still was recognized, but thirty years of cashing in on the fame of a single acclaimed novel cost her. Cost her dearly.

"You told me George Starks was the man I had to meet," I went on. "You said he was the key. I would never understand the book until I experienced him."

She said these very things to me, but I was not surprised now that she didn't remember. Even at the time she'd said it, making a great dramatic performance of it, arms sweeping as she paced, trailing purple silks behind her, voice rising and dipping ... even then I'd known it was only another rant. She popped her pills. She was taking big swallows of thick red wine. Cigarette tip glowing orange as she strode and wheeled about. Pouring out her larger-than-lifeness. George! Yes, George Starks. He's the key. He's the decoder. He's the Rosetta Stone. Without him you'll understand nothing. Nothing! Go find him, fairy.

So, I had taken her at her word. Knowing that her epiphany about this George Starks being critical to finishing our book was balderdash, I went anyway. He was in San Francisco, said the Purple Witch. Fine. To San Francisco I would go.

And, of course the incident short-circuited itself from her mind and memory, probably immediately after I'd left her yellow-shingled house and started my drive back to New York City that day. I'd phoned the airlines for a ticket on the way. I stopped in the city to pack my bags; then I flew west, reading *The Gap Through Her Heart* by Minnie F. Tucker during the flight.

"Is Georgie there now?" she asked, still in the little girl voice.

"I haven't found him yet." Absolutely the only clue to his whereabouts she'd provided was that he lived in San Francisco. Or had, some thirty or so years ago. And still I'd blithely gone along with this. For once, I would demonstrate to her the consequences of her actions. Send me away on your demented whim on the wildest of goose chases? Okay. Sure. Now—live with the results.

"Oh, oh ... find. Georgie. I." Blissful silence returned once more.

It had, perhaps, been worth this entire trip simply to have the experience of dumbfounding her.

But there were venomous agents in her bloodstream and misfiring synapses in her head that wouldn't allow her to remain docile too long. A moment later she came back, in more familiar form.

"And I'm supposed to do what while you're away out there? Probably having the time of your life, aren't you, fairy? We've got a book that needs working on! Isn't that important to you? Where's your work ethic? How am I supposed to ..."

I slouched a little deeper into the car seat. She had another cigarette going—of course—and I listened to her smoking it and didn't hear much else. I waited for the young blond with the dog to come home, but she didn't.

Finally it was over. I set down the phone. I programmed it not to receive any incoming calls. I had my pager if anyone wanted to try to reach me.

I hadn't started my search for George Starks. It hadn't occurred to me to start it. It was idiocy, of course. It had been entirely in the realm of possibility that George Starks was a figment, something fermented in the Purple Witch's putre-fying brain. Now I was a little more convinced of his reality. But what difference would finding him make? I certainly didn't believe that talking to him would do anything toward finishing the dreadful, derivative novel that I was aiding Irene I. Isis in bringing to fruition. The book was doomed. And, just coincidentally, so was my—mostly hypothetical—writing career. Doomed before it could ever have become anything.

I swung the car east and went back home.

NINE.

WARD: Wedding Bells

ON A LOVELY SPRING MORNING, exactly eleven months after our first meeting, Margot Jean Morton and myself, Ward Bartholomew Pentecost, were married in a Catholic wedding ceremony, at the same church that served at the nuptials of her parents.

The wedding was widely attended by friends of both families, and a spattering of local politicians, three supervisors, eight department heads (including mine) from local government, and someone from the animal shelter, all of whom were indebted to "the people's realtor," Drake Pentecost.

My father might have been a poor husband and parent, but he used his ability in the real estate market to help hundreds of working people move into decent, low cost, family dwellings, often taking a reduced commission, and in some cases, no commission.

From these grateful people and their friends and acquaintances, he wielded considerable political influence in the geographically small City and County of San Francisco.

The first rows of the pews were taken up by immediate family members, dwindling down to distant cousins further back.

On the bride's side Phyllis was seated, having been escorted down the aisle by the best man, looking fragile in a delicate, green dress, tastefully weeping, and sniffing at every errant breeze that came from where I stood on the altar. After escorting his daughter down the aisle, and symbolically kissing her goodbye, Harry Morton was impassive, and while I expected him to be uncomfortable in a tuxedo, he wore the formal clothing with considerable ease, reminding me of one of the family heads in *The Godfather*.

Ruth and her husband, whom I already dubbed "Inspector Pete," were there, right alongside the "uppity" Sarah and "Stockbroker Sam." From there the faces faded into nonentities, as far as I was concerned.

On my family's side, my mother was radiant and my father properly distinguished. My maternal grandmother, she of the marvelously aromatic kitchen of my youthful memories, had been brought down from the nursing home in Sonoma County, and in spite of the dementia that so heartbreakingly afflicted her latter days, I am certain she knew what was going on and approved.

My mother and father both were only children, my father because it was the custom in his family to limit the number of offspring, and my mother because her father had died of an early heart attack. So, the pews on our side were filled up by my coworkers and friends and acquaintances of my father and mother.

Margot was breathtakingly beautiful. After I finished shivering with sobriety, I shivered with delight and anticipation. That which I had been dreaming about for almost a year was about to be made true by the uttering of some phrases by a person I didn't know.

I remember saying, "I do." I kissed the bride on the lips, and somehow, in a state of almost complete euphoria, made it out of the church, shook hands with men I knew and didn't know, kissed many women, and exulted in feeling as wonderful as I have ever felt.

The reception loomed as a hostile wall of booze for me to overcome.

∽

As we entered the well-appointed hall at the Irish Cultural Center that Phyllis selected for the occasion, I grabbed a glass of water, and held onto it for dear life.

We made our way through the well-wishers, including those who arrived early to drink late, a contingent of which I had long been a distinguished member, and managed to be seated at the main table. Most of the wedding party preceded us.

The small, hired combo, struck up a few notes from the wedding march as we took our places.

There were a large number of small children running around. Evidently, the proscription on large families that marked my father's ancestry did not apply to the Mortons. Still, they all seemed happy. The children were boisterous and loud, as children in packs always are, but they were not rude, and used the words "please" and "thank you" a refreshing number of times. Everyone got on well with everyone.

Bill Berry, the best man, who was the closest I had to a best friend, and who shared a position in the mail room with me, offered a toast to the bride and groom, followed by a very funny monologue, which showcased his wit at the expense of no one. I breathed a sigh.

I felt that long before the first course of the nuptial meal I'd met everybody in the room at least twice. An endless number of people migrated to the head table, exchanged a few remarks with us and made way for the next wave.

It all was very pleasant. I refilled my water glass several times, and guarded the pitcher zealously from those drunken wags who might think that getting the groom drunk was the stuff of high humor.

The meal was not corned beef and cabbage. Instead the sirloin tips were properly cooked, not too dry nor too rare. The accompanying vegetables were crisp and not overcooked, the roasted potatoes excellent, and the salad tasty and freshly made. While everyone else toasted the bride and groom and just about everything else with glasses of wonderful smelling Chardonnay, I toasted the same everything with water, which tasted and smelled just like water.

It could not matter less. I was intoxicated by the day. With my bride beside me, I beamed out at all the people, including Phyllis, who tried to beam back, but couldn't quite make it.

I was very grateful for the time I spent learning how to dance, and for the new pairs of built-up shoes and half boots, which were a present from my father.

There was an order to be followed in these things.

First, of course, I danced with my wife. A momentous event. The first of many firsts, I hoped. Then I danced with my mother, and the bride's mother, who tried to lead.

Then everybody was dancing, some of the children doing better than any of the adults, exhibiting the natural grace that goes with unclouded childhood, and many old people doggedly doing their best, and, in some cases, carrying it off with aplomb.

It was very nearly another first for me. Once more I was sober and happy at the same time, as on my first date with Marge.

The afternoon reception seemed to be headed for early evening. I didn't care, but sometime around five o'clock the crowd gathered into a different ritualistic configuration and it was time to toss the bouquet and the bride's garter. We did it amidst laughter, and shrieks of joy from the bridesmaid who caught the bouquet. Bill Berry caught the garter.

To say that I was excited would be to definitely understate the situation. When we broke off from the crowd to change into our street clothes, I found myself placing both legs in the same pant leg three times before I got it right. I wondered if Margot was having similar experiences. I thought not. My experiences seemed to be a guy thing.

After being reassured twice that I was properly dressed, and my shirt and jacket were not on backwards, I finally took my best man's word.

I declined several invitations to go to the bar with guests who were obviously under no prohibition regarding drinking.

After a not so short wait, Marge appeared, looking lovely and appealing in a casual suit in blue tones. I took her arm somewhat possessively, and we began the final goodbyes. It didn't take that long, and it went smoothly, except for one incident, which no one explained to me.

An older woman, dressed informally and quite attractive, made her way towards us, and was intercepted by Phyllis and Harry Morton. Words were exchanged, the Mortons showing signs of irritation, and the woman smiled through it all. Before they led her away she made eye contact with both of us. Those eyes were of the clearest, brightest blue, like a high mountain lake on a sunny day, and except for the color, might have been my wife's.

Finally, we were in the doorway, all the hands shaken again and all the cheeks pecked again. I couldn't believe it. We were actually married, and we were going away to be with each other, in an answer to all my dreams, and forever after that.

The limousine that my father hired waited at the curb.

We honeymooned in a two level, executive condominium, on Monterey Bay, with all the accoutrements which we could not afford, but which my father negotiated for a reciprocal deal, I am sure. Meaning, no money needed to change hands.

Monterey Bay is beautiful, the nearby aquarium is also beautiful, the shops and restaurants are beautiful. It is all beautiful, I am sure. We did visit the beaches and the aquarium and ate out and shopped. I don't remember any of it.

My consciousness was overwhelmed by my happiness.

We had not had sex before marriage, although neither of us was a virgin. We'd seen each other dressed or in swimming gear only. When we first undressed I was sure that I died and gone to heaven. Marge was the loveliest thing I had ever seen, and amazingly, she was impressed by the fact that, although nature shortened my left leg, it had been generous elsewhere.

We made love on the bed, actually two beds, because there was no need to neglect the second bedroom, in the kitchen, the shower, the entrance hallway, and even one sunny afternoon, on the balcony.

We were in turn passionate and silly. We made love fully dressed, partially dressed, undressed, and sometimes wearing shoes or hats only or whatever struck our fancy or piqued our passion.

We laughed a lot and kissed tenderly even more.

I wanted it to last forever.

Although pure, undiluted passion is great, I think silliness wears better. It is almost always a shared emotion, and, on the rare occasions it is not mutual to start with, it usually infects the reluctant member. It is joyful and lighthearted. It doesn't preclude passion, but modifies it into something less intense, and less serious.

I think Marge and I enjoyed each other the most when we were being silly, or being tender with or without sex.

As Friday inevitably came around and time for us to leave,

my thoughts turned back to the wedding. Marge was already preparing a list of thank you notes she would write, each one personalized and written in her neat, calligraphic script with a fountain pen.

I was thinking of the lady with the piercing eyes, who disturbed the Mortons when we were leaving, and asked Marge about her.

She didn't answer me right away. I could see that she was considering how to phrase her answer. Apparently I was being admitted to the highest level of family security.

"That was my Aunt Chloe. She's my mother's older sister and we don't talk about her. In fact, she wasn't invited to our wedding."

I didn't say anything.

"You know that my mother is not just a devout Catholic," she said.

"Nothing wrong with that," was my careful comment.

"Mother is a strict Catholic, and Aunt Chloe is just as strict a pagan."

When was the last time I heard that word? Certainly sometime in the early years of my unpleasant parochial education. *Pagan* was a swear word then, practically.

There was more. "Aunt Chloe was associated with Wicca, may even have participated in their rituals."

Pretty harmless stuff, as I gleaned from my own later reading on the subject. It was mostly benign nature worship.

Marge halted. The great disclosure of the family disgrace had been passed on to the newest member.

"She does have beautiful eyes though," I said. "Just like you."

That seemed to comfort her. I examined the great secret in my mind. As I understood it, Aunt Chloe was being ostracized because she was a witch.

⤜⧉⤛

On the ride back home into San Francisco we passed the bar where, after my great reneging on my promise not to touch alcohol again, I would drink until my son was born. My son's birth, which would stop me drinking once again, would also signify the start of what I felt was, on a personal and real level, my own dying.

———∞———

TEN

NATHANAEL:
Come to The Table

"WELL, JUST ..." MOM STOPPED, TITTERED. "I was going to say, make yourself at home. Well, why not? Make yourself at home, Nathan. Do you need a plug for that?"

I was dry-mouthed yet again but finally past the point of caring if that was too cliché. I unpacked my laptop and brought it downstairs, looking for a spot to set up. Father's old study at the rear of the house was now a small library full of potted plants. I'd figured on commandeering the kitchen table. Instead, Mom led me in here.

"Nathan?"

"No. It doesn't need an outlet. Thanks."

She gave my arm a squeeze as she went past and out.

I continued to gaze at the dining room table.

It belonged to Father's parents, Drake and Alice, just like this house once had. It was a solid piece of craftsmanship. Mahogany. All one component. It exuded a kind of nineteenth century durability that set it apart from an "antique."

This was *furniture*, made at a time when merchandise in general was meant to last. It was a heavy mother too. As a boy I would test the limits of my manliness by trying to lift one of the legs off the floor.

I stopped trying after one particular morning in here, with Father. Probably, though, I would have been fourteen or fifteen before I could have hoped to do more than budge the thing. But I would never have been able to move it the way Father had.

A tiny storeroom off the hall upstairs, one wall slanted and bare-beamed, served as my office when I was butchering the short story as an art form as a teen; but it had since reverted to its original function. Neither was there really space to work in my old bedroom, not with all those boxes of Father's old gear.

Still, I stood, staring at the table.

I had a deadline to hit, but the situation was hardly urgent yet. April Gregoire, my editor, wanted five hundred words on *Gap Through Her Heart*. That was all. That was as critical as things were for me at the magazine at the moment.

How would I review Minnie F. Tucker's opus, anyway? It deserved a thorough savaging, no doubt. *Diamond*'s book reviews, however, had to have a particular, youth culture flavored panache. They also—at least mine, by my personal standards, did—had to give some genuine insight into why the book succeeded or failed.

Why had *Gap* failed? The grander challenge, of course, would be in determining where it succeeded. That would certainly tax my faculties ...

Was this one long stall or what?

It's a table. It's a big inert table. The wood died by a lumberjack's hands long ago, and it has never lived again. This is what I told myself.

I took another step closer. Then another. Then, forcing it, came up to the table and laid my laptop on the long lace tablecloth covering it. But I didn't sit. And, I realized, I wasn't going to. I went back out to the kitchen.

"It's all right in there?" Mom asked. She had on her reading glasses, the mail in a little stack before her on the kitchen table.

"Oh, fine." I did my best to keep any reaction off my face. "I just wanted to—to set up my machine. I'll work later."

"Another review?" she asked, interested.

"Yep." I did not, however, want to tell her about *Gap*; or, if she pressed, I would simply omit that the Bridge's disappearance figured vaguely into the book's plot. I hadn't told her I'd visited the site yesterday, and we had not mentioned the Bridge since I'd arrived.

"What would you like for dinner tonight?"

I waved my hand. "I'll take you out to dinner. You choose. Anywhere's fine."

She was weeding out the junk mail. The curtains were open, and the afternoon sun picked out the highlights from her dyed red hair. "We can go Dutch, you know."

"But the hell we will," I said in a cheerful tone. I wasn't rich or even well-off. You don't get rich living in New York doing what I do. But it felt good having at least enough to treat my mother to a meal.

Her gray eyes were suddenly quite fixed on a particular envelope. Her face wore the expression of someone who has just said "Oh my," only she hadn't.

"Something wrong?" I asked.

I was away at school when the Bridge disappeared. I was in the midst of a disappearance of my own. I was in New York, among what I considered my intellectual peers. When I told people my name was Nathanael, that was what they called me—not Nathan, not Nate. It was a heady experience for me.

I came home on the 9th of November, 2010, two days after the Golden Gate Bridge inexplicably, fantastically, terrifyingly, ceased to be. San Francisco was practically in quarantine, and if I hadn't had a father who'd been identified by traffic surveillance cameras as being on the span at the time, I probably wouldn't have been let through at the airport.

It was chaos in the city. People were afraid. *Very* afraid, in a way that not even Pearl Harbor or 9/11 evoked. It was like the vengeful hand of God swept down and scooped away something from the world. People prayed. People burst into hysterics in the supermarket, in elevators. People put their $800,000 homes on the market and moved away overnight.

I stayed with Mom here at the house. I helped turn away the news people when they came prowling hungrily for a human interest piece. Soon enough, I realized that I effectively dropped out of school; so I made the act official. Mom needed me. Very probably I needed her. I didn't go back to school until the following September.

"Mom? What's wrong?"

Her eyes finally rose, and there was a stillness about her. She took a further moment to make sure her voice was steady. Then she said, "It's the Memorial Society. Just a reminder about the anniversary." Her lips pressed together, then relaxed. "As if a reminder's necessary."

Yet the date slipped my mind.

"Are you going to go?" I asked quietly.

She regarded me. "I go every year."

When I was a kid, I remembered the gatherings every April 18, at Lotta's Fountain. 5:12 AM. The time when the quake slammed the city in 1906. I would see the news segments with the assembled aging survivors. Back then there had still been a number of them.

"Are you still going to be in town?" Mom asked.

In just over a week it would be November 7th. Would I have left San Francisco by then?

"I can't say," I told Mom. "This business I'm doing ... it's not—not up to me. It's not my own time. You know? I might have to leave, like, *before*." I was suddenly tongue-tied, off balance.

Mom, of course, let me off the hook. With a smile. With a few understanding words.

∞

She tried to convince me a hamburger would do, but eventually I persuaded her to pick a real restaurant; and we ended up having Chinese somewhere far down along California Street. I didn't recognize the place, but it was just the right mixture of kitsch and genuine Far East grace.

The short-term effects of the Bridge's disappearance in the Bay Area were visceral—upheaval and panic. The economic aftershock followed, less spectacularly, felt most especially north of the Golden Gate. Freight wasn't traveling through that region any longer. The real estate market there, over the years, quietly imploded. Malls went bust, and local industries suffocated. A lot of old money in Marin County was lost.

Neither Mom nor I were hearty eaters, but we strove through the courses gamely. We were comfortable in each other's company. I found I'd built up a surprising store of anecdotes from my time at the magazine. I'd stopped finding my work for *Diamond* interesting some time ago—though I didn't loathe the job by any means—but Mom soaked it up merrily. I didn't, however, tell her any further tales of my brief internship at the publishing house. (The flesh was still tender there; I might never be able to talk with detachment about that period of my life.) Thus we passed a very pleasant dinner together.

She pretended to forget this was my treat and made one last stab at splitting the check. I made sure no money of hers touched the table.

When I'd driven us back to the house, Mom surprised me by fetching a bottle of wine and two stemmed glasses. "Would you like one, Nathan?"

I blinked. "Sure. Okay." Sharing alcohol with a parent for the first time might be one of the great unacknowledged rites of passage.

The first of maybe four times in my life I've been drunk occurred—and I imagine this is a fairly common experience—the first time I tasted alcohol. I was sixteen; I'd been out at another of those chance social events, and this time somebody contrived to procure a bottle of Southern Comfort. We drank it mixed with warm flat soda. I recall it tasted like nothing so much as bubble gum. I lost control of my faculties in pretty short order, reeling in and out of a queasy awareness of my surroundings. One of the times I came up, I found myself stumbling into this house's foyer—the front door open wide behind me, my key hanging in the lock, my "friends" vanished.

I got to the kitchen, where I was suddenly on my knees; and just as suddenly my stomach decided to unload its contents. I was urgently aware that my parents were now present. When I was seized by the back of my collar and hauled—not gently—toward the sink, I assumed Father grabbed me. As the heaves overtook me, I realized it was Mom who had a hold of me. Her grip was shockingly strong.

When I'd eventually finished, in an absolute misery of shame, disorientation, and drunkenness, I found that Father had left the room. Mom put me into my bed, saying nothing but "Be quiet, go to sleep" whenever I tried to burble an apology.

Now, Mom and I brought our wineglasses into the front room of the house. The space was cozier without the tv, I decided.

It occurred to me that I might now remark on that incident of my debut drunk, and that we two might laugh over it, as adults. But I withheld it. Father, so I knew by the same osmosis by which most family legends are learned, flirted with a dangerous love of alcohol when he'd been younger. But, by the time I had any awareness of it, he was attending AA. Whatever the gene was, I hadn't inherited it. Or I'd resolutely refused to let it take root. Yet ... I had known, even as a boy, that Mom looked upon her husband with a sort of subtle, permanent disapproval. And that the disapproval had, at least in part, to do with his drinking.

I had no memories at all of Father ever taking a drink of anything alcoholic; and I, as with many other of his ways, made sure not to echo his old habit.

The morning following my first foray into the realm of alcohol consumption, I woke with what I imagine will be the worst hangover I'll ever experience. After vomiting yet again—just painful dry heaves this time—and brushing my teeth for five or ten minutes, I went to make a very contrite apology to my mother. I wouldn't do it again, I meant to promise. I'd been stupid, *real* stupid. I was so sorry.

But she wouldn't let me apologize. "You didn't let me down, Nathan," she explained, without any obvious tenderness. "You didn't let your father down. If you're disappointed, *you're* disappointed. Make your apologies to yourself. Promise not to do it again, if you like. To yourself."

It was an awfully adult concept for my sixteen year old, booze-blasted brain to handle that morning. As with all things in my adolescence, I brooded grimly on the matter. I don't know that I ever came to any conclusions.

In the front room, Mom and I chatted breezily, an extension of our conversation from dinner.

"How did you know about that restaurant?" I asked, slowly sipping my way toward the bottom of my glass of ruby port.

There was just a hairsbreadth of a lull before she answered. "A friend takes me there sometimes. His name is Bennet. We know each other from church."

I smiled. "Well, that's nice."

It *was* nice. I didn't give in to the freefall feeling that comes of hearing that your mother is seeing another man—no matter that your father has been dead, or at least cosmically absent, for almost seven full years. I could be happy that Mom had some companionship, and I would be happy.

For the moment, though, we both appeared content to leave the matter unplumbed.

Eventually she went upstairs to change into the uniform of the house—a fuzzy, comfortable robe and slippers. I'd had thoughts about writing my review tonight, but with the wine in me I was lethargic. Besides, I truly didn't know what I was going to write regarding *Gap Through Her Heart*. It wasn't as clear-cut as I would have thought it would be.

And anyway I didn't feel like sitting at my laptop at the head of that big mahogany table.

I went up to my room and kicked off my shoes. I looked around at the many, sloppily stacked boxes.

I spent almost a year here at the house after the Bridge disappeared; but this boxing up of Father's effects had been done sometime after that. Maybe Mom enlisted the help of a few of her nieces and nephews. I wasn't terribly well acquainted with my cousins. Maybe Mom had undertaken alone the task of removing Ward Pentecost's things from view and storing them here in this room.

I couldn't fault her for having waited so long to do it. It wasn't tidy and absolute, what happened. It wasn't as if Father had gotten shot or been in an auto wreck, not as if his body had been laid out solemnly for identification on a cold morgue slab. He, along with those hundreds of others, was just gone.

The things was, if you were gone, the inverse was that you might someday come back.

Not that anybody with any sense or sanity believed *that* after seven years.

I went across the upstairs hall and knocked at the other bedroom door.

"Mom ... how about I take all those boxes down into the basement? There's still plenty of room down there, right? It ... it seems more appropriate. Don't you think?"

ELEVEN.

———∞———

WARD: The Letter

MARGE WAS OUT GROCERY SHOPPING WITH NATE, one of his favorite activities, especially since he found that he could always prevail on either of us to purchase something sweet and non-nutritious, if he asked.

I was home alone on this Saturday morning in the spacious flat on 25th Street. My typewriter rested on a small desk we bought at a local garage sale, carried home for two blocks, and fitted into a corner of our large bedroom. I had written a total of one story at the desk, and was presently in a fugue, brought on by the dreadful sameness of yet another of those printed rejection slips I'd seen so many of over the years.

I sat on the chair in front of the typewriter and let my fingers drop to the desktop and linger there for a minute. Then I raised them, not wishing to take a chance of damaging the typewriter, when, and if, I managed to lift the desk.

It had been a long time since I attempted this. And for what purpose? I don't think I ever did it, or anything else involving what I referred to as *real magic*, for any discernable reason, except that it was fun. It was like stretching muscles in my mind. I can't define it better than that.

For a while, when I was very young, my mother used to tantalize me with stories of how her great grandmother, in Italy, could see things at a distance, find lost items just by thinking about them, and move objects without touching them. I was young enough that I believed all the stories. Who knows? Maybe they were true.

When I was old enough to ask my grandmother about her grandmother all I got was, "Nice lady." My attempts at persistence were all in vain. To this day those are the words that describe my great-great grandmother in my mind: "Nice lady."

I picked up the typewriter, with the partially used ream of paper on top of it, and put them both on the bed behind me. Without the weight of the typewriter and the partial ream of paper, the desk was not very heavy. Still, it had dimension and mass. It existed, took up a place in space and time.

Table levitating is what I was most familiar with, but it wasn't the limit of what I could do, or done. I achieved other effects when I was alone in the basement out on Santiago. With my hands atop the clothes hamper, I caused it to dance across the floor. It was a feat which required a different set of mental muscles, and was actually harder to do, needing more energy than it took to lift a table, no matter what that table's weight or dimensions were. That had been years ago. Table levitating was what I had once frightened my mother with.

I placed my hands loosely upon the desktop and lifted. The desk rose three inches. I guided it back down and released it.

Then I replaced the typewriter and paper and smiled to myself. Yes, it still was fun.

I heard the sound of a key in the front door lock and hurried to meet Marge and Nate. She was already on her way to the kitchen, the stroller laden with groceries and one small child.

"It would have been nice to have some help getting this up the front stairs," she said.

"Sorry, I was in the bathroom."

I helped her lift the grocery bags onto the kitchen table. Nate was happily munching on a red licorice stick when I released him from the safety harness and carried him over to his maple high chair. He continued to chew contentedly while I unbuttoned, unzipped, and unsnapped his going-to-the-store garments.

"Did we get any mail today?" I asked.

Marge finished putting the quart of orange juice and the half gallon of milk in the refrigerator. "My hands were full," she said.

"Oh, well, when you've seen one rejection slip you've seen them all," I said half-jokingly. The couple of story submissions I had out to various magazines' fiction departments were ones that had already been out several times each, and each time rejected. After a while you lose hope in these stories, one by one.

While she continued to put the groceries away, I let myself out the front door and went downstairs to the street level. Our mailbox was stuffed. I thumbed through the usual collection of catalogs, sales notices, and offers, didn't see any returned manuscripts, and carried the whole mess upstairs.

Marge finished with the groceries and was at the stove getting a kettle ready for some instant coffee. "Oh," she said, indicating the catalogs, "be sure to shake them. Letters get caught in the pages all the time."

I rifled the pages of the catalogs and found two bills and one pale blue envelope addressed to both of us.

"What's that?" I said.

"Open it and find out."

"Not right now." I shoved the letter aside and went over to the stove next to Marge, who was just finishing making her coffee.

"I'll join you." I got my mug from the sideboard, made my coffee, and took it to the table.

Nate chewed contentedly on his remaining third of red licorice. "Is that all he wanted?" I asked.

"I got off easy," said Marge.

She picked up the two bills and the letter and shuffled them absent-mindedly.

"Now who would be sending us an invitation?" she asked.

The blue envelope did look like an invitation to a shower, or a wedding. I glanced at the return address. It was over the hill in Glen Park.

Marge was also reading the return address. She dropped the letter and the two bills. "I can't read this," she said.

I picked up the letter. "It's addressed to both of us," I said. "Maybe I'll open it."

"Don't you dare!" She snatched the letter from my hands and crumpled it into a ball, which she threw in the waste container under the sink.

"Marge, are you all right?" There was real concern in my voice because this was something new in our relationship, and I was worried.

"Of course, I'm all right," she snapped at me. "It was from *her*. We don't read letters from her."

"Do you mean we, as in us, or we, as in your family?" I asked.

"Both."

"Well then, will you please tell me who is this mysterious letter writer?"

"Aunt Chloe."

"The lady with the beautiful blue eyes?"

"All of you men notice that," said Marge.

I was getting progressively confused. "Marge," I said as gently as possible. "Is there something else I should know?"

She took a deep drink from her coffee cup. Her eyes did not meet mine as she spoke.

"Aunt Chloe used to come over and visit all the time when I was little," she said. "I thought she was coming to see me."

"Wasn't she?"

Marge raised her eyes and looked directly at me, almost defiantly. I braced myself for the next revelation.

"She wasn't coming to see me. She was coming to see my father. Do you understand? My mother's sister was having an affair with my father."

"And nobody has forgiven her?" I asked. "Did she do something really dumb, like get pregnant?"

"No."

I kept silent, giving Marge the opportunity to restore her equilibrium. She cried a little and reached out to me tentatively. I took both her hands.

"That was a long time ago," I said soothingly.

"Not to my mother," said Marge. "It broke her heart. If my dad hadn't repented they would have separated. Mother would never get a divorce."

"I understand," I said, which was a lie, because I didn't know what she was talking about at all. My parents were casual about their religion, and they left me to find my own way. I was comfortable floating in a non-denominational world. Right now I was grateful to be there. The world of Marge's parents scared me.

Nate was acting up a little, disturbed by the strong emotions. Marge held him in her arms and soothed him. In a few minutes he calmed down and she took him into the bedroom. It was time for his afternoon nap anyway.

I reached under the sink and fished for the blue envelope. I would read it later.

❦

At two o'clock in the morning I woke up knowing that this was the time. I had put Aunt Chloe's letter in the inside pocket of my work jacket, intending to read it in the morning. This was earlier in the morning than I intended, so I moved through the bedroom like a cat burglar, extracted the letter from my jacket and slipped it into my bathrobe pocket.

Ten minutes later I came out of the bathroom and marched out into the kitchen, all traces of stealth forgotten. I made coffee, sat at the table and stared at the three objects in front of me—the original envelope, the long precise letter from Aunt Chloe, and a check, which in approximately sixteen years would pay for Nate's college education.

My God! Wicca or not, seductress, wanton woman (now that was an old one), or not, Aunt Chloe was definitely not the Wicked Witch. Margaret Hamilton could rest easily.

I thought of waking Marge with the news, but held back from the precipitous action. Let her sleep. There was the shock of the check for her to overcome tomorrow, and I didn't know how she would be able to handle the rest of it.

Nor did I know precisely how she would react to my reading the letter, but I suspected that I would have to do some clever talking just to get her to listen to all of it. The three page letter from Aunt Chloe had given, at least to me, an understandable explanation of those events from Marge's childhood.

∽

"I read it," I said as soon as Marge seated herself at the breakfast table. We both came close to being deluged by her serving of Quaker oats.

"What did you say?"

I was not looking at Margot Pentecost. It was Marge's body, but Phyllis Morton glared at me from across the table, upper lip pulled back from her teeth. For the first time since I met her, I asked myself the question: what in hell have I gotten myself into? Then the mask of her mother faded and my Marge stared at me, her lovely face filled with hurt.

"Aunt Chloe sent us a very big check with instructions on where to invest it. It's to pay for Nate's college education."

"I can't believe it," she said.

I took out the envelope and extracted the letter and the check. I handed her the check. "Read it and believe," I said.

Marge took the check and examined it. As the daughter of a warehouseman, this was entirely outside her realm of experience. "It's real?" she asked.

"Yes," I said, "it's real."

"The letter, please," she said hesitatingly.

I handed it to her and waited.

"It says she didn't seduce Dad."

"And that he didn't seduce her," I added.

"It just happened?"

"She describes it as a force of nature," I said. "They were both young and it just happened."

"That's hard to believe," she said.

"Remember on our honeymoon when we made love on the balcony?" I said.

"In the afternoon." A faintest blush tinted Marge's features.

"Yes, in the afternoon indeed. If someone in another condominium called out for us to stop, I couldn't have. I probably would have called back for him to get his own girl."

"Or *her* to get her own man," volunteered Marge.

"They only made love three times before Phyllis found out about it. So, you see, she *was* coming to visit you all those times."

"All right." Marge looked troubled.

"She's already made peace with your sisters."

"I read that," said Marge.

"So Nate now has another relative and we can keep the check?" I asked.

"Yes," said Marge.

"Our son is going to go to the college of his choice. Not bad for the offspring of the nearest thing to a high school drop out."

"What is the nearest thing?" asked Marge.

"Never mind."

We both laughed.

Nate heard our laughter and giggled at nothing from the bedroom.

I thought that *I had to meet Aunt Chloe.*

TWELVE

NATHANAEL: Down in the Basement

IT WAS COOL IN THE BASEMENT.

I realized I'd taken my pager off before getting in the shower yesterday morning and hadn't since put it back on my thumb. Neither did I do it today, though I did look at the circling numbers. 401 ... 401 ... 401. Nothing but the Purple Witch, paging me from her Rhode Island area code at wildly ranging hours. Possibly she'd forgotten our conversation of yesterday. Or maybe she was anxious for news about George Starks. Where is he, fairy? Did you find him?

Delusional, maniacal monster.

No pages from New York, which meant April wasn't unduly worried yet that I might go overdue. I'd earned that trust. A year and a half at *Diamond* without a missed deadline.

But it wasn't the only deadline in my life. On the 1st of December, a certain semi-reputable publishing house was going to want the novel it contracted for, for which it was forking out a substantial sum. December wasn't far away, and

I knew how easily the time could be consumed, misused, squandered. Irene I. Isis was under contractual obligation to deliver a manuscript of specified length. As yet, we did not have a full third of those pages, although a great deal of material had been tossed out as we'd gone. Of course, much of what there was I had actually written, all of it at the Purple Witch's behest. That was how it worked; that was our deal. She *created.* That was, she pulled the inspired vision for a scene or so-called plot twist out of her ass and I did the legwork. That was, I put the flimsy, hazy, or sometimes thoroughly deranged concept, on paper.

For my part in the novel's making, for which I would receive no byline, I was getting six thousand dollars. Less than princely I had come to think over the past months, upon reflection. Oh, but the honor of collaborating with—well, ghostwriting for—Irene I. Isis! Such an opportunity and thrill come but once in a lifetime.

I brought down the final box. I waited until this morning to start clearing out my old bedroom. Mom offered to help, but when I'd said I could handle it, she didn't offer again.

The general cool of the house's basement, with its cement floor and high slitted windows, felt good through my now slightly damp T-shirt. I sneezed at the dust I'd stirred up.

I put the Purple Witch's ideas on paper. I sat at the typewriter—an honest to God *typewriter*—that she set up in what she insisted was her house's "parlor." I touched fingers to keys and *thwack!* went the little staves of metal, leaving ink impressions on the sheet of paper wound into the roller. Wild.

At least it was an electric. She wasn't a total Luddite evidently.

I had to write as she would write. The reading public, seeing a new novel by Irene I. Isis on the stands for the first time in thirty years, would want to read *her* words. Or plausible facsimiles. Of course, I was an unqualified failure when it came to imitating her. I knew this because she told me so, repeatedly. I didn't defend myself by saying that only the one previous book of hers from which to draw my inspiration; or, at least, to gain insight into how she assembled a sentence or constructed a chapter. *Everyone Goes Away* was a dated but very readable novel. Its "found sound" dialogue technique was particularly resourceful. It served as a minor cultural touchstone in its time and stayed in print for thirty consecutive years. No mean feat. I read it, before I'd even met the Witch. I reread it since and consulted it often, trying to squeeze from it the clues I required to rebuild a writing style its author could no longer carry off.

She inserted a few contributions into our book—for which there was no definite title as yet—which were purely of her own making. The Purple Witch's writing, three decades after the publication of *Everyone Goes Away*, was raw and untamed. These are not compliments. "Raw" as in inedible; "untamed" as in unhindered by the most basic laws of grammar, a kind of chaos wherein nouns and verbs couldn't even find one another.

The thing was, I believed she actually knew how bad her unassisted work was. Behind the bravura and the tantrums, behind the seething arrogance, I think she knew shit when she smelled it.

Mom's gardening supplies were stored down here, along with the other household tools. A washer and dryer stood side by side toward the back. Private laundry facilities, as they do with all apartment dwellers, filled me with a quiet awe.

Also in the basement, was almost a full wall's worth of rough shelves that Father put up years ago. Here was where the house's overflow of books came. Father's old office upstairs was loaded with the sort of volumes Mom, who never met a biography of Ulysses Grant or a history of the Carthaginians she didn't like, favored.

Down here was the pulpier stuff. John D. MacDonald. Faye Kellerman. Philip Wylie. Row after row of paperbacks.

Some that had been bought in secondhand bookstores before I was born; some with "50¢" as the price on the spine.

I browsed the shelves, squinting at some of the flaking covers. I had grown up in a house of readers. It was some many years before I understood how rare a thing that is these days. I read on a college level at age twelve or thirteen. I'd devoured a fair number of these very books, reading almost indiscriminately—and no doubt obsessively. I realized early on that anything I read made me stronger. Stronger in ways that friends, classmates, probably even teachers didn't understand.

Down here was also a wealth of science fiction novels. Father had sworn by these, and—again, before I knew discrimination—I'd read my share. Science fiction is a ghettoized genre, of course, and frankly, with good cause. How much literary worth can be distilled from stories about alien invasions, computers run amok, and end of the world scenarios?

Father had been especially fond of that last category, and for a time, I too wallowed in those imagined worlds that were devastated by plagues, atomic wars, social collapse. But it was a strictly adolescent fixation. When you don't fit in with the world around you, it's fun to imagine yourself among the sole survivors of a cataclysm that has wiped just about everything away.

But, eventually, one must outgrow it.

I sneezed again from the mustiness of the aging paper. I certainly wouldn't want for anything to read during my stay here, although—I smiled—I couldn't imagine myself cozying up with a novel about robot armies or the doings on a planet populated by talking plants.

Ward Pentecost probably would have made a decent adult. But it was much too late for miracles now.

I turned from the shelves and looked at where I'd neatly stacked the cardboard boxes. There were a fair number altogether. Even so, at that moment it all seemed pitifully small to me, so mean and meager a collection of items to represent over half a century of living. Father was here, packed away into a dozen or so boxes of personal effects; now stored in the basement, out of the light, out of everyone's way.

I stifled my next sneeze and went back up the creaky wood steps, watching my footing in the dimness.

It was nearing noon. I toasted and buttered a day old bagel for lunch, poured myself some coffee and went into the dining room. I sat at the head of the table and powered up my wireless laptop. I didn't behave melodramatically. Watching, you wouldn't have guessed I'd given the table even a passing thought.

It wasn't like I'd *never* come in here after that time when I was eight years old. We'd always had Thanksgiving in here, with the extended family gathered at this same table. Other semiformal occasions called for me to take a seat at this rectangular slab of mahogany, and I'd done so, without fuss.

Still, I had been leery then, and I was leery now. The sort of disquiet that teases your nerve endings; dread, not fear.

Mom had gone out on errands. Among other activities, she was volunteering, through the local parish, at a nearby library. I'd offered to drive, but she dismissed it. Plainly she was independent, mobile. Also plainly, she had a private life. Just because I was stopping over at this house didn't mean I needed to know where she was every moment, what she was up to, who with. And of course, I didn't want to know. I liked that we were interacting as adults.

Daylight flooded the dining room, warming it. I went and snapped on the kitchen radio, left it on the classical music station I found it tuned to, cranked it so I could hear it in the other room, and settled in to work.

To the strains of Vivaldi, Mahler, and whoever else, I wrote out a review for *The Gap Through Her Heart*. I started out by awarding it its grade—I'd never tried it in this sequence before—which was a D-. Then I backtracked into the analysis of the novel's failure. I was witty. I was biting. My points were incontestable. No one could defend the book's sloppy structuring or sappy characterizations. I defeated it.

When I had my five hundred words, I read them over. Then I deleted them.

Normally I keep everything I write. Every last word. Normally I would have saved my perfectly passable review of Minnie F. Tucker's first novel, even if I didn't intend to hand it in to the magazine. Every word I wrote was an act of creativity, on some level. So I always told myself, since the earliest days when I'd realized I wanted to write.

But I didn't feel a pang as I wholesalely dumped the review I'd just spent an hour and twenty minutes putting together. *I failed*—never mind the book—and I knew it. This job wasn't my first choice of professions, but I had taken a professional attitude towards it. I was good at what I did. I cared about my work, even if it didn't stroke me off like I'd imagined being a pro novelist would.

But I wasn't going to do anything substandard or cut corners. Ms. Tucker had written a book. It deserved an even-handed evaluation, even if I was going to slag it.

I shut off the laptop. Now wasn't the time to try tackling the review a second time.

Mom still wasn't back. I was at loose ends and tried to enjoy it. I had a little too much New York in me, though, and felt I ought to be accomplishing something, even if it were just to be deliberately idle.

I thought about going for a walk or a drive. That set me to thinking about visiting old haunts around the city—coffeehouses, movie houses; and that got me thinking further about looking up old acquaintances. I had actually not given that any thought at all when I'd decided to come out here. I started ticking off relevant people I'd known, in childhood, during high school.

I didn't come up with anybody I wanted to see badly enough to actually seek them out. Bobby Berry, probably the best friend of my youth, moved to Seattle's outskirts years ago. Besides, did I need the questions? Such as: What've you been up to? And, worse: Did you ever finish that book you were writing?

Since the age of fifteen, my answer to "What are you doing with your life?" has been this: "I am writing a book." I've been saying it for over a decade now. Saying it with just a dash of smugness, of pomposity. Saying it to place myself—without warrant—into the category of WRITER in which I've so desperately wanted to belong.

Yet in all that time I never managed to *finish* any of those books I spoke of. And now, with the aid of the Purple Witch, I was not going to finish a book for which a publishing house had issued an actual contract.

I went back down to the basement. I took the first box off the first stack, set it down on the cement, opened it.

It was already nearly noiseless in the cool of the basement, but a stillness fell anyway. I slowly, carefully, lifted out the oversized book with the stiff cover and thick pages. Its edges were black from years of small smudged fingers handling it. I knew the cover. I knew the story of the golden tow truck and its kindly owner that lay beyond the cover.

In the rest of the box were the remainder of my childhood picture books. Every single one of them, which Father kept.

THIRTEEN.

—✦—

WARD: Trouble at Work

"WARD."

It was Bill Berry, and he looked concerned. We both were dressed in our new "official uniform," as dictated by the also new Commissioner, who prided herself upon being a micro-manager, meaning: I'm going to show everyone how *important* I am.

So, instead of wearing our smocks over comfortable casual shirts, we now had them on over white shirts and ties. It was the same thing I had gone through before in my employment. Following each election, appointment, or promotion; we were all conscripted into the army of "Let's clean up this mess" by the new boss.

It usually phased out in two months.

The current Madame Lafarge was still going strong after six months, and my job, which had been a source of mild delight for all this time, was becoming something to be dreaded and to take home and moan about. For some of us, myself not included, it had also become something to drink over. I maintained my sobriety since Nate's birth.

"What's up?" I asked.

"Have you heard the talk about computerizing our department?" Bill Berry asked.

"They can't computerize mail deliveries."

"Not yet," was his reply. "But after we all get computers ..." His voice trailed off. "You're smart. Why don't you get a computer. Get a head start on everybody."

"My wife assures me that you just don't get computers. You have to buy them."

"Well, if you can get your hands on the money, keep it in mind."

Then Bill headed off on an errand of his own, while I made my way into the file rooms. Although I was ostensibly working for the mail room, I was really a kind of unofficial and unpaid supervisor of the file rooms. As a veteran of my four high school years spent mainly in the public libraries of San Francisco, more familiar with the Dewey Decimal System, the plain vanilla filing system the City used was a snap for me. I was regarded as an expert, at least, I was until we were taken over by Ms. *Thou shalt have no experts before me.*

Bill caused me to start thinking. Aunt Chloe had taken care of Nate's education. We had already begun making mostly token deposits in a bank account devoted to that cause. So, just maybe, and without a major disagreement, which I was resigned to losing, we could manage a computer.

I lost myself in the cold and musty-smelling file rooms, and did my job with expertise and modest pleasure.

Later that day I was corrected twice for job deficiencies, which were not of my making, but it gave my immediate supervisor a chance to grandstand in front of his supervisor, and never mind the justice of the situation. Things were getting worse and worse.

Morale in the basement of City Hall was lower than the location.

I went home like many others, feeling defeated and dispirited by the hierarchal ethics that, this time, lasted much
longer than anyone expected. Perhaps it was a sign, something on the wind that blows through our minds at night,
that portends a great disaster.

My happy home at work was gone, and I missed it. What
possible reason was there for turning everything upside down,
inside out, especially as things were now very bad for the
whole department? Inefficiency was our newest, biggest,
statistic. Doesn't anybody realize that frightened workers are
bad workers? *But they are only workers and not important like
me.* I am certain I heard that somewhere in the basement
of City Hall.

Marge was home. She had already begun dinner, and something savory was simmering on the stove. Nate was on the
floor in the hallway, concentrating hard on his picture books.
He wasn't attempting to lurch down the hall. For just over one
year old you couldn't quite call what he was doing walking, but
what he lacked in grace he was making up for in enthusiasm.

This evening he was content to peruse his brightly colored books, acknowledging my greeting in his own already
developed, perfunctory manner.

I turned my attention to my wife. She was busy with the
dinner preparations but returned my kiss with a brief hug.

Still thinking about work and the possibility of getting a
computer, I hung up my jacket in the bedroom closet. When
I looked at my desk, I saw a large manila envelope.

"The perfect end to a perfect day," I muttered, opening
the envelope and ready to consign the rejection slip to the
waste paper basket.

There was a brief, handwritten note at the bottom of the
printed form: "Keep trying. This one is almost a story." It was

signed by the reader of the day at the small science fiction magazine I sent it to.

I didn't read any sarcasm into the message. I felt encouraged enough to go out into the kitchen and broach the subject of computers—and maybe also of visiting Aunt Chloe.

"Well," said Marge, "since you got the last raise, we're better off."

"And a year without drinking has got to make a difference."

"I've been able to set some money aside," said Marge. "Not a lot, but now we can do it steadily. Why don't you research the subject? You're good at that."

I was already figuring how I would do it. There's a method to good research. Get the latest magazines on computers, maybe from the public library, which was a block away on Jersey Street. There weren't that many magazines on the subject, and it didn't matter if there were. The thing to do would be to read each one from cover to cover, everything, the articles, the advertising, the editorials, and especially any mail columns they might have. That's where the real information usually is. See what the library has in books on computers and computing. There have to be some. Take copious notes. That was probably the most important thing of all. So much research has been wasted by fools who don't make notes. I know. Get sales brochures from the companies, Apple and IBM. Who else? Read the magazines, stupid. And don't forget the interviews. Find someplace where computers are being used and talk to the people. Maybe even get a little hands-on stuff. There, I thought, I set myself up with enough of the right work to make an informed decision.

"I think I can do that," I said. "It might even be fun."

Marge began to set the table. I helped her, getting the silverware from the drawer.

We sat down to a casserole dish, made with pork, which broke apart with the touch of a fork. It was seasoned with an herb I didn't recognize and was delicious.

"This is good," I commented.

"It's from the Wednesday food column in the paper," said Marge. "I've been wanting to try it out."

"Well, it's great," I said enthusiastically.

Marge smiled at me. "I've been thinking about Aunt Chloe," she said. "You know I sent her a thank you note?"

"Well, for that much money ..."

"I phoned her today," Marge blurted.

This was news. It must have taken real courage on her part. "Really?" I said.

"She's very nice," said Marge.

"Her letter was nice. Her gift to Nate's education was nice. Why shouldn't she be nice?"

Marge wasn't listening to me, which was different from ignoring me. I could tell. Images were bouncing around inside her head faster than she could find the words to describe them.

"Do you know she's a professional photographer?"

A memory of a magazine spread of black and white photographs teased my mind. I thought I remembered the name *Chloe* in fine print below it. And I might be imagining the whole thing. I decided to listen to Marge instead of myself.

"Yes." Marge was on an unstoppable run. "She took a job in a camera store after the experience with Dad."

Nice choice of words.

"She learned everything she could about photography and bought her first camera there. Within a year she sold her first photo to a newspaper chain, from an ad she saw in a magazine."

"Impressive," I commented enviously. Just what I had been trying to do with my writing for years. The next sentence really drove the nails in deeper.

"Pretty soon she was a regular contributor and got known. For years now she's been a freelance photographer, and works all over the world. That's why Nate's check came so late. She was in Africa when he was born."

"Impressive," I muttered again.

"She lives on a funny little side street in Glen Park. Her house backs right onto the canyon."

If I had a car we could zip right over there in five minutes.

"She offered to drive us over any time. All we have to do is call her."

Was Marge reading my mind?

It seemed that peace had been made with Aunt Chloe.

"How do you feel about her now?" I asked.

"Oh, I don't know," said Marge. "A part of me wants to stay mad about her and Dad, but that may be because I'm so used to feeling that way. Does that make sense?"

"Yes. Most people are hanging on to some old ideas that are liabilities in the present."

"You read that?"

"I read everything," I answered, returning the word to its present tense.

"Smarty."

Marge turned some apples into a delightful cobbler.

It was a great meal and one of the best days at home in months. If only my job and home would work out the same way at the same time. That would be wonderful.

We cleared the dinner table, including Nate's tapioca pudding, which dropped from his high chair onto the table somewhere between my wife's mentioning of Africa and Glen Park. We hadn't noticed.

Was Aunt Chloe really a witch, or was that simply Phyllis' hyperbole? I myself am not very good at hating people, although I would make an exception for the new commissioner.

"Did you and Aunt Chloe make any arrangements?" I asked.

"Of course not," said Marge, slightly offended by my question.

I grinned, trying to make light of the faux pas. "I guess the subject of witchcraft didn't come up."

"I wouldn't make any arrangements without your input," said Marge, not letting me off the hook, "and we did talk about witchcraft, and it's none of your darned business." She grinned at that one and so did I in relief.

We were still in the world of the present and not reliving Phyllis' tragic past, as relayed through her daughter.

"I'd like to meet her," I said.

"She wants to meet Nate," said Marge. "He's her youngest grandnephew."

The Mortons were family-oriented, something nobody ever accused Drake Pentecost of being. I felt a twinge of jealousy, but wait a minute, wasn't that one of my reasons for getting married? It was, but my love for Marge had to be number one by any scheme of reckoning. Nate was proof of that love, never mind what had gone before, bad and good.

I asked myself again for the hundredth time: Then why did you start drinking again? Why I reneged on my promise, those months after the wedding when Marge learned she was pregnant? It wasn't because my wife was carrying our child. That was just an excuse. The answer always came out the same. I had gotten drunk again because that's the kind of drinker I was. For me there were no *reasons* to drink, but the world was full of *excuses*.

I remembered the look on Marge's face that morning after my great slip. I remembered waking up on our bedroom floor with a pounding head and no memory of coming home from the bar where I'd betrayed her trust without warning, apparently without any consideration for her at all ...

"How is Saturday for you?" I asked.

"If I grocery shop early ..."

"I'll help you."

Marge laughed. "And you were asking me if she was a witch, Mr. Already Spellbound without even meeting her."

She was right and I felt kind of silly. I figured that this was not the time to tell her of my relatively innocent fantasies about another blue-eyed woman. This one was in the movies.

"You win," I conceded.

She reached out and hugged me, which I returned. All thoughts of aunts and witches vanished temporarily from my mind.

She raised her lips and I kissed her and was kissed back. My body responded with its own imperatives. Nate could play with his picture books a while longer.

Just before we went into the bedroom I thought of the name of that movie and of the principal character, *Ladyhawke*.

FOURTEEN

NATHANAEL:
Fractured Fiction

OVER A DINNER THAT EVENING of stroganoff, in which I could taste the wine we'd had last night, and salads, Mom asked if I wanted to see any of my relatives while I was here in the city.

We didn't eat in silence at the kitchen table. She had the radio on, tuned this time to a doo-wop station, and we chatted and chuckled right through the meal. This was a radical departure from my teenaged eating habits, which had been to come sullenly to the table, force food into a stomach twisted by anxieties and resentments (both real ones and ones I was trying out for size), answer any questions in a monosyllabic monotone, and be done with the meal in about six minutes.

I paused to sip at my orange juice, considering. Relatives. I had two aunts on Mom's side of the family. From childhood, I could remember voices like magpies intruding on the dreary hush that was the accustomed ambience of this house on Santiago Street. Those aunts were both married and had kids, and back then I found the concept of brothers and sisters luridly fascinating, though the whole dynamic looked awfully noisy and messy.

The Pentecosts weren't diligent breeders, and so Father's side of the family had no relatives to offer.

The whole slate of grandparents had been wiped. Mom's folks gone more recently—and less violently—than Father's parents. It was Mom's father, Harry, who'd been the last. He was the one I'd liked best out of them all. I managed to connect with him as an actual person, not merely as a family elder.

That left, I believed, a great-aunt on Mom's side of the family as the oldest surviving member of the entire clan. Chloe was her name.

"Oh, I don't know ..." I said with a bit of a sigh.

"It's up to you," Mom said, letting it gently drop. She hadn't just laid a "motherism" on me, those acts of subtle psychological torture or guilt inducement that I knew some parents gleefully worked on their children. Whatever else happened in this little family of ours, Mom had never been deliberately unkind to me.

I could not also say, however, that Father was innocent of mistreatment, deliberate or not.

"Any plans for tonight?" Mom asked as we finished up the meal. She snatched up my empty plate before I could get up and take it to the sink myself.

"Not really. I do have to get that review done, though." I'd botched it once this afternoon, and that deadline was only getting nearer.

"That sounds so exciting. Hearing you say that. Oh, I know it's boring to you by now"—I'd said as much when we'd gone out to dinner last night—"but that the words you're going to write will be put into print in your magazine. That *is* exciting." She sounded unapologetic and proud.

I laughed. "If you say so."

"You know ... or maybe you don't, completely ... but your father wanted so badly to experience that. Not book reviews, of course. But books. Short stories. Seeing one get into print. He would talk about it sometimes like there was no better thrill possible in this world." Her tone was now mildly wistful, though not melancholic.

A chill tingled its way over the nape of my neck.

"Oh," I said, but it was as if I'd just recited a letter of the alphabet, nothing more. I was sitting very still.

Mom demonstrated quite a motherly talent at sensing my moods since I'd arrived two days ago. Each time I became uncomfortable, she backed off the subject at hand.

So I was surprised when she said, "Your father had some talent too. I don't know how much. His stories—a lot he'd written when you were just a baby and even before you were born—didn't seem completely like stories. They almost always seemed to be missing ... *something*. I never knew what it was. He didn't seem to know either." Her clear gray eyes met mine directly. "Actually, now, you could probably understand his stories, being a reviewer. You could see if he went wrong somewhere."

From the radio, spunky rhythms and rhymes. In my head mental static was trying to come between me and any immediate thoughts of Ward Pentecost and the things he'd done in his life.

"His stories didn't get thrown out?" I listened, after a significant pause, to myself asking this question. Why was Mom pressing this? I didn't need to hear about Father's amateur writing antics.

"No. They're in those boxes you put in the basement. Thank you again for doing that. I should've had them put down there, out of the way, in the first place. I'm going to brew some decaf. Do you want anything?"

"No. No. No." I pushed up from the table, an uncomfortable smile pinned to my mouth. "I'll ... be upstairs."

I fairly fled.

◦∞◦

I hadn't looked inside any of the other boxes after I'd found my boyhood picture books earlier today. I sat there in the basement, on the cement flooring, and read each one of them, cover to cover.

When I reached my room, I checked my pager, purely as a distraction. The Purple Witch was still demanding contact with me. I felt a sort of giddy freedom from her, though, as I hadn't experienced in the eight months of our "professional" relationship. I was remote from her, from her thrall, from her secondhand smoke, from her diatribes and senselessness. I was far from her seething delirium, and that distance gave me nerve. Or maybe it was just indifference I felt, finally. Our book was going to fail. Had, by all reasonable estimates, already failed.

I'd also received a page from another source, in the 212 area code. New York. A glance told me it wasn't from any of *Diamond*'s offices, though the number did look vaguely familiar.

Goddamnit, I didn't care about unpublishable fiction that Father had written a couple decades ago! I'd written reams of unreadable trash all by myself that would never see print. What had Mom been circling around about? Did she want me to look over her husband's work, get it to a publishing house, use my "insider" influence to get it posthumously published? Did she actually think I could finagle something like that?

Although ... scaring up interest in the unpublished fictional writings of an individual who himself, later disappeared along with the Golden Gate Bridge, would likely be fairly easy ...

No. Christ, no. We Pentecosts, including all the supplemental family branches, stood steadfastly silent throughout all the years since the Bridge's vanishing. Mom told the extended family and all the friends of that family how she wanted things, and, in a poignant show of total solidarity, nobody ever submitted to an interview or allowed themselves to be exploited by the media in any way. No one ever cooperated in a human interest piece about Father, about Mom, about me. Bill Berry, who'd been Father's friend and coworker, allegedly pushed a reporter down a flight of stairs several years ago when the overly assertive man wouldn't take "go to hell" for an answer.

When I was staying here at the house for the year following November 7th, 2010, I once received a letter, addressed directly to me, from the president of a West Coast *People*-type magazine. He wanted to do a cover feature about me, entitled "Where Is His Book?" By this time the barely perceptible grace period of shock and bereavement was over, and publishers were glutting the market with every breed of book that pertained to the Bridge's disappearance. It swiftly became known, not courteously, as Bridge lit.

Someone evidently had illicitly plundered my college records and discovered the English lit. and creative writing courses I'd taken. If I had an interest in being an author, why hadn't I written a book? I needed only to tie my work in with what happened to the Bridge, and my instant credibility of having a relative—a *father*, which was just about perfect—on the span that day would carry my book into print. Guaranteed.

What this magazine publisher wanted to know was why hadn't I written such a book?

I didn't respond, naturally. By then I was very deft at hanging up the phone and slamming the front door on news people. I would never capitalize ghoulishly on my father's tragedy just to get myself into print. No. Never.

Abruptly I snatched up my pager again from the bedside stand, squinted at the second number. I now recognized it. A bitter queasiness, different from the cold gut-twisting I'd felt only a couple days ago on first seeing the Purple Witch's number, coiled through me.

Here was another bid for my attention from back East that I felt no urge to respond to just now. The hell with her.

I had a lot more space in the room with the boxes gone, but suddenly it was still much too small in here. I checked the time, still feeling a ghostly hint of jet lag. Then I started getting myself ready.

I unpacked a nice-looking shirt, put on slacks, applied cologne tastefully and told Mom I was going to be out for a while.

I had vague recollections of Union Street being a hot spot, and though this was a weeknight, I saw a sufficient amount of the bustle I was looking for.

Parking, this close to the Marina district, was bad; but I eventually got a slot. San Franciscans are first in line to hop into the latest environmentally sound transport, and so the neighborhood was fairly littered with a decade's worth of vehicular experimentation in electric engines, alcohol-burners and whatnot.

On foot now I headed for the clubs.

When I'd gone back to school after my hiatus and resumed my studies, I found myself taking a critical theory course. Later, I was minoring in the subject. My ambition to be a professional writer hadn't waned, not a detectable degree; yet I'd given myself a cushion for after my graduation. An alternative. A backup.

Had I suspected back then that I wouldn't make it? Had I feared that all those years of writing short stories and those unfinished novels and all those words, words, *words*, would amount to nothing?

My critical theory professor, Mrs. Carstens, told me I was an exemplary student.

I was a good age for these clubs, I discovered. It was mostly a college-age crowd, but of the aspiring-yuppie variety; and these were kids with the trust funds and family connections to back up their aspirations. At twenty-seven I was older, mildly exotic, yet I was also younger than the forty-some-things trolling for midlife crisis companions.

Besides, age didn't mean much in the game I was playing tonight. Neither, for that matter, did looks.

I was handsome enough and well-dressed enough. I knew how to smile and how to carry myself. I learned these things during college, in studies no less critical than what was on the curriculum. At school in New York, far away from everything I had known before, I adopted an air of confidence, suavity, and radiated a sense of sexual entitlement that reversed every trend that kept me—mostly—solitary throughout my adolescence. I'd never had a genuine girlfriend before I went away to school. Once there, I had several. At the same time. I slept just about with whomever I liked, and the utter meaninglessness of it was part of the allure.

It was all a shuck, but that didn't matter.

I breezed in and out of two places, eyes darting in the dimness. At the third I realized what I was doing wrong and ordered a whiskey and water, picking one of the better brands. I'd been drinking club sodas at the other joints; I needed to show that I belonged to this scene.

The girl who jostled my elbow was actually chewing gum, and when I remarked on that, I did so in a friendly manner and in a way that made her giggle. I asked if I could get her a drink. She had just seen a documentary on PBS about Newfoundland and wanted to talk about it. I wanted to listen. She had dark hair, very dark eyes. She wore a yellow top and a coat with furry black buttons. She dared me to guess her age, but I demurred. (She was twenty-two.) I told her I was a realtor. I took two swallows out of my glass. She finished her cocktail. I didn't want to buy her another and didn't; she'd had enough. We left the club after she went to tell her friends she was going.

In my rental car she laughed, loud, like you would on a roller coaster, when I told her I lived with my mother.

I had a joyless hard-on, and she was the ideally indifferent corresponding component.

FIFTEEN.

WARD: Aunt Chloe

FRIDAY NIGHT WHEN WE PUT NATE TO BED he was feverish, and had a rash covering most of his body. A hasty call to the pediatrician's answering service brought an answering call within the hour. The news was reassuring. Nate was having a reaction to the few strawberries he had eaten with dinner. The rash would go away in a few days. In the meantime, apply calamine to any blisters.

I found myself unexpectedly annoyed that this should happen now. But, there was no need to worry.

Marge was on the phone when I rose at ten o'clock in the morning. From her end of the conversation I could tell that she was talking to Aunt Chloe.

"Yes," Marge was saying, "an allergic reaction to strawberries. The doctor says it'll take several days to go away, and we're supposed to treat the blisters with calamine. So, I'm sorry but we won't be able to make it today."

We were supposed to go over to Aunt Chloe's today, stay for lunch and dinner, with time out in between to play in the adjacent park with Nate. Thinking about that kept me awake much of last night.

"Really," said Marge to Aunt Chloe, "I don't think there's been any change this quick. He was still covered with them when I checked an hour ago. He's asleep now. If you think so, I will."

I listened to the one-sided conversation. Marge clarified with her next statement. "Ward, would you check on the baby?"

"Right away." I went down the hall to the bedroom and found Nate in his crib, awake and wide-eyed. I opened up his pajamas and found no trace of the rash that covered him last night, and the thermometer confirmed his appearance. No fever at all.

I carried him out to the hall phone with me, showed him to Marge and stuck the thermometer under his tongue again.

She took him from me and extracted the thermometer in that effortless way men can never manage.

"Just a minute, Aunt Chloe," said Marge. She handed Nate back to me. "Twelve thirty will be fine."

I mouthed the words silently.

Marge picked them up. "And Ward says thank you. We'll see you at twelve thirty. Goodbye.

"We're going. Aunt Chloe will pick us up."

"On a broomstick, no doubt."

We both chuckled at that one, with Nate joining in with a happy gurgle.

The next two hours were spent vacuuming the carpets that had been vacuumed yesterday, and dusting every reachable surface.

It was not a broomstick, but a ten year old, tan Mercedes Benz. The car showed some signs of wear, but overall was still an elegant machine. The same held true of the driver.

I don't know what I expected. The woman who got out of the automobile and climbed our stairs, with a spring in her step, was in her early fifties or late forties. She was not Michelle Pfeiffer nor Margaret Hamilton. She was not even the wicked witch in the cartoon version of Hansel and Gretel.

She was slender, with a strong body and striking face. Not exactly *Ladyhawke* but not that different. The eyes were certainly Michelle Pfeiffer's. There was much living in the face. The years spent globetrotting on freelance assignments showed, and it was very attractive.

Her voice was musical as I opened the door before she had time to ring the bell.

"You can't be Margot, so you must be Nate," she said.

Marge came down the hall cradling Nate.

I smiled, a face-splitting grin. "Wrong," I said. "He's Nate. Hello, Aunt Chloe."

"Hello, Ward." I received a kiss.

"Aunt Chloe." Marge reached out with one arm and hugged her aunt. Nate slid gracefully from one woman to the other. He focused his attention on Aunt Chloe's face and grinned happily as she shifted her grip a little, making his perch in the crook of her arm more secure.

"You've made a conquest," said Marge. Then she paused and blushed. "I didn't mean ..."

"Margot, you've grown up just the way I imagined," said Aunt Chloe. "You're a beautiful young mother."

Her attention moved to me. I was standing like a wooden Indian, without a perky statement with which to make an impression. In fact, I really wasn't thinking about making an impression at all. The lady mesmerized me.

"Ward, you're very handsome."

I felt like a commoner who has just been noticed by the Queen Mother. Wrong country, but after all, Aunt Chloe was a globetrotter.

Marge gave no sign of being threatened by the remark. The ghost of her father's indiscretion had evidently been dispelled.

"If everyone is ready, why don't we go?" said Aunt Chloe.

⁓

While Marge carried Nate, I acted as pack animal with an amazing assortment of traveling supplies, which she deemed necessary for a day away from home with Nate.

Aunt Chloe opened the front door of the attractive, rustic house under the trees. It nestled at the end of an unpaved street, which had a sidewalk dating back to the 1906 earthquake at least.

There was a subtle smell of herbs the moment we entered. The house was beautiful, with old, comfortable furniture. I saw a genuine Tiffany lamp in the dining room. Everything seemed to reflect the occupant, and glowed.

Marge and Aunt Chloe directed me where to place each item of my burden. Nate had been put down on the floor in the living room, and on wobbly legs was beginning his exploration of this new environment.

Aunt Chloe showed no sign of concern.

With every third step Nate looked in Aunt Chloe's direction. If she looked back and smiled, he did a little dance. I felt the same way but did not give in to the feeling.

We ate lunch in the spacious, light-filled kitchen at a massive old table. The adults ate tasty Eggs Benedict and fruit bowls at room temperature, instead of the refrigerated version I usually had. Nate had a smaller bowl. I am used to very big meals. It came to me as a surprise that it felt better to be filled rather than stuffed.

After we finished, Aunt Chloe took us on a tour of the house. It was very old and immaculately kept up. Not in the snobby, antique showplace way, but in a more comfortable, lived in with happiness way. The scent of herbs that greeted me I attributed to the kitchen rack full of jars and cloth bags. They gave off a medley of aromas.

When Aunt Chloe opened the backdoor a large, orange and white tabby, sauntered in as if he owned the place. Aunt Chloe produced a can of Friskies from under the sink and transferred its contents into one of three bowls on the kitchen floor.

The large cat ignored us and proceeded to heartily enjoy its meal.

"What's his name?" Marge asked.

"I don't know," explained Aunt Chloe. "He's one of the feral cats from the park."

Marge immediately looked around for Nate. The action was not lost on Aunt Chloe. She smiled. "Perhaps I should have said that they're not feral to me."

As if in acknowledgement, the cat rubbed against her legs, purring loudly.

Aunt Chloe opened the backdoor again, and with his tail held high and haughty, the cat marched out. "You come back after dinner with no more than two of your friends," said Aunt Chloe.

The cat turned for a minute and seemed to nod. Then he disappeared into the high grass facing the park.

Marge offered to help clean up the luncheon settings. She and Aunt Chloe set to work together. Nate preferred to stay with them, so that left me free to wander about the house.

The study held the information that I wanted, with three of the walls holding floor to ceiling bookcases. This was my world, a place as natural to me as my own shortened leg.

I recognized all the twentieth century philosophers. Freud and his whole school were represented, and Jung's books, in the section allotted to psychology. There were alternative schools of thought too, Korzybski's *Science and Sanity*, the definitive volume on General Semantics, and some of the so-called space age religions. Count Korzybski's book looked well-read; the space age religions had probably been read once.

There was a whole bookcase devoted to the pagan religions. Evidently Wicca was not the only form of worship that piqued her interest. I especially was intrigued by the books devoted to spells. This was far removed from my own small collection of books on sleight of hand and other parlor magic books. I suspected that her books might have more to do with majik of the ancient spelling.

As I continued to mentally inventory the contents of the bookcases, Aunt Chloe, Marge, and Nate, came into the room to break my concentration.

"We're ready to go over to the park," said Marge.

I turned away from the bookcases. "How about that, little fellow?" I asked Nate, not really expecting an answer. He reached out and gripped Aunt Chloe's hand.

"Animals and little children," she said scooping him up and receiving one of his biggest smiles.

Glen Park was reached by a dirt path.

"Can you really talk to cats?" I asked as we stretched out on the large cotton blanket we brought to the lawn area opposite the playground. Marge was introducing Nate to the equipment cautiously, ready to snatch him to safety in a second. He giggled happily.

"So can you," said Aunt Chloe. "If you had the nerve you could talk to your left shoe."

My left leg seemed to twinge in reply.

The woman noticed everything. "You've made a remarkable recovery," she said.

"How did you know ..."

She smiled. "A lucky guess?"

Her eyes supplied the punctuation. We both laughed.

The afternoon moved toward early evening. It was not quite dusk when we gathered all of our gear and one tired little boy, and made our way back to Aunt Chloe's house.

I hadn't seen her set up the crockpot before we left, but when she removed the lid the whole house was filled with the hearty aroma of stew made with fresh vegetables.

Marge set the table. Aunt Chloe seasoned the stew with a dusting of powdered herbs and a handful of fresh ones.

The meal was lighter than most stews I've had, with less meat and more taste experiences, which I attributed to the herbs. I once again found myself full but not stuffed, extracting my enjoyment of the food from the wonderful variety of tastes.

Throughout the meal, Marge and Aunt Chloe carried on an enthusiastic conversation, which I happily ignored until I was finishing up and realized Aunt Chloe was speaking to me.

Aunt Chloe finished her meal and was looking directly at me. "I don't want anyone to know about the college check, including Nathaniel," she said. "Please promise me you'll keep it secret." Her eyes fell on Marge. "Both of you."

"But when he's old enough to go college, surely ..."

"I believe that gifts should be given anonymously," she said. "Don't break the charm."

Marge was the first to agree. She held her hand up like a little kid and said, "I promise."

I followed suit, but without holding my hand up. I knew that I was not going to mess with *her* charm.

"I promise," I said.

"Good," said Aunt Chloe. She pushed back her chair, walked to the stove and opened the oven. She drew out a tray filled with joyful aromas. "Who wants some homemade chocolate chip cookies?"

I ate two of them; Marge and Nate each ate one. We took the remainder home in a paper bag.

It might have been one of the best days of my life.

—⊗—

SIXTEEN

NATHANAEL:
The Review

THE GAP THROUGH HER HEART
by Minnie F. Tucker
Paternus Press
422 pages
$29.95

The main characters in Minnie F. Tucker's debut novel, a 26-year-old paralegal living in Sausalito and her married lover, a 38-year-old architect residing in San Francisco, find themselves spiritually disengaged after the Golden Gate Bridge's disappearance.

Couldn't they just have taken the ferry?

Moira Astin is the paralegal. Tucker, evidently exhaustively unfamiliar with this profession, glosses over whatever it is Moira actually does at the office. Outside work is more interesting, feuding by phone with her mother, who lives in an unnamed flyover state. The mother advises her daughter not to "wear too much lipstick. Your lips have the wrong grain for it."

There are other painstakingly quirky characters, including a mailman who talks about his UFO abduction in the future tense. Moira's interactions with these one-noters are written with satisfying punch, if not believability. Set-dressing hints of the region's very real economic downturn presage darker, more substantive story elements.

Still, it's 108 pages before we actually meet her paramour, Harry Hartford, and then only over the telephone. Moira's affair with Harry, a hard-drinking but never drunk frustrated architectural visionary, is in its second year and going nowhere. Harry is baggaged with a dragon lady wife, Sophia, who may or may not have her husband hopelessly blackmailed. A subplot regarding incriminating photographs is creakily *noir* and entirely without payoff.

The meat of the matter, however, is the melodrama between Moira and Harry. True, their affair is "going nowhere, like a bullet shot at a cloud" (though bullets fired into the sky *do* land somewhere), but each regards the other as the ideal emotional complement. Flashbacks throughout demonstrate the tenderness and passion between the two. Harry has Moira's face sculpted into a rock wall on the secluded hillside where they first made love; Moira tells Harry about the (shamelessly contrived) girlhood trauma that sent her fleeing to the West Coast as an adult. They stand against the silhouetting sunset on the Golden Gate Bridge and declare their intense love for each other.

It's headlong goo. Sure. Harry Hartford embodies a checklist of vintage *Playboy* predatory attributes; yet he waxes postfeminist Hallmarkisms as if from a NOW fever dream. Moira Astin's Big Issue past is the cheapest character crutch in recent memory. The age dynamic between the two characters is vaguely squirmy. Sure.

Yet, the novel lingers, with a not-quite-disagreeable aftertaste.

We never meet Harry in the present tense, and this is where the novel succeeds best. The Bridge's disappearance signals an absence of hope. But it is also a sobering end to pretense. These two characters have no future. The backdrop of the Bridge's vanishing, more artfully evoked than anything else in the book, looms over the fore shenanigans and lends the histrionic proceedings a solidity and pathos they most certainly wouldn't have otherwise possessed. Judging whether this is another tawdry ploy or an apt minor-key counterpoint is wholly a matter of taste. But the novel's unflinching verdict, which resonates throughout and nearly makes the whole mawkish mess worth it, is this:

Love will not put the Bridge back where it belongs.

Rating: C+

NATHANAEL PENTECOST

Pentecost seems like a name that ought to have some quip readily attached to it. Bullies in my grade school certainly thought so; and when they realized "Pentecostal" didn't really ring true as an insult, they grew impatient.

It is a name that looks good on the printed page, though. Atypical without being bizarre or, such as in the case of Irene I. Isis, flamboyantly phony. Early on in our association I asked her about her name. The Purple Witch, adopting what I would come to know as her "wise woman on the high hill" countenance, replied, "By the third eye, I see. By the third I, I *am* seen."

That this bit of pontification was also nonsense I didn't point out at the time. At that New York literary cocktail party stage of things I was still quite dazzled by the woman's stature and significant presence. She knew how to capture and hold a room. Her every move and word were performance.

Her anecdotal reserve was bottomless, and I could never tire of private accounts of Norman Mailer, Gore Vidal, Doris Lessing, the whole hallowed pantheon.

I was struck. She was breathtaking. I would have thrown myself at her feet, had she so bid.

As it happened, I had to first pay for the privilege of groveling at the altar of Irene I. Isis. I had to bring her a sacrifice. And so I did.

I had come in late last night, very late, having left a small meaningless part of myself inside the latex sheath of a condom in the bedroom of a female who I would never think of as an individual again, but only a member of a category. She would regard me the same way, which was good. If it had been otherwise, I wouldn't have gone through with it.

I'd woken in the morning, nonetheless, and spent the three hours until noon writing the review. It was harder work than anything I could readily remember, but I was also particularly satisfied with it. It wasn't a cheat, not to anybody. *Diamond* hadn't hired me for my prejudices and partialities. I was there to dole out erudite analyses, with a dash of hipster snarkiness perhaps, and that was what I consistently delivered.

I zapped it off, then rang New York to let them know. I got Terry instead of April. Terry disliked chitchat. Was it five hundred words worth of copy? Yes. Then why was I bothering him? He clicked off.

It was another very warm day, though with a bit more overcast, and Mom was in the backyard again. We both broke for lunch. I took over the stove and made us omelets.

I had a suspicion that she somehow knew what I'd been up to last night, but the worried guilt that went along with that was totally misplaced, a throwback to the instincts you learn in adolescence that tell you to keep all sexual activities secret from your parents.

Or ... was my guilt something more?

I fried a little bacon and onion, grated some cheese, folded these and a few other ingredients into the omelets and served.

"When did you learn to do this?" Mom asked, enjoying her first bite.

"Sometime during adulthood."

I married Janeane Youngblood a little over one year ago, a civil ceremony before a judge, with unsentimental vows and no idolatrous rituals. Both of us were repulsed by the very thought of a church wedding and made our disdain known to any who asked. Janeane's mother was in and out of posh rehab spas, and her father lived in Tokyo; neither was informed of the nuptials. Janeane and I were independents. We were equals, intellectually and emotionally. We detested the same things. Our courtship was fierce and fast. It was also, ultimately, as stoic as our marriage vows.

From the day we rationally discussed and agreed to marriage until a full month after we were legally husband and wife, it did not once occur to me to tell Mom about any of it.

Only after it had and I'd phoned her with the news, did I realize how deeply I'd wounded her. I was at first surprised by her reaction, thinking it unreasonable. That's a perfect indicator as to how deep into our selfish, hermetically sealed world, I had gone with Janeane.

My wife paged me yesterday. That was the other New York number that appeared on my pager. I had no idea why she was trying to reach me.

"Was that your review you've been working on?" Mom asked.

"Done," I said, my mind still elsewhere; then, realizing I'd lapsed into my old monosyllabic meal conversation, I smiled, met Mom's clear gray eyes and said, "Yes. I finished and sent it off. To New York."

"Sent ...?" Her red-haired head tilted a degree. "E-mail?"

Mom wasn't a member of the Plugged-In Generation

(actually Wireless Generation is more apt) and saw no need to become too acquainted with our ways. "Right," I said.

We had toast to go with the omelets. She jellied a piece modestly.

"Can I read it?"

"What?" I was startled.

"The review."

Of course I knew what she meant. "Well ... you haven't read the book, I'm sure, so ..."

She chuckled. "I hadn't read any of the books in those other reviews of yours. I still enjoyed what you wrote. Unless you're not allowed to show anyone the material before the magazine comes out ...?"

I waved my hand. "No. That doesn't matter." How to warn her about the Bridge's disappearance being a feature of *Gap*'s plot? Hell, surely I could just keep her from reading the review easily enough.

But who was I protecting?

"I don't have a printer with me," I said. "You'll have to read it off the screen. That's okay?"

We were done with lunch. I cleared the table, and she reached for her reading glasses. "Not blind yet," she said cheerfully. "I can still feel my way around."

❦

This, I imagined, was how I might have felt if my mother had ever inadvertently gotten hold of any of my off-limit teenhood writing, the short stories containing the feeble sex scenes or the racy language.

I sat at the kitchen table with the last tepid cup of coffee from the morning pot, waiting while Mom read my *Gap Through Her Heart* review in the dining room. It seemed a long while for someone to read five hundred words, but she never quite inhaled books like Father and I.

"How do I turn it off?"

My eyes, aimed at my coffee, snapped up. "Just leave it." Tension tugged a lone tendon in my upper right arm. I hadn't heard her make her chuckling-squealing sounds. I hadn't heard anything at all from the other room.

She came back to the kitchen table, which seemed to be her base of daytime operations.

"You hated that book, didn't you?" She asked it seriously.

"Personally? Yes."

"But professionally ... you gave it a fair shake?"

"That's right," I said with a quiet note of pride.

She nodded, plainly approving. "I like what you do, Nathan. I like how you do it."

"Thanks, Mom."

"Is this a better job than what might have come from that publishing house?" She reached out, patted my hand. "I mean, a better job for *you*."

It was a good question. In fact, it was a stumper.

"I don't know. But I just couldn't stick it out in that awful internship. I have to say ... I'm glad you're not disappointed."

Her brows rose slightly. "Disappointed? Have you killed anyone? Are you smuggling drugs? No? Then I'm not disappointed. You're doing something you're good at. And if you're happy with it—even if it's just a stopover to someplace else—well, Nathan, that's all I care about."

It occurred to me there, quietly but with great and sudden force, that this was probably much better than I deserved. I hadn't been an especially loving son. I'd foregone warmth and affection for the peace that results from a stalemate. Father and I were oppositely charged particles, and whenever I'd noticed the tiniest similarity between us, I realigned myself diametrically.

Mom unfortunately got more or less shut out in the

process. Collateral damage. Unavoidable. But it was also mean-spirited and small and stupid. As an adolescent, I hadn't let myself care, as I brought home ridiculously dazzling grades and planned for college from the age of twelve.

Now ... now I could feel different. I could regret how coldly Mom had been treated.

"There was a time when your father enjoyed his job, when he was a file clerk," she was now saying. "I remember it. He was good at it, and he was almost content." She was shaking her head, as if not quite believing herself, despite her own reassurances. "I hope things never go bad for you."

Once more I was sitting very still, the way you do when you're waiting for a wasp to pass you by. Didn't Mom understand by *now*?

I was nothing like Ward Pentecost.

SEVENTEEN.

———❁———

WARD: The Computer

"I'M GOING TO MISS HER," I said. "Do you know when she'll be back this time?"

We spent two more warm and sunny days with Aunt Chloe, before the Indian summer ended and she'd left for another round of globe spanning assignments.

"No," said Marge. Her eyes checked on Nate who was playing Pong against the hallway walls with himself as the puck.

"Well, I'm glad I made my notes," I said, referring to a list of titles and publishers of some of her more arcane books.

"I didn't know you were interested in that sort of thing," she said.

"It's not what I am used to, like sleight of hand and parlor magic, but it is interesting."

"Don't get them mixed up with your computer notes. It would be awful to bring it home and have it disappear."

"I think not," I said. "If there is one thing I do know, it is how to file." All of my notes were broken down by subject alphabetically, each with its own folder, and then classified further alphanumerically by date.

We tentatively agreed that an Atari 1040ST would be the computer to purchase. I especially liked their slogan: "Power without price."

Marge was more inclined to play it safe and go the way of Big Blue, or IBM, which I researched in magazines and books. She didn't realize that the Atari ST was a game machine par excellence, exceeded only by the new AMIGA, which cost more than we were able to spend. There was a program available that could read and write PC documents by emulation, and it was affordable. I had seen some of the IBM machines at work, in the executive offices, and I understood that with this program I could run WordPerfect, and take work home if I wished.

The last thought convinced Marge.

I had never taken work home in my life.

My mind was occupied with anticipation of the great stories and novels I was going to write, classified under the subheading of Wishful Thinking, and the more immediate thoughts of gloriously colored medieval computer games.

On a rainy Saturday morning Bill Berry, only slightly hung over, drove the three of us down to the Tanforan Shopping Center, south of San Francisco.

I felt at home as soon as we entered the store. Indeed, I read so much on the subject in the last few months that, I didn't doubt, in some areas I knew more than the very young man who waited on us.

In spite of Bill's whispered admonition to look out for the "razzle dazzle" from this guy, I was neither razzled nor dazzled. We entered into a conversation between equals, as soon as he realized that I knew that software was not necessarily something which old men have.

I looked at enough computers in my research period to be able to bypass most of the usual new user stuff. In fact, strictly speaking, I was not a new user, as I managed hands-on experience on some of the machines at work during my noon hours, with the help of friendly secretaries and office assistants.

Within the hour we were on our way home, Bill talking about nothing in particular, and Marge and I both experiencing the numbness of cash outlay.

We had a 1040ST computer with a color monitor, a printer, a ream of fanfold paper, a word processing program, the game of *Phantasie*, and *PcDitto*, which I intended to use with the WordPerfect disks I clipped from work. Not exactly a great theft from City Hall as they had one legal copy of the program, and it was used on twenty-two machines. My disks were a copy of a copy.

Bill dropped us off with our merchandise, promising to come by when I had it all working.

While Marge retrieved Nate from our upstairs neighbor, I went to work, setting up the computer and printer with a minimum of confusion. The manuals were readable by a slightly knowledgeable layman, unlike the cryptic operating system binders that drove everybody crazy at work.

When she came downstairs I was happily exploring the world of *Phantasie*.

Nate watched me for most of the afternoon, temporarily fascinated by the colors on the screen. I continued my adventures in the fantasy world, with rich sound effects, up to dinner, after dinner, and on and on until ...

"Ward, it's two-thirty. Aren't you ever coming to bed?"

I maneuvered my character to the nearest town and saved the game.

My dreams were in color.

The only disappointing thing that weekend was that Bill didn't call. I was anxious to show off my toys and even called him twice Sunday afternoon. The phone somehow sounded like it was ringing in an empty house.

He was not at work on Monday.

By Tuesday morning I was worried enough to discreetly ask if he called in sick. I knew all about calling in sick on Monday, *and* Tuesday. Then Bill did show up. Late.

I myself hadn't had a drink for over a year. Not since Nate's birth. I was mildly surprised to find that the milestone passed unnoticed.

Bill looked like he hadn't had one for fifteen minutes. He wore the regulation smock, shirt and tie, but they didn't do much to improve his appearance. His skin had a grayish color, he had two days growth of beard and his eyes were bloodshot. To make matters worse, he was shaking visibly and his breath was almost lethally alcoholic.

I grabbed his arm and guided him into the file rooms.

"Have you checked in?" I asked.

"Yes," he mumbled.

"Did they say anything to you about being off?"

"No, they were busy with something."

"Did they give you an assignment?"

He looked at me. "No."

I breathed a sigh of relief. "Someone told you to help me out in the old file room. Can you remember that?"

"Sure, Ward."

"All right," I said. "Go into the old file room and try to look busy. Take files out of the drawers and put them back. It doesn't matter which drawer."

"I can do that," said Bill. "Thanks a lot, Ward."

"You've done the same for me."

"Yeah." I left him to find his way to the old file room. The air freshened considerably.

What was I going to do? I noticed that after I'd stopped drinking with him, his escalated.

I wanted to help.

But wanting to help and actually helping were two different things. I had the advantage of having been a drinker, yet when I tried to capitalize on it by talking to him, it didn't help at all. From what I read on the subject of alcoholism, it should have worked, one alcoholic helping another ... except, then it hit me, I wasn't talking as one alcoholic to another. I could cheerfully admit that my friend was an alcoholic, but not me. Never.

What a hypocrite.

Suppose Bill and I were exactly alike, and that the only difference between us was that I stopped drinking, but that our thinking was still the same? It was a scary line of thought.

I still had the same likes and dislikes. Authority still frightened me, as did so-called normalcy. Without any merit, proven by my actions, I had a good case of intellectual snobbery, based on nothing except an IQ, possibly enhanced by four years of marathon reading, and those years were retreating with every passing day.

I read the book, *Alcoholics Anonymous*, during a phase when I was cataloging my father's failings. But that type of thinking wouldn't help me now.

Although I mentally cringed at the thought, the next step was clear. If I was to help Bill, I would have to take him to an AA meeting. Considering all the times he helped me, it had to be done.

I just wished it didn't have to be me doing it.

For the rest of the workday I kept Bill in the old file room and kept sneaking him black coffee from the dispenser. At quitting time he was ready to float out of the building, but he was sober enough to drive, and his eyes were open.

I extracted a promise from him not to drink for the next few days. His physical condition was so bad that he agreed willingly.

Friday night we went to our first meeting. It was held in the basement of a downtown church. I phoned a number I found in the phone book to find out where to go. That call required a tremendous will on my part.

Bill loved the meeting.

"I felt like I belonged as soon as I walked in the door," said Bill, his eyes glowing. "I've never felt like that before in my life."

"Yeah."

"Didn't you like that speaker?" he asked as he fired up the engine and we drove out of the parking lot. "Before she spoke, I couldn't imagine her taking a drink."

"Yeah."

He was so high on the experience of the meeting that my comments were lost. Or maybe they were ignored.

He rambled on and on about the meeting, about the speaker, about the attendees, about the program, although he hadn't even read about it before today.

When we got to my place he came in with me. Marge had been alerted before we left, and she had coffee and some pastries ready for us. She had been more or less silent on the matter of this AA attendance, and that silence had been ambivalent. Perhaps her Catholic upbringing had trouble with a devoutly secular organization that nonetheless dealt in spiritual matters; after all, the Lord's Prayer was said at each and every meeting. I think she was as emotionally confused about it all as I was. AA never seemed like an option while I was drinking. God knew I wasn't going to *belong* to anything, even if it could get me sober. When I thought of organizations, I thought of hierarchies. I didn't know at the time that AA was unique in this respect.

"It was great!" Bill replied to Marge's first question. Then, as she skillfully listened, he poured out his unbearable enthusiasm, except that she didn't find it unbearable or boring.

When he left, a little after midnight, I booted up the computer and played *Phantasie* until Marge got irritated by the noise, and asked me to quit.

I went to bed feeling bad, without quite knowing why.

Did my friend's happiness threaten me? No, I wasn't possessive about friendships. What was it then? I didn't know, or I wouldn't admit what I knew.

I dreamt grim dreams in black and white.

Saturday morning I woke feeling better, and looking forward to a day with the computer. At great personal sacrifice, I intended to forgo *Phantasie* for the day and experiment with the word processors. Maybe I would start a story.

The word processor that came with the computer took a little while to master. Getting it to work with the printer took longer, in spite of my extensive experience with printers at work.

At last, after dinner, I had my story title and author's name printed, just in time to get ready and head out with Bill to another meeting.

He was still aglow with the same excitement he manifested last night. Tonight's meeting was in my neighborhood in another church basement.

I went, by actual count, to ninety meetings in ninety days with him. He found them wonderful. His health continued to improve. People were starting to respect him at work. They were even asking his advice on projects, in deference to his long experience in the basement. They had never done that before.

I remained the same—clever, smart, knowledgeable, and remote. I won't say it was lonely. I don't allow myself to feel that emotion.

Finally, the night came when he was asked to be the speaker at a meeting, and, of course, I had to go. It wasn't a little meeting, and it wasn't a big one. There were enough people to fill up the tables.

He was nervous until he was introduced and when he spoke I saw that *something* happened to him. The drinking

Bill I knew had been replaced by a sober stranger, calm, clear-eyed and self-assured.

He smiled in my direction and began. "My name is Bill, and I'm an alcoholic," he said.

He was terrific.

On the drive home I listened to his nonstop enthusiasm without resentment. Even when Marge hung on his every word, when he came up for a coffee as the conquering hero, it didn't bother me.

Though perhaps I envied his newfound celebrity just a little bit.

EIGHTEEN.

---◆◇◆---

NATHANAEL:
Toll Taking

A LONE SKELETON, the threads of an almost mili-
tary-like uniform decaying on the crosspieces of its ribs and
shoulders, occupied the fourth toll booth from the left, one
of those that met the traffic incoming to San Francisco. All
the other booths were empty. Dirk Krieger, when he walked
with his lantern in hand across the cracked asphalt of the toll
plaza, was helpless to look in on his only companion. The
name tag was gone, and Krieger had never rooted around on
the floor of the booth, among the dust and shards of glass—
and the sifted, powdery remains of human flesh—looking
for it. He wouldn't disturb his companion's abode. Neither
would he award the booth's skeletal resident a pet name
of his own devising. *This* had been someone, once, this toll
collector who'd had loves and hates and all the rest, who had
apparently stayed faithfully on duty to the very end. Krieger,
in his vast loneliness guarding the San Francisco end of the
Golden Gate Bridge, was grateful even for this bone face

to gaze upon, with its hollow eye sockets that played tricks with the lantern light, letting him believe sometimes that the world hadn't really been destroyed by germ warfare almost twenty years ago.

∝∞∝

It was entitled *The Toll*, and the paper on which it had been printed was the brownish yellow of an antique document ... which was indeed what it was, in more than one respect.

It was of that breed of end of world short stories that was popular in, say, the 1960s. The lip-smacking excitement over the world's devastation was there, along with the mandatory grimly determined survivor, in this case fortified with the über-manly name of "Dirk Krieger." The rusting, slowly buckling span of the Bridge was described in florid detail; and even with an overabundance of similes in the story's latter half the imagery was still effective.

The story, such as it was, oozed along unencumbered by any serious plot points. Dirk Krieger, it turned out, was not in fact the world's sole survivor. He was a carrier of the biological bug that had been loosed in the war, and his duty was to guard the Bridge against any infected scavengers from the north. For, as it turned out, in San Francisco, there dwelled a colony of "clean" survivors that he could never join but which he was sworn to protect.

I neatened the edges of the pages and returned the manuscript to the Manila envelope in which I'd found it. The address on that envelope showed it originated from the old family apartment on 25th Street. Inside as well was a rejection form from a—doubtlessly—small press magazine. Below the mimeographed kiss-off some bygone editor written in ballpoint: "This has a real emotional jolt but needs stronger plotting. Try us with your next."

I wondered idly if Father had done so. But it was moot, of course. These weren't the early archival works of an author who had gone on to best-selling eminence. These weren't even efforts that resulted in the humblest ½¢ a word sale to a three hundred subscriber geek fanzine.

The box I'd opened in the basement yielded a trove of short fiction by Ward Pentecost. Hundreds and hundreds of pages worth. At least as many stories as I'd written in my teen years.

A real emotional jolt. The story had that, no denying. When at the end, the character—Krieger—scratched beneath his beard and felt the scar tissue there that signified he was a carrier of the war germ, it was stirring and revelatory. So at least one editor thought—I checked the date of the canceling imprint over the return envelope's stamps—back in 1991.

How much more of a jolt would the story, authored by someone who disappeared with the Golden Gate Bridge on November 7th seven years ago, have today? What publishing house wouldn't eagerly snatch up a short fiction collection with *The Toll* as the kickoff story, even if the other works were garbage? Such a book was ready-made for the market. One more prime example of Bridge lit.

In 1991 I had been a year old. Starting at the age of four-teen, I regularly submitted my short stories to magazines. With the initial Internet revolution already more or less fought and won by that time, I was able to do much of my submitting via e-mail.

Electronic rejection, I discovered, wasn't especially different from the tangible paper rejections Father received so often.

I picked another 9x12 envelope out of the box, undid the rust-brittle little clasp and read the contents. I was sitting on the cool cement floor, cross-legged, a bare forty watt bulb— which I'd replaced earlier—burning in an old socket overhead.

When I finished the story, I pulled out another, read it.

I read more after I'd read those.

A good percentage was science fiction. Some horror and fantasy. Some mysteries. A romance. A juvenile morality tale. Mom said that Father's fiction was always missing something; and of course it was. There was no discipline to the structure. It wasn't maverick writing. It wasn't *meant* to be unconventional. He just hadn't understood the basics. His colors were often vivid, but he drew too often and too far outside the lines. Those rejection forms that included actual notes from editors agreed. "Needs a tighter plot." "Good, but where's the ending?" "If this had a better buildup of suspense ..."

Taking note of the dates, eventually arranging a chronology, I saw that Father never learned the ABCs of the craft. His unschooled promising talent remained just that.

The rejection letters I received in my time were of another order, naturally. *I* had been endeavoring to reinvent the wheel, and it was small thinking on the part of editors that kept me out of print.

Right. Of course. For all my efforts I'd gotten no further than Father ... except to mire myself in a contract for a new novel by Irene I. Isis which was due in less than a month and which could not be completed on time. The Purple Witch was notorious throughout the industry for non-delivery, for reneging on agreements and promises of every sort; she could wave off this fiasco with a flutter of her nicotine-orange fingers. I, however, would have failed in my best and perhaps only chance to break into the world of professional fiction writing.

I found I'd culled about a dozen of Father's stories, including *The Toll*. They sat stacked beside the open box. Strung together with, perhaps, an introduction by the author's sole surviving heir these stories—for the most part diverting, despite their poor structuring—would make for a handsome volume. Hell, I could walk this compilation into the same publishing house where I'd so briefly and unpleasantly been an intern and watch my former overlords and taskmasters fall over themselves to be the first to kiss my ass.

And once the collection, along with that lengthy self-aggrandizing forward by Ward Pentecost's son, hit the stands? What then? Why, then the book reviewers would be on it, and what sport they would have vivisecting the various stories' rickety plots. What righteous literary pique they would express over the fact that yet another such opportunistic book, exploiting the grief and intrigue of the Bridge's disappearance, was being foisted on the reading public ...

In the course of the second to last—and very vitriolic—conversation I'd had with my wife, Janeane, I, desperate to inflict any damage, resorted to cliché. Our argument started over the unwieldy amount of time and effort I was giving to the Purple Witch. Janeane wasn't jealous, though by this time we were both seriously involved—or at least preoccupied—with others. I was sleeping with a *Diamond* junior ad exec, and Janeane was ... doing what she was doing. We each knew of the other's affair.

Janeane teaches at a high school in Brooklyn, a private school. I wrestled our increasingly heated dialogue about so that I was accusing her of standing in the way of my literary career. (Pure crap, since by then we both knew the Witch was a dead end; worse actually—a fatal yoke.) This did allow me, however, to shout, "Those who *can, do.* Those who *can't, teach!*" That I employed such triteness that day now only shames me.

It was pointless anyway. Janeane, having mapped out my vulnerable places thoroughly by then, had a lethal comeback.

"And those that can't do anything, *criticize!*"

I hadn't heard the basement door open, so when Mom called my name down the stairs, I started sharply. I had been sitting so long in the same cross-legged posture that pain cramped instantly through me.

"What is it?" I called toward the rectangle of warm upstairs light that the door let into the basement's relative murk.

"Telephone for you." Terrible thoughts of the Purple Witch having somehow gotten hold of this house's number flashed through my mind, but Mom allayed these with, "It's Aunt Chloe."

I frowned, nonplussed, and told her I'd be right up.

⤷⤶

I looked a question at Mom as I picked up the receiver from the kitchen counter, but her shrug of perplexity and innocence was totally convincing. She hadn't informed anyone of my presence in the city behind my back.

"Um ... Aunt Chloe?"

"Hello, Nathanael." The voice was robust but at ease, and for all the world I swear I heard her pronounce the "ae" in my name.

"Hello." I checked my memories, but mental snapshots of Aunt Chloe—actually Great-Aunt Chloe to me—were few and far between. She hadn't been as frequent a drop-in to this house as Mom's intrusive sisters, Ruth and Sarah, and their kids. Chloe, instead, *visited*. Occasionally.

"How are you?" she asked now.

"Oh. No complaints." What was I supposed to say? "How did you know I was in town?"

"Well, how could I know?"

I blinked, feeling I'd missed something. "Exactly ..."

"I keep in touch with your mother. Not enough to crowd her, just to stay apprised." She evidently felt that was some sort of explanation; she went on, "But, here you are."

"Here I am."

"How long will you be in the city?"

If I wanted to get away before the 7th and the Memorial Society's annual ceremony at the Bridge site, I had a week to do so. "At least a few days more." I glanced around, but

Mom had left the kitchen, giving me privacy.

"You're busy?" Chloe asked. Despite her evasion of a moment ago, there was something fundamentally straight-forward about her manner. Not confrontational … just candid.

"Well, I'm in town on business." The lie flowed easily by now. "I write reviews for a magazine in New York."

There was a beat of silence from the line; then, "Books? You review books?"

I was blinking again. "How did you know that?"

"Sorry? Oh, I thought that was what you'd said—you were a book reviewer. Good for you. Do you get to meet famous authors?"

I chuckled, taking care that it didn't sound bitter. "Usually I don't get to meet the *un*-famous ones."

"Well, they're not all they're cracked up to be." And instead, in her voice, I heard a caustic note, as if she truly knew what she was talking about.

I recalled then that she was—or had been—a photogra-pher. A professional photographer of some repute, a globe hopper. Odd that it slipped my mind, considering she was easily the most professionally successful member of our family tree. Or maybe envy helped blot out the fact in my mind.

"So," she said in her normal hardy voice, "tell me straight. Do you have time to pay me a visit while you're here?"

I hadn't come to San Francisco to see my relatives. Mom was doubtlessly the only individual to whom I was tied by blood that I genuinely cared about. She was my mother, and she mattered. Yet, my feelings were belated. I'd pissed away my boyhood following Father around like he was a god and my teenaged years canceling him from my life and, coinciden-tally, cold-shouldering Mom. As for the rest of the family, in all their cousinly sets and subsets, what did I honestly care?

"Yes," I heard myself say into the phone, sure and steady. "I have time to see you."

"Outstanding. I'll leave my schedule clear. You decide when. Your mother has my number and address. Call, drop by—whatever you like. I'm looking forward to seeing you, Nathanael." Again, that distinct pronunciation.

I set down the phone.

I had a date with Great-Aunt Chloe.

NINETEEN

WARD: Dare To Be Average

I WAS WORKING QUIETLY ON RETRIEVING SEVERAL DOCUMENTS from the files that were needed upstairs in a hurry. The request was from one of the Supervisors, and requests from elected officials were given top priority. This was not necessarily respect for authority; although that did exist, it was scarcely epidemic. It was more like fear. There is a lot of fear in City Hall, any City Hall.

The job was surprisingly simple, or maybe my filing system made it that. I brought the folder back to my boss, who had given me the assignment, watched him hand it off to a messenger, and forgot about it.

The next morning, when I arrived for work, I was told to see the boss right away. This sort of thing has always given me butterflies in my stomach, so I approached his office with more concern than the situation warranted.

I opened his door and entered, managing to look more composed that I was. "Ward," he said. He picked up a sheet of paper from his desk and handed it to me.

I stared at the brief note written on the Supervisor's private stationary: "Your timely work yesterday was very valuable. Thanks." It was signed with a flourish by the Supe who initiated the document search yesterday. He was one of our more conservative officials, although he would be regarded as flamboyant anyplace but San Francisco.

"You made the department look good," said my boss. "Good work."

I almost did my Gary Cooper "Aw shucks" but thought better of it. It was the first time I had ever been complimented by anyone upstairs, and it frightened me a little. I worked many years, happy for most of them, partially because I had always remained in the background. My childhood experiences with my father and grammar school teachers taught me that the best thing to be was invisible. Now I was in the spotlight. It was nice, but I could feel danger in the situation.

"Thanks, Mr. Thomas," I said.

He waved me out of the office.

I hid in the file rooms for the rest of the morning, coming out at noon to join Bill in a corner of the employee lunchroom. He was impressed by the note when I showed it to him.

"You'll be a supervisor within the week," he said. He was referring to a department supervisor. I did not like the idea at all, even if it was presented jokingly.

For the rest of the work week I tried to evade anything that even looked like it was for upstairs. On Friday morning my boss caught up with me.

"Ward," said Mr. Thomas, "they can't find this. Will you please help them out?" One of the secretaries from upstairs was standing by his side. She was pretty, young, and scared.

"Oh, Mr. Pentecost, my boss needs this right away. We lost our copy, and I put the file copy in the wrong folder."

I indicated for her to come along with me, and side by side, we walked through the double doors into the file area.

The problem, which was complicated only in the telling, proved easy to solve. I went through all the folders from the department, even though there were a lot of them, ignoring the date and scanning for subject. I caught it on the second pass.

"You'll have to sign for this," I said, handing her the signature sheet. She scribbled a hasty signature and took off down the hall, sighing in relief as she went.

"You made a lot of points with that one," said Mr. Thomas, when I returned to his office to report the results. "She's the mayor's niece."

For the rest of the afternoon I was incommunicado in the file room.

Bill came over Saturday, on the way back from a morning meeting. We agreed that it might be better if we went to separate meetings for a while. He went to his five days a week and I went to mine zero days a week. He still looked great.

"Still shook up about work?"

"No." I got up from behind the keyboard, stepped back and led the way into the kitchen.

"Where's your sidekick?"

"Nate's out, at a tribal mother-son ritual called grocery-shopping-for-the-week."

"That's a lot of words to say so little."

I didn't recognize the expression on Bill's face. It was grown-up and it made me feel defensive.

"Words are there to be used. I use a lot of them because I like them."

"Okay." Bill was smiling at nothing.

He was beginning to irritate me. I made the ritual cup of coffee for AA guests and had one myself, hot and black.

"I don't mean to upset you, Ward. What you did for me can't be overstated."

"Careful with those words," I said.

He drained his cup and slammed it down. "That's what I mean, Ward," he said. "You hide behind words."

"Oh, thank you, Mr. Roget. How's work going on the thesaurus?"

"Why don't you dare to be average?" he asked.

There was no answer to that one. I didn't have a glib answer. I looked quickly up and down the path of my life. Smart, glib, alone. Wow, what a wonderful life.

My shoulders dropped.

"You're the smartest man I know," he said.

"Me too," I said, but it was a jest offered to ease the intensity of the situation.

He brushed it aside. "You've got to put something else in your head, Ward. You're almost running on empty."

He was right. How I wished I could recreate that excitement I felt as a youth in the San Francisco Main Library. The joy of discovery, of all the possibilities of learning. But that was another world. This was the adult world, my father's world, and I was trapped in it.

"Think about it," he said. Then, as a true friend would, he left it at that.

We moved away from significances and talked of lighter things. I expounded on the challenges and joys of computing. "Yes," I said, "it's the wave of the future now, but very soon it'll be the wave of the present."

"Show me."

We were in front of the computer when Marge came home with Nate and the groceries. He was chewing on his usual red licorice.

"Got off easy again?" I asked.

Marge laughed.

One of my stories was showing on the monitor. I was taking Bill through some of the basic commands of WordPerfect.

I closed the file and gave him a clean screen. "It's all yours," I said. Then I helped Marge with the groceries, right after I gave my little sidekick a big hug.

While Marge and I were putting the groceries away, he drifted into the bedroom and stood, watching Bill. I observed him through the open door. Those intent eyes never moved from the screen. I usually had him with me when I was playing games, but not when I wrote. He would find the colors temporarily interesting and then wander off. This morning it was different. He was associating the appearance of the letters and words on the screen with Bill's typing.

He was two months shy of his second birthday and, evidently, the right side of his brain was already running on overdrive. I felt a surge of pride for my son. His IQ was going to be more rooted in the real world than mine, and I suspected it would be higher.

Marge moved to look too, pushing me aside a little to make room in the doorway. "Is he reading that?" she asked with a kind of awe.

That made me smile. "No," I said. "Not yet."

Bill's remark worked in the back of my brain all day. At five thirty I called him and made arrangements to go to a meeting.

Twice I almost called him back to cancel, but that would be more embarrassing than going. The butterflies were back in my stomach and I would not admit I was afraid, even to myself.

"You look nervous, Ward," Marge said after dinner.

"Is it that obvious?" I asked.

"Yes."

We went to a seven thirty meeting across the hill, on a side street, off of Monterey Boulevard. It was in another church basement. I whispered to Bill that there were obviously more church basements in San Francisco than churches, an engineering marvel if there ever was one. He took the joke in the spirit it was offered and laughed heartily. "I'll have to remember that next time I speak," he said.

Then we went inside and the usual round of handshaking and hugging began, with Bill participating heartily. I managed to shake a few hands but avoided the hugging. I got a laugh from some of the people as we shook hands and made first name introductions at the same time.

"I'm Bill."

"I'm Fred."

"I'm Nick."

"I'm desperate," I said.

I had a good time. I didn't board that pink cloud of epiphany and fellowship that so many in AA talk about—all the clouds in my life are black—but I found myself listening to voices that weren't in my head, and lately that was a change.

AA *was* an organization, I'd discovered, but not a hierarchy, not in the way a bureaucracy was. There was no authority here for me to fear. But still I didn't feel like I belonged entirely to these people. Even when their accounts of the shambles alcohol made of their lives sounded awfully and intimately familiar to me, I couldn't quite make that leap that would let me admit I was an alcoholic. I'd been a drinker. A heavy drinker, to be sure. But I stopped, on my own. Did that fact preclude me from belonging here?

Bill didn't attempt to proselytize me on the way home. We exchanged pleasantries about the evening and that was that.

I went to bed without playing a game for the first time in weeks. My sleep was dreamless and restful.

Sunday I spent most of the day trying to finish a story that was proving obstinate. Nate was in the room with me much of the time, fascinated by the cause and effect of type-and-watch-the-words-appear.

Once I picked him up and let him press one of the letter keys.

He wriggled to get down as the letter appeared on the screen. For the next hour he avoided me and the computer, but then he was back, standing at my left side watching with those piercing eyes. Evidently it was all right for me to type. I was the one doing the magic.

This time when I started one of my *Phantasie* games—I was up to *Phantasie II*—he stayed, as if trying to reestablish our earlier camaraderie. Or maybe I was imagining it all.

There was one thing I was certain of, and that was that I better be careful about pushing him beyond his limits.

I played for less than an hour before I shut down the machine and carried Nate out to the kitchen. Marge wasn't serving red licorice, but I had a hearty bowl of lentil soup, as did Nate, and he only left a quarter of it on the tablecloth.

After lunch I went back to the story. My little shadow took his position.

Monday morning I kissed and hugged Marge and Nate goodbye and headed forth to slay the dragons.

While on the second of the two buses I usually took, I suddenly realized that I had been sober long enough to think about buying a car. I would have to research it in the near future.

There was a note waiting for me. I picked it up, sure it was another summons to Mr. Thomas's office. It wasn't. It was a summons to see *his* boss.

"Do you know what this is about?" I asked, stopping by his office before heading upstairs.

"Not a clue, Ward. But, considering the quality of your work lately, I suspect it's good news."

To me that was bad news. This violated my personal precept of invisibility. Color me absent. This time I had no trouble admitting it. I was scared shitless.

His boss' office was up on the first floor, amidst the marble columns and gleaming floors. As soon as I was ushered into his office he jumped up and shook hands with me.

"Hello, Ward. I've been hearing great things about you from the Commissioner."

That was the new Commissioner; Madame Lafarge had been kicked far upstairs recently, much to the relief of everyone on my tier of the bureaucracy. "All I've been doing is my job," I said.

He heard the words but not my attitude. "Don't be modest," he said. "Word came down from the big man. He thinks you deserve a promotion and I agree."

The bottom fell out of my world.

TWENTY

NATHANAEL: The Son

"NATHAN?"

"Yes?"

I looked up from the newspaper, from accounts of local doings that read like quaint, vaguely unreal anecdotes to me. I'd been in New York a long time. News was multiple homicides, gang turf wars, garbage strikes, police scandals.

Mom had been waiting to say something, I realized as I looked across the kitchen table. She was still fine tuning the phrasing as I watched.

"It's Thursday ..."

I folded over the paper, set it aside. Anything I might say would, I sensed, only make her more nervous. So I waited quietly.

"Usually I meet Bennet—you remember I mentioned ...?"

"I remember."

"Usually, on Thursday, not every week but most, we meet and go—oh—to a movie, to dinner, sometimes a jazz show."

"You like jazz?" I asked, smiling softly and wryly, looking to put her at ease.

"I like to watch it being played. Live. It's the interactions among the musicians—when you can sit and see it happening, so spontaneously, it makes the music richer."

I nodded. "I agree." Mom's hands lay on either side of her morning coffee cup, her fingers drumming erratically. As she had done to me several times now, I reached out and patted her hand. I asked, in as reassuring a tone as I knew how to use, "Where's he taking you tonight?"

"Actually"—she drew herself a little straighter in her chair—"nothing's definite. He knows you're visiting, and he doesn't want to take away any time you and I might have together."

"Come come," I said, smiling expansively now. "You *must* be getting tired of me by now ..."

"Don't be silly."

"... and I've got things to do. So, go. Enjoy yourself. I insist."

Her hand, looking for something to do, stirred a spoon idly in her cup. "Would you like to meet him?" She asked it levelly, without nervousness now; but her voice was just above a whisper.

I met her clear gray eyes. I let this woman down, many times. Sins of emotional omission. She was asking now for something from me, something a bit costly perhaps ... but something I could still afford.

"Yes. I'd like to meet him."

Relief showed, delicately, in those eyes. "Good," Mom murmured.

We finished our coffees leisurely.

The sun and salt wind faded the ink, but the leaflet stuck to the phone pole—where thousands, whole generations' worth of staples were embedded and rusting—was still readable.

They're S.I.T.ting on the truth was the assertion.

I crossed the street, went under the Great Highway through the pedestrian tunnel there—a different one than last time—and stepped out onto the sand. The wind was up, and I slid on my sunglasses. The beach was spread with a predictable array of dog-walkers, joggers and loiterers. I started slogging my way down toward the water.

San Francisco still fancies itself a haven of left-leaning Bohemia, even though it's been about as authentically radical as a country club for the past few decades. It simply doesn't know any better. So it's locally fashionable to presume that the Scientific Investigation Team, which has probed the Bridge's disappearance for seven years, actually knows perfectly well what happened to it and is—of course—party to a complex conspiracy to keep the truth from The People.

I'd seen one of the SIT members the day I arrived and visited the Bridge site. I remembered. The powder blue jumpsuit, the clipboard. He looked across the empty Golden Gate, made a mark on his clipboard and gone on his way.

I never, not even in the immediate aftermath when the Team first came on the scene, expected the SIT or any other scientific, government, or military agency, to provide a definite explanation for what happened. It honestly never occurred to me that a perfectly rational accounting might even exist. The Bridge's vanishing was just too big, too extreme. It was beyond the realm wherein humans could safely surround it with *facts*, with the known.

It was, simply, out of our mortal league.

I brought along my pager and phone. I intended to make another call to the Purple Witch. With amazement and no small pleasure I'd realized earlier it had been several consecutive days since we'd spoken. My sense of liberation from her was, if anything, stronger now. It felt good. Very good.

I had the breadth of North America between me and that miserable, thoughtless, bombastic, lunatic.

So it was that when I reached the irregular line of dark sand, I left the phone in my pocket and just stared meditatively out over the Pacific. A ship was plowing along, northward, out near the horizon. I drew in long breaths, the ocean smelling cleaner than it probably was.

The Witch would not be in thrall to anything so tiresome as a work schedule, so I had been on call these past months. My job at *Diamond* didn't often require my physical presence at the offices. I would receive calls at all hours. Sometimes these were "story conferences;" sometimes they were summons. I made the drive, many times, up Interstate 95 after having been dead asleep only a half hour earlier. I arrived at that yellow-shingled house with the Cantonese character on the door to find its resident unconscious in bed and quite unreasonable when woken. (I insisted on my own key to the place after the first two times of being locked out.)

Janeane, whenever these calls came when we were both sleeping, always got up with me and told me I was letting myself be abused by the Purple Witch; she would tell me so until I'd dressed, grabbed the car keys and left the apartment.

But those late night calls hadn't disturbed her for almost three months now.

The manuscript of the novel that was meant to be Irene I. Isis' thirty year delayed, hungrily anticipated follow-up to her best-selling debut was a collection of pages, actual paper, that sat stacked beside the Smith Corona on the desk in her parlor. Those pages, about a third of the number necessary to hit the contractually obligated minimal word count, had been scribbled upon and slashed at in pen, amended by the Witch with the grace of Jack the Ripper wielding garden shears. Much of that scrawling was illegible, even to her—ideas for plot points and subplots and characterizations that likely evaporated hours or seconds after they occurred.

She enjoyed pacing about while I sat interminably at that desk, fingers on the typewriter keys. She strode through the parlor, layers of loose purple silk flowing but no longer concealing her weight as such getups must have, once. Cigarette butt after cigarette butt filling the room's ornamental ashtrays. She wore nail polish the color of wine and a foulard—purple, of course—high about her neck to cover the flaccid aging flesh there. While she promenaded, she held forth. Sometimes her vast windy lectures had to do with the material we were currently working on; sometimes the topics ranged dementedly far.

She also enjoyed hovering often at my shoulder, exuding alcoholic fumes, while I struggled to put her bleary ideas into words that could be read and understood. Often, at such times, she would abruptly seize the sheet of paper and rip it from the roller. It made a kind of *zweeeeeeet* sound.

The first time she'd done this, eight months ago, I thought I was witnessing an act of eccentric creative genius. I was still very thrilled—if not crack-brained delirious—to be collaborating with an actual name author, one who made her literary bones before I was born ... even if she'd since produced absolutely nothing. Hell, she'd written one more published successful novel than everybody else I knew, collectively.

In those first months, still aglow with my good fortune, I solemnly accepted the tirades that followed her tearing pages from the typewriter in mid-word. I was determined to learn everything possible from this woman.

Later, I would still sit at that desk while she raved and stalked about the room, ripping those pages to violent shreds, accusing me of being an incompetent hack, of undermining her ideas, of many other offenses that her onetime literarily inventive mind concocted on the spot. I sat, I heard, but I no longer listened. I watched the pieces of paper flutter to the carpet.

The manuscript stayed with her, always, at her house. She threatened to burn it so many times—screaming it, cooing it tauntingly—that the threat meant nothing anymore. She would, or she wouldn't. Either, it was due in five weeks, and it was several tens of thousands of words short.

The Pacific was the color of metal, but nearer in it churned with colorful seaweed, starfish. Sand dollars lay about on the border of dark sand just past my feet.

I sat, removed my shoes and socks, rolled up my pants. Hot sand turned immediately cool as I took a step toward the waves. I watched one tumble in. The foam touched my toes. I turned and strolled northward, following the direction of the tanker or whatever I'd seen earlier. The Cliff House and the inviting ruins of the Sutro Baths lay that way.

I took out my phone and dialed. I had to check my pager for the number.

After the third ring:"Hello?"

"You called me."

A lull back there in New York, during which strategies were no doubt assembled. Finally she said, "We should see each other."

"I'm clear on the other end of the country."

"Are you coming back?"

A heavy wave came in, and foam broke around my ankles. "Eventually."

"What are you doing out West? Are you in San Francisco?"

"Are you trying to make chitchat?" I heard and liked the hardness in my tone. Too many times I'd let this woman verbally mistreat me. I'd just taken it, initially too amazed that it was happening to defend myself.

"No," Janeane said, and in her voice was a mirroring hardness. Something lay beneath it, though, something ... frail.

"Why did you want to talk to me?" I asked. Spray dotted the lenses of my sunglasses. A pair of male joggers passed me.

It was a game of chicken we'd been playing the last few months, I mused now, feeling detached from this conversation, from my wife, from myself. Whoever said *divorce* first was going to be the game's loser.

A stupid game. Just now I absolutely didn't care who won. "Nathanael ..."

Janeane was forthright, blunt. She didn't withhold thoughts, views or judgments. But she was hesitant now.

"What?" I didn't snap it; I was actually curious.

"I'm going to have a child."

Someone, much further down the sand, was getting a kite aloft. I'd never seen anyone put one up into the air before. It was an interesting procedure.

"Did you hear me?" A very uncharacteristic note of panic sounded in her voice. I'd been silent some time.

"I did," I said. I stopped walking. I faced toward the water again.

I'm going to have a child was, I noted, profoundly apart from saying *I'm pregnant.*

"I'm going to ask you something," I said. I thought myself detached a moment ago. Now, that distant kite, if its owner were to cut it loose into the snapping winds, would not be more disconnected from things than I was now.

"Ask," Janeane said.

"Do you know what I'm going to ask?"

"Ask it."

"You do know. You know, and you're going to make me ask anyway."

"Nathanael, ask me."

A wave crashed loudly. A surprisingly big chunk of driftwood came in with it and beached itself.

"Am I the father?"

She let out a pent-up breath. "Yes ..."

"It couldn't be anyone else's?" I hadn't wanted, especially, to ask this follow-up question. Above all else it was crude. And it did nothing for my dignity.

"No," she said. "I haven't had any other man inside me since we were married."

I examined that statement carefully but found no cloaked put-down there. That surprised me; and *that* was perfect evidence of our marriage's advanced state of decay.

I asked my questions. There were many, many more to ask. There were long discussions ahead. I was going to have to see Janeane, when I got back East. I had not, during the last three months, satisfactorily imagined ever seeing her again, not even to end the game of chicken and be the first to say *divorce*.

At this moment, though, I was gazing out on an entirely different ocean than the one that washed against New York.

A facet of that difference struck me now, and I said, "You're not at the school." It wasn't yet noon here. She should still have been at the high school where she taught.

"No. I had a doctor's appointment."

"Is everything all right?" Something went quietly weightless inside me in a way I never before experienced. I came back into myself at that moment.

"I had an amniocentesis."

It took me a few seconds to dredge up the meaning of the word: fluid drawn from the uterus, then tested. "Is everything all right?" I repeated.

"There's a history of spina bifida in my family. Mild, though. Occulta. Dad's mother had it."

I didn't know these terms at all. They were alarming anyway. "Does the ... baby ... have it?"

"No. We do know the sex now, though."

We. I wasn't a part of that.

"Do you want to know?" Janeane asked.

I tugged off my sunglasses. I made a cursory swipe at my eyes, then just let the tears flow.

"Tell me," I said.

"It's going to be a boy."

The bottom had fallen out of my world.

—⊷—

TWENTY-ONE

WARD: Back Page Miracle

I DIDN'T HEAR ANYTHING ELSE ABOUT THE PROMOTION THE NEXT DAY, although my boss began treating me with deference. My fellow employees became a little remote. It was not the time to cozy up to a prospective boss. I understood. It made perfect sense.

That night I went home too distracted to play or write and picked at my dinner. Marge knew what I was worried about and she left me alone, although she made it clear that she was there for support in case I needed it.

My silences were neither sullen nor resentful. I needed to think. I needed to exercise my mind, like move a table, except that the desk was covered with the computer stuff and so was the small table we added to hold the printer. I always did it alone, except for one time, and that had not been good.

I picked up one of the books from my list of Aunt Chloe's library, a book I located in a used book store, and found myself in a fascinating world of spells and magic. As I read, I had to keep reminding myself that this stuff was regarded as real by a whole lot of people, and that there might be something to it. This went beyond the showoff stunts of my boyhood and I would have to evaluate the dangers of practicing it. Nonetheless, I skimmed over the Admonition to the Amateur, because I was above that.

I felt at ease as my psychic muscles stretched and then relaxed. I knew what I would do. It would take a little more study and thought, but I knew I could do it. Friday would be the time of maximum effectiveness, so I chose instead Thursday afternoon. Start easy was always good advice. That's probably what that warning said anyhow.

With my mind engaged, the fears of my forthcoming promotion lessened and I was able to devote the rest of the evening to Marge and Nate.

We made a bowl of popcorn and the three of us settled down in the living room to watch a movie, Nate on my lap, laughing with the movie, Marge sharing the popcorn with me, and the spell book on the sofa beside me, like a talisman.

Half of my mind was on the movie and I joined in the laughter at all the proper times. Neither Marge nor Nate perceived my preoccupation. The other half was in downtown San Francisco, in the Civic Center.

Underneath my intellectual excitement was another feeling, something building, which I did not recognize.

I felt well enough to go to bed with Marge, and for a while the job and the promotion disappeared into a hazy future, and I was conscious only of my wife and her beautiful body.

⚭

Wednesday I went to work. Nothing was happening on the surface, but Mr. Thomas grinned a lot whenever he saw me. I hid out in the old file room as much as possible. The only person I had anything to do with that day was Bill, and we simply shared our lunchtime. If he noticed my preoccupation he didn't say anything.

The day ended and I rode the two buses home in a state of dizziness. I didn't know what was happening to me, but by the time I entered the front door of our flat I was nearly unconscious.

Marge greeted me warmly, still showing a glow from last night, and Nate ran to hug me. Then she noticed that I didn't feel good and led me down the hall.

I went into the bedroom and stretched out on the bed. This was not the time to pass out, I told myself. Reciting silently to myself and by memory, I tried to cast my first real spell, self-conscious enough to hope that Aunt Chloe wouldn't find out. Just like a little kid.

ൟ

I woke up in a hospital. Marge was beside me. "Oh, thank God, you're back with us," she said.

Back from what? I thought. Even more frightening was the next unspoken question:back from where?

"Hi, Marge."

She hugged me fiercely.

"What's the date?" I asked. Not the usual "Where am I?" that you hear in all the badly written movies and teleplays. Ever since the convulsion I'd induced in myself when I quit drinking, during those dark days of our separation, I had woken up next to Marge with a need to know the date. That part of my brain was broken. That was why I had calendars in every room of the flat, and in all the places they would allow me to put them at work.

"It's later," she said. She fished a pocket calendar out of her purse and held it in front of my face, pointing to the date.

"Nine days?" I asked. My math was still all right.

She nodded.

"What happened?"

"The doctors say that you were totally exhausted. Running on empty was the term they used."

Not exactly the latest thing in diagnosis. It was the same observation Bill made. Bill was right when he said it. If the doctors were also right, something had happened.

I tried not to let the anxiety show in my voice. "What's the news of the world?" I asked casually. "Any great news events?"

"No."

I was shocked.

On Friday morning they let me go, with instructions to take another week off before returning to work. I had eighteen days of sick leave left, so the instructions were agreeable. I was anxious to get home and research those missing days. They were unable to locate used newspapers for that period in the hospital. Marge sent ours to recycle heaven.

I needn't have worried.

I rested in bed the whole weekend. I was still weak, but could detect tendrils of strength creeping along my limbs.

Monday, Marge brought in the mail. She shook a blue envelope out of one of the catalogs.

It was postmarked North Pole Station, Alaska. Aunt Chloe was making a return engagement to the Eskimo village she had chronicled ten years ago.

Dear Ward, the letter read. *I read about your exploit. You're lucky to be alive.*

I blushed at that sentence. There was more.

Next time read the instructions. It was signed by Aunt Chloe. *P.S., the newspaper story is enclosed.*

I unfolded a torn out article from the back pages of our local paper. I decided not to wonder how she'd gotten a hold of it in Alaska.

On Thursday afternoon, the day after I collapsed, the Civic Center garage, which holds eight hundred and forty-three parking spaces, was visited by a yet unclassified, pressure related weather phenomenon. All of the five hundred and ten vehicles that were parked in the garage that afternoon suffered an immediate loss of air pressure in all their tires, including the spares. The two parking attendants on duty were startled by the sound, and watched as all the vehicles in sight settled onto their rims. Police investigation has ruled out the possibility of vandalism, as the valve stems were not tampered with. It took several hours for service trucks to reinflate them all.

⸺

It worked! I felt exaltation.

Marge reached for the letter. I shook my head and slid it into one of my pockets. "Personal stuff, babe," I said, folding up the article and sliding it into the same pocket.

Marge frowned but did not contest my action.

When I stopped being exulted I started being scared. I could smirk all I wanted to, but I was carrying a letter from someone who knew a lot more than me in this area, and she didn't think my action was worth cheering.

Marge and Nate tucked me in for my afternoon nap. I was still conscientiously recuperating. I looked at her. "The letter's nothing personal," I said. I thought about it for a minute, realized that this was not the time to estrange my wife. "Hell, read it. They're both in my robe pocket."

Just before I fell asleep, I remember her taking out the newspaper article, and then the letter. My sleep was full of undefined, frightening dreams, and it was with a sense of relief that I woke up. Marge was sitting on the edge of the bed regarding me carefully. Her usually clear eyes were cloudy. She had been crying.

"Did you do this?" She held up the newspaper article.

"I think so," I said.

"Your mother told me about the dining room table."

That startled me. "When?"

"It doesn't matter," she said. "Don't you see how dangerous this is?"

The table wasn't dangerous. My effort to levitate it off the floor wasn't dangerous. The danger arrived with my mother.

It happened many years ago. I assumed that the house was empty, and that my mother would be out for a while. With my twelve year old enthusiasm and a whim to test my limits, I removed the tablecloth and levitated the table two feet into the air, and that would have been that, except that Mother was in the basement and she took that moment to come into the dining room.

I can still hear her scream as she took in the sight of the table, which weighed a whole lot more than I did, apparently obeying my command to float above the floor.

Her scream startled me and I lost control. The table banged back onto the floor, shaking it, and I was grabbed by my mother, who inadvertently bruised my forearm.

My father, later that day, was not pleased with my explanation. Nor did he believe it. At the time, his reaction seemed sensible, perfectly in keeping with Drake's generally impatient manner. Now, in retrospect, it's fairly incredible. Here I was telling him to his face that I performed a feat of magic, with my mother as a witness, and he chose to believe I was making it up, like a kid caught with matches who has set a garbage can on fire. Drake didn't want to hear it.

"I won't do it anymore," I said now, to Marge. "I promise." It was the same promise I made to my own mother, later that same day.

The book that started it all? Where was it? I glanced over Marge's shoulder at the desk. It was there, shoved almost out of sight, under several returned manuscripts.

I said I wouldn't do it again and I meant it. That did not mean that I didn't want to know what happened, including my mystery illness.

"I think I'll read for a while," I said.

"Can I get you something to drink?"

"Please."

"My polite magician."

Marge was certainly taking it better than my parents. Was that another measure of her love for me, or simply an indication of a more accepting spirit? Whatever, I was damned lucky to have her.

She went to the kitchen and I got up from the bed and retrieved the book. It was small, less than three hundred pages, and the print quality was poor, as if somebody tried to imitate an ancient font. As I examined it closer, I realized that this was not an imitation of any sort. Had I struck gold in a neighborhood book store? There was no copyright date on the fly pages. This was appearing more and more like the real thing. A genuine magic spell book.

I stood there, belatedly reading the Admonition to the Unwary (not Amateur, as I mistakenly read in my intellectual arrogance), when Marge came in with my coffee and set the cup down on the desk.

The book didn't trigger any associations for her. She went back out as I dropped into the chair.

I read over the passage I used as a basis for my downtown garage spell. I had taken a spell that was to be used for draining pus from wounds, and adapted it to draining air from tires.

I skimmed the rest of the book. Then I put it away. All the spells in it were for healing, and I perverted one of them.

This was a look into a very real world, and the laws of it were different. The Admonition made sense. I had shown a lack of caution by skipping it.

I hoped that my psychic whiplash was over. Without any fanfare for myself, I tucked the book into one of the desk drawers, never intending to use it again. I'd sworn off alcohol; I could swear off this.

I opened the door and called for Nate. He came running down the hall, showing off his newfound powers of speech.

"Daddy."

"Nathaniel," I said, emphasizing his full name.

He hoped on my lap and watched for the next hour, while I continued on my quest through the computer landscape of *Phantasie II*.

Dinner was my favorite, the pork dish that Marge made so well.

It's my habit, picked up no doubt during my childhood meals, to eat quietly, drawing no attention to myself. Tonight, I pushed all that old caution aside and participated in the conversation. Marge was glad to suddenly find that the dinner conversation was not to be another long monologue on her part.

I don't know how much of it he understood, but Nate hung on every word, his eyes flashing from Marge's face to mine, like a tennis match. Emotions are hard for me, but tonight I was suffused with the joy, pride, and affection of our family. It was a new experience.

After a small dessert of tapioca pudding, with none left on the table, Nate and I adjourned to the bedroom, where I tried to edit one of my manuscripts, to make it saleable.

As always, he stood at my left side, his eyes tracing the patterns of words that appeared on the screen. I wondered how many of them he understood.

Like every father in the world before me, I sensed within my son my own obsolescence. It started the day Nate had been born, but for the first time it did not feel unpleasant to me. It felt, instead, like the natural flow between one generation and the next, between a father and his offspring. Nature designs replacements. Nature had given me Nate, for whom I was profoundly grateful.

---∞---

TWENTY-TWO

NATHANAEL: Fever All Through the Night

"I OWNED AN AUTO GRAVEYARD, OUTSIDE OF CHICAGO. I sold that, went into pet supplies ..."

I was making a man thirty years my senior ill at ease, in the manner of the adolescent helplessly squirming before the father of his date.

He was reciting his résumé for me. Bennet Conerly tried his hand—almost always successfully—at quite a few businesses ... or "lines" as would have been said fifty years ago, the time when his breed of entrepreneurial gadabout was more common in this country. He appeared possessed of nothing so much as *gumption*.

He was respectably handsome in the way that any male of any age can look if he grooms and carries himself properly, dresses with a little style. Bennet had confidence but no detectable shred of arrogance.

I didn't play the situation for laughs, pretending to be the protective parent and warning him to have Margot home at a "decent hour." I sincerely wished them both a fun evening and walked them to the door. Bennet shook my hand a second time as they went out. Mom kissed my cheek. I'd already forgotten where they were going.

I had to sit down when they were gone—sit right on the floor of the foyer. Every part of me felt out of kilter, as if my components had been removed, recast defectively, and replaced. Limply and struggling, I got my shirt off, but the rash hadn't appeared yet.

There was no reason it should. I hadn't had strawberries today.

The last time I'd had any was in my first semester back to school after my yearlong hiatus. It was purely an accident, but I remember it scaring the hell out of whichever girl was around at the time when my temperature hit 101°. I'd told her not to worry. I popped aspirin, I applied calamine, I missed two days and then was back in class.

I felt hot, but I couldn't actually feel it on my forehead or face.

The baby was due April 14. There was a new deadline in my life.

I got up off the floor. My movements were weak, but I wasn't panicky. I just went slowly. I eventually got up the stairs and took the bottle of aspirin from the medicine cabinet into the room with me. I got onto the bed, dragging the tv's remote, and made myself comfortable.

With the set on, I hunted up a movie, set the volume low, and watched the images and colors dance feverishly.

⤫

Irene I. Isis' novel *Everyone Goes Away* was adapted for the screen and released in 1987. It starred Brooke Adams and John Savage, who both deserved better material and did their damnedest with what they had. A minor character in the book, the heroine's older brother, was awkwardly fleshed out by the screenwriters and played—again, gamely—by Bruce Dern, strictly to insert a deathbed scene (he dies of cancer in the film) and cash in on a similarly tear-jerking set piece in *Terms of Endearment*, which had just happened to sweep the Academy Awards a few years earlier.

When I mentioned it to her, the Purple Witch flat-out forbade me to see *Rosemary Leaves*, which was the unfortunate Hollywood translation of the title of her novel. The movie was poisonous, I was told. It was an affront. I was absolutely, under no circumstances, to ever *ever* watch it. Nor would I be permitted to allude to its existence again in her presence.

I visited three different video rental stores that same night before I found a copy.

This was early on in my association with the Witch. I took her overstatements as intentionally absurd, so my viewing *Rosemary Leaves* against her wishes was mere mischief. My reservoir of bitterness and resentment hadn't yet built up. I was still stunned by the opportunity that so unexpectedly come my way. I'd met Irene I. Isis at a cocktail party—one on a circuit of literary parties I'd been relentlessly trying to schmooze my way on to for a solid year—only a month ago. Now, unbelievably, she wanted me as her coauthor. We were going to write a book together. The contract would be easy to come by, she assured me with authoritative indifference.

I do not claim to have any real critical knowledge of movies. But *Rosemary Leaves* is tripe. It succeeds, thirty years after its release, only as camp. Rosemary Parrish, the heroine, is presented as a model of Women's Lib era independence. The polemic-rife dialogue was probably dated when the film came out, and time hasn't been kind to it since.

It wasn't, to be fair, a particularly good adaptation of the source book, but what could one have expected? *Everyone Goes Away* wasn't the first novel to be pillaged by Hollywood hacks.

The movie was critically pummeled, but it was also the eighth highest grossing film that year. The Witch had cut a very shrewd deal for it, and despite her outspoken denouncements, I doubt she felt many pangs when she spent the back-end money. Her book had since been optioned twice more, though a remake had yet to actually be shot.

So it was that one novel kept her in mood stabilizers and vodka for thirty years. Her literary standing, though, was another matter ...

Whatever I had been watching earlier morphed into something else. The colors were gone. Black and white now. A soundtrack that crackled with age. Every man in the movie wore a hat. I recognized an actress who repeatedly pressed the back of her hand against her mouth, but I couldn't name her.

Irene I. Isis was a punch line. She could still dazzle in her way. Her presence was commanding, and her tales of the high jinks and roguery of the literary world were still riveting. But her reputation by now preceded her. She reneged on one too many contracts, thrown more legendary tantrums than was permissible. She was a diva without the required talent or body of work to back it up.

But she'd written *Everyone Goes Away*, a real book, a book I'd read, and meeting her thrilled me deeply. I too had heard the gossip about her. I even credited most of it. But when she nonchalantly mentioned she was shopping about for a worthy collaborator for a follow-up, I breathlessly threw my hat in the ring. Without hesitation.

She regarded me in a thick silence while she fired up a fresh cigarette, despite the host's earlier attempts to tactfully remind her that this was a no-smoking soiree.

"Tell me the single best line of prose you ever wrote," she said. "You have eight seconds."

Again I didn't hesitate. I didn't even think about it; I shot from the hip. "'There was a tract in Vincent's memories of his first schoolboy crush where mental insecticide guaranteed nothing would ever grow again.'"

It was the same—and only—sentence from all my unpublished work that my wife ever commented on, favorably or otherwise.

Irene I. Isis appeared to be absorbing it. Then she turned away, shutting me off, and allowed someone else the honor of her presence. The party was, of course, lousy with writers. Mostly the wishful kind.

Nearly a month later I heard from her. I was once more thrilled and awed. I was told I had to bring her something. She wanted some unique thing of mine—a trait, an aptitude, an item of personal history. Some distinctive proof that I was different from any of a thousand aspiring writers in New York who would give their proverbial eyeteeth to work with her.

So I brought her something. Then, later, I signed the contract she procured, and we went to work on the book.

I woke up knowing I'd dozed only twenty minutes or so. I hadn't inherited Father's total lack of time sense. I didn't start each morning needing to look at a calendar, and I didn't wear a watch twenty-four hours a day.

My forehead was now hot to the touch. I lay on the bed listening a moment, but the house was quiet. Mom wasn't home yet. I wasn't worried or uncomfortable about anything she and Bennet might be doing. He seemed like a pleasant fellow.

I had no appetite whatever. I refilled my glass of water from the bathroom tap, moving my feet slowly and carefully. On the way back to the bedroom I grabbed the phone book that was by the extension at the top of the stairs.

I rested up from my excursion, watching the tag end of the old thriller on the tv. Then I opened the phone book and flipped pages. There was no George Starks or G. Starks with a listed number living in San Francisco. Not even a *Georgie* Starks, as the Purple Witch referred to him. I tossed the directory to the floor.

There. I'd tried. I now had no reason for being in San Francisco.

George Starks ...

It jumped out of my fevered head at that moment. The name hadn't been familiar before. I was weary of the Witch when she'd put me on to this quest. Worn out by her. Go find George Starks, fairy. Fine. I'd gone, not caring who this person might actually be, not even especially curious.

Now, despite the temperature I was running—or maybe because of it—the name popped up suddenly in my mind's catalogue.

There was a novelist by the name of George Starks. I knew nothing more than that, not anything about him or what he had written. Had he known Irene I. Isis in the old days, just before she hit with *Everyone Goes Away*? Was he a former lover?

I would get a hold of one of his books. Even if nothing of his was still in print, I could troll the used bookstores. On the short list of San Francisco's virtues is the fact that there are still many such shops here. (Hell, there might be a George Starks novel in among the veritable trove of books in this house's basement; but I wouldn't make all those stairs just now.)

So, I could justify my stay in the city awhile longer at least.

∽

It was Thursday. This Sunday was the end of daylight-savings time. Set back your clocks. Seven years ago it had fallen on the 7th. This year, November 7th was a Tuesday ... this coming Tuesday.

We'd gone through a roster of titles. Nothing stuck. Needless to say, the Purple Witch rejected my every suggestion, but she was no more satisfied with anything she dredged up. To give credit where it's due, I must admit she put forth—and then promptly discarded—what I considered the best title for our book so far, which was *Everyone Goes To Hell*.

I woke again, sharply this time. Mom was home, moving around downstairs. I meant to shut off the set and the lights the minute I heard her key in the front door; now it was too late.

I wasn't going to try the stairs, so I pushed myself off the bed and onto the overstuffed chair. A few minutes later she came up.

Even though the door was open, she knocked softly on the jamb. I smiled.

"How was your evening?" I still couldn't remember where she'd said they were going.

"Oh, just fine. Fine."

"Did you cab it home?"

"No. Bennet has a car." Mom had removed the earrings she'd been wearing when she left. A tiny frown made an indentation between her brows. Her lipstick was nicely offset by the shade of her hair. "You're flushed. What's wrong?"

"I'm not flushed."

She came into the room, peering at my face. "Are you running a temperature? Just *let* me."

I stopped trying to evade her hand as she felt my forehead. "It's okay, Mom."

"You're very hot, Nathan."

"It's okay."

"Did you get into some strawberries sometime today?" Her tone was firm and concerned.

"Mom ..." I took her hand and pressed it between mine. "I like Bennet. He seems like a straight shooter."

Her face went still. "He's been very kind," she said softly. "Good."

I was too weak to easily stand up and didn't want to alarm Mom by doing so. But she perched herself on the arm of the chair, meeting my eyes.

We looked at each other in silence for a while.

Finally she said, just a bit tiredly, "I am a widow, Nathan."

"I know." I pressed her hand tighter.

The gazing silence returned.

TWENTY-THREE.

—◆◆—

WARD: The Boss

EARLY TUESDAY EVENING BILL CAME OVER WITH NEWS of current events in the basement of City Hall.

"They've taken part of the old file room and built a small office," he said. "The sign painter showed up this morning."

My stomach began to knot.

Bill didn't take note of my increasing anxiety as he continued. "Congratulations, *Mr. Ward Pentecost, File Room Supervisor.*"

We were sitting at the kitchen table and Marge was nearby, cleaning the stove top. Some spilled sauce vanished under the dishcloth. "Oh, that's wonderful news! Ward, I'm so happy for you."

"I've talked to most of the clerks," Bill said. "They're all behind you one hundred percent."

"Mr. Thomas?" I asked.

"He said he's glad to get rid of that responsibility, and that they couldn't have picked a better person for the job."

"You?"

"With you one hundred and ten percent," said Bill.

Everybody was happy with my promotion. Everybody except me.

"I'd like to go to a meeting tonight," I said.

"I thought you might."

Marge made three mugs of coffee and joined us to pass the time until we had to leave. Nathaniel was in the living room perusing his books.

"Do you realize that this means we can buy a car?" Marge was excited by visions of sugar plum faeries. I know what it's like. I used to have the same visions whenever I submitted a story.

"We don't know how much of a raise this means, Marge," I said.

"Oh, but it's bound to be substantial." There was no stopping her enthusiasm.

I felt like I had been roped, tied, and dragged kicking and screaming towards a terrible kind of adult world. With a little more bad luck I could be just like my father.

After my marriage, a lot of things in my life changed, for the better, but my relationship with authority remained the same. I simply *did not* want to be placed in a high profile position. I didn't want to sign time cards, approve vacations, reprimand employees, kiss around the higher-ups. In short, I didn't want to supervise anybody. Why hadn't they left me alone?

When it was time for us to leave, I glanced over my shoulder, as we paused in the doorway. Marge was already on the phone, calling Phyllis, no doubt, to spread the glad tidings. I fled down the front stairs.

∞

I don't know what I expected from the meeting. The speaker was moderately interesting, but I heard her story before at other meetings we attended.

In some unfathomable way I was comforted simply by being there. The dynamics of the group were different from the dynamics of the individuals present. The group was an entity itself, and it had no private agenda, as did some of the people present.

It was a commonplace experience that I heard described often, during the three months Bill and I attended that marathon series of meetings. I didn't do anything. I didn't directly participate in the meeting. I was there and nothing else. It was only vaguely that I even followed the discussion without contributing. I felt better. Leave it at that. *Utilize. Don't analyze.*

I was quiet on the way back. Bill sensed my need for silence and we drove home without conversation. He declined to stop by for coffee and a snack.

I opened the front door to be surprised by the sight of Marge still on the phone. Usually at this time of night, she was either watching a movie or was curled up with a non-fiction book. I waved and she waved back. Her face still bore the excitement I fled from two hours ago. The animation in her voice made me sure that Phyllis was not at the other end of the line. In two hours she should have been able to work her way down to second cousins.

My problems with authority began at home, the point of origin for most minor and major disabilities. Dad was violent. Dad was authority. It was as simple as that, except most children get over it when they get into the school system.

I spent the first four years of school in a state of unconsciousness. To this day I can't remember the name of a teacher or a classmate. In the fifth grade I met my new teacher, my dad's twin, in Christian Brother's clothing. I hope he was atypical of the species. The gentleman seemed to nurse a personal grievance over my inability to learn. He was also a violent man. The least thing that happened to me that frightening year was that on three separate occasions I was slapped across my upturned palms with a wooden ruler until the ruler broke.

This did not make me a better student.

It did not prepare me for the work force, unless there was a place for galley slaves in this century. And now I was a boss? I wanted to cry.

Marge finished her phone calls and came into the bedroom to find me sitting on the edge of the bed with downcast mouth and reddened eyes.

She sat down next to me and put an arm around me. "What's the matter, Ward?" she asked. "I thought you'd be happy."

I managed not to laugh at her.

"Marge," I said as gently as possible, "I do not want to be a boss."

"Why not?"

"I can't say right now."

"But you've got the position. Your name is on the door." The excitement left her face to be replaced by worry. "You're not going to refuse it?"

"I'm not going to refuse," I said. "It's too late for that."

She looked relieved.

"But don't expect me to be happy about it."

Thus, I laid down the rules. Yes, I was going to take the job. No, no, and no, I was not going to enjoy it. This was many degrees worse than my travails under the commissionership of Madame Lafarge. Gone forever were my happy days of anonymity, hiding in the files. I would still be there, but it would be different.

Nate was already asleep. I tucked the covers closer around him in his big kid's crib, newly placed in the second bedroom complete with his own star-shaped nightlight.

My son and Marge would somehow make it bearable.

My father's political influence made it possible for me to get the clerk's job in the first place, leapfrogging to the top of the list. The same influence saved that job time after time during my heavy drinking days, which were really *all* my drinking days. Now, I suspected that that same influence was a factor in my unwanted promotion. There was nothing I could do about it.

The powers that be promoted me, a qualified employee, to the position, and also just happened to pay off a political debt at the same time. Such is the way of government at every level.

I wanted a drink so badly that I could taste it.

Either Bill was psychic or he sensed my discomfort with the situation. The next day he called right after work, even before he went home. "Meeting tonight?" he asked as soon as I came on the line.

"Yes."

"I'll be a little early," he said. "Is that okay? There's something I want to ask Marge about."

"Okay," I said.

He hung up the phone.

I went back to the computer. Nate stood beside me in his usual position, while I attempted to straighten out the opening of my latest rejected story. It was getting very discouraging. Since the time I received the unwanted news of my promotion I also received four of my manuscripts back.

I did something unusual. I muttered, "The hell with it," and turned off the machine. This was getting too much like an exercise in self-flagellation. I was starting to slip into the delicious waters of the sea of self-pity. Then I grabbed Nate and carried him out to the kitchen, where we each had a store-bought chocolate chip cookie. It's impossible to concentrate on self-pity, the most luxurious of emotions, and a chocolate chip, the most luxurious of cookies, at the same time. Marge said something about spoiling our dinner, and we both laughed happily.

The dinner was so good that a whole package of cookies wouldn't have spoiled my appetite. Nate devoured his smaller share of the casserole, made with pork, potatoes, and sauerkraut with equal enthusiasm. I did not brood any further over my unfulfilled writing ambitions.

"That was great," I said.

Marge smiled broadly, and then the doorbell rang.

It was Bill. He carried a paper bag and handed it to Marge. "Nuts and Chews," she exclaimed as she looked inside.

"I hope you like them," he said. "I can always exchange them for something else."

"Don't you dare."

He sat down at the kitchen table. "I need your advice," he said to Marge.

"I hope I can help." She cleared her place at the table and sat down. "Is it a problem?" she asked.

"No," said Bill. "It's more of a question." He managed to look embarrassed and hopeful at the same time. "It's about Eileen Duvall. She's the girl who caught the bouquet at your wedding."

"I know who she is," said Marge.

"Do you know if she likes me?"

Marge smiled. "Now that is a coincidence," she said. She paused teasingly.

Bill shifted awkwardly in his chair.

"Really, Bill, it is a genuine coincidence. Last week Eileen asked me if you were seeing someone. I told her you were seeing Ward—as a friend."

Bill relaxed visibly, as if a load had been taken from his shoulders.

"Do you think it'll be all right for me to call her? Maybe ask her out to dinner?"

"I think that would be very welcome," said Marge. "You're one of the most charming men I know, especially since you stopped you know what ..."

"Drinking," I interjected.

"I was going to say that, Ward," said Marge.

Bill sighed. "You really think so?" he asked.

"I really think so," Marge reassured him. She moved away from the table. "Let me make us some coffee, and open that wonderful box."

The coffee was good, a new blend Marge encountered on one of her shopping trips down 24th Street. We drank enough of it for me to hope that there were two bathrooms at the meeting.

For the rest of the week, Bill and I attended a meeting daily. If I was on-again, off-again with AA, this was definitely one of the very *on* times. It had the effect of calming me, of pushing away those unwanted thoughts of my new position. I started to listen—a little. Maybe one day I would get the words "I am an alcoholic" past my lips, but that day wasn't today.

Bill noticed the slight modification of my attitude, and, if he found it amusing, did not comment. That could have been concern for my feelings, or else it was simply because he was busy most of the time talking about Eileen Duvall, and they hadn't even had a date yet.

But meetings or no meetings, the days passed swiftly, and one dark morning when I woke up it was Monday.

Marge checked me one last time. I was standing reluctantly in the hall while she took a clothes brush and attacked some nonexistent dandruff on my collar.

"All right," I said. "Enough." I kissed her. I lifted up Nate, warm and earthy-smelling in his sleepers, and hugged him tightly.

"Daddy is going forth to slay some dragons."

I was nervous enough, as I rode the bus and the Muni Metro downtown, to have shaken any dragons to death.

Outside of City Hall, I paused and wished that I had a magic spell for this situation. Just a simple incantation to make me disappear. It shouldn't be too hard.

When I got downstairs I realized that it was too late for wishful thinking. My stomach did a flip-flop when I saw the banner. It was lettered in a cheery red and it stretched across the entrance to the file rooms:

WELCOME MR. PENTECOST

TWENTY-FOUR

NATHANAEL:
Book Hunting

NO EXOTIC MEDICINES, NO EMERGENCY ROOM VISITS. Just aspirin, to keep my temperature relatively at bay, and bed rest. I dutifully showed Mom my arms and chest. No rash.

"I'll be fine this time tomorrow," I promised.

Psychosomatic or not, I was sure this bout would last no longer than if I'd actually eaten a strawberry.

Mom was hardly prone to hysterics. With a husband and son who both responded poorly to conspicuous emotional displays, she learned to mete out her feelings a bit more carefully than was probably natural for her. But she was still a mother and would be as long as we two were alive.

I spooned up a little of the cup of broth she'd made, even though my enfeebled body was telling me plainly that it didn't need any sustenance right now. I good-naturedly accepted it when she said I couldn't have coffee.

"Weakens the immune system," she said, in a very *un*-old

189

wives' tale tone of voice.

I lay there, I sweated, I saw the world through the fisheye of my fever. Reading was too much of a strain, so I watched more television, which served to remind me why I usually watched so little. Between catnaps I did stumble on a public television documentary that caught my interest. It was about New-foundland, and I couldn't figure out why it was so familiar.

That was Friday.

The name Pentecost, as it connected with a victim of the Golden Gate Bridge's disappearance, didn't follow me to New York. Not to school and not into my professional life. I left all the connotations out here, in San Francisco. It was as Mom had wished: no one in the family was to cash in on the tragedy.

I told Janeane about it only on that same day we calmly discussed marriage. She digested the fact coolly, then opined that my not taking advantage of my father's misfortune was somehow comparable to her not being on speaking terms with either of her parents these past two years. I didn't quite see the correlation, but I went along with it. I loved Janeane Youngblood after all, and if we found one more thing to feel indignant about and superior to, so much the better.

Janeane, naturally, retained her surname when we wed. We wouldn't even give thought to the barbaric practice of the woman assuming the male's name. Even the phrase "maiden name" was nebulously revolting to us.

Now, however ... what name was our child, our son, to have? Was Suzette, who was Janeane's girlfriend, going to have some say in this? How many hyphens would we be subjecting him to?

Poor little fellow.

I dreamt of a wide sky full of dark floating rectangles. I don't have nightmares often, but when I do, they're vivid and vicious. Even so, I normally need only open my eyes for them to dispel completely, leaving no aftertaste.

Which was why it was strange that when the fleet of mahogany tables overhead suddenly felt the grip of gravity and plummeted straight for me, I found myself shaking and cringing for minutes after starting sharply awake.

The daylight at the window was frail. It was very early. I got up anyway, in part because I was too rattled to sleep again but also because I *could* get up, I realized happily. My limbs felt like they belonged to me again. I showered and shaved, and that restored me all the more.

I glanced at my pager, but it was only idle curiosity. By now I couldn't easily count the accumulated pages from the Purple Witch. I wasn't inclined to try. No one else tried to reach me.

It put me on to thinking about George Starks, though. With my temperature gone, my head was clear, and George Starks still registered as the name of a novelist. I even found further information in my mental file. He was a genre writer of some sort. Mysteries? Maybe.

I set a pot of coffee to dripping, knowing Mom would be awake soon but not waiting for her to officially check me out of the sick ward. I felt fine. I drank off a quick cup and set out, more excited by my undertaking than I should have been. Probably I was just grateful for the positive distraction.

I had a good feel for the city by now. I drove over and past the Peaks and down into the valley, Noe, then the flatland, the Mission. Parking was shockingly easy, or maybe it just didn't compare to the demolition derby of New York street parking. I was suddenly, savagely hungry. Valencia Street had been gentrified in the past decade or two to within an inch of its onetime barrio life, but I didn't care. I don't like Mexican food anyway. I found a diner—a retro punk-themed one—and ate sausages, eggs, toast; then I ordered pancakes. The faces of punk rock icons snarled and sneered from the walls, but the anarchic three-chord guitar music on the sound system was at a gentle volume at this early hour and the tables and floor were squeaky clean. I left my waiter with the fire engine red hair and meticulously torn jeans a good tip.

Nobody in the place, including myself, had even been alive when the Sex Pistols' Sid Vicious stabbed his girlfriend to death.

I hit the bookstores along Valencia. There were a few Halloween decorations still in the windows of the apartments above the businesses. The holiday had been several days ago. Halloween, as in New York, is a big deal here.

George Starks didn't show on the computer at the first place. At the second a leathery woman touched her forefinger to her nose and stared intently past my left shoulder.

"Detective writer," she said suddenly and sharply, slapping her counter with an open palm. The sound echoed in the narrow shop where there was only me, her, and an uncaged cockatoo. The bird didn't flinch.

The place was dense with the smell of paper and print, but there wasn't enough dust to make me sneeze. You couldn't see the walls of the store.

We talked as she homed in on the books. She looked like she might have spent considerable years in this neighborhood; she and the shop both appeared to have deep roots. Her passion for books was something more than a vendor's love of profits. We talked for twenty minutes while she excavated, and I would have thought three had passed.

"Smart, smart stuff," she said, handling each of the three used paperbacks before passing them to me. "He doesn't underestimate the intelligence of his readers. He's honest too—in the plotting, in the emotions he elicits. I haven't read any Starks in years." She was sitting on part of a pile she'd dislodged.

"You don't mind me buying them, then?" I asked with a droll smile.

She returned a look more somber. "I *sell* books, friend. They are supposed to find as many readers as possible."

There was something of a perfectly legitimate credo in that. I bought all three novels.

On the way back to Santiago Street I hunted for and found 25th. I slowed at the address of the apartment where Father, Mom, and myself lived through what turned out to be some of the best years we had as a family. Another car glided up behind me, though, and I pulled away before I'd even satisfied myself as to which unit in the building had been ours.

∽

When Mom gave me a somewhat stricken look when I came in, I felt a surge of annoyance as intense and pre-programmed as a racial memory. I realized only then that I should have at least left a note before heading out. The last she'd seen, the night before, was me bedridden and running an almost dangerously high fever. She'd woken up this morning and found me gone.

She was, of course, overreacting.

"Sorry," I said. "That was thoughtless." I didn't really mean it until I'd actually said it, though. My irritation evaporated at that. Too often in my adolescence I'd been subjected to those long-suffering gazes from her, as she pined about her stoic morose son who wouldn't give his father the time of day.

"You're feeling better?" Her voice was a bit remote.

"Just fine."

"Well, good."

I lingered in the kitchen awkwardly.

"Why is it, Nathan," she started, breaking the lull but not making things any more comfortable, "that you can commit some very insensitive acts, when I know that you're a kind, generous, decent, person?"

That was, I mused, more than I knew about myself.

A wide range of replies came to mind. I didn't deserve this, I decided. And I wasn't going to play out some sort of showdown here with her. Mistakes had been made in our little family on all sides. Crimes you might call some of the deeds. Well, *one* of them anyway. Now wasn't the time to blame or apologize or to try, so very belatedly, to restage the past.

"Nobody's perfect. I said I was sorry." I spoke both trite platitudes with all the blandness they merited.

Mom shook her head, stopped and met my eyes squarely. "You got married without telling me. I've never told you how hurt I was by that ..."

"I think I know."

"How could you know? You're an imaginative person. But I don't think anyone could imagine that."

My face felt stony. It was the face of my teen years.

"My marriage has fallen apart, Mom. It's gone completely to hell."

A new silence came, pitched to a different frequency. Sadness showed on Mom's face, and in that moment, I saw the almost bottomless well of sympathy and compassion she harbored; and I wondered how I'd contrived to inherit so few of her traits. I'd gone to such extremes to be nothing like my father. But I hadn't followed the other ready example nature provided me.

It was a can of worms. I opened it, let out a few, then resolutely resealed it. I said nothing about the child—Mom's *grandson*—that my wife was carrying. I omitted many other details. I told her, basically, that Janeane and I married hastily and unwisely. It was, basically, the truth. But it was ultimately as cursory as a plot summary in one of my reviews. It was hard to communicate it unless you'd lived it.

And what, in the end, could Mom know about a failing marriage?

She said sincere and supportive things, which I thanked her for. Then I excused myself and went upstairs with my paperbacks, saying I had to look them over as part of the business that brought me to the city. I surprised myself when I realized this was true.

I rolled my eyes heavenward when the protagonist's name was given as August Purity, but that was the last time I was anything but captivated by what I read. George Starks' third person prose was tidy and effective. He had that rare knack for full-fleshing walk-on characters in two sentences. His scenes jumped vividly off the pages, but he accomplished this through restraint, not verbiage.

A very strange thing happened while I read the first of the novels—it was entitled *Pale Semblance*—over the course of that day: I did not read it as a critic; I read as a reader.

It was indeed detective fiction, but the dearth of fatal clichés inherent to that genre made the story fresh. After some short while, even the flowery affected name of August Purity started to make literary sense. As a character, he couldn't be summed up by a few neat traits and tics. He had complexity. The predicament in which he found himself was totally plausible. I didn't have to suspend my disbelief; I already knew that everything August Purity was doing was real.

Before starting in reading the book, I, of course, scrutinized it for clues. The copyright was 1982. There was no bio, but the dedication was ...

to Dorothy Shields, a damn good sport

The other two books were 1983 and 1986, both August Purity mysteries as well. (I was already looking forward to devouring them.) Dorothy Shields was mentioned again on the dedication page of one; the other was dedicated to an editor, since retired, acclaimed in the industry for consistently getting a writer's best work.

The '86 novel, *Black Bones*, was a much later edition, indicating the series had come back into print in recent years. It had a photo and bio. George Starks looked to be in his sixties, with piercing eyes and a mostly gray beard. He was smiling, and it looked very natural. He was a native New Yorker. That he "resides in California" was the only clue offered to his present whereabouts. In addition to the mysteries, he'd written at least four nonfiction titles, about various aspects of the Industrial Revolution, it looked like. I wondered if Mom read any of those.

George Starks was of the right age and profession and had been born in the right geographical location to have perhaps consorted with Irene I. Isis in the mid-1980s, when her novel splashed onto the scene. George Starks evidently hadn't hit big with any of his works—hadn't plucked that vital cultural chord that meant literary celebrity—but his list of titles showed he'd worked consistently for over thirty years. It was an admirable accomplishment in the field.

The leathery lady at the bookstore had been quite right. His work was intelligent and honest. If he'd even remotely kept up the quality through the years, he had an impressive body of work to his name.

We had soup and salad for dinner. Mom didn't press me for details about Janeane. That was predictably tactful of her.

Late that evening, in the middle of *Pale Semblance*'s last gripping chapter, a thought occurred, but I didn't act on it until I'd read through to the satisfying, very credible conclusion. Then I fetched the phone book again and found the number for Dorothy Shields, who had an address on 23rd Street in Noe Valley.

That was Saturday.

TWENTY-FIVE.

WARD: Changes

"TIME CHANGES THINGS." That was a line from George Pal's *The Time Machine*, uttered by Rod Taylor. He could have said that time changes people and been just as right.

Five years ago to the day, my name changed at work. From that point on I was no longer *Ward*, but had been elevated— or demoted, to my way of thinking—to *Mr. Pentecost*.

"Mr. Pentecost, you have a call," said my new secretary.

The city administration changed in the last election. The supervisor who'd favored me with a compliment years ago was now mayor, and by some political alchemy it translated for me into a bigger office, a bigger staff and more responsibility.

"Who is it?" I asked.

The girl smothered a grin with her hand. "Mr. Pentecost, it's Mr. Pentecost calling."

I hadn't seen my father since the time he attended Nate's fifth birthday party, and he hadn't been able to stay for all of that.

"Yes, Father," I said with a false heartiness.

"Son ... your mother and I need to talk to you and Margot."

When was the last time he called me anything that hinted of family? Now I was *Son* again? Something about the voice was wrong. It was my father's voice all right, but not exactly, more like the way I imagined Drake Pentecost would sound as an old man, without the bravado and contagious self-assurance. I could not conceive of my father being that old—never.

But he continued, dispelling my doubts. "Something has happened," he said. His voice made me afraid that he would break into tears at any moment.

"Mother?"

"No, nothing like that. We're both all right physically." I did not choose to think of the possibilities that left open.

"Could you and Margot come out to Santiago tonight, please?"

My father asking me to please do anything? No, this was not the Drake Pentecost I grew up fearing, and then avoiding. This was a frightened old man I didn't know.

"Take it easy, Dad," I said gently.

The calmness in my voice seemed to diminish the fear in his. "Thanks, Son," he said. "Eight o'clock tonight? You can bring the baby."

For God's sake! Nate hadn't been a baby for years. "We'll be there," I said. I put down the phone and stared into space. We were going out to the house I grew up in. My father and mother were currently enjoying their sixth (and still counting) reconciliation. They halted their divorce proceedings of several years ago at the eleventh hour, for reasons neither explained to me. Maybe they'd been afraid, on some primal level, of being separated from each other. Whatever, they had still not figured out how to keep their marriage stable. Or how to end it.

My father was still in the realty game, though he didn't need to be anymore. He was still successful and on the affluent side. Maybe he wanted to prove something to himself and my long-suffering mother. But he hadn't sounded either rich or happy just now on the phone.

I called Marge during the day to prepare her for tonight, and to make the necessary arrangements to leave Nate for the evening with Bill and Eileen Berry. I did not expect that tonight would be a good thing for him to witness, and he always had a good time with them and their three year old son, Bobby.

At quitting time I drove directly home in our second brand new used car. Picking out the first car confirmed what I suspected for a long time, namely that some things can't be learned from books.

I got the last parking place on the block.

Marge met me at the door and she was visibly upset. "Oh, Ward, I called your mother. It's very bad news."

I stepped inside and closed the door.

"Let me put these things away," I said, and headed for the bedroom. Minutes later, more comfortable in my civilian garb, I sat down at the kitchen table with Marge.

"Now," I said, "I'm ready for it."

"I talked to Alice this afternoon," she said. "Your father made some bad investments."

"He's done that before," I said. "He always recoups, usually with a profit."

"Not this time, Ward. According to your mother, your father is broke."

I held up my hand. "I'd like to hear it from him," I said.

"Very well." She recognized my obstinate mode and withheld the rest of whatever my mother told her.

"I don't mean to be rude," I said. "But something this important I would prefer to hear from him. My mother might be exaggerating."

She accepted my apology. "Let's hope she is," she said.

Bill and Eileen were glad to take Nate for the evening, or, for the night if this took too long. I walked Nate to their door with Marge. Bill was beaming happily and Eileen had that glow that comes from steady good sex.

"I hope everything works out all right," Bill said as we left Nate and made our farewells.

"So do I," I said.

We drove in silence out to the Avenues. I was wearing my old leather jacket like a suit of armor. Marge smiled about that but it made me feel better.

The sight of my father did not. Whatever Marge left unsaid at my insistence couldn't have prepared me for this.

"Ward, dear," said my mother, almost running to embrace me as we entered the house. Her eyes were puffy. I immediately turned my attention to my father. No, he hadn't beaten her up. That had all been a long time ago. She had been crying, though.

I gently broke the embrace. "What's the problem, Mom?" I asked.

She indicated my father. He was lying back on the couch with his mouth open. A bottle of Jack Daniel's lay on its side on the floor. It was empty. I wondered if he'd drained the whole thing in the hours since we'd spoken over the phone. His clothes were disheveled and he had a heavy growth of stubble. No matter what, drunk or sober, peaceful or raving angry, he never let himself look bad. I was scared.

"He would hate it if he knew anybody saw him like that," said my mother, reading my mind.

"He looks so old," I said.

"Your father and I are each in our mid-sixties," she said.

He looked more like the mid-nineties. I caught Marge's eye and shrugged, as if to say *I don't know what to do.*

"Can we go into another room?" asked Marge.

"Why certainly." My mother got a better grip on herself. "Where are my manners? I picked up some pastries earlier."

We went into the dining room. The table was decorated with a vase of white roses and a platter of pastries. I recognized blueberry muffins and orange scones.

"Ward," said my mother, leaning over my shoulder before she went to put on the coffee, "the table is for sitting at. Do you understand?"

In spite of the gravity of the situation I smiled as I squeezed her hand. "Yes, Mom."

"I'll give you a hand, Mother," said Marge and accompanied her into the kitchen. I remained *at* the table, the same one I once scared my mother with by levitating it impossibly off the floor. I was still smiling to myself, although there was little to smile at tonight.

Mother and I each had a scone with a delicate overtaste of orange while Marge had one of the large blueberry muffins.

After a slight hesitation, Mother began to talk. Her voice was measured and under control, but the tightness in her neck muscles revealed her strain. Good for you for holding it together, old girl, I thought.

"Your father was swindled," said Mother. "There's no other way to put it. It was perfectly legal. I've already been to several attorneys with him." She, having answered my question before I even asked it, continued, "Drake is too old for the pretty young things to want him any longer. I imagine he used to be quite the prize."

"So he wanted to prove that he still has it? Is that why he did it, Mother?"

My mother raised her head; it threw her jawline into a regal frame, but not haughty. "He wanted to impress *me*," she said.

For her mid-sixties my mother was still a very attractive woman. I had no trouble imagining a man, even a middle-aged man, or an old man like my father, wanting to impress her.

"He'll be asleep for hours," she said. "Maybe until tomorrow morning. I think I better show you what happened."

She left the room and returned with a bulging briefcase. When she deposited the contents on the table, my first thought was that it was lucky we left Nate with Bill and Eileen. This was going to be a late one. She laid the contents out in chronological order.

My father had been jobbed real good. As I read from document to document, page to page, I was appalled by his gullibility. Couldn't he have seen it coming? The light glinted off the silver frames of Marge's new glasses as she took each paper and read it.

"See how they masked it right up to the end," she said.

I was using the gift of hindsight. Suppose I looked at it from my father's viewpoint for a few minutes? I was repelled by the thought but did it anyhow.

He had been roped in by the presentation of a perfectly credible business deal, although a richer one than he was used to participating in. A consortium of rich men in Marin County were in the way of acquiring the land to build a shopping mall/multiplex theater/restaurant complex. They'd already had the ground surveyed, secured the necessary permits for an environmental impact study, and with the acquisition of the land, were ready to go ahead. The profit for each member of the consortium could be measured at over five million each, more if the land sold cheap enough.

My father would not have to be comfortable with the type of wealth that could be measured in hundreds of thousands of dollars. No, he would be rich. What a hook for an aging lothario. He bit the hook.

In the rest of the documents, I got a chance to look at what it cost him. Essentially, it was everything. When they demanded the final contractual assessment to allegedly buy the land, he didn't have it and he couldn't get it. He defaulted on the contract and the cost was everything he put into the pot, and everything he promised to put into the pot. Everything.

Marin County was a community of the rich, just north of San Francisco. It was a kind of oasis of elitist wealth that put to shame just about everyone else in the Bay Area. I never had a fondness for the place. Greed is a grotesque human impulse, and it is something we as a species will have to overcome if we ever intend to evolve beyond our current state.

"The house is in my name," said my mother. "We have that and my own bank account. It's adequate to live on and we're both eligible for Social Security."

"Is he going to live with you?" I asked. I knew all about alcoholics and money. How long could she be expected to get by taking care of a drunk who was used to high living?

"He has nowhere else to go," said my mother.

I felt sick to my stomach.

"Mom ..." I said.

She was still regal-like. "No, Ward, I know your objections. Can you give me a serious alternative, because if you can't, we are not going to discuss this."

"What can I do to help?" I asked.

"What can *we* do?" corrected Marge. I reached across the table and gripped her right hand. *Thanks,* I mouthed silently. She nodded.

I dreaded the thought of it but I had to ask. "Can I help put him to bed?"

My mother smiled at me. "Thank you for that, Ward. It won't be necessary. I can take off his shoes and put a blanket over him and a pillow under his head. Don't you remember?"

"I remember, Mom."

She rose from the chair and I took the opportunity to hug her. "You're a very classy lady, Mom."

"And you have grown up," she said.

She went into the kitchen and returned with a large paper bag into which she put all the pastries.

"For breakfast and for Nathan," she said.

"Thanks, Mom."

We said goodbye and left the house with my mother hovering over my father like an angel of mercy. Why not? That's what she was.

"I like your mother," said Marge. "A whole lot."

"Me too." I wasn't crying, but I was close to tears.

I brought my mind into focus. Think of those fat cat swindlers. Over there in Marin County. Across the bridge.

—⊗—

TWENTY-SIX

NATHANAEL:
Great-Aunt Chloe

"ARE YOU GOING TO GO OUT and see Aunt Chloe?"

Convening the morning at the kitchen table, the coffee maker's noises, the radio softly playing classical or jazz or '50s pop—these were new familiarities. Mom was comfortable with me back in the house; I too slid into the routines. It would be easy to stay here. The thought chimed suddenly and gently from a corner of my mind. Just stay.

"I told her I would," I said.

"Then you ought to."

I told Mom what Great-Aunt Chloe said when she'd phoned the other day. That conversation had taken place on the other bank of the great river that had since surged through my life, dividing it, as nothing before it had, into two parts. I'd talked to Chloe before Janeane told me about the baby.

"I will," I assured Mom. "I'll see her." But it all seemed incredibly frivolous.

Janeane and I had always been strongly attracted to one another physically, and so we were still having sex right up to the split. Now she was three months or so pregnant. It must have been one of the very last times, before she packed off to Suzette's place. We used birth control from the get-go, without fail. Instead, *it* failed us, evidently.

She waited quite some while before telling me about the baby. Probably she used that time to decide whether or not she would keep it. Now the decision was made. I wondered how much of a say Suzette had in the decision-making process.

"Well, I'd better be off," I said.

"You work on a Sunday?" There was just a whisper of churchy disapproval in her tone.

I had the last bite of a lemon-flavored scone and stood. "No rest for the wicked book reviewer."

Mom was on the verge of asking something further, I saw. I realized right then that she didn't entirely believe my shuck about being in the city on business. Her expression shifted, though, and she told me to come back for lunch if I wanted. Why on earth had I thought I could totally dupe her? She read my short stories as a teenager. She knew the tone of my lies.

I smiled back at her and left.

I drove past Twin Peaks again, following the same route that eventually taken me to the Mission district yesterday.

When Janeane first told me about her bisexuality, *Penthouse Letters*-type fantasies inevitably crossed my mind. She was militantly unapologetic about her carnal inclinations, so I learned about them after only the second or third time we'd slept together. She preferred her male lovers to be bi also and was, rather candidly, disappointed that I didn't share her indiscrimination regarding genders.

When she said she wanted to introduce me to Suzette Lasome, her ex-girlfriend of many years and still her occasional lover, I entertained an overheated thought or two of polyamory. I could've saved it. Janeane had a very fine figure and a range of recognizably female attributes. Suzette was of that squat, deliberately unfeminine mold, virtually the "dyke" stereotype. Which would have been fine if she was pleasant or even remotely civil. Instead, I was treated to an hour's worth of her glares and much possessive pawing of Janeane as we sat around drinks in Greenwich Village.

Later, I asked Janeane why the hell she'd wanted us to meet.

"Suzette's a big part of my past and a smaller part of my present," she said, "and if the two of us are going to be together, you need to understand that you can't satisfy *every* part of my life."

I stopped sleeping with Lucy, the *Diamond* junior ad exec with whom I'd had my affair, immediately after Janeane vacated our apartment. I'm quite sure now I'd only been seeing Lucy to cash in on the verbal infidelity clause in my marriage contract. Janeane and I married in order to pledge ourselves to each other ... only we saw no need to go through with any of the contemptuous conventions of normal marriages. "Forsaking all others"? Screw that. We were above that. Janeane could go on seeing Suzette and whoever else now and then, to gratify her particular itch; I too was free to romp about at will. We would keep nothing from each other. We didn't truck in jealousy. Our love—which was love's next, intellectually valid, forward evolutionary leap—would sustain us.

And it hadn't lasted a year, that marriage. It's very, very possible Janeane and I loved each other, once. But I doubt if we ever liked one another.

I pulled to the curb at a pleasant little park with a firehouse at one end. Toddlers and parents were milling around the playground equipment. A young couple went by, laughing, teasing each other, making a minor spectacle and not caring.

I didn't want to seem like a creep, staring at them from the car, so I busied myself with my phone.

From here I could either drive down into Noe Valley or go the other way down to Glen Park.

An answering machine picked up, but it was an older man's voice telling me what number I'd reached. I hadn't misdialed.

What the hell.

"Hello. This message is for Mr. George Starks. My name is Nathanael Pentecost, and I work for *Diamond* magazine out of New York. It's important I talk to you."

I recited my number and clicked off. If the Dorothy Shields in the phone directory wasn't the same one in the dedications to the George Starks novels, no harm would come. She would think I was selling subscriptions.

I wanted my marriage to be the antithesis of Father's marriage. I wanted an assertive wife, one who would disagree vehemently with me occasionally, who had her own spirit, who would challenge me, intellectually and emotionally.

My marriage had been nothing like Father's. Technically it was still operative ... although it would soon surely become strictly a support system for Janeane's and my child, an arrangement of custody and visits and finances ...

I started up the car. I made sure no kids were playing nearby, then pulled out.

I got lost in Glen Park, which is another of the city's valleys, this one very residential and quiet. The streets wind, and I ended up on a number of dead ends, even though I had the address written down.

I was considering just giving up. This was a minor obligation, after all, and I had enough serious pressures on me to justify blowing it off.

When I glanced up again from the paper with the address, I was startled to discover I was finally on the right little unpaved street. I was further surprised that I was idling past the very house. I braked.

A woman in jeans and a purple and blue striped blouse stood on the short pathway into a country-style house. A warm mild breeze was blowing across the valley, stirring the branches that spread over the home and rippling the sunlight across her. She gave me a casual wave.

She hadn't come out at the sound of my motor; she'd just been standing there.

I parked behind a several decades old, tan-colored Mercedes, and stepped out.

She smiled and came toward me. The face on which that smile was spread was weathered, in the best sense of the word. It was a face that felt foreign climates and come away stronger. It showed no signs of abuse or resignation or even especially the frailties of age.

Her eyes were fantastic.

"Well," she said, "sizing each other up is all well and good, but a kiss from my grand-nephew is what I'm after."

I recalled that mild awkwardness I'd experienced with Mom at the door of the house on Santiago when I'd first arrived—that hug that hadn't quite come off. Chloe, however, entangled me neatly in her arms, embraced me strongly, maneuvering me into a stance where my arms had to go around her as well. I kissed her cheek; she kissed mine. It was as smooth as a waltz.

She was a few inches shorter than me and easily as lean. Her hair, which was spilled around her shoulders, was white, not gray, and it showed no signs of brittleness.

"Come on in. Watch out for the kitty there."

A fluffy white cat was suddenly underfoot on the path of yellow stones that led to the open front door. I'd been adding numbers in my head, not looking where I was stepping. We went into the house.

The smell of herbs added to the rural feel of the place. There were no sounds of passing traffic. I was looking at everything as we moved through the house. The furniture was old; but it was old because it lasted, in good repair, from the time of its manufacture and was still usable.

"I've got a pot of tea all set. Want a cup?"

"Sure."

I was still ogling when I sat down at the big kitchen table.

"What do you think of the place?" she asked. Her voice was easy, almost melodic. She poured dark steaming tea into the handle-less cup in front of me.

"It's ... familiar." Gooseflesh had risen on me, I realized. It wasn't an unpleasant sensation.

Chloe sat opposite me. Her movements were as easy as her tone. She was still smiling. "Well, you've been here before."

"As a child, though. Right?"

"A boy. Yes."

"And I remember ...?"

She shrugged. "We remember everything. At least, it's all recorded in the brain. Some things we choose to remember and preserve them carefully. Other stuff just hangs around. Or is stuff we *can't* forget."

Her statement had none of the long-winded pomposity with which the Purple Witch spoke. Chloe's was just a chatty observation—astute, not pontifical.

I was still doing numbers in my head, rechecking figures I couldn't believe.

"It's a very nice place," I said.

"Thank you. I don't mind leaving it, but it's always good to come back to it."

"Do you go away a lot?" I sipped at the tea; it was rank with herbal flavors—startling at first, then very tasty.

"All in all, I'm gone about six months out of the year."

My eyebrows went up. "Still?"

"Still." She was amused.

I still couldn't quite get myself to believe. Great-Aunt Chloe was in her mid-seventies. She looked for all the world like she might be thinking of celebrating her sixtieth birthday in a year or two; and it would be a healthy vital sixty at that.

"You look great," I said, without hint of condescension.

"Thank you again."

Irene I. Isis was in her sixties. She was overweight, she had respiratory troubles, her liver was probably going to burst like a cherry bomb, and it was a neck-and-neck race to see which would get her first—stroke or heart attack. Also she looked every one of her maltreated years and then some.

Chloe was the polar opposite. And Jesus Christ, those eyes ...

"You're quite the handsome young man."

That actually got me to blush and avert my gaze. There were framed photographs hung on one wall of the kitchen, opposite a rack of jars and fragrant little sacks. The pictures were good, possibly sensational. Light and shadow looked to have been brushed in by a Renaissance master. I recognized Jimmy Carter in the elder years after his presidency, Jack Nicholson in a greasy T-shirt and—it took me a second—a young Annie Lennox sitting beside a somber German shepherd.

"These are yours?" I asked.

"Some of my showoff pieces. I started hanging them a couple years ago."

"Wow. I'd like to see the stuff your proud of."

"I didn't say I wasn't proud of these. I am. But these don't really represent my work."

I took another sip of tea, by now quite hooked on the stuff. "I should've called. I'm sorry for just showing up ..."

"This is for you."

I looked down at the envelope she slid across the broad table. I frowned. I frowned harder when she told me what was inside and for what amount the check had been written.

"Aunt Chloe ..." I was deeply confused.

Her eyes drilled into me. "Nathanael"—and once more I heard that very particular pronunciation that included my name's new spelling—"it's not whimsical. If I'm to have a *great* grand-nephew, I want him to have the decent things this world has to offer. I even want him to have some of its comforts."

I just stared back. I was walloped.

Her eyes were bewitching. Bright blue and penetrating. I thought I was remembering them from childhood. Maybe I was. But I realized now they were also reminding me of another similar set of eyes, which belonged to a film actress. Her name escaped me at the moment, but she'd been in that silly fantasy movie about the hawk and the wolf, the one Father liked so much.

TWENTY-SEVEN

WARD: Old Money

I'D TAKEN OFF THE LAST WEEK, SINCE FATHER HAD CALLED ME. It was all true and there was nothing to be done about it. Father was sheared and fleeced within all the applicable laws and statutes. I didn't know that, but the lawyers on the city payroll I checked with put in enough time to look at me, shake their heads, and say, "I'm sorry, Ward, your father has been screwed."

Marge had also been busy. "The man's name is Rudolph Pring, and he appears to head the consortium," she told me as we shared a late Chinese meal out of paper containers. As soon as Nate began school last year, she had gone back to work at her old job at the insurance office. The hours had been reduced, which was perfect for picking Nate up after school. She seized a whole prawn with her chopsticks. "He's *old* money in dear old Marin County, old *important* money."

I filed that away in my mind. I would not forget it.

"He's been involved in a lot of land transfers, and they've all been legal," she continued. "Not even a single suit against him."

"Which means he's completely honest, or very clever," I said.

She lifted a mass of green stuff with her chopsticks and popped it into her mouth. "Clever," she said. "Your father should have been informed of the risks."

"That's it, then," I said, knowing full well it wasn't.

"I'm sorry, Ward." Marge finished the prawns and vegetables. She pushed the containers aside. "I'm sorry for your father and mother."

"They'll make it," I said.

We cleared the cartons from the kitchen table and I went down the hall to look for Nate while Marge washed out the tea cups. He was sitting on the floor in his room, first grade school books spread out before him.

"This is dumb stuff," he said.

He had to be reading on a fourth grade level on his own by now. No wonder the school books were *dumb stuff.*

"It's not dumb stuff to those who need it, Nate," I said. "Not everybody has your brains. Do you understand what I mean?"

"Don't be a snob?"

"Exactly. Sooner or later it will even out and you won't be so uncomfortable."

"I'm not a little kid," he said seriously.

"True," I said, "but you are a kid and you are little."

He laughed and started writing in his brand new notebook. As I started to leave he looked up. "Daddy?"

"What Nate?"

"Someday, do you think I'll be able to write stories?"

"I hope so, Son."

"But not the make-believe kind," he added. "I don't like that."

"Okay, Son."

He didn't cotton to fiction. He didn't like it. Even the

stories in his old beloved picture books had become suspect to him recently. His mind was rooted in logical thinking; great stuff for an article writer, a biographer, or an historian. I was getting too far ahead of him. He's a kid, I thought. *A little kid.*

"How's our little genius?" asked Marge as I joined her in the living room. She tossed the *TV Guide* aside and was hunting through our collection of VHS tapes. "Honestly, Ward, haven't we got anything to watch that doesn't start with an earthquake, a flood, or a worldwide epidemic?"

"I find them restful."

"Very funny."

"Try the second shelf."

She rose from the cabinet holding a copy of *Love Letters*, starring Joseph Cotton and Jennifer Jones, one of my favorite films.

The phone rang at two o'clock in the morning. At first I thought it was the alarm clock. I felt for it in the darkness, and only succeeded in wiping out the settings. The ringing persisted until Marge reached across my body for the phone.

"Hello."

There was an ominous silence.

I clicked on the table lamp. Marge's face had gone chalk white.

"Yes, Ward Pentecost lives here." She handed me the phone as if were a deadly snake.

A minute later I was an orphan.

After a long conversation, I hung up the phone and sat there in silence for over five minutes until Marge spoke. "For God's sakes, Ward, talk to me."

I shook myself into something like wakefulness, while all I wanted to do was go back to sleep and wait for this nightmare to end. It felt like every atom of my being had been smashed. I was more unconscious than I had ever been while drinking.

"Mom and Dad were killed in an automobile accident earlier tonight. I have to go to the hospital and officially identify them."

"What hospital, Ward?"

The words came out just above a whisper, a cold, furious whisper. "Marin County General," I said.

Then I began to dress.

⁂

The rest of that long night I remember in bits and pieces. I recall we awakened Bill and Eileen and begged them to take Nate for the night. I recall driving across the bridge, the *thrumming* of the tires as we crossed the expansion joints at each tower, and the feeling of isolation as we rolled along the nighttime roads.

The white lights of the hospital.

The solicitous doctors.

The concerned clerk, who was more concerned with insurance than anything else.

Finally, in one of the waiting rooms, we met him.

The other driver was teenaged, bloody, and had that vacant, slack-jawed expression that goes with the chronic drinker and user.

"It was an accident," said the uniformed officer. He tried to look very officious but did a poor job of it. "Mr. Pentecost cut off Mr. Pring at the intersection ..."

Pring? Old Money. Important money.

I remember calling him a liar and then being subdued as I lunged for the driver. Later, they sent me home with a sore shoulder. Marge also got into it and managed to scratch the cop before being pulled off him.

She drove the car on the way home. I neither saw nor heard anything on the way back.

❧

Sometime after ten o'clock in the morning I rubbed the sleep from my eyes. I didn't get up right away, preferring to let my mind assimilate last night's events at a tolerable pace. My left shoulder ached terribly, probably as a result of the restraint hold that husky orderly clamped on me.

"Marge," I called.

She came hurrying into the bedroom. "You should rest some more," she said. "They sedated you pretty heavily last night." She came over to the bed and opened my pajama top. "That's a bad bruise," she said.

I looked down. "Tell me," I said, "did I get him?"

"Which one, the cop or young Pring?"

"Either."

"Neither."

In spite of the gravity of the moment we both laughed, a kind of gallows humor, an escape valve.

"The young Pring is named Alec, and yes, he's Rudolph Pring's son," said Marge. "There will be an official investigation of the accident."

"I doubt it will change anything," I said. *You can't change it. Your father's been screwed. Old money.* I refused to believe it. There would be justice. There would be an accounting. I was certain of it.

"We'll have to go out to the house," I said. "Mom probably left papers that we'll need. She was that way."

I blinked away the tears and got to my feet.

Marge made arrangements for Bill to drop Nate off at school. She picked him up after school every day. Today wouldn't be different.

While I showered and got dressed, Marge prepared a late breakfast for me. She had coffee while I had my oatmeal and orange juice. I used to have much bigger breakfasts, before I learned how to eat at Aunt Chloe's. This morning I ate slowly, not savoring every spoonful of the porridge, but simply using it as a delaying tactic, to put off what promised to be more heartbreak.

We had to come back before we had gone ten blocks because I forgot my keys. Mother insisted that I keep my keys when I moved out of the house. "You can never tell when you'll need them," she said. Now I was face to face with the worst never of all.

I don't know what I expected when I opened the front door, but no apparition greeted us. It was just an empty house. Correction. *A neat, empty house.* Never let it be said, even now—especially now—that Mom was anything less than a world-class housekeeper. The very normalcy of it affected me more than I anticipated. I'd tried to steel myself against the unexpected, perhaps the bizarre. Instead I was greeted by an empty house, just the way I remembered it, but without the lady who was its soul.

I stood there in the doorway with my shoulders slumped and tears running down my cheeks. The sense of loss was paralyzing.

Marge waited until the tears slowed down and I was able to take one hesitant step into the house. She slipped an arm around my waist and steered me into the dining room. "Sit down," she said. "I'll get you a glass of water."

From the kitchen I could hear the sound of a glass being filled from the tap. So normal.

I accepted the glass of water greedily and drank it in two swallows. "Thanks, honey."

She pulled another chair out from the table and sat down. "Ward, I'm going to look for the papers." She patted my wrist. "I know what I'm doing. You just sit here. Is that all right with you?"

"Yes."

"Would you like some coffee before I start?" she asked.

"Hot and black," I said.

"I'll be right back."

She vanished into the kitchen and returned in a few minutes with a steaming cup of coffee and a small plate containing one orange scone. Mother must have really liked them.

I sat there, sipping at the coffee and nibbling at the scone while Marge went off to search for whatever papers Mother kept.

Before I finished, Marge came back holding a thick manila folder. "It's all here," she said, "including a letter for you."

I took the letter and began to read.

Mother left it all to me—*my darling son, Ward*—the house, her little car, a Toyota, and her bank account. Everything was free and clear of any encumbrances. In case of legal questions, I was to contact her attorney. An embossed business card was enclosed.

I handed the letter to Marge.

"We better call the attorney soon," she said, "just in case *they* try to get their hands on anything else."

"Good idea," I said.

Marge picked up my empty cup and plate and took them into the kitchen. "I'll wash these and put them away," she called.

Just like Mom.

After we checked all the doors and windows in the house and brought in the mail we were ready to leave.

"I better drive, Ward."

I sunk back in the seat. The safety belt was the only thing holding me upright. It was not like me to become this emotional over anything. Where was the wiseacre young man who dreamed of a beautiful Oriental woman at the time of his son's birth and resented being awakened? Mom was right. He had grown up.

It was too early to pick up Nate, so we went directly home. I was glad, because I did not want him to see me all done in like this. I understood that grief is a part of life and that the young need to witness it as a necessary part of their experience, but I looked so awful and acted so dispirited that I felt it would affect our relationship. I simply did not want my son to carry those pictures in his head.

Later in the afternoon Marge brought him home and carefully explained what happened. He cried a little because he liked Grandmom Pentecost.

Then, while I sat at the kitchen table, staring into an empty cup, Marge set about making the necessary arrangements.

In the hectic days that followed, amidst the confusion and the strained nerves, Phyllis Morton came over to help and was a source of strength to all of us.

———❈———

TWENTY-EIGHT

NATHANAEL:
Time Runs Short

THE STUDY WAS ALMOST AS DENSE WITH PRINTED MATTER as that Valencia Street book shop where I'd picked up the August Purity novels. Here, things were tidier, though. There were three walls of those floor to ceiling bookcases you always see referenced in literature but so rarely find in real life. I didn't focus on the spines on those shelves, but the atmosphere alone was familiar and soothing. I'd been around books all my life; they were a separate sort of home to me.

There were comfortable reading chairs in here, but neither of us sat.

I looked at the fourth wall. It was absolutely bare, except for a single framed photo.

"How the hell did you get this shot?" My lips were wood. I couldn't even feel my tongue.

But I must have made myself understood. "I didn't," Aunt Chloe said softly behind me. "That's a movie still."

I could see her head of white hair reflected in the glass, atop the profoundly disquieting black and white image of the Golden Gate Bridge lying empty of traffic. The shot was taken on the span itself, and those six lanes were so stark, so peaceful, so sad, that I was almost as wrenched as when I'd visited the Bridge site a week ago.

I was also, as before, using this melodramatic impression to distract me from my genuine feelings.

I realized the movie was *On the Beach* before I even noticed the caption at the bottom. I recalled it now from the mass of old VHS videotapes that Father collected. Like his library, a lot of his movies concerned the end of the world. In *On the Beach* nuclear war was the culprit. One of Father's favorite scenarios. In the film a submarine—captained by Gregory Peck?—visits a depopulated but eerily preserved San Francisco. I, naturally, preferred the novel by Nevil Shute.

"Why would you hang this?"

"It's a reminder," she said. "Of consequences."

From the Purple Witch, this statement would have rung grandly with impenetrable pretentiousness. While I didn't understand it any better from Chloe—and didn't for the moment try to—I knew her words were sincere.

I turned to face her. From the kitchen, I'd brought along the envelope containing the check she'd written.

"My wife, a few days after we agreed to get married, and after I told her my father had been on the Bridge that day, asked me why the Bridge hadn't been rebuilt. I was dumbfounded—literally. I just stared. The Bridge *disappeared*. What if a replacement was put up and that one went too? But that wasn't it. It was the ... the sacrilege of what she'd suggested. The Bridge was gone, with all those people, so inexplicably. That empty space is a graveyard now. She didn't have any thought that she'd said something inappropriate."

My mouth was working better now. I could feel my nerve endings again.

I said, "There's no way in hell you could know my wife is pregnant with my child. With my *son*."

She didn't flinch. "According to what you believe ... no. No way."

"What I believe. What does that mean? *What does that mean?*" It barked out of me, along with a wild surge of anger. It was one of the emotions I was least competent to handle. I am much better with anger's more sluggish counterparts—sullenness, bitterness.

I scared myself in that moment. I didn't appear to have also scared Aunt Chloe.

"Sit down. Sit."

I blinked and found myself in one of the deep plush reading chairs. It was like a cradle. My blood stopped hammering in my carotid.

Chloe sat in the facing chair. "Time might be running short."

"How do you know about the baby?" But I asked it calmly now.

"That's not the most important issue."

"Maybe not." There was an old oak stand between us. I set the envelope atop it. "But I want to know."

A sigh lifted her shoulders. "Okay." She gave me the full effect of her eyes—which was potent—and said, almost apologetically, "I keep in touch with you. Like I do with your mother and her sisters, Sarah and Ruth, and their kids. Like I used to with your father."

"Keep in touch? You mean ... keep tabs on."

She shook her head. "Nobody's been spying on you."

As she said this, I realized that very same paranoid thought had just been unspooling in my head.

"I mean," Chloe said, "that having a feel for what is happening in one's own family is nothing extraordinary. And nothing to be frightened about."

But I *was* afraid, suddenly and violently. I felt strangled, fragile, threatened, and all the other things you're supposed to feel when a panic attack hits.

But I was also still looking into those fantastically clear blue eyes.

Once more my pulse slowed. "So," I said, "it's not important how you know. You just *know*." I even managed to sound a bit droll, which made me proud.

Her smile was comforting. "That's right. Tell me about being a book reviewer. What's it like?"

"Isn't this an even less important issue?"

She shrugged again. "Maybe."

So I told her, describing it in much the same way I first had to Mom. Chloe listened. Eventually her white-haired head tilted quizzically on a wattle-free neck. "Didn't you want to be a writer?" she asked.

"I did."

"Do you still?"

I nodded solemnly.

"Are you doing anything about it?" Her tone was interested, concerned.

I still hadn't gotten up the steam to broach the subject with Mom, but somehow the notion of confiding in Great-Aunt Chloe was uncomplicated.

"I'm under contract with a publishing house to co-write a novel with a woman named Irene Isis. She's a professional writer ..."

"*Everybody Goes Away*—her?"

I smiled, a little thinly. "*Every*one. She bites heads off when people make that mistake."

"What else does she do?" Again I heard melodic rhythms in her voice, lulling.

"She has all the toilet seats in her home in Rhode Island

bolted down, so that her male guests have to pull down their pants and squat if they want to take a piss."

Chloe mulled that over. "I suppose that's easier than emasculating every man that comes by for a visit."

"Yet somehow, *that* wouldn't be as humiliating."

"How do you handle it?"

"I do it standing up and mop up with toilet paper."

She nodded firmly. "Good."

And I told her more things. There was plenty of stuff I hadn't told Janeane—partly because it was too mortifying, partly because I'd had no guarantees of sympathy from her.

The story of the Purple Witch was a long one, but it was only so because I was unloading so thoroughly, in such gruesome detail. Irene I. Isis was a pathetic spoof of a stale caricature. She was simple. She was *boring*. She knew full well how ridiculous and inept she was, and she fought every desperate second of her existence to keep the covering scenery and histrionics in motion, lest someone figure out there was nobody on the stage but a frightened, mean-spirited, under-talented little girl.

I was blinking rapidly. "Jesus ..." I looked levelly across at Aunt Chloe, who just summarized every private and subconscious estimate I'd ever made of the Witch. She *nailed* the purple-wearing bitch.

A very grateful smile took hold of my face.

"Thanks."

She nodded.

When my smile faded, it was only because I realized it was time to get down to business ... whatever exactly that might be. I straightened in the chair.

"You said time was running short," I said.

She nodded. "It might be."

"Might."

"I'm not an oracle. I don't know all, tell all. Guesswork and intuition—they're as useful to me as to anybody."

"I don't much care for intuition," I heard myself muttering. It felt like a reflex.

"Yes. I gather." She edged forward on her chair. "But your writing—that's an intangible, basically intuitive practice."

"That's different."

"Your father told me that as a child—and you were very bright, very young—you were already interested in writing, when other kids were still shaky on the alphabet. But you didn't like fiction. Didn't like *stories*."

"Made-up stuff," I whispered.

"How did that change?"

I was very still. It was what I did, my personal defensive measure.

"Nathanael?"

Mom would have seen my discomfort and glided on to some other matter. Chloe, absolutely no doubt about it, sensed my uneasiness too. But she held me on the spot.

"I ..." I looked at the tips of my shoes, at the shelved books, but I kept coming back to her eyes. "I wanted ..."

My picture books—the same ones I'd found in the boxes I put in the basement—were the last "make-believe" stories I read after I started grade school. I liked my schoolbooks much better, even though I was well ahead of the curve. I liked turning the information I readily absorbed from them into correct answers in the classroom and on tests. I had known I was smart.

Stories were just dumb, because they couldn't be *proven*. They couldn't be logically evaluated and codified. I didn't yet know what a book critic was.

My bent changed when I was eight. Hell, what hadn't changed when I was eight?

"I wanted to write better stories than my father." I said it in one very fast breath and softer than I guessed the human ear could hear.

But of course Chloe heard. "And did you?"

Good question. I thought of the yellowing short stories in their Manila envelopes in those boxes. I thought of Dirk Krieger with the moldering skeleton of a tollbooth collector for company as he guarded the Golden Gate Bridge. I thought of Father's other stories, the dozen or so I'd set aside, the ones that nearly overcame their own awkward plotting and amateur pacing.

Then I thought of my work. The dark, experimental, ultimately artificial short stories of my teen years, when I'd meant to do nothing less than recreate the art of literature. They were followed by seven unfinished novels. Eight, if I now counted the one with the Purple Witch. And even so I felt that, on some level, somehow, my work wasn't entirely worthless.

"I'd say we came out just about even," I said, still whispering. I looked at my hands, at the fingertips pressed together in my lap. Then I found my way back to those eyes.

"You're a lot like Ward," she said.

Since coming into this book-lined room, I felt anger and fear, both intensely. Now, quite abruptly, I felt nothing at all.

Great-Aunt Chloe was shaking her head at me, her impossibly unaged face gone quietly sad.

"That's a trait you Pentecost men all share, in addition to your good looks. I met Drake, your father's father, a few times. He had it. So did Ward. So do you."

Feeling *nothing*.

"You never matured into your emotions," she said. "You grew up ... but just for show."

I looked away. Then I jerked up onto my feet. "It's been lovely seeing you, Aunt Chloe ..."

"*Wait ...*"

But without the eye contact I was freer to move, and I did, crossing the study toward the door. Chloe, though, was suddenly in my path. She seized my wrist—really *seized* it, her grip strong—and yanked my hand forward. She slapped the envelope I'd left on the oak stand onto my palm.

"Take this."

"I don't ..."

"Goddamnit, Nate, I said *take this.*" The melody was gone from her voice. Now it was thick with frustration, disappointment.

I closed my fingers around the envelope and the money for my son. Feeling nothing.

"We have a lot more to talk about," she said urgently. "I meant it about time getting short."

"And I meant it about it being lovely to see you." I pulled back my hand, and I walked past her with heavy, even strides. A cat, this one orange with nicks in its ears, watched me as I passed through one of the outer rooms, heading for the front door. Chloe's footsteps were behind me.

"It's almost certainly the Majik of Sevens," she was saying. "Damnit, you've got to listen ..."

But the truth was something else. I didn't have to listen. I didn't have to listen to any of it.

I got into my anonymous rental car and made my escape.

TWENTY-NINE.

WARD: The Last Table

THE NIGHTMARE WASN'T OVER. It never would be for me, but it had receded to the darker places of my mind, where I carefully stored all those things that I someday would take action on, if the opportunity ever presented itself.

My parents had been laid to rest, and during the long afternoons and evenings of wakes, I think I understood that sometimes, euphemisms are the kindest words you can use.

My mother left many friends in the neighborhood; most of them came to say a last goodbye. They were not just elderly people. There was a sprinkling of all ages. The kindness of Alice Pentecost had not been squandered on any particular age or group. I was comforted by these people who were repaying kindness for kindness, and often found myself unable to do anything but sob in return.

The real surprise was the turnout for the final tribute to my father. The dignitaries from City Hall and local government were in attendance, but they were joined by others, those who benefited from "the people's realtor." There were people from all over northern California, not just San Francisco, but as far south as Santa Cruz and as far north as Redding, with one family taking the train from Reno, Nevada. Marin County was not represented. My father helped so many working people. Drake Pentecost, I hardly knew you.

My friends from AA also came to pay their respects. They were quiet, courteous, and often dressed in the clothes they'd worn to work. They shook hands with the family and introduced themselves most often by their first names. The sign-in books bore not only the names of dignitaries and families, but a sizeable number of names like Danny D., Edna, Phil, Martin, Jimmy G. and Fred. Sometime during the past two years, with surprisingly little fanfare, I realized I wasn't just a sober drunk, but an alcoholic. At the meetings I went to, I was even able to finally say those magic words: "My name is Ward, and I'm an alcoholic." The words were easy. I admitted who I was, and like most miraculous revelations this one was almost mundane. I found that oddly comforting.

My parents' deaths were a difficult time made bearable by the support of friends. I forgot to think of myself for hours on end.

At last the burials had taken place, the ritual feast had been held, and well-meaning friends and neighbors finally stopped bringing casseroles to the house. After all, Marge was an excellent cook and so was I within my limited repertoire.

The funeral costs had been defrayed entirely by two small policies my mother had taken out years before in preparation for this occasion.

That left my mother's money and the house. Everything my father owned was gone to cover his debts to the consortium, including his million dollar life insurance policy, meant to provide handsomely for his wife and family. They would have taken his car too, if it hadn't been totaled in the wreck.

What had father been doing in Marin County that night? Was it a last ditch attempt to beard the lion in his den, or country club? If anyone knew they were not telling.

A week after the burials, a Mr. Joe Pucci came to see me at my office. He was middle-aged, obviously Italian, with a wonderful head of jet black hair. There was a hardness in his face that belied his soft manner. "Mr. Pentecost," he said, "your father helped me and my family greatly. I would like to express my gratitude."

I shook his hand. "Your being here is gratitude enough," I said. "I saw you at the funeral. *I* am grateful." I pumped his hand again.

"You do not understand," he said. "My family would like to do something. I am Sicilian." The hardness in his face was more prominent now. "This Rudolph Pring is a bad man. Something could happen to him."

When you come face to face with the real thing it isn't at all like the movies. I was looking at death—calm, polite, death. It was chilling.

I didn't want anybody else to execute my justice, although I had no idea of what that justice might be, or when it would occur.

I shook his hand one more time. "I appreciate your offer, Mr. Pucci, but it will be taken care of differently."

"Very well." He moved toward the door. "Your father was a good man," he said.

The door closed behind him.

I told him what I would not tell myself. *It will be taken care of differently.* I shrugged off similar thoughts that threatened to overwhelm my consciousness and went back to work.

For the next several days Marge and I considered what to do with the largesse from my mother. Although Marge hated the idea of moving from the sun of Noe Valley back to the gray of the Sunset district where we'd both grown up, in the end she agreed with me, and we made the decision to move into the large house on Santiago Street.

Nate was noncommittal about the move. He made no lifelong friends during his school years, preferring his schoolbooks to any chums. He had my trait of being comfortable with himself, but didn't share my taste in writing or in movies. He was becoming his own person, and I should be happy about that.

Harry Morton offered to drive the U-Haul truck for the move. I estimated that it would take three trips to empty out our large flat and transfer everything to Santiago. I didn't count on Harry's expertise as a warehouseman. He fitted things into that truck that I knew wouldn't fit. He wasted no space, no matter how small, and as a result we finished the moving in two trips and hours less than we planned. "There are tricks to every trade," he said, brushing aside my compliments about the ease of the job.

Phyllis and Marge made a hearty platter of sandwiches just in time for Bill Berry's arrival. The rest of the day was spent in bringing items from the truck, moving other items, and, of course, arranging and rearranging furniture.

At long last, on the other side of several scraped knuckles, bruises, and unexamined injuries to our legs, we were finished for the day. The rest of the work would take place in the near future with Marge telling me just what went where—again.

Then, since we moved everything except the Great Pyramid, Marge ordered three large pizzas. Next to my spaghetti and meatballs, pizza was Nate's favorite food, and his stomach learned to accept an amazing amount of it without protest. It was a good ending to a busy day and we all devoured our shares.

Mercifully, the ladies disposed of my mother's belongings while I was at work. Of my father's things, I found several leather coats and jackets to my liking. There was a whole bureau drawer full of testimonial plaques, which I decided to keep, after moving them to a back closet. We arranged, discarded, and rearranged. We settled comfortably into the larger quarters, and I felt very much at home in the house that had already once been my home.

Nate was still establishing a routine with the new school. It was easier for Marge to pick him up after work on this side of town, and day by day he regained his former scholastic reassurance.

We celebrated his eighth birthday in the house on Santiago. Those years had been pleasant and mild.

The next day I mentioned my persistent concern over his lack of imagination to Marge. Nate's sharp mind was, if anything, more logically attuned than ever. His grades were exceptional.

"He has an imagination," she said. "It just isn't your kind."

"What kind is that?"

"No need to get upset," she said. "There's nothing wrong with it. You have a sense of make-believe. Nate doesn't."

She put her finger right on it. How in the world could he ever write if he didn't have a sense of make-believe? If only there was some way to lead him into an appreciation of that other world, the one that children are supposed to inhabit, the one that, for us, had become reversed.

After school he greeted me as I came home. "Daddy, can we start learning to write?"

I hugged him. "What do you want to write first, a dictionary or volume one of the encyclopedia?"

"Very funny."

We never talked down to him and occasionally we had

cause to regret it. I went into the dining room and indicated that he should follow me. Wide-eyed, brimming with eagerness, he scrambled onto one of the chairs and placed his writing materials on the table before him. He had two brand new pencils, a pristine notebook and an eraser. He was ready for big time composition. I hoped I wouldn't let him down.

"First," I said, "you have to have a sympathetic character, somebody the reader will like."

"Do I have to make him up?"

"Yes."

"I don't want to do that," he said.

"Well, then maybe we better talk about article writing," I said, hastily regrouping my thoughts. "Do you know what an article is?"

"It's when the writing tells you about somebody or something. Like the newspapers."

"Very good. Do you like that kind of writing?"

"Sometimes I don't understand it, but I like it fine."

I wondered if he had a secret subscription to *The Scientific American*.

"If you read enough articles you'll find out that they have their own rules, just like fiction writing. You need to tell the reader what you are going to say, when it happens, and where it happens. There are more rules but that should give you a start."

"Thanks, Dad." He opened his composition book and immediately set down a title: "Moving Day."

The ninety-seven word "article" he did was head and shoulders above my first effort at a similar age, an even shorter work which I proudly called a story, with the highly original title of "A Narrow Escape." Nate's work, of course, documented our move, three years ago, to this house.

"That's very good, Nate," I said.

"Thank you, Daddy. Can we do some more tomorrow?"

"Absolutely, Son. I'm proud of you. Now, let's go and show your mother what you've done."

⌒∞⌒

The next day was Saturday. Marge and I were both off work, and Nate was up bright and early. He had his notebook, pencils, and eraser, all laid out on the dining room table, even before I finished my breakfast in the kitchen.

"You've got an eager student," said Marge, indicating the door to the dining room.

"Yes," I said. "I wish I had been that good at that age."

"I'm sure you were."

"Thanks, but I wasn't." I took my cereal bowl and spoon over to the sink. "The new Bob Woodward is waiting," I said.

"You're doing a good thing," Marge said and kissed me.

I stepped into the dining room. My prize pupil greeted me warmly. "Good morning, Daddy." He hunched eagerly over his notebook, pencil in hand.

"Good morning, Nate."

I took my seat at the end of the table and paused before beginning.

"Today I want to show you something before we start," I said.

"What, Daddy?"

I'd given it a lot of thought, not just last night, but for some time, and I was convinced that all that was needed to kindle his sense of make-believe, of *my type* of imagination, was a demonstration.

"This," I answered. I rose from my chair and took a place directly opposite him. I folded back the tablecloth so that my hands hovered over the bare mahogany of the table.

"Watch carefully," I said.

He sat there looking intense and vulnerable at the same time. Perhaps for a second or two I had misgivings.

Then I lowered my hands, the sense of power almost audible. I could feel the contact being made. My strength was certainly up to it on this bright morning.

Slowly I began to raise my hands. My forearms ached. My upper arms and shoulders ached. Fatigue was settling into my torso. My vision dimmed. I was distantly aware of Nate's mouth opened in a scream as my connection with the table faded and it crashed eighteen inches down onto the floor of the dining room, spilling his writing materials. The shock to the house rattled all the dishes in the kitchen.

Then I passed out on the floor with my son screaming, his eyes wide with hysteria, and Marge hurrying in from the kitchen.

THIRTY.

—◦—

NATHANAEL: A
Pale Semblance

WHEN I GOT BACK TO SANTIAGO STREET, I withdrew with August Purity and involved myself in a complex tragedy that only started with the forty year old drowning of a prepubescent boy. *Grey Hands* was, if anything, even better than the extraordinarily well-crafted *Pale Semblance*, the George Starks' novel I'd read yesterday.

Mom and I had each purposely tipped our hand a little, and the balance between us had shifted and resettled on a new level. I had met Bennet; she knew my marriage to Janeane was fast circling the drain of divorce. There was something very *un*-mother/son about knowing the details of our respective love lives. It wasn't uncomfortable, though. Actually it felt like the natural course for our mutually adult relationship to follow.

I might even eventually tell Mom she had a grandchild due in April. But I wasn't up to it yet, not today.

I still hadn't decided if I was going to stay in the city ... if I was going to accompany Mom to the Memorial Society's

annual ceremony at the Bridge site on Tuesday. As an immediate family member of a victim, I would hold a privileged
place. I'd never attended before. I would need to decide soon.
Time was running short.

Time was running short. So Great-Aunt Chloe said earlier
today. Why?

I pushed away all thoughts of Chloe.

Dinner with Mom was another simple affair. I didn't talk
much, but it wasn't the same harsh uncommunicativeness
of when I'd been younger. Tonight I was just preoccupied and could only toss back simple comments to her
conversational overtures.

I sat up fairly late with *Grey Hands*. Not only did the
story resolve very credibly, as with the last book, but to my
surprise and pleasure, August Purity's character took several
forward steps in development. He was not the same person
now as when the novel opened, which was remarkable for a
lead character in a series.

I went to say goodnight to Mom, then climbed into
my bed.

She was gone when I woke up. She left a note for me,
which made me remember how upset she'd gotten when
I ducked out the other morning without leaving one. The
note said she was at her church, where she and others in the
parish volunteered to do some cleaning.

Faith in God is, whatever else, not intellectually satisfying
to a child. I valued logic at perhaps much too young an age.
Mom, recognizing this, hadn't seriously foisted anything
religious on me. I appreciated it.

Many people around the world had inevitably taken the
Bridge's disappearance for a miracle. Here in San Francisco,

in the days and weeks following November 7th, places of worship of every variety were jammed. SRO. Disturbances erupted in some, and news viewers were treated to clips of police in riot gear pouring into local churches and temples.

Mom knew Bennet from her church. She had been donating her time there for several years now. Certainly, she didn't need to be working, not with the money from Father's life insurance, but total idleness wouldn't have suited her.

The telephone rang—and kept right on ringing, once more past the point where an answering machine should have picked up. (Mom evidently did fine without one. Incredible.) I was amused by the quaintness. I counted off the tenth ring and picked up the receiver in the kitchen.

"Hello?"

"H ... Who the hell is this?"

I nearly retorted by hanging up. Instead I said, "You don't get to ask that. You're the call*er*, see? I'm the call*ee*. It's incumbent on you to identify yourself—politely. After that you can make inquiries. We'll try it again. Hello?"

There was silence; then, "Uh ... this is Pete Jarman. Who the ... Who, may I ask, is there?" I was about to respond when he burst back in with, "Holy crap! Is that you, Nate?"

Pete was married to whichever of my aunts was Mom's older sister. Pete was a San Francisco cop, a blustery but decent fellow. When the Scientific Investigation Team was first hastily put together, they sent an agent around to this house. This was before they started wearing those nice powder blue jumpsuits. The agent was named Phil Moses—I remember to this day—and he wore a cheap conservative suit, and he asked Mom and me a lot of questions about Father. I pretended not to remember everything.

"It's me, Uncle Pete."

"Well—how the hell are you, kiddo?" His voice was hardy. He sounded genuinely happy to hear my voice.

Pete accompanied Phil Moses that day, and I had the impression that the SIT agent didn't want him around but that Pete applied leverage. He was a sergeant in uniform then; I believed he'd moved up to plainclothesman sometime after. When Mom, tearing up, asked for a moment to collect herself and the agent continued to press her, Pete stepped in. Mom got her moment.

"I'm fine. You're still on the force?"

"Keeping the city safe from the likes of my children," he said. It had the sound of an old joke. The youngest of his kids must be at least thirty by now. "But what about you? You're … working for a book company, right?"

"A magazine actually."

"My mistake."

It wasn't, but I didn't correct him. It would be mannerly of me if I now asked about his wife (still couldn't remember which aunt she was) and kids (couldn't pull up a single name at the moment), but I settled for, "I hope your family's well."

"Why, indeed they are, sir. Hey, is your mother around?"

"Church."

"Natch. I do believe she has stock in that corporation. Well, it's nothing important." But I had the sense, in the haste with which he said it, that it was. "Say, are you in town for a while?"

The eternal question. "A little while," I said.

"Ruth and I'd love to see you. The boys too. Oh." His tone suddenly went hush and solemn. "You're here for … for the thing at the Bridge, right? Jesus, the 7th just creeps up. Somehow I never see it coming. I'm always thinking about Halloween." I recalled then that Pete gleefully did up his family's home as a haunted house for the neighborhood kids every year. "Damn, I'm sorry, Nate. That's a damn stupid thing to say. *Halloween.*"

"It's okay, Uncle Pete," I said sincerely. "It's okay."

"Well"—he gathered himself—"maybe we can see you, y'know, afterwards. If you're still in town."

It was too much trouble to waffle about it. I would be here, or I wouldn't. "I'll let you and Aunt Ruth know."

"'Kay, Nate."

"And I'll tell Mom you phoned."

"Thanks, kiddo. Bye."

When it was my turn to be grilled by Phil Moses about Father's habits and associations, Pete sat with us in this house's front room, staying in the lines of sight of both me and the SIT agent. But I hadn't needed a break during the questioning. I didn't even come close to crying.

That meant it was Sarah, Mom's other sister, who was married to the stockbroker. Sam was his name. He did very well for himself and his family. He seemed content with that, but his wife took their prosperity as an excuse to act the blue blood. Their kids were an uneasy mix of those two attitudes.

During the year I'd spent here at the house after the Bridge went, the relatives showed up regularly. We were a united front against any exploitation of the tragedy at the center of our family, and that sense of solidarity was steadfast. It was a good feeling ... and quite like nothing I could remember experiencing before. Imagine, finding consolation and support from one's own family.

Samuel Hardy, the stockbroker, consorted with an array of local business people, and he was the one who—to my memory—first predicted the economic decline for the precincts north of the vanished Bridge.

"Sausalito, Tiburon, clear up to San Rafael, really," Sam said during a visit to the house a month after November 7th, "it's all just a big bedroom community. Those people mostly work in San Francisco. They aren't going to add hours to both legs of their commute by going all the way around east to the Bay Bridge. It's not practical. It's not even physically possible. It would make the Eastshore Freeway permanent gridlock. And the ferries—even with the new boats they're talking about commissioning—won't be able to handle the huge flow that used to cross the Golden Gate every morning. None of the work force up there able to reach their jobs in the city anymore. No commerce passing through, what with 1 and 101 being rerouted. Believe me, Marin County is going to be hurting—badly."

I could remember the speech like I'd heard it yesterday, though I hadn't thought about what Sam said in a long time and didn't know why I was doing so now. But it struck me powerfully as I was idling around the house; and, strangely, it gave me a sudden purpose.

I made myself a late breakfast, got dressed, made sure I left a thorough note for Mom and hurried out to my car. I considered at the last second phoning for a cab, but the parking gods had been kind to me since I'd hit the city. I didn't think they would abandon me now, not even at Fisherman's Wharf.

The Bay Bridge, which connects San Francisco to Oakland and the East Bay environs, is a mighty and sturdy structure ... and utterly devoid of romance. It's big, it's gray, it carries traffic.

I gave it a look as the ferry chugged out from the pier, but it just wasn't worth much more than that look, and my gaze wandered.

I experienced a veritable parking miracle, finding a space just blocks from the Wharf. But somehow it didn't surprise me. The strong impulse that was urging me on this journey also reassured me I would meet no petty difficulties.

Normally I did nothing on impulse. What was I in the grip of?

Fisherman's Wharf, hideous and touristy, receded. A lot of people were out on the ferry's deck, where I was. Cameras clicked, and 'corders whirred, most getting shots of the empty Golden Gate in the distance. Here, unlike at the old toll plaza, the mood was lighter, even festive. Children monkeyed around. Adults on weekend outings relaxed. I couldn't remember the last time I'd been on the water, and I enjoyed the swaying movement. The sun was hot, but the breeze straight off the water was nice.

There were other ferry lines that connected eastward to Oakland. This one went north, though.

Inside the boat, occupying the seats and reading newspapers, were Marin County natives—those coming home from housecleaning jobs or graveyard shifts at diners or whatever other gigs brought this lot into San Francisco on the weekend. Gloomy faces. Just the normal resentments of not having much money and having to scrape for what you did have ... and also having to share your boat ride with people who *did* have money and the leisure time to take a trip across the Bay for fun.

Once, things had been different.

We put in at a ramshackle pier in Sausalito. I blinked at the panhandlers, the litter. Minnie F. Tucker hadn't done the Bayside community justice in *Gap Through Her Heart*, which made mention of the decline in the local economy but evidently missed the scope of it ... or maybe the dive was simply growing steeper and gaining speed. Whichever, this wasn't Marin County as I remembered it. Certainly its time as a rather elitist enclave of imperious wealth was past.

I walked a few blocks inland, counting FOR SALE signs

on the homes. A trio of teenagers, gathered around a semi-dismantled car at a curb, looked up at me like—so help me—wolves protecting a fresh kill.

I went back to the water and managed eventually to flag a cab out in front of a closed-down restaurant with actual boards on the windows.

It wasn't a long ride, but the state of the road, on top of everything else, was pretty depressing. The cab rattled violently on the final climb, then swung into the parking area. I paid the fare, with tip, and asked the driver—a big, mustached man—to wait. I realized I was over-enunciating my words, like I was speaking to a foreigner. He left the meter ticking and stepped out, glaring around at the cheaper pedicabs haunting the lot. He needn't have worried; I wouldn't have trusted any of those underfed adolescents to keep control of their oversized tricycles.

In my third year of college, I went to Mexico City on the Christmas break with a girl and another couple. The other male in our quartet had family there, and that family put us up, and there was much hospitality and merrymaking. But all I could really remember now from that trip was the city's grinding poverty and implacable decay.

Vendors hawked bags of peanuts and T-shirts. They were aggressive about it. I crossed the lot, detouring around these merchants when I had to. Out on the closed-off highway were National Guardsmen. A bunker-like structure stood off to one side. It was recently built, as opposed to the ancient World War II bunkers that still pepper the coast on both sides of the Golden Gate. I saw a Guardsman feeding scraps to a pair of stray-looking dogs by some trash barrels. An unmarked, brightly polished SUV was parked in one of the empty lanes of the unused highway. SIT, I figured.

The road's drop-off was as sudden and utter as it was on the other side of the Gate.

I got to the edge of the lot, where other sightseers were taking in the view. A ten year old tourist girl was complaining loudly about how hungry she was. I had my look, getting a clear view of Fort Point and the old Presidio. It was only a little over a mile across, but the ferry boats couldn't handle the current here. Promises to extend the underground Bay Area Rapid Transit system—BART—northward had come to nothing. The expansion would be very expensive. Besides, this region needed the Bridge to survive. There was no sense pretending otherwise.

I went back to my cab and my mustached driver. My thought was the same one as when I'd viewed this stub of land from the other side on the day I'd arrived in the city.

Poor Marin County.

THIRTY-ONE.

WARD: Explanations

I WOKE UP STILL LYING ON THE DINING ROOM FLOOR. By the wall clock I estimated that I'd been out for less than an hour, a big improvement over the last time. Then a picture of Nate's terrified face flashed through my memory.

"Marge?" My voice was loud enough to be heard in the adjacent rooms. No voice answered mine. I was becoming frightened. I struggled to my feet, using the table to brace myself. A brief period of vertigo passed and I was able to let go of the table. A minute later I took a couple of steps. My legs were a little rubbery, but held my weight.

I looked around the room. The tablecloth was still folded back. Nate's writing materials had been removed. The short drop to the floor hadn't visibly harmed the table.

I went through the open door to the kitchen. No one was there. Several broken cups, obviously hastily picked up from the floor, were on the sink board. Nothing else appeared to be broken.

"Marge, where are you?" This time I really raised my voice. No answer.

I went through the house room by room. Marge and Nate were both gone. Peering through the living room curtains, I looked outside. The little Toyota, which Marge was using wasn't at the curb.

I found the note on two large Post-It pads stuck to the computer screen in the rear room I was using as an office.

Dear Ward, I've taken Nathan out for a while. You gave him quite a fright, but he isn't physically injured. I didn't know what to do about you, so I called Aunt Chloe and explained what had happened. She said to let you sleep it off. You should call her when you wake up.

She left her address book on the desktop. It was opened to Aunt Chloe's entry.

I didn't call immediately. I wanted to prepare what I was going to say and thought about it until I realized that I'd better stick to the plain, unvarnished truth. No excuses, not to Aunt Chloe. Simply stated, I screwed up royally.

In spite of the situation, I found myself looking forward to talking to and seeing my favorite aunt.

I went into the kitchen and made myself a cup of coffee in one of the undamaged cups, had a blueberry muffin, and a glass of orange juice. I was feeling clearer-headed when I finished and made the phone call.

∽∞∾

The trees over the house muted the sunlight. I parked in front of Aunt Chloe's house, making sure that my car was out of the direct rays of the sun.

When I got out it was like entering a different world. Gone was the gray of the Avenues. It was warm but not hot. Everywhere there were growing things, trees, shrubs, patches of grass, weeds, all alive with the sounds of miniature life. A soft light diffused everything.

"Ward, come inside." She stood in the shade of the doorway.

"Aunt Chloe," I said. I did not realize the state of my own tenseness until I saw her and the rigidity left my muscles instantly.

"I've made some tea for you," she said as we entered the ever-aromatic kitchen.

I preferred coffee, but I thought it might be some curative for me she'd brewed, that is until I saw the Lipton tag.

She smiled. "No, Ward, your little escapade doesn't warrant anything stronger. It's the boy I'm more concerned about."

She got up from the table and went to the backdoor. A beautiful black cat was waiting. It looked to be purebred Persian. "He lives around here," Aunt Chloe explained. "But he likes to visit me from time to time."

She fixed him a bowl of dried cat food.

"What did I do wrong?" I asked.

She sat back down and took a sip from her tea cup. "Just about everything," she said. "First, you frightened the child. Second, you impaired his creative imagination, probably for years. Third, you could have injured yourself badly." Aunt Chloe paused. "What you call magic is not a toy."

"I wasn't playing," I interjected.

"You need to develop a sense of balance," she said. "That's what this is all about." With an airy wave she took in the kitchen, the bags of herbs and the shelves crowded with jars of the same.

My eyes and mind followed the direction of her gesture and suddenly I was also seeing the study, the room full of books. I don't know how she did that, since there was a wall between the kitchen and that room.

"Take that as a lesson, Ward."

"What just happened?" I asked.

"A little bit of the old majik. There will be no repercussions."

"Why not?" I knew she was making a point, but my ego

kept getting in the way of seeing it.

"Because there's only you and me here, and a glimpse of my books from a distance isn't likely to have any effect on either of us."

She was right. I put my ego aside and *really* started to listen.

"What happened at the garage?" I asked. "It was mostly just cars. I may have frightened one or two people, but why would that knock me out for nine days?"

"After lunch," she said. "We'll talk about it after lunch."

We had some stir-fried dish, made with bits of chicken and shrimp that was tasty, filling, and I was assured was guaranteed not to put on weight. Judging from the way Aunt Chloe looked, it was worth listening to her dietary advice.

I helped her clean up afterwards. We chatted like the good friends we'd become, without a single statement of significance between us. It was as refreshing as the lunch had been.

When everything had been put away she surprised me by suggesting that we continue our conversation while walking back into Glen Canyon. It was a real canyon, with the older homes backing on it like old friends, and the newer ones, further up, taking up space as intruders.

"Up at the top of the canyon, off Portola Drive, there used to be a golf driving range," she said. "All the children in the neighborhood made pocket money by hunting up lost balls." We crossed a little creek by means of a rickety wooden bridge. "I love living here."

By now I felt truly relaxed and receptive, without even being aware that my attitude shifted. On the way back she finally broached the subject of the flat tires. "It wasn't necessarily as harmless as you think."

"Oh?" I was falling a little short on witty repartee.

"Just imagine that one of those people who had to wait for tires to be reinflated missed an important appointment, and a business deal was lost, or even worse, an engagement was broken because someone became tired of waiting on a street corner. There are a hundred variations, and, judging from your coma, some of them must have been true. A pattern was broken. Your coma balanced that out."

"And with Nate?" I asked.

"He'll get over most of it," said Aunt Chloe.

"Most of it?"

"Don't expect your relationship to continue to be the way it was."

"That's not fair."

We arrived back at the house. "Oh, yes it is," said Aunt Chloe. "*You* shifted the balance. It's a different relationship now."

She led me into the room with all the books and sat down in one of the plush chairs, indicating that I should do the same.

The chair was comfortable in a way that all of the designer furniture at work missed by a mile.

"Ward, why don't you drink anymore?" she asked. "Remember, I know about your involvement in AA."

"Because I can look ahead and see how it will end up."

"Clairvoyance?"

I saw what she was driving at. "Not a chance," I said.

"One last question," she said. "For whom do you stay sober?"

"Me, of course. It doesn't work any other way."

"I wonder about the table."

Something happened. I was staring into those startling blue eyes one minute, and the next one found me outside my body looking at myself in the dining room. Nate was screaming. Power poured through my arms and the table was over a foot off the floor. God, what a glamorous figure I was. I was using magic, and I was having an *effect*, like no other action ever let me do in my life.

Then it was like a rubber band snapping. Immediately I was back in the bookroom with Aunt Chloe. I had to take several deep breaths before I could speak. "I've been auditioning for myself my whole life," I said. "Look what I can do, look what I can do."

"End of lesson," she said. "Some very talented people never learn that."

⚬⚬⚬

I left Aunt Chloe's house with the scent of herbs on my cheek where she kissed me goodbye. As I drove up O'Shaughnessy on my way to Portola Drive, I reviewed the events of the day. I was deeply embarrassed—no, make that ashamed. I traumatized my son badly, using help for his potential writing as an excuse to cover up my grandstanding, which misfired.

Marge's note didn't hint at any hostility, but I felt apprehensive anyhow as I swung on to Portola Drive. My actions certainly called for some response on her part and the only responses I could call to mind were from unpleasant to dire.

Far too soon, I completed the journey and sat in the car across the street from the house. Marge's car had the spot immediately in front of the house, and although I didn't want a drink—I never wanted one anymore—I realized that if ever there was a good excuse for one this was it.

I got out of the car clutching the bag of peanut butter chocolate chip cookies Aunt Chloe handed to me on the way out of her house. "Peace offering," she said.

Some peace offering, I thought as I crossed the street. But when I opened the front door Nate came to meet me, his eyes on the large brown bag. The only thing that was different, was that he didn't call me Daddy, or even Dad.

"Oh, boy, Father," he called. "Cookies."

I had the feeling that I had been demoted. A degree of the warmth that had been between us was gone. I felt the same about him, but he obviously didn't feel the same about me.

"I'm sorry about this morning," I said to him. Marge stood in the background, arms folded on her chest. There was no fire in her eyes or anger in her expression, but something changed there also, and I knew I was going to hear about it soon.

"I'm sorry," I said again to her.

"Accepted," she said. Then she took the bag of cookies from me and led the way to the kitchen with Nate eagerly following.

Marge and I each had a cookie with coffee, while Nate devoured two of them with a tall glass of milk. He excused himself from the table and that left the two of us.

Here it comes, I thought.

Marge got up from the table. "Please, wait here, Ward." She left the room to return in less than a minute holding several legal-looking papers.

"Relax," she said. "It's not what you think."

I truly didn't know what I thought, but she handed the papers to me and clarified the issue. "These are insurance applications," she said. "I want to take out a policy on you."

"Isn't this rather sudden?" I asked.

"No, I've had the papers for a while."

I examined the papers. They were, of course, from the same insurance office where she worked. The policy application was rather large. The other paper was an appointment form for a physical examination with the insurance company physician. The date had yet to be filled in.

"You've been thinking about this," I said.

"Yes, for some time."

"And it's important to you?"

"Very."

"Go ahead and make the appointments."

"Thank you." She gathered up the papers.

"It's a large policy," I said.

"We can easily afford the premiums," she said.

"But why so much?" I asked again.

"Because you seem determined to do away with yourself with your *majik*." She spat out the word like a bad-tasting piece of fruit.

The one thing I could do that was truly extraordinary ... and it was a dirty word to my wife. Not that I blamed her for her attitude.

"I'm thinking of Nathaniel," she added. "Perhaps you should think of him also, and not whether or not his imagination matches your expectations."

THIRTY-TWO

NATHANAEL: The Key

MY PHONE RANG WHILE I WAS IN TRAFFIC, startling me momentarily. I'd gotten used to it being quiescent these past few days. But I'd since reprogrammed it to accept calls from only one number.

"Nathanael Pentecost here."

"This is George Starks."

"Thank you for returning my call, Mr. Starks." A driver in an adjacent lane gave me a disapproving look for talking on my phone while I was at the wheel.

"I'm curious how you got my number."

I explained it to him. "I apologize for the underhandedness."

"You write for *Diamond*." His voice was unhurried and on the rich side, the same older man's voice from Dorothy Shields' answering machine. "I spoke to an April Gregoire."

I was impressed. "I'd be curious as to how you got *her* number."

"I know one of the CEOs of the corporation that owns your magazine." Again, impressive. It's a big corporation. "Ms. Gregoire tells me you're not on any sort of assignment concerning me."

"No. I'm not." I was heading south on Van Ness.

"Then, your interest in me is ...?" His voice remained level and patient.

I drew a breath. "I'm writing a book with Irene Isis. She ... recommended I meet you."

Silence on the line. I came to a red light at the big intersection with Market Street.

Finally George Starks said, "I've got some time, right now. Would you like to meet?"

"I would. Where?"

"Here at the house." He gave me the address on 23rd, which I'd already cribbed from the phone book.

"Thank you, Mr. Starks. I'll be there in twenty minutes."

I turned on to Market and headed for Noe Valley.

It was saved from being an overly picturesque pile by the house's natural wear and tear. People *lived* here. The place didn't get repainted every other year, and the small front garden abutting the sidewalk had a healthy number of weeds in it. Other homes on the same street oozed museum-quality false charm: San Francisco reimagined as a yuppie fable. The house was just a few blocks from my family's old apartment on 25th Street.

George Starks looked remarkably like his bio photo, though his piercing eyes appeared a little weary. He had heavy shoulders, and his grip was strong when we shook hands. He brought me into the front room. Compact discs and LPs were heaped around an old, complex stereo console. Edith Piaf, Bartók, Cat Stevens, Led Zeppelin, quite an assortment. A great deal of opened and unopened mail was scattered across a coffee table.

"Coffee?"

"God, yes." I hadn't had a cup since I'd left the house that morning. The few open restaurants I'd seen on my visit across the Bay looked too seedy to order anything from.

He brought in the cups, and we sat. I heard no one moving around the kitchen or the upstairs, but amiable feminine touches to the decor told me that Dorothy Shields still lived here as well.

"So ..." George Starks said, "Irene." He was comfortably slouched in his chair.

"I'm afraid so," I said a bit faintly.

A smile moved his mostly gray beard. "Well, that answers a thing or two right there. So, you're collaborating, you and Irene."

"Yes. On a novel."

Surprise showed in his eyes. "Oh. I thought it would be her memoirs, and you were doing research."

Thoughts of the Purple Witch's memoirs ever being written were almost enough to make me shudder.

"Am I right, though," he went on, "that she's still only got the one novel?"

"*Everyone Goes Away.* Yes."

"No follow-up?"

"That's what we're hoping to write. I'm assisting her. Ghostwriting." I didn't spit the word out; I showed commendable restraint.

He took a sip from his cup. "Forgive me, but you don't sound too confident about that."

I had a sip too. The coffee tasted like almonds; I liked it. "Well, it's not going well." Suddenly I wanted to laugh, to just guffaw uncontrollably. Understatements are great sources of humor.

He seemed to sense it and chuckled, but it was very cordial. "I have to sympathize."

"That's nice of you, Mr. Starks." I joined him in the chuckle.

As when I'd talked to Aunt Chloe yesterday about the Witch, I felt myself relax, felt the noose give a little.

He gave me a wave. "It's George. If you're let in past the front door, it's George."

I nodded. "I'm Nathanael. Before this goes any further, I absolutely must express my admiration for your work. I've read two of your books in the past two days, the August Purity mysteries. They are superb."

"Why, thank you," he said mildly but sincerely. "Impressing a critic is always an accomplishment."

"I didn't read them as a critic."

It was his turn to nod. He understood. Then he straightened slightly in his chair. "But—to whatever business brings you here. Why exactly did Irene send you to me?"

I'd met a few professional writers in the course of my job and on the cocktail party circuit, but none had the name recognition of Irene I. Isis. The others were mostly authors with one or two titles, desperately promoting themselves. They were imagining—or frantically pretending—that what they'd written was going a huge hit, was going to *make* them, that once that happened they'd never have to write another word in their lives.

George, instead, was obviously the genuine article. Writing was his livelihood, his craft. He'd made his bones, stood the test of time. His ego was secure, and nobody had to pay a price to be in his presence.

I'd never met his like before.

"I don't know exactly why she sent me," I said. "She tends to speak in flamboyant generalities and doesn't take well to being cross-examined. She said something to the effect that George Starks was the *key*, then told me to go find you. I honestly don't know what she meant by it."

"Yet you came all the way out here."

I smiled softly. "I may have had other reasons for making

the trip. I've got family here. And a respite from her ... seemed appealing."

He chuckled a little louder. "She's still in New York?"

"Rhode Island."

He nodded, as if there were a backstory there that he knew or could guess about. "Well, suppose you tell me what this novel is that you two are working on."

I drew another long breath, then gave it a brave go. It wasn't easy. Our untitled project was essentially a redo of *Everyone Goes Away*, though the Purple Witch adamantly refused to acknowledge it as such. In it, a character very much like the Rosemary Parrish heroine from the first book—now thirty years older—undergoes trials and tribulations in her social and romantic life remarkably similar to those experienced by her earlier counterpart.

It was, however, very difficult for me to describe the story in linear terms. Pages and whole chapters of our book had been summarily expunged by the Witch over the past eight months, whenever a gale-force mood and new schizoid vision for the story line overtook her. So much material had gotten scrapped, in fact—several times the amount which had been retained—that it was hard to sort through all the rejected scenes and subplots. Some of that abandoned work was quite passable, in my insignificant opinion ... insignificant because the Witch so regularly reminded me it was so.

In talking about the book I relived it in part, and a cold queasiness moved through my gut.

Finally, I just gave up trying to explain the goddamn thing.

George regarded me, still sympathetic. "Forgive me, but that sounds an awful lot like a retelling of *Everyone Goes Away*."

I nodded. "Frankly, I don't think she has any more real ideas in her. She acts as though these are fresh, but obviously they're not." I finished my coffee, set down the cup. "To be even more frank ... if she would just accept that the book *is* a retelling and let the Rosemary Parrish-type character *be* her thirty years later, I believe the story could work. It would have a very humanistic resonance, as the heroine engages life's tireless and repetitive crises—but from an older, though not necessarily wiser, perspective."

George's tired eyes showed a little more animation as he continued to gaze at me. "Nathanael," he said at last, "that's not bad."

The uneasy coldness in my middle warmed noticeably at that.

"But," he added, "it still doesn't explain why Irene put you on to me."

I pressed my lips into a line, then said, "Truth be told, I wasn't even sure you would turn out to be a real person."

He looked down at his hands where they enclosed his coffee cup, absorbing that. "She's that bad nowadays?"

I had a strong feeling I wasn't telling tales out of school. "She's not a well woman." I tried to put the depth of my meaning into those words.

George sighed. "Man, what a fucking shame."

We sat for a silent moment. Finally I asked, "Can I ask how you know her?"

His eyes had gone melancholy. "Oh, from the old days, of course. We were all there in New York, your typical slew of young aspiring writers and poets, the whole grab bag of ambitious artists. Some had success eventually, some didn't. But we pretended we were the Algonquin Round Table. I was lucky enough to be learning my trade on the job. I fell into my first two book contracts and had an editor who was very hands-on. She taught me a great deal."

He drained his cup and put it on a clear corner of the cluttered coffee table.

"Anyway, Irene was in our circle. She was the most passionate one of us. She was like an elemental. She was going to be a writer. No doubt about it, simply because no one could imagine anything getting in her way and surviving. I ... was fond of her." He smiled somewhat sheepishly. "I used whatever little leverage I had to make some introductions, then I helped her pitch a book proposal to a publisher. Those things were easier to do in those days. It was a different market. But Irene got her contract ..."

I looked at George levelly. "And then she couldn't write the book."

He met my eyes. "She had the talent. She had the energy—more than enough energy. She had the *image*, burned into her being, of herself as a writer. But she didn't have the organizational abilities. Didn't have the discipline. She couldn't sit down, day after day, and produce pages, which is how books get written. Not by magic. No smoke and mirrors. Just work."

"Then how did *Everyone Goes Away* get written?" I asked, though I already knew.

He shrugged his heavy shoulders. "I wrote most of it."

I nodded.

"If that little detail ever turns up in your magazine, I'll deny it. Vehemently."

"You needn't worry," I said.

"I genuinely consider it her book, though," George said. "She had the concept of it—full-blown, I believe—somewhere inside her. But it only came out in jagged spasms. I helped to herd the ideas ... then later, as she became dependent on me, I put them on paper for her."

I imagined his experience of that particular process was different from what I had undergone.

"You don't take credit for the book?" I asked.

"No."

"And you don't begrudge her the success she's had, considering you're responsible for it?"

"I never wanted what she seems to have achieved."

"Cutting a movie deal, coasting on royalties from one novel for three decades—that's the success you *didn't* want?"

He shook his head solemnly. "No. I didn't. I don't. Writing is part of the reward of writing. For myself, anyway. If I make a perfectly decent living at my work, which I do—work I love, work that means everything to me—then I don't have to go back to selling carburetors and truck axles. Which means I get to go on writing, uninterrupted, unimpeded. Purpose and fulfillment."

An enormous and profound envy filled me. It wasn't jealousy. I didn't resent this man. I only wanted what he had.

He let out another chuckle. "Incidentally, they did want to put August Purity on film, possibly even turn him into a franchise. I carefully explained to my agent and to several other people who represented great amounts of money, that there was only one actor who could have portrayed August. And that was Basil Rathbone, circa 1940s. I wasn't being a smartass about it. He was simply who I'd had in mind when I created the character. Anyone else would've rankled me till the day I died."

I didn't know the actor he'd mentioned. Father had been the film buff, so naturally I regarded the medium suspiciously.

"Irene had the *gift* inside her," George finished. "But it was wired to a demon. Poor girl."

Once more we sat in silence. George Starks was feeling pity for Irene I. Isis; and, almost unbelievably, for that moment, so was I.

⚬

He was gracious enough to ask me about my own work and to seem truly interested, but when a handsome woman in her sixties came in the front door, I took it as my exit cue. Evening was settling. Dorothy Shields wound her arm through George's and asked if I was staying for dinner. I wasn't. I smiled, said my sincere thanks and went.

When and why George Starks moved out to the West Coast and come to cohabit (neither wore wedding bands) with Dorothy Shields were irrelevant background particulars. Thirty years ago, though, he'd held an important place in and drastically altered the course of the Purple Witch's life. Probably they'd been lovers; but it didn't really matter.

What had once been the woman's passions and eccentricities had since calcified into something very close to true madness. George hadn't asked for details about her current state of mind and body. Probably he could do the extrapolations all by himself. Neither had he given me a message of any sort to convey back to her.

Of course, a very secret and very desperate part of me hoped that George Starks actually *was* the key, just as the Purple Witch claimed ... that he could somehow miraculously unravel the terrible tangle of the book the Witch and I were supposed to be writing ... that my single chance at being a professional writer hadn't been utterly squandered.

I found my car and drove back to Mom.

THIRTY-THREE

WARD: Time Flies

I AM ALWAYS CONFUSED BY TIME. I have calendars to keep track of the days, weeks and months, and clocks to measure the march of minutes and hours, but I rarely know what year it is. I know that the year is usually printed on the pages of calendars. However, unless I make it a special point to look for it I don't see it.

The mirror is much more dependable for me. I am probably too acquainted with the geography of my face and body. I certainly fall far short of the ideals of humility I hear discussed at AA meeting after AA meeting. The face that stared back at me this morning was neither proud nor humble. It was older, with new lines running vertically down my cheeks and a liberal sprinkling of gray in my hair.

How did it happen? When did it happen? Was it a sudden event, or a creeping change, making minute alterations in my appearance day by day, underneath the threshold of consciousness?

Of course there was a simpler explanation for my Friday morning malaise. All I had to do was remember the non-event of last night. It had finally happened. Correction. The problem was that it had finally not happened.

Nature, which had so faithfully kept me operational for so long, seemed to have been on vacation last night. The routine we settled into, after those first awkward days when she finally returned to me following Nate's birth, had been broken.

We went to bed last night. We slept. There was nothing in between. This was not due to lack of trying on my part. The event I'd been dreading, since those early times when instinctual drive had taken the place of mutual sexual attraction, had come to be.

Marge was still excited by and thoroughly turned on by sex, and made an enthusiastic partner, but the enthusiasm lately seemed to be for the act itself. Not for me. That was a livable situation as long as I could supply what was required. She either couldn't or wouldn't supply me with any kind of initial physical stimulus if I needed it. I think, considering her background, that she couldn't. Indeed, she stopped deliberately looking at my naked body years ago.

Sex was great. I was chopped liver.

I think I was facing the echo of the solution that Phyllis Morton adopted in her own marriage to prevent her humiliation from ever happening again. Harry betrayed her; if her husband ever wanted to be intimate with her again, all duties of the act fell entirely to him. Phyllis, unwittingly or otherwise, passed this attitude on to her impressionable daughter. When I thought of Marge's initial reaction to Aunt Chloe's letter there seemed to be little doubt about the inherited carnal perspective.

I turned away from the mirror and prepared to address the day.

My small bowl of oatmeal, orange juice, and coffee, were on the kitchen table. Marge joined me as I took my place. It was hard for me to meet her eyes. Last night had been just about the most demoralizing time of my adult life.

"Good morning, Marge," I said.

"Good morning, Ward."

With those greetings a tacit agreement was made. We would not talk about *it*.

Nathaniel passed through the kitchen without speaking. His arms were laden with school books. He was the brightest kid in his high school freshman class. The front door clicked shut as he went out to meet one of his very few friends from school.

He's a loner, I said silently, feeling a little bit stung by being snubbed by my son. It was a long way from the days of him running down the hall on 25th Street calling, "Daddy, Daddy." The years were suddenly very heavy on my shoulders.

Where had they gone? A common measurement of time is how much you have accomplished in an allotted span. The unknown term in that particular measurement is *accomplished*. I had an attractive wife, an incredibly bright son, a best friend, a host of other friends through the AA fellowship, a prestigious job, a good home, and two cars.

But I hadn't sold a single story since the time I started writing, and I so wanted to sell one, at least one. Writing, seeing my name in print in a magazine—was that so much to want? Whether it was or not, I hadn't managed to cash in on whatever promise I'd once shown, when editors sent me genuinely encouraging rejection slips. So, had I really accomplished anything? I'd not even tried to write since that long-ago day on 25th Street when I'd said, "The hell with it," and abandoned what degenerated over the years into a self-flagellating hobby.

Perhaps someday I would try again.

I kissed Marge goodbye and headed out to face the dragons.

There are busy Fridays, when everyone in the building seems to be trying to line up their ducks for Monday morning. More pleasant by far are the usual Fridays, which are more of a winding down from the busyness of the week, and a time of mentally preparing for the weekend. This was number two.

I used the time to further review my life. It was not, I hoped, an exercise in masochism; because I believe that a review of the past can lead to intelligent decisions in the present.

Nathaniel was on my mind. There were two periods in my relationship with my son—before the table and after the table. After the unfortunate event, I treated him the same way as I had before. I used the same language to address him, was neither more nor less courteous, and still showed up for all his school events. I also tried to help him with any class projects that came along. This was acceptable as long as those projects were intellectual and basically impractical. For the more hands-on projects, those requiring manual dexterity and a strong sense of reality, he sought out his grandfather Harry, who always came through for him.

Thankfully, Bill stopped by my office in time to halt my ruminations from becoming hopelessly maudlin. I was skirting the shores of self-pity, and that, for an alcoholic, is dangerous. His infectious good humor cheered me into the present, which was neither good nor bad; simply tolerable.

In the old days, we would have headed for one of our favorite bars right after work, earlier if we could get away with it, as we often had. On this Friday, we each drove home alone under the darkening December sky.

I made another pass through the back parking lots at the Stonestown Mall. Luck was with me this time and we snagged the suddenly opened parking slot before anyone else spotted it.

"Friday night shopping is bad enough," I said, "but in Christmas season it is impossible."

"Inaccurate," said Marge. "We got a parking spot."

"Difficult?"

"Very."

We both laughed. Evidently we both had come to our separate peace with last night's debacle.

We joined the crowd surging into the upscale cavern. I love shopping malls. While Marge embarked on a search for the gift items on her list, I took the escalator up to the Electronics Boutique on the second floor. I was looking for an updated version of the encyclopedia software I installed on my PC. This was going to be part of Nathaniel's surprise present.

It was easier to find the software than to get waited on, and I spent the time in line looking at all the new game titles. With the passing of the Atari machine, due to a marketing decision, I'd been led into a whole new world of games, and it was exciting, although I missed the old workhorse. I recognized the clerk and we both commiserated briefly about the death of the Atari before concluding our transaction.

The change in our relationship hadn't affected Nate's appreciation of my cooking, though he was careful not to express too much in the way of enthusiasm. Even knowing this lifted my spirits as I hovered over the stove, stirring the sauce, tasting and adding herbs as needed. I was cooking enough spaghetti and meatballs to have some left over for the rest of the week.

A Christmas ham was Marge's choice for the main course, and the aroma of the slowly simmering glaze filled the house. Between the two, the kitchen was a delicious olfactory experience.

We held off opening the presents until the whole clan was assembled. This Christmas, my sister-in-law, "Society Sarah," and her husband couldn't make it, so we didn't have a repeat of the last four times, which entailed waiting and waiting for the grand entrance. I found such behavior inconvenient, but I am sure that certain of the customs of my tribe were equally strange to Marge.

At long last, after a sumptuous meal which was enjoyed by everyone, we got to the real business at hand.

Pete and Ruth had come alone. Their children, according to Pete, were enjoying a late teenage revolt. Since they were all approaching their thirties, I considered that an accurate statement.

We had a happy time that day and evening. Whatever her other failings, Phyllis Morton had a strong sense of family and the strength of will to make it real for all of us. After all the cold, frightening, Christmases as a child, spent dreading my father's appearance, I appreciated it.

After the floor was littered with wrappers, bows, ribbons of all colors, and scatterings of the ubiquitous Styrofoam packing, and the separate loot was piled around each participant, I handed Nate the key to the upstairs storeroom, which he had his eye on as a future *office*.

I knew that he was disappointed with the quality and quantity of his small pile of presents, but like all the Pentecosts, he tried not to allow his feelings to show.

"Son," I said, "will you please check the storeroom. I may have left a present or two there."

"Sure thing, Father."

He left the room.

Marge and I waited anxiously.

It took longer than I expected and I was about to get up

and go after him, when he returned. His face was the happiest I'd seen in years. I gathered that the presents were acceptable. "Merry Christmas, Son," I said.

He stared at us with his mouth wide open. "It's a brand new computer and a color monitor." He could hardly contain himself, choosing between the urge to express his gratitude and the to-hell-with-everything need to run back there and start playing with his new toy.

"You've got the latest version of Windows," I said, "and a trackball, instead of a mouse, and a fast modem ..."

"Enough, Ward," said Marge. She also was beaming with pleasure at the sight of his happiness. "... and the storeroom is now your office," she added.

"Thanks, Mom," he said. "Thanks, Dad."

There was more to come. "The boxes I asked you to look for are against the wall," I said. "I bought a few reams of paper to go with your new printer."

"A printer too?" He looked equally dazzled and stunned.

"On the floor in the box with the blue bow. Do you want a hand setting it up?"

"No. I'd like to do it myself—for the practice. But thanks, Father."

My brief foray into Dadhood was over. But he couldn't take away what had been said. For a brief moment on that wonderful day I had been Dad.

Phyllis, Ruth, and Marge, cleared the kitchen and dining room of dishes and silverware, while Pete, Harry, and myself, gathered all the leftover wrappings and debris from the living room. Nate would have helped us, I am sure, if he hadn't been called to his *office* on urgent business.

It was with glad hearts that we all said goodnight.

⚬⚭⚬

As Marge and I prepared ourselves for bed, we could hear Nate's enthusiastic cries, as he installed the printer and got it going. I hoped he would be happy with my old copy of WordPerfect for a while, at least until I could acquire a copy of Word.

Then I forgot all about software and all things computer as Marge came out of the bathroom and climbed into bed stark naked.

She's trying, I thought, and by God, she's beautiful.

I went to the bathroom and deposited my pajamas, top and bottom on the tile floor. Then I went back into the bedroom, hoping strongly that my present condition would stay long enough for both of us.

Sometimes nature is kind. What I feared did not come to pass, and what we both desired did.

THIRTY-FOUR.

———✖———

NATHANAEL: Septem

SAN FRANCISCO, AS I WOUND THROUGH IT heading back to the Sunset district, was peaceful and sleepy and so unlike New York's tireless hive-like bustle. Houses dreamed under what looked to be a moon very near its fullness, either waxing or waning.

Marin County had suffered, worse even than I'd known until today; but San Francisco abided. The Bridge's absence hadn't fatally cut it off from anything. San Francisco was a self-contained destination, its own site of commercial power and socioeconomic stability. Even the rerouting of the highways hadn't damaged it seriously. Tourists still flocked here, still came to see the legendary Golden Gate ... even without that fanciful suspension bridge painted that curious orange color spanning it. Hell, maybe the city got *more* tourist trade now.

When I put my key in the lock on Santiago Street, I figured Mom must be out. The lights weren't lit. Even the porch light, the beacon for the trick-or-treaters I was already seeing in the neighborhood, was off.

I was wrong. She was home. I found out when I flipped the light on in the kitchen.

Once I would have thought, from the look she gave me now from where she sat at the table, only of what trouble I might be in. Did she want to have a Talk? (That was what they'd always felt like.)Was she going to try, yet again, to encourage me to be friendlier with Father? Was she going to lecture, plead? And how long was I going to have to hear it, until she ran out of breath and energy while I sat there like a stone, until I was excused, with nothing at all changed?

But those were leftover thoughts from adolescence, and I wasn't that kid anymore.

"Mom ... did something happen?"

The bottle of ruby port was on the table, along with a half-empty glass. I waited tensely, prepared to hear her mumble and slur, but her voice was unimpaired. I had the sudden and distinct impression that she hadn't gone to church this Sunday, an omission of some magnitude.

"Dexter McBride died."

I waited to connect the name up with some distant relative or elderly friend of the family, but my memory was a blank. Mom didn't look mournful, precisely. Her face, while melancholic, was almost steely.

Gently I said, "I'm afraid I don't know who that is."

"Dexter McBride was one of seven enterprising individuals who came from old money and wanted nothing more but to gather *more* money about themselves. Rather than going into business or making legitimate investments in others' business efforts, though, these seven, for the most part, swindled people. Their stings weren't complicated, and by the letter of the law they weren't even illegal. They relied on other people's carelessness and trust. They did very well for themselves. And today there's one less of the bastards."

Mom knocked back the rest of the glass.

I slowly pulled out a chair and joined her at the table. I was looking into deep waters here, it seemed.

Something occurred to me, and I asked, "Was that the news Uncle Pete had for you?" I'd mentioned he called in the note I'd left.

Mom nodded. The sad hardness in her normally cheery eyes was disturbing.

"What does it mean?" I asked. "Who did these seven swindle?"

"Your grandfather. Drake. They took everything he was worth. Absolutely all of it. Can you imagine what that must've been like—to be truly *destitute*?"

"I can imagine." But I didn't know if I could, really. My way had been paid all through college.

I had been five or six years old when my grandfather and grandmother died in a car wreck. I remembered both of them—not in any detail, but I did remember. The deaths of Father's parents were probably upsetting to me, but like many events in my early childhood the experience was eclipsed by a much bigger injury, one done to me at the age of eight.

"Penniless," Margot was saying.

I'd taken my SATs and sent out my applications. I so wanted to go to college, recognizing it as my natural element. But ... had I just assumed I could go, without once truly considering what it would cost? I couldn't remember.

"Broke ..."

She wasn't slurring, but she'd had more than the one glass of wine.

I lifted a hand. "Wait. Why did Pete call to tell you that this McBride guy died? And"—an uneasiness suddenly stole through me—"what did he die of?"

Mom regarded me with those hard melancholy eyes. "Cerebral hemorrhage," she finally said. "He was pronounced dead at 3:16 PM yesterday. At Marin County General." She nearly smiled, saying it. But it was a cheerless smile.

I thought it over. "And this was one of those seven that defrauded Granddad Drake?" I had some memory of Drake suffering a financial mishap, so someone must have told me some part of the story once; but I'd never understood the extent of his troubles. I'd liked Grandmom Alice—memories of smiles and warm hugs—better. "So McBride died at Marin County General. He must not've been doing very well money-wise anymore."

"He was old Marin County money."

"I guess old money isn't any better protected when the local economy goes bust." Images from my impulsive visit across the Bay earlier today were still fresh in my mind. What a sad sight.

Mom was shaking her head slowly. "Oh no. No. Old money is *very* protected. Old money buys things regular money can't. But"—back came that smile—"eventually, over time … over, say, seven years … it runs out. And you try to sell off valuable properties that suddenly nobody wants to buy. And you're going into debt and heading for bankruptcy. And your home, your family estate, suddenly has fry cooks and drug dealers and low-income families for neighbors. And you can't do anything to stop any of it. You're helpless. And when your evil old brain up and ruptures one day, they take you where they take everybody else, and you die among the riffraff, the junkies, the mugging victims, the *commoners* …"

Her shoulders were rising and falling rapidly. She gasped. Then she refilled her glass and took a swallow.

I was unnerved, but I stayed at the table with her. I thought some more, then said, "Uncle Pete has been keeping track of this group of seven, for—what?—the past twenty years? How could that be possible?"

"They were never secretive," said Mom. "They never had to be. Pete's been on the force for almost thirty-five years. He has all the connections he needs. He couldn't do anything legally about your grandfather's troubles, of course, but he's kept tabs on the people that hurt Drake ... just so I can know whenever another of them is gone. It's four down now, three to go."

She took another drink. That was what she had been doing for some while, sitting here as the sun went down, not bothering to turn on the lights. Just sitting alone and drinking over the death of a man named Dexter McBride.

Incredible. Nothing I knew about my mother could have prepared me for this scenario. Yet it was obvious that this news stirred something even deeper than memories of her in-laws' financial misfortunes or even their deaths.

I fished mentally for something else to say, something that might lead her to switch to a cup of coffee or eat some food. Maybe I could talk her into taking a nap, sleeping it off.

But before I could speak, Mom jumped back in with, "If your father were here, he would celebrate too. Not with a drink, of course ..." Her smile grew wistful.

I felt myself go automatically still.

"Their deaths—Drake and Alice's—they affected your father. Deeply. In that emergency room, when we saw that Pring boy. I believe your father would've ... would've ... well, he didn't get the chance to." She was shaking her head. "Drake was a harsh man. To your father, when your father was young. When he was a child. Drake mistreated your father. Did you know that?"

My silence and stillness said nothing; I made sure of it. But Mom was carrying on without me.

"But eventually, somehow, against all the odds—your father reached a peace with your grandfather. It took a long time. But it did *finally* happen."

I didn't want to hear about fathers.

Suddenly Mom's gray eyes shot toward mine sharply.

"You do that every time," she said, not trying to mask her accusatory tone. "Are you even aware of it?"

"Of what?" I asked stonily.

"Don't play that game, Nathan. I had enough of you being stoic and mute and—and *callous* when you were a teenager. Enough!"

It was like the hypnotist's code word that activates the preconditioning. A raised voice, an emotional display ... and I only went colder. I gazed back at her with dead eyes.

"Damnit, I ... Nathan, Nathan. You can't even stand to hear your father mentioned. That's not good. That's no good at all. Ward was your father, and he's gone. He's been gone now seven years ... and *still* you're—you're ..." Her hands bunched in frustration.

I wasn't going to hear it. My chair was pushed back, and I was on my feet.

"Ward loved you, and he was very sorry for what happened, but *you* just couldn't forgive it ..." She was talking to her fists where they lay on the table. Her tirade had the sound of something long pent-up.

I didn't want to go back out. I'd had a long day, and at the moment I didn't especially trust myself to drive.

I crossed the kitchen; now I opened the basement door. She was still talking behind me. I would not hear it. I pulled shut the door and went down the creaky wood steps to Father's boxes that waited in the dark below.

I'd already been into the box with my childhood picture books and the box full of Father's rejected short stories. Under the delicate, stark glow of the basement's bare forty watt bulb, I now pulled another box off the top of the stack. Roughly. Smacking it down on the cement floor. I heard glass tinkle. I tore open the box's flaps.

I lifted out the curiosities. They looked like awards. One,

framed and behind glass, now had a crack down the middle. I held a plaque under the light and squinted at the tarnished plate that ran along the bottom: DRAKE E. PENTECOST. It had been presented by something called the Geer-Mayfield Fellowship. Granddad Drake also received accolades from the Sons and Daughters of the City of Oakland, the League of North Beach Bakers, a testimonial from the city editor of the *Chronicle*. Several of these organizations named Drake "Man of the Year" at various times over a span of several decades.

Drake had been in real estate, right? Yes. Apparently he'd had quite an impact in his day, before being swindled. I wondered, as I handled several more such tributes, why nobody had told me about his legacy.

Then it occurred to me that somebody probably did ... and that I had probably ignored it as irrelevant data.

I yanked down another box. What Mom had said upstairs ha touched off a fierce frigid anger in me. But it wasn't anything I knew how to process. I was only sure that she should have known better. I wasn't about to relive a twenty year old crime.

A box of unfashionable ties. A pair of leather gloves, a dark red ceramic mug with the handle missing, a worn deck of playing cards with a train line's logo on back. Some knick-knacks. The playbill for a community theater production of *The Iceman Cometh*. Probably one of Father's AA acquaintances had been in it.

Father and that goddamned table, and that's *my* fault? I'm supposed to forgive ...

Another box crashed to the ground. It was still cool in the basement, but sweat was gathering on me. I tore off the sweatshirt I was wearing and chucked it into a corner.

Systems manuals for computers, for those asinine roll-playing games Father devoted so much time to. I scattered the books across the floor, digging deeper into the box.

Then I found a very ragged copy of a book about sleight of hand. I jumped like I'd come up with the body of a stiff dead rat.

At the age of ten, I humiliated myself at a school chum's birthday party when the hired magician started doing his act. I had to be driven home by my friend's father.

There were more such books. Some I could even remember being on the shelf at the apartment on 25th Street. I removed them from the box carefully, picking each up by its corner. My right eye stung suddenly and sharply. I wiped sweat off my forehead. I sneezed several times in a row from the stirred up dust.

The last book inside the box was larger than the worn trade and pocket-sized paperbacks. I lifted it into the pale light. It was bound in old imitation leather—or maybe *real* leather. How often had I handled an actual leather-bound book? It was fairly heavy, as much from the size as from the bond of the paper. It looked old but not ancient. The corners were badly battered. It wasn't anything a dealer would pay a good sum for.

In the center of the graying black cover it said, in raised silver script, *Septem*.

And I thought: Latin.

And then, the definition detaching from some obscure mental file, I thought: seven.

I heard the basement door open at the top of the stairs. I told Mom to go away. I said it loudly and emphatically. After a few seconds the door quietly closed.

I sat myself on the floor and, handling it like it was something alive and poisonous and only slightly dormant, I opened the leather-bound book in my lap.

THIRTY-FIVE.

WARD: The Majik of Numbers

THE TITLE OF THE SLIM VOLUME was *Numbers 1-6*. The list I gleaned from Aunt Chloe's bookshelves had finally run out. I acquired copies of all of her books on the subject of magic that interested me. Now I was searching for more exotic information. I stood there in Fred's Used Magazines and Books knowing that I'd succeeded.

Something compelled me to take the book from the shelf, glance at its innocuous title and open it. The glossy, hard leather cover, gleamed with newness, which made it even more unlikely that it contained anything of interest to me. When I opened the book, I found not newness, but the same blurry ink and primitive print style I encountered time and time again in my pursuit of like volumes. The newness of the cover was a sham.

I skipped the usual admonition to the reader—this one had something to do with Beware the Impatient—and began to savor the contents. It was all about six ways of accomplishing the same extraordinary thing. The six methods were listed in fair detail. A seventh was outlined, but directed the reader to another book, which treated the subject at depth, with complete instructions for the usual unwary user. I wrote down the name for a future research junket: *Septem*, by Augustus Crowe of Ayres Rock.

I was reading more these days. Nature, which had been reliable for so long and charitable for a shorter period, now became indifferent. As a result, Marge and I rarely went to bed at the same time. To begin with, I found excuses, mostly far-fetched, for staying up later, but eventually it became the new norm.

On this February evening I was reading and making notes from *Numbers 1–6*. I acquired some number-crunching skills with the computer at work, and the use of a spreadsheet was going to make things a lot easier.

It was my intention to write my own instruction manual for the event I had in mind and then to test out the result. This was going to be more spectacular than any number of flat tires, and it was going to take place in dear old Marin County.

If my penciled calculations were proven correct by the computer, what I had in mind could be brought to bear in a short amount of time.

I had been as overpowered as any working class person would be by the wall of wealth that faced me following my father's financial ruin, and later, during the aftermath of my parents' deaths. That consortium of old Marin County money was simply beyond the reach of someone of my social class. I didn't like that. But it was possible that *I* had recourses that others of my station did not.

The ordeals of my parents' financial downfall and deaths had been three years ago, and throughout and since both tribulations I remained, on the whole, admirably calm. I'd taken what happened more as acts of nature.

But there is—hey, call it what it is—an impotency to such acceptance of tragedy.

Lately, however, I'd become disenchanted with my mature resignation to an implacable enemy, and I'd started to ask myself, *"What about the sonsofbitches that caused all this misery and pain?"* It was a perfectly admissible question. However, that this new attitude of mine paralleled the decline of my physical relationship with my wife and the disintegrating emotional relationship of my son escaped my immediate notice. I had good reasons for the undertaking I was preparing for.

The only nature that presented itself to view was an evil nature that was shared equally by members of the consortium. Actually, I'd come around to thinking of them as accomplices. They were proof of what most thoughtful people already know. Namely, that we have the best system of justice in this country that money can buy.

It was not my intention to *physically* hurt anyone, although one member of the consortium, Rudolph Pring, was going to encounter a financial loss of magnitude, if this worked.

Reluctantly I put down the pencil and paper. Even though I usually skipped all admonitions and warnings with which majik books seem to be populated, I did notice and agree with the one that made it clear that only a fool tries to cast an important spell while tired.

When I went to bed, Marge was still awake but didn't say anything. I pretended not to notice, and went to sleep—lonely, frustrated, inadequate and guilty, all at the same time. Strangely enough, I had wonderful dreams.

The next evening it was more of the same. I scribbled notes until it was time to sleep.

Friday did away with the need to go to bed at any sort

of reasonable hour. It was refreshing not to have to pretend tiredness and I used the time to complete my notes. The next morning, right after breakfast, I went to my study, and began the long, careful, process of creating the formulas necessary to manipulate the information I assembled.

It was tedious work, and more than once I was tempted to give up. But then I thought of my mother and father, and suddenly, tedious or not, I was not that tired.

It took all of Saturday and Sunday, sitting in front of the cathode ray tube monitor, with my eyes starting to burn and my rear going numb in the chair, to do the job. The only way to check the results of my efforts was to actually cast the spell according to the specific instructions that emerged from those efforts, and it had to be cast in an open field, far out in western Marin County. I was looking forward to it.

The following week, I adjourned to my home office right after dinner each night and checked and rechecked my figures. I didn't anticipate any disastrous effects to people as a result of my action, but I had to make sure.

I would have to be careful, much more careful than I'd been with the Civic Center garage. That I'd survived that debacle was sheer luck. I'd been an infant playing with a loaded Uzi. Thanks to the gravity of Aunt Chloe's scolding, I hoped not to repeat my mistake. After all, people were not to be involved, and if they happened on the scene, they would be blocked out of the effect. Or so it said in fine print.

As far as what I'd come to call "the pendulum effect" went, I wasn't worried this time. The event would not need to affect me in any way to balance out the energies of reality.

Nevertheless, I was glad that Marge had taken out that insurance.

The weekend drew nearer. My son's stoic exterior did not turn me away from expressing warmth when complimenting him on his latest school project. As far as his response was, I could have saved it. Marge and I gamely went to bed together, and there was at least a degree of mutual warmth there. Fulfillment was another matter.

Friday night, I rechecked my figures again. The results were the same as they'd been all week. If my basic premises were correct, there was nothing to worry about. The formulas I'd used on the spreadsheet were pretty standard stuff.

If I'd made a mistake, or a series of them, the spell would most likely fizzle. There was also the possibility that the whole project was the product of an old book and my deranged thinking. After all, who could actually expect to find a book of *real majik* in a store on outer Mission Street? In that case, nothing could or would happen.

For a moment I almost hoped that was true. This obsession was driving my life down a dark road, and I didn't know where it led.

I wished I could talk to Aunt Chloe, but I knew that any conversation with her, at this time, would result in my giving up the project. Besides, even if I were willing to forgo revenge and let those bastards get away with it—and I wasn't—there was still the obsession to see it happen. It would be a marvel!

Saturday morning arrived. It was raining slightly and I hoped it would abate by the time I got to western Marin. I was up at six o'clock in the morning. I couldn't help it—just one more trip to the computer to run the final numbers, as a kind of precaution. The results were the same as they'd been all week. If I went out there and cast the spell, *it would happen*. With luck, nothing would happen to me in return.

That was too much like the fellow who jumped off a ten story building, and as he passed the fifth floor downward was heard to say, "So far, so good." An old joke indeed. As long as it wasn't prophetic in this case ...

I made a breakfast of hot cereal, bacon and eggs, orange juice, and two cups of strong, black coffee. *And the condemned ate a hearty last meal.*

I cleaned up after myself. Then I peeked through bedroom doors at my wife and my son. Both were sleeping soundly. I hoped to be home not too long after they awoke.

The distant rays of the morning sun lit up the eastern sky as I opened the front door and let myself out. I was, I realized, scared to death. I carried a cheap briefcase that was crammed with my notes. In separate folders were the results of my calculations and the reason for them.

The reason consisted of several slick paper magazine articles, and a personality piece in the local Marin County daily news. It was all about *Rudolph Pring, A new breed of gentleman farmer.*

I tossed the briefcase onto the front seat of the car. It was still early enough to avoid the later heavy traffic on 19th Avenue and I swung onto that thoroughfare.

In a short time it gave way to the approach to the Golden Gate Bridge. The light rain stopped. Then the claustrophobic, concrete, canyon-like approach fell away on both sides and I was at the toll plaza with its view of those dazzling international orange towers in the morning sunlight. The traffic heading north rolled smoothly through the toll gates. No toll was collected going north; it was going south that they really got you, like a prison where you had to pay to get back in.

The last time I crossed the span had been to view my dead parents, start the arrangements for their burial, and to be smirked at by the younger Mr. Pring, who was so loaded he could barely stand, but who was innocent of any wrongdoing. After all, *Mr. Pentecost cut off Mr. Pring at the intersection.* That was how the uniformed cop at the hospital explained it to me that night, and that assessment stuck all the way through the justice system.

I crossed the bridge and continued along Highway 101 until I came to the underpass and swung off the main highway onto Sir Francis Drake, which ran west.

The sleepy morning towns of Ross, San Anselmo, and Fairfax, first appeared in front of me, and then were visions in my rearview mirror. Other, smaller places joined them. I wasn't interested in a place with a name. I was looking for rolling hills in an area with a history of dairy ranching.

Eventually I reached Olema. Now I was a short distance from the Point Reyes National Seashore Recreation Area. In one of his rare moments of fatherhood, Drake Pentecost had taken me out there for a hike along the Bear Valley Trail. It was wonderful until we got home and he saw the mess the trip made of my expensive shoes. End of hiking experience. But I always remembered the day itself fondly.

The road crested and dropped. Off to the right was a well-cared for, large pasture. A dirt road ran along its edges. Munching the dark green grass were thirty or forty cattle. Rich, purebred cattle, who were going on a trip.

I drove on for a quarter of a mile and parked near the entrance to Point Reyes. From the trunk of the car, I took an orange day pack, rain parka, sunglasses and a baseball cap. Then, disguised as a day hiker, I began to walk back to the pasture.

THIRTY-SIX

NATHANAEL:
The Witch

I DIDN'T SLEEP, and I didn't come up to eat.

I saw daylight at the high slitted windows through swollen eyes. My back was an elaborate knot of pain as I finally got to my feet. I took the leather-bound book, *Septem*, with me as I climbed the stairs. Mom hadn't disturbed me a second time during the night.

I found her asleep on the couch in the front room. She was bundled in her fuzzy robe. I moved past quietly and out the front door.

The sun was just up. I drove pale unpopulated streets. It was Monday.

Eventually I parked, and I swayed out of the car with the big book still in hand, and I rang the bell half a dozen times in a row, then started banging on the door, hard. It was a sturdy door, but of course it was the strength of the lock that would matter.

I finished hammering. I stepped back onto the yellow stones and gauged my stride. I would take two momentum-building steps, then stomp my foot on the wood immediately next to the knob. I would give it everything I had. I gathered a breath.

The lock slid and clicked. Chloe pulled open the door. She wore white satiny pajamas. She looked a bit disheveled and rudely woken, but even at this hour she still appeared nowhere near her right age.

I strode into the house, pushing her aside with my shoulder and upper arm. I bumped some piece of furniture, and something broke across the floor. I entered the study.

I hadn't looked at the titles of the books on her three full bookcases when I'd visited before. I looked now. Lots of psychology, lots of philosophy. I moved to the next case. Religions. At the third, I started pulling out the books. Cabalistic symbols on the covers. Some of the books were old, some very cheaply printed. *Wicca* flashed at me repeatedly among the titles as I swept books off the shelves. They thumped the hardwood floor. I was still holding *Septem* in one hand. That hand was shaking. So was the other as I finally snatched up one of the volumes from the shelves I was ransacking. A spiral was drawn on its cover. There was also the word *Witchcraft*.

When I spun around, Great-Aunt Chloe was standing in the doorway into the study. She was composed but not unaffected by my display. Worry and maybe even fear showed in her striking blue eyes.

I thrust both books out toward her. "Did you do it? *Did you?*" I wouldn't have recognized my own voice.

"Nathanael ..."

"No! I don't want to be calmed down. I don't want cleverly worded evasions. I want you to answer!"

"Then you should ask a question." Her voice was rough with sleep, but she put an edge on it.

"Did you do it? Did you make my father into ... into a witch?"

Chloe's response was unexpected. She put back her tousled white-haired head and laughed. It was hearty and genuine.

I lowered my hands. The books dangled at my sides.

She brought herself quickly under control. When her eyes met mine again, there was compassionate pity in them. "Oh, you're so wrong. You're miles off. Heavens, I didn't know ..." She was shaking her head.

I found it comforting. I liked that there were things in my head she knew nothing about, though it certainly didn't erase the shock she'd given me on my last visit, when she handed me that check meant for my unborn son. I looked at that substantial check only once before filing it in my briefcase and sliding that case under the bed.

"Are you going to ask if I'm a good witch or a bad witch?" There was no trace of irony in her voice.

"Are you a good witch or a bad witch?"

"I'm a good person. That makes me a good witch. The two don't separate."

"How do you define good?" From one of the other rooms I heard a cat meowing.

"I try to do good deeds," Chloe said. "I prefer that to fighting evil."

"Subtle difference."

"The hell it is."

I was no longer shouting. Somehow it was very difficult to raise my voice with those eyes on me. But she still hadn't answered my question, so I asked it again. "Did you ... did you *influence* Father? Did you"—I held out the book from her shelves on Wiccan practices once more—"fill his head with this stuff?" I held up *Septem*. "Did you give him this book?"

She looked at the leather-bound volume. "No. I have, however, read it. The fact is, I never actually gave your father any books. He did make a thorough inventory of my library once, though."

"You did influence him," I said.

Chloe sighed. She raked fingers through her hair. "Enlarge that far enough, and we're all influencing each other. Every time we meet. You influence me, I influence you ..."

"I don't want your influence." The unwieldy anger that drove me into this house at this early hour was gone; I reverted to a more familiar device—coldness.

She shook her head minutely, as if pitying me all the more.

"I didn't make Ward into a witch." Chloe took a step into the room. "Your father had basic abilities ... and a very distinct aptitude. They were completely natural talents. That's really what you must understand. There was nothing *un*natural about what he did. It was all according to his nature."

I dropped the Wicca book onto one of the reading chairs. I held on to *Septem*. "What do you know about what he did?" My voice was an icy rasp.

She made to come another step closer, then saw it wouldn't be a good idea. She stood still, folded her hands and said, with a great deal of tenderness, "I know about Ward and the table. When you were eight years old."

Suddenly, it seemed that Chloe's standing in the study's doorway meant she was blocking my exit, my escape route.

"Did he tell you about it?" I could barely put any breath behind the question.

"No. Your mother did. Though she didn't have to."

"I don't want to talk about this." Now I was sure I was speaking too softly to hear.

I was wrong. She said, "Yes, you do. You came all the way to San Francisco from New York to confront this."

I backed away and bumped the other chair. I sat, feeling weak from more than just lack of food and sleep.

Chloe came forward and carefully knelt in front of the chair. Her eyes, so near now, burned gently through the darkening haze I felt closing around me.

"Why did it frighten you so badly?"

My fingers clutched and tightened around the aging leather surface of the book I'd spent the night reading.

"Lifting a table is a parlor trick," she said.

Muscles jumped at random in my back. I'd really done a job on it. "It was no trick," I whispered. I hate sleight of hand. I hate card tricks, hate disappearing hankies, hate bouquets of flowers that turn into doves. It's cheap, and it's stupid. But Father hadn't used any such "magic" that day. I was absolutely positive of it.

"No," Aunt Chloe agreed. "Not a trick. Not a wise thing to do either. Not a mature thing. It *was* something he regretted, though. He regretted it very much."

I dropped my eyes to the book in my lap. "I read about ... about the—the—the Majik of Sevens." I wanted to speak in a colorless monotone. If I was going to address this, I wanted to do it unemotionally, on my turf. But I was shaking now, deep in my bones.

"*Septem* is the definitive book on the subject," she said, sounding a bit rueful. "It would've been best, of course, if it had never gotten into circulation."

"I didn't believe what I read," I said.

"It doesn't matter if you believe. Someone else who read it did believe. And they were that drastic rarity able to work the metaphysical apparatus."

The text hadn't been what I'd expected. It wasn't full of New Agey gobbledygook or impenetrable occult musings. Actually it was quite straightforward in its way. It took many of the reader's beliefs for granted, but then, who other than a true believer would be reading such a thing?

Who indeed?

In fact, the how-to manual prose was so unpretentious that the book didn't date itself in any way. It might have been written five years ago; it might have survived multiple retranslations since the fifth century. That the copyright said 1933 was virtually irrelevant.

"Why did that table frighten you so badly?" Chloe asked again.

I felt warmth on the back of my hand. I'd squeezed my eyes shut. I opened them now, saw that she was gently touching the back of my hand, just like Mom was in the habit of doing. I snatched the hand away.

"Frighten me? Yes. Indeed. It frightened me. Eight years old. Eight. A table lifts off the floor there in front of me. It's a big table. A big, very heavy table. I used to try lifting the legs when I was a boy, pulling on them one at a time with all the strength in my little body. I could barely budge it. Father didn't have that problem. I watched the table when it rose, and I watched his face, and I knew he was doing it. There was no doubt. I also knew that what he was doing wasn't possible. I was eight. I knew about gravity. I also knew about inertia and a lot of other basic concepts of physics. I was a very smart kid, and I thought very cleanly and clearly. The world was full of wonder and mysterious adult things, but I was satisfied I would eventually be able to figure it all out. Everything in that world was within the realm of logic. Nothing was outside it."

I'd stopped shaking. I felt my nerves calming, and it wasn't the composure of detachment, of deliberate indifference.

"That ended. For me it ended, that day. What could I trust after that table? Nothing in my schoolbooks could rationalize what happened. Nothing in the logical world, in which I felt at home, could offer any explanations. After that, I thought, maybe the sky wouldn't be blue anymore, maybe water wouldn't flow downhill. And even when I saw that they still did, I wondered if maybe *tomorrow* they wouldn't. I was frightened. Yes. I stayed frightened. And I did not trust."

I lifted my eyes and met Chloe's.

"If I was on a high-wire, the net had just been cut from under me, permanently." It was a bit of imagery I'd worked repeatedly into the garish self-indulgent short stories of my adolescence. If Mom—the only one who read those stories, not counting the magazine editors who wisely rejected them—ever understood the allegory, she'd never said.

When Chloe pried one of my hands from the book and pressed her strong fingers around it, I let her.

"What your father did was wrong," she said in that tender voice. "But you, Nathanael ... you reacted very poorly."

It jarred with the compassionate expression on her aged but firm features.

"You've lived your life as a *response*," she continued. "Whatever Ward was, you weren't. Whatever he did, you went the opposite way. You got a different education than he did. You married differently than he did. You both wanted to be writers, but you made it a personal competition. And you wrote differently than Ward—wildly, carelessly—while he wrote simply and sincerely. And what happened? You both failed."

I nearly asked how she knew about what I'd written; then I decided not to ask.

"Your trust was violated, Nathanael. Yes. But you've lived a life devoid of spirituality ... by which I mean, empty of life's best ingredients. Charity, camaraderie, all the diversities of love."

"I loved my wife," I said, wincing at the defensive tone of my voice.

"And now you don't."

"And now I don't."

"But you can love your son," Chloe said; and after that, she had to hold me as the leather-bound book slid off my lap to the littered floor and my body nearly followed.

∽⧜∾

She told me what Father had done. She reiterated that it didn't matter if I believed or not.

I asked her what she'd meant the other day about time running short, though I could guess by now, which was why I wasn't surprised when she explained it.

I helped clean up the mess I'd made. She got me to sit and drink a cup of tea, which I suspect was laced heavily with herbs meant to knock me out. But I still had a mile or two to go before I slept. I drank the tea down like Rasputin, gave Great-Aunt Chloe a fierce hug and a kiss, then excused myself and, taking Father's copy of *Septem* with me, left her in her Glen Park sanctuary.

THIRTY-SEVEN

WARD: The Herd

BEFORE I LEFT THE CAR, I folded my notes and the articles into one of the cargo pockets of my rain parka.

Now I leaned on the white-painted fence and stared at the pastoral scene. Most of the cattle I read about were in sight, with some more over the hill, but in the same grazing land. These were the prized bovines of which the *gentleman farmer* was so proud. In the larger magazine article, entitled *How Now Gold Cow?*, the writer made a point of Rudolph Pring's sentimental attachment to his four-legged money makers. With everything faultlessly logged into the appropriate herd books, along with supporting certification on every animal, the herd was a money machine in perpetual motion. The Pring herd served to sell semen, embryos, and calves, shipped to buyers all over the world.

I was almost ready.

Pushing back my sunglasses, I took out the sheaf of papers and separated my notes from the articles. There were only four double spaced pages. When the formulas had been reduced to the written word, something meant to be spoken aloud, they were not complicated at all, and I expected to have no trouble saying them.

I looked carefully all around as I prepared to cast the spell. It was just me and the cattle. Nevertheless, both articles said that the land was heavily patrolled.

I took a deep breath before I began. The book made the point that spell casting was not recommended for those with any kind of speech impediment. I wondered if that was behind the medieval barbarism of cutting out tongues? Then, speaking slowly, in carefully measured cadence, I recited the four pages of words that were the spell. They were not in some strange argot, but in standard English. They followed a logical sequence, and with my experience of table levitating, I could see that they appealed to the same forces, although they displayed a more conscious knowledge of them.

As the words rolled off my tongue, the pasture changed before my eyes. The grass and the cattle seemed to darken. Then I realized that it was just a seeming. The color was not *in* the grass or the cattle. It was *over* them, a canopy of the lightest lavender that began about a hundred feet above the pasture and shrouded everything with a gentle hue. It didn't do anything. It just hung there. As I watched, a small pickup truck came roaring over the hill on the dirt road just outside of the event. It appeared that he intended to enter the affected area. Before that happened, a tendril of lavender extended from the main colored mass and the truck stopped. Even though it must have been going at forty miles per hour, it just stopped. No skidding. No items flying from the back seat into the windshield. No whiplash. No inertia. The driver sat there looking perplexed.

The color was becoming thinner. It took a minute to disappear. When it was gone, the cattle were no longer there.

The spell worked, and the safety measure against outside intrusion that was an integral part of it worked flawlessly. I walked casually back down the slight grade to where my car was parked. The guard—if that was what he was—in the pickup truck, was still gathering his senses as I left. I'd not physically hurt him, or anybody.

I am certain that I was unnoticed.

When I reached my car I put the day pack, parka, sunglasses and baseball cap back into the trunk. My notes and the articles were returned to the briefcase on the front seat.

I sat there for a while before starting the car, half waiting for the enormous energy drain that felled me after the Civic Center garage spell. It didn't seem to be coming. I followed at least one admonition when I'd cast this spell—one that came from Aunt Chloe. *I followed the directions.* There's a lot to be said for that.

As I drove back the way I'd come, one thought kept recurring to me. What would Aunt Chloe think of what I'd done?

When I arrived home, Marge had been up for a couple of hours and Nate was incommunicado in his storeroom office. I could hear his printer grinding away. I knew he was writing fiction these days, short stories. He was flexing his imagination, which was what had been behind that incident with the table those years ago. He was even submitting his stories to magazines. But I hadn't read any of that fiction. I hadn't been invited to. Nate showed some of that work to his mother, and she told me something of it. It sounded like dark, gruesome, early adolescent stuff, but I *still* would have liked to have seen it, to perhaps comment on it and share whatever it was that I knew about writing with him.

But Nate wasn't going to let me read a word of it, of course. And I wasn't going to come to him, hat in hand, asking.

Right now, I was practically dying with the need to tell someone about my accomplishment.

The excitement hadn't grown less on the ride home. My attention had wandered from the road, time after time, whenever I saw a County Police car or a Highway Patrol vehicle. I don't know what I expected, but I thought at the very least the Army, Navy, and Marines, should have been deployed along Sir Francis Drake, considering the magnitude of what I'd perpetrated.

Instead, the ride was uneventful to a fault, except for my really bad driving. At last, just before I crossed back onto U.S. 101 South, I was able to wrench my attention back to reality and complete my trip in safety.

Marge looked at me curiously as I made a cup of instant coffee and started to carry it and my briefcase back to my office.

"You're not going to tell me, are you?"

"Tell you what?" I asked.

"Where you went this morning," she replied.

"I've been to Marin County." I placed the briefcase and my coffee cup on the kitchen table. "Would you like to hear about it?"

"Does this have something to do with the computer work you've been doing for the last week?" She sat down at the table opposite me. "Is it magic stuff?" There was some fear in her eyes when she said it, but she met my gaze unflinchingly.

"It has everything to do with the computer work. In fact, it wouldn't have been possible without the computer," I said. I smiled broadly. "Yes, Marge, it was magic stuff, *successful* magic stuff. *Without* repercussions."

"Ward, what did you do?"

I opened the briefcase and withdrew the articles. "Have you seen these before?" I asked her.

Marge examined the articles.

"They're not there anymore," I said.

"What!"

"The cattle aren't there anymore. They're gone, and I did it."

"How did you do it?" she asked.

I fanned the spell papers across the table. "This way," I said.

"I think you better see Aunt Chloe."

"You don't want to hear about it?" I asked, feeling somewhat chagrined.

"It frightens me, Ward."

"Then maybe I *had* better see Aunt Chloe. I won't scare her half as much as she scares me."

"I thought you liked her," said Marge.

"I do."

She shrugged. "I talked to her last week. She's in town for a few months."

"In that case, I'll call her and get ready for my scolding."

"That's a great story title for you, Ward, if you ever take up writing again—'Scolding the Wizard.'"

"I love your sense of humor," I said. I stuffed the papers into my briefcase. I took it and my coffee into the office.

My big moment really fizzled. Perhaps I should go and make Nate's computer disappear. Now, that would give him a reason for his icy attitude.

What was happening to me? I'd never thought that way before. Had I become impressed by my own greatness? And what had I done—really? I'd done nothing on my own, certainly nothing to brag about. *I'd followed directions. No more, no less.*

I picked up the phone, dialed the number, and prepared for my scolding.

It took four rings, and I was just about to hang up when I heard the familiar voice. "Hello."

"Aunt Chloe, it's Ward. Can I come over?"

"Right away," she said. "I'll put on lunch. You do want lunch?"

I glanced at my wristwatch and then at the battery operated office clock. It was twelve thirty-eight by both of them. "I'm looking forward to it," I said.

It took me several minutes to make up my mind whether to bring my notes or the articles. In the end I elected to bring both of them and take my chance of being lectured.

Marge kissed me goodbye.

The midday sun was muted by the tree cover and I found a nice, shady place to park on the quiet little street that was so much like a country lane.

Her front door was open and I entered without hesitation, closing the door behind me. It sounded like she was in the kitchen. I advanced towards it and entered the room just in time to see her letting a large, gray tomcat out the kitchen door.

"My poor, dear Ward," she said.

That was my scolding? "It's nice to see you, Aunt Chloe."

She noticed the briefcase under my arm. "Is that what I think it is?" she said.

"I cast the spell this morning and there were no repercussions," I blurted out.

She smiled. "Perhaps we should sit down while we discuss this," she said.

I took a seat at the kitchen table while she made some last minute adjustment to whatever was simmering on the backburner of the stove. "It won't do to have it boil," she said. "The recipe calls for a slow simmer for half an hour."

I automatically checked my watch. That's how time was for me; if I didn't monitor it carefully, I lost all track of it. I couldn't even remember now what it'd been like before my alcoholic fit so long ago, when the normal time sense in my brain had been fried.

"Now, what have you been up to?" Chloe asked.

I opened the briefcase and spread all the papers out on the table.

"You used *majik* for revenge?"

"Somebody had to do something," I said.

"It would have been done anyhow," she said. "In the great balancing out, everything is paid for."

"I didn't want to wait."

She didn't comment on that. Instead she asked another question. "You used *Numbers 1-6* for the spell?"

"How did you know?"

"Please, Ward." She smiled at my question.

"It's a safe spell," I explained.

"No, Ward," she said. "Understand this. *There are no safe spells.* Spell casting is dangerous, all the time, very dangerous."

"But you use it," I said.

"Not as much as you might think," she said.

"You know what people are thinking."

"I'm a good listener," she said. "I pay attention to what people are saying and how they say it. If I can see them, I factor in their expression, their body language, and their breathing. I do all this in seconds because I have been practicing for years. You don't need a spell to hear or see."

"I'm confused," I said. "Why should there be books on the subject, if we are not meant to use them?"

"There is no meant to use them or not meant to use them. That's a childish notion. In one translation or another, those books have been around since man learned to write. The people who wrote the books were genetic freaks. They were among those wild anomalies nature comes up with from time to time. If they are evolutionary leaps forward, their kind hasn't quite taken hold yet. Just as likely, of course, is that they're dead ends of evolution. Impractical. Unwieldly. I am not one of those."

"Then how do you do what you do?" I asked.

"I don't use those books because I can't," said Aunt Chloe. "I use a natural majik that is available to anyone who believes they have the power. I use it to make things better for people. That's all it really is good for."

"Are you saying I am one of those genetic freaks because I can make it work?"

"No, Ward," she answered. "I am saying that, for whatever reason, genetic *or* spiritual, you have an ability that is not shared with anyone."

"No." The fear in me grew and grew.

She looked at me tenderly and reached across the table to capture my right hand and caress it. "My poor, dear Ward," she said again, "you are the most dangerous man on the planet."

THIRTY-EIGHT.

NATHANAEL: Phone Calls

I BREATHED IN THE SALTY AIR. I noticed for the first time that it was markedly cooler today. October was through. Mid-November would bite the city, then December would usher in the long gray of a sullen snow-less winter.

New York's winters are white. Its other seasons also are their proper colors, even in the steel and concrete maze of the city.

The variety of people on the beach was no different than from my two previous visits; there were merely fewer of the joggers and Frisbee throwers. Maybe the city was collectively hung over from the Halloween revels of last night. Again, I went down to the water, and again, I stepped out of my shoes, rolled up my pants' legs, and let the Pacific wash over my feet. A strand of seaweed came in with the first wave and manacled my ankle. I shook it off.

Gulls cried nearby. The ocean brought something small and dead onto the sand. It struck me as fitting that whatever it was wasn't going to waste, and the thought made me smile.

Surely that was some bit of homespun spiritualism left over from my contact with Aunt Chloe.

I punched the only Rhode Island number programmed into my phone. The Purple Witch's answering machine—the message it played couldn't have been more pompous if it had royal trumpets blaring behind it—picked up on the fourth ring. When it did, I cut the connection. Then I hit the redial. Hung up on the machine again. Redialed. Hung up.

Eventually I made enough racket in that house with the yellow shingles and the Cantonese character painted on the front door. In the eight months of our collaboration she'd told me dozens of contradictory definitions for that symbol. Christ, now that I thought about it, it might not even have been Cantonese.

The ringing stopped. The line engaged. She knew my number, knew it was me calling.

Just returning the half a hundred pages you've left for me over the past week, my dear.

I heard the unhealthy wheeze of her breath. I heard the insane anger in it, even before that breath turned into words.

"God! Damn! You! *Fairy!*"

If one were to drag, say, an ancient gas-guzzling Cadillac to a high peak of the Rockies, invest it with a human voice, then shove the car down the sharp stony mountainside, it would, on the way down, probably sound much like what I heard pouring from my phone.

She wanted to know where I'd been and why I hadn't responded sooner. But before that, she wanted to tell me how useless I was, how incapable. All of that, however, got mixed up with paranoid ramblings and some out-and-out babbling. She screamed everything. Even the puffing of her cigarette was a furious sound.

Irene I. Isis habitually calls me "fairy." This isn't any indicator of my sexuality. She might as easily have picked "virgin" as her pet insult for me. It was the mentality of a twelve-year-old bully that governed her actions and supplied her vocabulary.

Whatever curious shred of sympathy I'd experienced for this woman while at George Starks' home had plenty of time to utterly disintegrate during her diatribe.

I didn't stand there and take it. I didn't try to outshout her. I said into the phone, steadily, over and over, never raising my voice, these words: "I found George Starks."

And eventually she shut herself up.

She spoke once more in that eerie, little-girl-lost, voice. "Georgie?"

"Yes."

"Is ... he ... there?" How frail she sounded. He must have meant something to her—truly meant something—though imagining the Purple Witch possessing genuine warm-hearted feelings for someone was perhaps a bit beyond my creative capabilities.

"No," I said.

"Where ...?"

"He's living here in the city. He's very happy."

"Happy?"

"Yes," I said. How far did I want to go with this? I could tell her about the August Purity books (maybe she knew about those); I could tell her about Dorothy Shields (had Dorothy been part of their old New York crowd?). Maybe I could hurt the Witch with some of this news.

I shook my head.

"George Starks is very happy," I simply repeated.

"But—but *I want to talk to him!*" It wasn't her normal, thunderously demanding tone. It was the pre-tantrum whine of a child.

"He gave me no sign that he wanted to talk to you." It seemed there was no need, after all, to go out of my way to hurt her with the truth.

"Bullshit, fairy!"

"It's true," I said quite indifferently. "Also, he didn't see how he could help us with our book."

"Help ...?" Despite the volume at which she'd been shrieking earlier, she sounded very much like I'd woken her up. Awakenings for the Purple Witch could be unpleasant episodes, particularly if she wasn't sufficiently detoxified.

"You sent me out here," I said, "because George Starks, you claimed, was the *key*. He was the—how did you put it?—the Rosetta Stone. He was going to fix our book for us, somehow." She didn't remember. Her sending me across the breadth of the continent on a manhunt simply slipped her semi-demolished mind.

"Bullshit," she said reflexively.

"It's true," I said in the same indifferent tone.

"You"—she sucked savagely on her cigarette—"you lie. You lie so much. I—don't—believe your bullshit! I ..."

"The deadline for our book is a month away, Irene."

"I don't *care* about deadlines!"

"I do. Tell me. How can we finish our book on time and at the right length? How?"

"You child. You pathetic smudge of a boy. You untalented little ..."

"Do you think we can finish it? To the publishers' specifications. Can we, in one month?"

"I've faced down editors before! They mean *nothing*."

I hadn't received any advance on the six thousand dollars I would be earning for the book. I would owe no money to the publishing house if the novel didn't materialize. I would only be stigmatized throughout the field for nondelivery.

The Witch claimed that New York was replete with aspiring (read: "wannabe") writers, like myself, who would give their right arms to coauthor a book with her. No doubt, she was right. But any writer professional enough to recognize her reputation for what it was would not, under any circumstances, have entered into the alliance I had. Irene I. Isis wasn't a genius. She'd hit big with a single book. A person had a better chance of winning the lottery and being struck by lightning within the same hour. So, her luck was noteworthy. Nothing else was.

Imagine what the New York literary circles would think if they knew she hadn't even written that single book.

"Can you give me a straight answer?" I asked. "An honest, realistic, one."

How do you *know* the leopard can't change its spots, unless you ask it?

"I can do anything I want," she declared, and that, in its way, answered everything.

More gulls were wheeling, settling over the dead thing a hundred or so yards off to my left. Beaks flashed on fast necks.

"You never appreciated the privilege you had," said the Purple Witch. She now adopted a self-righteous disappointed tone and was actually carrying it convincingly. "You were lucky. Incredibly lucky. How often in your life do you think you'll be given an opportunity like the one you've had? It'll *never* come again. It shouldn't've even come the one time! You don't appreciate. You don't respect the honor of it. I chose you. I allowed you to participate in the greatness. You never understood the magnitude, the eminence, the distinction ..."

I was the wayward one. I hadn't given the book—or her—the appropriate respect. Rightfully, I should be ashamed of myself.

She might even have carried this argument through with some dignity, if not logic; but of course, she couldn't preserve a single mood for any length, to say nothing of a line of reasoning, even a faulty one.

So, soon: "Damn you to hell, fairy! You sniveling, snot-nosed, second-rate ..."

"What about the book, Irene? What do we hand to the publisher on December 1st?" I wasn't trying to get a realistic answer from her anymore about the feasibility of meeting the deadline. Our book was dead. Now it only remained to arrange the funeral.

"I'll hand those greedy bastards a pile of ashes!" she screeched.

"What do you mean?" I asked tonelessly.

"I'm going to *burn* the goddamn thing! You hear me, fairy? It's going to burn. Burn! BURRRRRNN."

It was as she'd threatened to do many times over the past months, mostly as a means of terrorizing me. It was why the manuscript pages that emerged from the Smith Corona always stayed there at her house, stacked on the desk.

And because any other thing I might have said could possibly have led her to reconsider the idea, I said, in my very best schoolyard standoff voice, "You wouldn't dare."

She, naturally, told me she *would* dare, she *did* dare. She raved. She dropped the phone. I heard things crashing around in that yellow-shingled house in Rhode Island.

Finally, a white-hot gibber loose in her voice, she came back on the line and said, "There! It's happening, fairy. It's burning. And you can't stop it. You're through! Do you hear me? You! Are! *Through!*"

Indeed I was.

"Very well, Irene. I've only got one last thing to say to you." I hadn't rehearsed this in my head, and it struck me the very instant I spoke that I'd just tipped my hand fatally, that if she wanted to do me one final cruelty, she could right now hang up the phone. Thereby giving herself the last laugh.

I also realized in that same instant that I didn't honestly give a damn.

The surprise was that she said, "Go ahead, fairy." And there was fear in her voice, beneath the sneering fury. Real fear.

Because, abruptly, she didn't know what she was going to do without me.

I said, "You're a lousy writer."

The Purple Witch wheezed in a seething breath, meaning to expel it as more abuse, more insulting insanity.

I clicked the line dead.

∽

I phoned Janeane, who would be teaching her high-schoolers in Brooklyn right now. Luckily, Suzette didn't pick up; and I realized then that I'd no idea what Janeane's girlfriend did for a living. But if she was going to play a role in my son's life—even just as a background player—I was going to have to get to know her. Whether either of us liked it or not.

I left a message on the machine about the check Chloe had written. I also ended, then and there, the juvenile game of chicken my wife and I had been playing for some months now. I said the word *divorce*, and I was the first one to say it. So, I lost the game. But I said it calmly, reasonably, and I briefly explained, though it didn't really need explaining, why it would be for the best.

My goodbye was very cordial.

∽

The Witch raved against computers as tools for writing merely because they weren't in common usage when *Everyone Goes Away* was being written. Her outrage had no basis. It had no more relevance than any middle-aged person railing against the peculiar accoutrements of the latter-day culture. It only pointed up the decrier's fundamental fear of change and its portents of personal obsolescence.

So I'd been allowed only to do work on her old Smith

Corona there at the house. No copies were permitted. Her threat of burning the manuscript had to be absolute.

She didn't understand microtech. It was much easier for her to simply dismiss anything that made her culturally uncomfortable.

So it'd been decidedly easy to smuggle in the text scanner—since the device was neatly hidden when it lay in my palm—and to record the pages as they were produced. I'd even saved those that the Witch had torn out of the typewriter's roller in my mid-keystroke. I'd started my clandestine campaign of preservation early on, even before I'd realized the depths of her instability and malignancy. I'd simply been unable to abide the thought of my words being destroyed … words I was putting together according to the Witch's instructions, yes, but *my* words nonetheless. A small prideful part of myself wouldn't accept the erasure of anything I'd created.

Thereby, every discarded page and chapter, every one of the book's abandoned subplots—those whimsical and those, perhaps, worthwhile—was safely preserved as a computer file. I had that file with me on my laptop. I also had backup copies at my apartment in New York.

I had a month to work with the material. There was more than enough to reach the book's contractually obligated minimal word count. I needed only to shape the mass into a coherent story, along the lines I'd discussed with George Starks. It wouldn't be easy. Time was tight. I wasn't sure I had the skill. But perhaps I deserved the chance to try.

All the while, I'd been standing, leaving deepening footprints in the wet sand, and feeling the foam break around my ankles. All the while, I'd had Father's leather-bound copy of *Septem* tucked under my arm.

Now I strode forward. The water crashed higher up my legs, spattering my pants, then soaking them as I waded further out. The day's mild chill and the iciness of the water brought out gooseflesh. The outgoing tide pulled at me. It was insistent, but I stayed upright.

When I was waist-deep, I halted. I turned at the hips, cocked my arm like a discus thrower and hurled the book as far as I could manage.

I nearly did lose my balance then as the undertow hauled against me; but I stood and watched the book which meticulously documented the Majik of Sevens as it bobbed briefly on the surface, looking much like driftwood. Then a wave smothered it under, and I never saw it again.

I waded out of the surf, onto the beach, grinning, tired, dizzy. My clothes were wet and heavy.

A jogger slowed long enough to scowl prissily at me and say, "You couldn't find a garbage can?"

I grinned all the brighter at him. He had that archetypal look of a transplanted San Franciscan who'd come to the city with money, an attitude, and within six months was calling himself a native.

I collected my shoes and staggered steadily toward my car

—⊗—

THIRTY-NINE

WARD: The Goodbye

I DID NOT WANT TO BE the most dangerous man on the planet. I wanted to be Ward Pentecost, husband to Margot, father to Nathaniel, File Chief at the Hall, and recovering alcoholic. For now, I did not want to hear about or think about Rudolph Pring, his band of merry men, or his prized cattle.

Those thoughts crossed my mind as Aunt Chloe released my hand and went to the stove and prepared to serve the aromatic dish that'd been simmering throughout our conversation.

"Ward, will you get two soup bowls?" she asked. "The silverware is in the drawer over there." She pointed to one of the many cabinets. "Better get spoons *and* forks."

We needed the forks. This was no broth. Aunt Chloe's dish was half stew, half soup and all delicious. I felt calmed and energized by the time we'd finished.

"We'll have lots of time to talk," she said as I took my leave with the usual bag of cookies. Nate had always enjoyed her cookies. I wondered if stone-faced *Nathaniel* still would.

I would soon find out. I turned the car around and headed for home. The late afternoon had turned gray as I parked in front of the house.

Nate was busy with his computer in his office and Marge was out visiting her mother, according to the note in front of the coffee pot. I went to the refrigerator and got a carton of milk. I drank two glasses while eating two of the cookies.

Then I went to my office and stretched out on the sofa, intending to take a short nap. Marge would certainly be back by the time I woke up.

When I opened my eyes I was immediately conscious of two things. Someone'd covered me with a blanket, and it was dark outside. I fumbled for the nearest lamp. The clock above my computer console said three ten, presumably in the morning. What morning? I felt a stab of terror. Had it happened again? Then I realized that I was still in my office in my house on Santiago. This wasn't a hospital room. My clothes were not a hospital gown. My heart stopped racing and resumed its measured beat.

I got unsteadily to my feet and went out to the kitchen. There was another note in front of the thermal coffee pot.

Dear Ward, it said, *I made a pot of decaf just before I went to bed.*

The note said nothing about food. I was suddenly very hungry. Safety factors notwithstanding, spell casting requires large amounts of energy, even when it is done according to directions. I was too tired to cook and looked around for something to munch on. We are not very big on munchies, preferring to take our calories at meals. Aunt Chloe's cookies? I opened the cookie jar. It was empty. I guessed Nate still liked them. I wonder how he reconciled his taste for my spaghetti with his attitude towards me?

I poured a cup of the decaf and made myself a salami and cheese sandwich. A half hour later I went to bed.

Another gray morning greeted me when I opened my eyes shortly before noon. I put on my robe and made my way to the kitchen. Marge placed a frying pan on the stove and was frying bacon. A bowl on the sideboard contained three eggs.

"Good morning," she said. "How did it go with Aunt Chloe?"

"I wasn't scolded, I said.

Marge kissed me lightly on the lips, a peck really. "Should you have been?"

I grinned. "As soon as I glance at the paper and catch the noon news, I'll let you know."

"You never watch the news," she said.

"I'll force myself."

The bacon was removed from the pan to drain on paper napkins and the three eggs were broken into the pan. The aroma made my mouth water.

A few minutes later I was staring at the steaming plate in front of me. A piece of buttered toast had been added.

Marge had already eaten breakfast, but she filled two cups of coffee and sat down across from me. "I looked at the paper," she said. "There's nothing about magical events in it."

I was startled. "No?"

She shook her head.

"It might be listed under something else," I said.

"For God's sakes, Ward, what else could magic be listed under? I checked and there isn't anything."

"There has to be something," I insisted.

Marge left the table for a minute and returned with the very big Sunday morning newspaper. She dropped it on the table. "Help yourself," she said.

"Thank you." I finished my bacon and eggs. "That was delicious," I said.

She didn't stand there watching me as I took my time thumbing through the paper. In the back news section I found the story and started to laugh.

Rustlers in Marin County was the heading. I laughed again when I saw that the lone witness—the pickup truck driver—was being tested for substance abuse, after he told his story of the lavender haze. I did not laugh at his description of the day hiker, although I was thankful for the sunglasses I'd worn, and that I'd parked a distance from the event. Authorities had checked with the Point Reyes staff but the description was too vague. Everyone wore sunglasses and a baseball cap.

Marge moved so that she could read over my shoulder. "You did that?" she asked.

My moment of recognition finally arrived. I nodded my head, grinning broadly. "With my own little spell book," I said, suddenly more interested in Ward the Wizard than Ward the husband, father, etc.

"You didn't have a coma this time," she said.

"No," I said. "That happened because I didn't really know what I was doing the first time."

"I understand that," said Marge, "but are you going to keep on doing it? I'll tell you up front, Ward. It frightens me very much, and if you have any sense, you should be frightened yourself."

My moment of triumph was short-lived, and perhaps that was right. I'd gotten even after a fashion with Rudolph Pring. Why not let the whole thing go and dare to be average, as Bill Berry said long ago? A part of me wanted very much to be *average*.

"I'll stop," I said.

The story was a three day wonder. On Wednesday, when I checked, there wasn't even a mention of it.

Time began to move swiftly again. My job hadn't changed, even though there was a new mayor in power. I had become an institution in City Hall. I knew where all the information was, and as a corollary, I knew where all the bodies were buried. I never abused that power or used it to threaten. As a result of that attitude on my part, I was considered an asset by each succeeding administration. I tried to be just that. I still disliked being the boss, though.

My home life had changed also. I chalked it up to some witch-like intervention on Aunt Chloe's part. I never questioned her about it, but the problems with lovemaking lessened, rather than increased as I aged. My body functioned as it might have with some external encouragement, although there still wasn't any of that. Marge was set in her ways, and I couldn't fault her for that. But she was also happier, and the frustration, which dogged my days and nights, disappeared. I not only felt better, but I felt *male* again. It was wonderful!

What was not wonderful at all was the state of society in general. After the horror of 9/11, the country'd been caught up in hysteria. Anything that *promised* to prevent a reoccurrence of the event was swiftly enacted into law, without discussion or debate. Fear and repression rode across the United States unchecked.

On the surface it didn't affect me or my family. But some of my friends lost their jobs as the wealth of the country migrated to the rich, away from the middle class. These were the new thoughts that kept me awake some nights. Other nights, sex drove such bleakness from my mind.

But not far from the conscious part of the mind were the nagging questions about how long this would last. Would there be a future for my son, or for Bill Berry's three children?

Would there be a future? I remember my mother telling about the nationwide fear, when nuclear war seemed imminent. People dug hopeless shelters in their backyards, made hidey-holes in their basements. Contrived complicated plans to escape from the city before the bombs struck—and in San Francisco, stuck out on a peninsula, that is quite a trick.

Nate graduated from high school, not marginally like his father, but at the head of his class scholastically. Socially, he was regarded as a bit of a cold fish. He wasn't unpopular, but lacked the necessary degree of warmth to draw many to him. He was respected. His teachers wrote enthusiastic letters to the college of his choice, just as they attended the graduation party hosted by Marge and myself, and managed to drink the bar dry. Considering their salaries, who could blame them?

I got by on bottled water, and, thanks to a connection in the kitchen, several pots of dark roast coffee. Nate handled himself well and socialized the right amount of time with everyone, except me.

Marge raised her eyebrows the fourth time my son passed me without acknowledging my presence. When she stepped toward him to comment on the obvious slight, I shook my head. I didn't think it would help. It might make matters worse. Besides, what had he done that he hadn't been doing in one form or other for ten years?

I was becoming tired of the whole charade. If Nate wanted to go on playing his game, he would have to play it without my participation. I knew that Marge spent a lot of time trying to get him to change his attitude, and I'd been grateful for the attempt. Now, I thought that it was wasted time.

On the last week of August the house was in an uproar as Nate prepared to go away to college. Thanks to Aunt Chloe's money, wisely invested, also according to her, there was never a question about being able to afford the schooling, including residential expenses for the entire four years.

It almost seemed that Marge was going instead of Nate, because every time I saw her she was carrying something of his. I'm certain I saw the same pile of sweaters packed and repacked at least three times. He was enthusiastic in picking out the things he wanted to take. High on the list was the new laptop computer I'd purchased, for which I'd received the usual, "Thank you, Father." The warmth of it did not overwhelm me.

As the week drew to an end the chaos became manageable, and then organized. Marge and I would soon have to face what parents faced before us for centuries. What would we do now?

The ideal answer was that we would take care of each other. It would be an interesting subject to bring up at an AA meeting.

Finally, the day arrived.

Nate's excitement was evident in his expressions, his body language, and his nonstop dialogue with his mother. He planned to take a shuttle to the airport in preference to being driven by Marge and me. Although I was caught up in the same excitement, it was as an outsider. Marge was busy being the mother and I was busy being an onlooker. I had no resentment at her for the situation. I would not have wanted her to behave differently.

We moved to the front of the house and I helped bring down the luggage. Most of the stuff would be shipped after he was domiciled.

Suddenly, the shuttle came around the corner and it was goodbye time. Marge kissed her son goodbye with much weeping. I turned and went back into the house.

FORTY.

NATHANAEL:
Undertow

I GLANCED AT MY WATCH JUST OUTSIDE THE HOUSE, feeling that something was out of joint, something wrong with the sunlight. Perhaps my jet lag was still nagging me. My watch automatically reset itself, but I hadn't noticed yesterday. Daylight-saving time was over. The clocks had all fallen back. Back on standard time.

The memory radiation was visible now. It soaked from the house's seams as I approached, and when I put my key into the lock and pushed open the door, it streamed onto me. It was white, black, red, blue, everything. It had texture now as well. I waded against it, feeling its living silkiness on my body.

Disappointments over my rejected short stories, moody teenaged days and nights, clipped conversations with Father devoid of all warmth, punishing him endlessly for the profound mistrust he'd invested me with—it washed me, like the ocean would have done if I'd lost my footing in the surf when I'd thrown *Septem* into the waves.

And like the oceanside, where a short while ago I'd settled accounts with Irene and initiated the formal end of my marriage to Janeane, there was an undertow. I felt its strong pull. Of all the places in this house that held memories, it was of course hauling me toward the dining room.

But Mom appeared in the foyer, blocking my way.

The stricken look in her eyes gave way to immediate worry when she saw the state of me. I was unkempt, unshaven. My clothes were wet and sprinkled with sand. I hadn't slept or eaten since yesterday, and today had already been a long day. But it wasn't over yet.

"I didn't mean to give you a scare," I said. Then I smiled.

It must have been a rather ghastly smile. Mom said, "Nathan, were you...in a mishap?"

Laughter suddenly unknotted itself in my chest. I imagine it was even more unnerving than my smile, judging from the expression on Mom's face. I couldn't help myself. I felt this same urge sometime recently (I remembered—when I'd told George Starks that the book with Irene "wasn't going well") but hadn't acted on it. Now, doing so, it felt good. But once more I was excluding Mom. She deserved to be let in on the joke.

"Yeah. I had a mishap. C'mon, I'll show you."

I strode into the front room, through the sliding doors that were standing wide, and entered the dining room. I turned, with my arms spread.

"I had my mishap right here, about nineteen years ago."

Mom, of course, followed me, and the concern she wore on her face intensified.

"My father—your husband"—how easily it was coming, words I'd never spoken before—"he demonstrated to me that reality was poppycock. Right here, with this table. It was a watershed moment. What came before was that part of my life where I got to be a child. Granted, something of a snobby intellectual little brat—but a genuine *child* nonetheless, one who could discover the wonders of the world bit by bit and be assured that they'd stay the same from day to day. What came after was everything else, and that's the child—and the teenager, young adult, and adult—who disappointed you so badly, who treated his father so coldly. I remember screaming that day. Did I scream?"

Mom said, "You screamed."

"I thought so." I swept aside an edge of the white lace tablecloth and planted my hands on the slightly oily mahogany surface.

"We should've gotten rid of this thing," she said, shaking her head, looking at where my hands met the table. "Should have chopped it into kindling."

"It would've been too late," I said, meaning it as a comfort. I was still on my feet, but I was reeling, seriously lightheaded now. The undertow sucked me into one of the chairs, and I found myself in the seat Father occupied that day. My hands remained on the table surface. I had images, strobed mental snapshots, of the movements he'd made, the basic mechanics. It seemed, really, a simple thing at the time, though no less frightening. Actually, maybe it was because it seemed so simple that it was also so drastically terrifying. That simplicity precluded any sleight of hand trickery. I'd watched Father's face, seen him turn his concentration inward, seen—somehow—the *connection* ...

"He was so sorry for what he did, Nathan."

"I know."

Warily she sat opposite me. It was the chair I'd occupied that day, in my eighth year. Her gray eyes shone. Her jaw trembled slightly.

"*Do* you ...?" she asked fraily.

I let my hands relax. Whatever Father had done that day, I couldn't duplicate it. I wasn't interested in trying to. Chloe explained Father's awesome and appalling uniqueness to me. It wasn't something I could have inherited.

I attempted another smile. My damp clothes were drying on me, and I itched here and there.

"Ask me what I've been up to," I said.

"What have you been up to?"

I didn't tell her the specifics of my day. Instead, my answer was broader. "I've been writing a book."

Mom nodded slowly.

"No," I said cheerfully. "The real thing this time. With a book contract with a real publishing house. It's supposed to be in collaboration with a woman named Irene Isis."

She was, I realized, wondering if I was babbling nonsense at this point. I couldn't much help how I looked or sounded, but I could, finally, speak the truth.

"She's a semi-famous author," I said. "I saw my association with her as my big break. I was very excited by that prospect. I've never given up the idea of being a professional writer. Not with those endless rejections of my short stories. Not with those books I could never finish writing. Not even with a wife who was absolutely unsupportive of my work. I kept that dream alive."

"I'm glad you did," Mom said. "I always liked your work."

Incredibly, she wasn't merely humoring me. I felt a rush of warm gratitude.

But I still had a truth to tell her.

"Irene's a demanding woman. She demanded something of me. She wanted me to prove I was different. That I had something *exotic* to bring to our partnership. I had to give it up ... to her ... had to. If I wanted to work with her, if I wanted to move into the field professionally ... I—I—I. I ... had ... to ..."

Dry-mouthed. So dry-mouthed I couldn't swallow.

Mom held the tears in her eyes, held her jaw even. She asked quietly and firmly, "What did she make you do, Nathan?"

I spoke through the terrible dryness.

"I told her that my father was on the Golden Gate Bridge when it disappeared. When I did that, she allowed me to become her collaborator on the book."

It was, arguably, the worst thing I'd ever done in my life. It was also a betrayal of the pledge Mom exacted from everyone in the family—the promise never to exploit Ward Pentecost's tragedy. Everyone else, so far as I knew, kept that pact.

I watched my mother absorbing it. The smile was long gone from my face. I felt intense shame and guilt ... but, no matter how she would respond, I had the spiritual satisfaction of unburdening myself, of admitting I'd done wrong. It certainly wasn't an experience I'd often had in my life.

Finally Mom said, "That was wrong of you."

"Yes. It was. I'm so sorry for it. If I could, I'd undo it."

She was once more nodding slowly. "But then you wouldn't be writing this book?"

It wasn't necessary just now to tell her what a disaster that book had become ... or about the slim possibility of redeeming it.

"I don't care," I said. "It was a mistake. A stupid blunder. Worse, it was an offense." I was feeling the righteousness of my repentance. I could understand now why some people found it intoxicating.

"Yes, Nathan. It was all that. But—you said it was your opportunity? Your big break?"

"I thought so at the time."

She eyed me a bit quizzically. "Do you still?"

I considered. "If it gets handed in on time ... yes. I think so. But the deadline's tight." It would come as quite a shock to Irene when she learned that she hadn't possessed the only copy of our novel. Probably she would renounce it. She might even be so unhinged as to try to block its being published. (She wasn't short on crazy; that was for sure.) But once that commodity was in an editor's hands—a semi-genuine Irene I. Isis novel!—it would be very difficult to pry it away. She might eventually see reason ... or get a taste of that new revenue. Christ knew her earnings off her first book, no matter how shrewdly she'd strung out the profits, couldn't sustain her forever.

And what about me? What would I get from the book, besides the six grand I'd contracted for?

"Will it lead to other things?" Mom asked, as if following my thoughts. Maybe she'd inherited some small part of Aunt Chloe's talents. Maybe she was just a mother.

"It could," I said. "Handing it in on time and at the right length would give me some professional credibility. It would certainly make getting something of my own published that much more feasible."

"Then maybe it wasn't so bad," she said softly.

I blinked.

"Using your father ... as a bargaining chip. It *was* bad. Wrong. But—if good might come from it, especially something like this, like real success for you at your writing ... then it's not so bad. Your father always wanted you to succeed."

"Did he?" I was caught quite off-guard by that.

Mom nodded vigorously. "Oh my, yes. Very much."

"But I never showed him my work." The last thing of mine he'd seen was a miniature essay I'd painstakingly printed in my old composition book. It was entitled "Moving Day," and it was about the epic journey of our family from 25th Street in Noe Valley to Santiago and the Sunset district. I'd been eight.

"It didn't matter. He was still proud."

I sat there, as though waiting for her words to be translated. Father, *proud* of me?

"I suppose ... I shouldn't be so surprised. Should I?"

Gently her head shook. "No. You shouldn't."

I thought again of *The Toll* and of that forlorn character's lonely vigil guarding the Bridge. I thought of the other stories I'd pulled out that box in the basement. Father's stories. Images from them, scenes and snatches of dialogue whirled slowly around me now. They were vivid, as alive as the memories that this house was keeping.

Jesus, I was tired. I should also get some food into me. But I still had news for Mom, and now might as well be the time.

"Mom, I've got something to tell you. I only found out about it a few days ago...."

"Yes?" She was waiting patiently.

Suddenly my smile returned. It pulled wider, into a grin, and a hot giddiness surged through me. I had thought a lot about the thing I was about to tell to Mom—thought pragmatically and sensibly—but this was the first time I was consciously, deliberately, happy about it. And I *was* happy. It felt very right to be so.

I said, "You're going to be a grandmother."

I cleaned up, I ate, then I collapsed into bed. I woke up in the evening, my time sense askew, partly from the setting back of the clocks. I did know the date, though; and thereby I knew tomorrow's date.

A slight chill seeped into the house. I put on my shabby sweatshirt and wandered downstairs, following the smell of coffee. I found Mom on the phone and backed out of the kitchen to give her her privacy; but she waved me in, finishing up the call with, "Okay, Bennet, yes, bye-bye."

I crossed to the coffee pot.

"Sleep well?"

"Yes." I filled a cup; it was a fresh pot, not reheated from morning. I regarded Mom. "Is Bennet going to the ceremony tomorrow?"

"No. I've invited him, but he doesn't want to be an intruder."

I thought it was understandable why he might feel like one. I also thought it was decent of Bennet to give Mom the space for this occasion to publicly observe the loss of her husband.

"Are you coming to the ceremony tomorrow, Nathan?"

I took a sip of coffee. I vacillated about it for a week; but things were much different now than when I'd arrived in the city. I'd read *Septem*. I didn't know if Mom had. I wasn't going to talk to her about the Majik of Sevens.

I'd never attended the Memorial Society's annual observance at the Bridge site.

"I'll come with you," I told her. She smiled and started putting dinner together, humming intermittent happy noises over her impending grandmotherhood.

FORTY-ONE

WARD: "The Girl Who Loved Basil Rathbone"

SEPTEM.

I held the large book with the leather-tooled cover in my hands. Its dimensions and weight seemed to affirm its mystic status, as if to say, "This book is important."

Fred, of Fred's Used Magazines and Books, bought a collection of old books at an estate sale, and while there were several boxed original editions of classical fiction, *Septem* was the odd part of the rest of the odds and ends. He knew I was interested in such things, especially since my purchase of *Numbers 1-6*. He called me and offered it at a reasonable price.

Buying the book seemed in no way to violate my stated intention to give up spellcasting. It was simply a way to round out my collection.

I thought that it would make interesting reading. My thoughts already ran along mystic channels and it might be just what I needed to bring my mind back into focus. In the two years Nate had been away at his New York college, I'd let myself become mentally lazy. Work, old movies, and AA meetings seemed to dominate my life, with very little time devoted to reading. Perhaps that was because the current crop of post-Armageddon books was slim and mostly done in a modernistic argot that turned me off.

I'd already worn out two copies of *Lucifer's Hammer* and two copies of *Earth Abides*, both fortunately replaceable. My tattered paperback of Pat Frank's *Alas, Babylon*, however, was irreplaceable.

I paid Fred and headed home with *Septem*, and a mint condition copy of Eric Frank Russell's extraordinary *Wasp*.

Marge was out shopping when I got home with my loot. Somewhat sneakily, I placed the copy of *Septem* on the lowest shelf of my office bookcase. I placed *Wasp* in plain sight on top of the computer console. Then I wandered out to the kitchen.

It was one fifteen in the afternoon. Should I wait for Marge to come home, or should I cobble some lunch together from leftovers? I decided to wait; made myself a cup of coffee and took it back to the office.

My eyes kept going to the lower shelf of the bookcase. *Septem* was really a handsomely bound book. I ended the suspense by picking it up and skimming the list of contents. It was more complex than I anticipated. However, with *Numbers 1-6* to fall back on, I figured that with a lot of time and a lot of hard work, I would be able to decipher it. "Then what?" I asked myself out loud.

No answer to that one.

Learning for the sake of learning is always an answer, I amended, even though I knew that it was often just an excuse, like in the old days when generations of teenagers "read" *Playboy* for the articles.

Septem had no illustrations, even though I'd hoped for some woodcuts illuminating certain passages. I moved from the computer console to the sofa, turned on the floor lamp, and settled back with the book.

It was complicated, yes, but it was also fascinating. This old volume was a look into the mindset when people saw spirits everywhere, a time of dragons.

My medieval fascination was interrupted by Marge's voice. "Did you get anything good at Fred's?" she asked.

In my surprise—I hadn't heard her enter the room—I slammed the book shut, looking, I suppose, like a kid caught with his hand in the cookie jar.

"On the console," I said, "a mint copy of *Wasp*."

"That's nice," she said. "It's one book I would like to read over." She looked down at the heavy leather volume in my hands. "What's that? A new dictionary?"

"It's big enough," I said. I smiled. "It's a companion piece to something else."

"What?"

"*Numbers 1-6,*" I answered.

"Isn't that the one you used when you ..."

"... I didn't buy it for that," I interrupted. "I just need the mental exercise." I hoped my reason didn't sound as weak to her as it did to me.

She turned and walked to the door. "Come to the kitchen whenever you're ready to eat." She left the room.

I put the book back on the lower shelf.

It was decision time again. I hadn't had many of them in my lifetime, and I always dreaded them, because like almost everybody else, I almost always made the wrong one.

Was I going to go out to the kitchen and have a late lunch with Marge and put the book out of my mind, or was I going to stay here and pick up where I'd left off?

For the first time in my life I was able to see the two choices that faced me with clarity. It was obvious. The real question was, why hadn't I seen it before?

I went out to the kitchen, my step quicker, my voice heartier and my complexion youthfully flushed. "What's for lunch?" I asked.

Marge turned to look at me. What she saw was a different man than the one she'd left in my office ten minutes ago.

"Sandwiches," she said. "Bacon, lettuce and tomato." She smiled. "If you're nice about it, I could be persuaded to throw in some sliced avocado."

"I'll be glad to persuade you any way I can."

"Is that a promise?"

"If you're not cooking the bacon, why don't we save it for dessert?"

She turned off the stove burners in two graceful movements. I took her arm.

It was a wonderful afternoon. Even the sandwiches were wonderful an hour later.

We don't smoke, but we both are avid coffee drinkers. I'd gotten the habit when I used to write at all hours of the day and night. Marge contracted the habit from me, but she drinks more decaf. I preferred dark roast, sometimes with a pinch of chicory.

Today, in a mutual warm afterglow, we nursed our cups and let ourselves enjoy our own company.

"Have you given any thought to writing again?" she asked me.

I hadn't given it any thought since 25th Street. I told her so.

"Maybe you should," she said.

"It was so discouraging," I said.

"You're not a bad writer, Ward."

"According to some editors I'm not any kind of a writer."

"It's not how you write that's the problem."

"Tell me more, Madam Editor," I said.

"You can make fun of me if you want, Ward," said Marge. "But if you let yourself go instead of being so logically perfect ..."

"... like Nate," I interjected.

"In a different way. Concentrate on the emotions. Nobody cares how smart you are. They want to read about *people*, not *characters*."

One of those cartoon light bulbs must have appeared above my head. She might be right. Oh, forget the pride! She was right.

"That Golden Gate Bridge story you wrote, the science fiction one—that was good. I got feelings from it."

"It wasn't good enough."

"But I bet it was for technical reasons. You had a genuine human protagonist."

"I remember," I said. "I liked him. I *felt* for him." I reached across the table and squeezed her hand. "Thanks, Marge."

From the way I felt, dinner would be late and tomorrow I would sleep very late.

∽

Sunday morning I didn't get up until just before noon. I was well-rested and more satisfied than I could remember being in years. Marge was at church, so I made myself a cup of instant coffee and a piece of toast and marmalade.

Writing. How long had it been since I woke up thinking about it? Too long. But considering my new mindset—courtesy of my wife—possibly just the right amount of time. I lingered over the coffee and toast with thoughts of my one-time avocation.

I was fifty-three years old. At this stage, for how long would I have to sell short stories before I achieved sufficient success to have book publishers notice me? But I'd *never* sold. Yet even so, I learned something of the trade, simply from hacking away at those stories for so long. I'd been like a competent house painter who only painted homes in one color scheme, which nobody liked.

Today I was going to enlarge my palate. I was going to use all the available colors. What had been a stifling, boring box of colors, would become a rainbow. I would view the world through a prism of light.

I was not having what they used to call "book dreams"— that is, daydreams of an improbable success. I wasn't thinking in the distant and frustrating long term, like I always had before. Forget about becoming a successful *writer*, and just *write*, just this one story. I even knew the title of my new first effort, a post-Armageddon short story with a very catchy title.

I hurried to my office and booted up my old favorite word processing program, WordPerfect 5.1. The familiar screen never looked so inviting. I began.

The Girl Who Loved Basil Rathbone
By
Ward Pentecost

La was only half a name. The other half, something sumptuous, unpronounceable and African had been given to her by her father along with the disease of the immune system she had been born with. There had been some hope of a cure before those final days when the bright nights came and the bombs fell.

She was nine years old yesterday. Ma had scavenged the cake from a store freezer that still operated. Together they had donned party hats, lit the nine candles and made as merry as they could. There were just the two of them in the whole city.

Pa had run before the bombs fell. His activism, which had caused him to give her the unpronounceable name, was symbolic rather than real. "I believe in survival," he had said on the way out the door. "My survival."

That had been a week ago. For some reason the bombs had

spared the power and some of the lights remained. Perhaps they were smart bombs designed to kill people and spare the real estate, Ma had said.

Four days ago Ma had gone scavenging for the first time. She returned with a backpack crammed with canned goods and a canvas carryall full of videotapes. "I passed the video store and this is all I could find, Honey," she said. "I hope you like them."

That was how La fell in love with Basil Rathbone.

I continued to type like a man obsessed—maybe because I was. The painfully learned formulas and plot skeleton fitted themselves underneath the prose, invisible to the eye, yet holding the whole structure perfectly together.

The videotapes were all of the old black and white Sherlock Holmes films: *The Voice of Terror, Escape to Algiers, The Spider Woman, The Hound of the Baskervilles, Dressed to Kill*, and more.

I raised a few false hopes, a voice in the distance that was probably the wind, and eventually came back to La watching the films, her interest turning into fascination and finally into affection. The stories were old-fashioned, some of the characters were right out of the cookie cutter school of screen writing, but Basil Rathbone always came through with his incorruptible professionalism. La's favorite part of all the movies was that two minute period at the end of some of them when Holmes would make some stirring speech to Watson, usually about the inevitability of right winning over might.

These were not corny to La. When you are young and dying, such sophisticated thoughts do not occur. He simply lifted her out of her despair and transported her to a place of hope and decency, a place where America did not try to "liberate" one oil-producing nation too many.

The end of the story was simple. La asked her mother to play one last tape. Watching it, she died with peace and dignity and hope.

It was eight thirty in the evening when I got up from my chair and stretched. Marge heard me and was at the door when I turned around.

"I saw you were working," she said.

"It wrote itself," I said.

"Long day?"

"No," I said. "A good day. The best day." I looked at the screen. "I've never written that many words at one time before."

"Is it saved?" she asked.

"Hard drive and floppy," I answered.

"Can I read it?"

"Please do," I said.

Marge took my vacated spot. I leaned over her and backed the story up to the beginning. Then I went out of the room.

She found me in the kitchen. Her eyes were red and puffy, but she was also smiling. "Beautiful," she said.

The next day, after work, I picked up a newsstand edition of *The Writer's Digest*. It had a notice of a new small press, slick paper magazine that would accept submissions from new writers only, and none electronically.

I printed, enveloped, stamped, and deposited the story in the mailbox before dinner.

FORTY-TWO

NATHANAEL:
Bridging the Gap

THE MORNING STARTED OUT WARM, then wind chilled the city. It was true San Franciscan weather—that familiar 55° to which the thermometer so often dips—and the reason it's rarely a good idea to leave the house without your jacket, no matter how deceptively inviting things temporarily feel outside.

Mom wore a smart dress of dark blue and pearl gray. I was neatly dressed and groomed as well. We headed out at quarter to three, not trusting the traffic.

We had a sticker for the windshield that Mom received along with the reminder from the Memorial Society the other day, and with it we were waved into a reserved lane of Park Presidio Boulevard that was guarded by orange cones and police on motorcycles. We were escorted all the way to a lot for Bridge personnel where olive drab military vehicles were parked. No doubt it was where the toll takers and executives and maintenance crews once parked when there was a Bridge.

A National Guardsman with somber eyes formally checked our IDs, then we started across the toll plaza on foot.

It was a different scene than when I'd visited a week or so ago. Many people showed up ahead of us. Many were sporting those familiar loops of reddish orange ribbon pinned to their lapels—symbols of ... well, I don't know what. Ribbons weren't going to bring back the Bridge. Mom didn't wear one. The grassy common and the area surrounding the Memorial were cordoned off. More police were guarding those perimeters, behind which the public inevitably gathered to gawk at this affair, a private party for the immediate families of the Bridge's victims, two thousand or so people.

Everyone appeared to be behaving themselves, though. I reconsidered the presence of the public. Some, but certainly not all, would be tourists. The rest were locals ... San Franciscans come to pay their respects at the site of what, despite its absence, was still their city's most treasured monument. Perhaps they were also here to acknowledge—humbly—the fact of the irrefutable mystical event that indelibly punctuated the year 2010, dividing time for many into what had come before that day, November 7th, and what followed.

Certainly they were also here to honor the hundreds whose names were inscribed on the Memorial.

"What's with the platform?" I nodded toward a dais that had gone up next to the Bridge-shaped Memorial. Engineers were busily checking sound equipment.

"There'll be speeches," Mom said. She was holding herself somewhat stiffly, but her voice sounded natural. "The Mayor always calls for silence at 4:14."

Naturally. 4:14 PM, a time as encoded into San Francisco's collective consciousness as 5:12 AM, that moment over a century ago when a mighty earthquake pitched the city off its foundations and set it to burning. Seven years ago, on a late Sunday afternoon, there had been traffic on the Golden

Gate Bridge. But how much more there would have been if the disappearance happened, say, during the peak of Monday's commute the next morning. Just as how much worse the fires would have been in 1906 if the fire-fighting crews hadn't dynamited houses to create a firebreak.

Pessimism is a learned reflex, but I believe our first instinct as humans is to see things in their best light. It is a nature that is deprogrammed by parents, siblings, teachers, friends, lovers. These people don't all specifically intend to turn us into cynics … just as we ourselves might be acting unwittingly when we snuff out the idealism in those closest to us. The optimist is that individual who has never had any sort of relationship with another human being.

I shook my head. Christ. I was still doing it, speaking the thoughts in my head as if they were going to be set into print and read by untold numbers. How often had I integrated my sophistries into the short stories I hacked out as a teenager? How many "insights" into the human condition served as the bases for novels I'd been unable to finish?

Yet, now I had a chance. A real chance. If I could put together the snippets and aborted vignettes that were the residue of my collaboration with Irene Isis, I could produce a book. One I would receive no public credit for, but one that would be published and read and—at least by some, surely—enjoyed.

And as George Starks said to me, the writing itself was a great part of the reward of writing.

"You're shaking your head *and* smiling," Mom said.

"Just seeing the two sides of things."

"Are you now?" She lifted an eyebrow slightly.

I didn't know how deep into that she wanted to read. I said, "What do we do here? Do we sit, stand?" We'd reached the common. I could see now there was a cluster of chairs set up before the small stage.

"Those are for whatever dignitaries show up. The President was here the first year." The crisp wind stirred through Mom's red hair.

I glanced around for Secret Service agents. If they were doing their job, of course, they could be standing right next to me. There were quite a number of police. I wondered if Uncle Pete was somewhere among them. I saw a few powder blue SIT jumpsuits in the crowd. There were several news camera crews on the far side of the common.

The assembled mourners were, predictably, a perfect cross section. The Bridge, in its disappearing, had shown no discrimination. It took with it whichever luckless individuals happened to be on the span at that particular tick of the clock seven years ago, and those victims belonged to all walks of life. Here might be the husband who'd had Sunday dinner plans with his wife. Here—this woman with the bent burdened posture—might be the mother of one of that busload of Novato school kids on a special weekend fieldtrip into the city, a reward for the success of the school's canned food drive for the Bay Area needy.

And these were just the ones, like Mom and myself, who were immediately related to someone who'd vanished. How many thousands more—thousands upon thousands—were nephews and aunts, cousins, longtime family friends, lovers, best friends? How far did the ripples of this event extend, into how many lives? How much damage resulted? Lost relationships, lost opportunities ...

It opened outward in my mind. It may be that this was the first time I'd ever *really* considered what the Bridge's disappearance had done. Not just to me; to everyone. Even to those people who had no intimate claim to the event, who felt for the victims without needing to have actually known any of them personally.

As a boy, I'd seen a table levitated before my eyes, and it shattered my basic trust in reality. The world had seen the

Golden Gate Bridge vanish into nothingness. The world, more or less, absorbed the trauma and gone onward.

Many more people arrived, on both sides of the barricades. I continued to watch them. I watched the tech crew finishing with the speaker setup; watched the politicos and celebrities and other notables milling about, and I thought: it almost seems normal, routine. This ceremonial observance might be a political fund-raising affair or the dedicating of a public building for all the decorum and familiar banality of the event. No one was running about tearing at their clothes, shrieking about "God's vengeance" or the physical impossibility of what happened. That sort of behavior had been commonplace once, in the direct aftermath of the disappearance; it no longer was. These people ... the world ... *accepted* what occurred.

And they didn't even know what I knew.

Or was fairly sure I knew.

Eventually, the speeches started. Important people introduced other important people. I think one was the U.S. Vice President (I guess we didn't rate the top dog anymore); another was an aging screen actor I eventually recognized. He looked frail and rather wan in the unflattering weakening daylight, but he spoke eloquently and with much feeling. I didn't realize until the end of his comments that his sister had been on the Bridge seven years ago.

Mom and I were standing toward the rear of the assembly and to one side. She was listening politely to the speakers but not hanging on every word. Father was in her thoughts. It couldn't have been clearer if she were broadcasting those thoughts. I stood a half step behind. I held my head still, but I let my eyes move. Their gaze tracked past the Memorial, past the dais—where an archbishop (or *some*body in a mitre) was now speaking—and slid out over the water. The ceremony had been underway for some while now.

There were a lot of craft out on the Bay, but nothing was moving. All were lying to. 4:14 was creeping up, and there were probably people out there on sailboat decks, heads bared, misty eyes blurring the still awesome sight of the empty Golden Gate.

I had cried, here, at the Memorial, the day I arrived in the city. I hadn't cried for Father before that time, not even once. I don't honestly know now if I was crying for him then. It's possible I wasn't. It's very possible I was crying for me.

Across the Bay's entryway, overhung with sharp-sloped hills, was Marin County and its corresponding tongue of amputated roadway. I could just make out the assembly over there. I wondered if the T-shirt sellers were working the crowd during whatever speeches were being made. No doubt, it was a second-rate affair.

The toll plaza lanes were all clear on the far side of the rank of booths. The National Guardsmen stood in their customary places along the margin of the road. My gaze moved to where that multilane road ended—ended so completely—where the lip of the precipice was preserved, without barrier or rail ... giving full view of the spectacular absence beyond.

I heard the timbre of the Mayor's solemn words. I couldn't recall if this was the same one who'd held the office seven years ago. I didn't pay attention to the speech nor look at my watch, but I listened for the call for silence. My eyes stayed fixed where they were.

I wondered—the thought a droll tickle—if Minnie F. Tucker, author of *The Gap Through Her Heart*, was somewhere in this crowd or among those onlookers behind the barricades.

The Mayor's speech reached its grave, carefully timed, climax. I heard her say, "Now, I think it is fitting that we all observe a moment for loved ones, for friends, for our fellow human beings. Let none be forgotten or omitted as we silently reflect."

The human silence was intense. No voices, no one coughing, no one shuffling feet. Everyone was stock-still. Everyone was evidently indeed contemplating those tragically vanished hundreds and the holes they'd torn into countless other lives. On the cool wind were the distant calls of gulls.

A few seconds into the ceremonial silence I saw lavender.

It was, for that first instant, just the unexpected but perfectly explicable darkening that comes of a fast-moving cloud blotting the sun. That the air itself changed color took another second for the first of the others in the crowd to register, those obediently reflecting on San Francisco's famous tragedy. Then the silence was prematurely broken by sharp whispering. Hands lifted tentatively, fingers pointed, elbows jostled as people alerted those standing nearby. Someone cried out shrilly.

The lavender was above, but it was descending. I was watching below, at the level of the roadway. I saw the suspension cables appear—quickly, but not instantaneously—against the waning afternoon sky above the far hills. They resembled the taut strings of a harp. I looked for the massive towers, and they too returned. Specifically, I picked out the south tower, the nearer one, as the voice of the crowd now rose wildly. Beside me, Mom gasped, and her hand flailed outward. I caught it and held it without looking away from the returning Bridge, just as the proper orange-red color restored itself.

One forgets how *big* the thing is. No photograph in the world, not even one of Aunt Chloe's, could ever really do it justice. It loomed majestically. Immortally.

The inertial arrest that occurred seven years ago—which kept any vehicles from tumbling into the Bay in those first seconds after the Bridge was gone, and which was an effect almost as incredible as the disappearance itself—did not now prevent the Bridge's traffic from continuing at the very same acceleration and with the same momentum that had been moving it seven years ago. The cars started to roll off, into a toll plaza that had since become a museum, a preserved shrine ... one, fortunately, that erected no obstacles on the way to the toll booths.

I didn't watch the traffic coming off the Bridge. I didn't look toward the northbound lanes that were this instant also spilling their contents off the other end of the Bridge. I didn't hear the wild primal sounds of the crowd nor the first fumbling words of the Mayor over the speakers.

I felt Mom's fingers clutching mine with fearsome strength, and I picked out the white Dodge as it cleared the south tower and came toward the city, toward San Francisco, toward Mom and me. It was still in the center southbound lane. It was moving at a good clip. I saw the yellow plastic daisy bobbling atop the aerial.

I believe I even glimpsed the figure who sat at the wheel.

The enormous, gently hued lavender umbrella that hung over the scene vanished for several seconds; now it returned. When it swiftly faded once more, the Golden Gate Bridge went with it. So, once more, did Ward Pentecost.

The reappearance lasted seven seconds.

During the uproar, and near-chaos that followed, I held Mom tightly and protectively, and when my tears came, they were this time purely for Father.

FORTY-THREE

WARD: The Golden Gate Is Empty

LIFE HAD BECOME ALMOST IMPLAUSIBLY GOOD. My writing was going well, and although I hadn't sold anything yet, that first story of the new me—"The Girl Who Loved Basil Rathbone"—was still at the small press magazine to which I'd sent it.

My marriage had probably never been better, or more healthy. Marge and I were enjoying each other in a way that we'd never experienced before. There was an ease between us that wasn't, surprisingly enough, the ease of resignation.

I felt like an adult, in the best sense. I was mature, but not stuffy. I enjoyed what I enjoyed, and did my best to tolerate that which was unpleasant, knowing that most things were never as bad as they seemed. This was another of those deceptively simple and quietly emerging revelations that changed my life for the better.

It was into this idyllic time that a phone message intruded. I received a request to call a number back. It was not a telemarketer. They usually don't leave messages on the answering machine. I looked up the first three digits of the number in my old phone book, the one where that information was still available. The caller said it was urgent and personal, and the call had come from San Rafael, in Marin County, across the bridge.

With slight misgivings I returned the call, and my life made another big change.

His name was Arthur Flogle. He claimed that he was a witness. A witness to my parents' deaths. He wanted to talk to me about it because it had been on his mind and conscience all these years. Could I come out to San Rafael and talk to him?

I could. Of course I could. After explaining to Marge what it was about and adamantly refusing to take her with me—I remembered what happened to my father *and* mother—I drove to San Rafael.

The light breakfast I had sat heavily on my stomach. I don't know what my thoughts were as I crossed the bridge, headed down the Waldo Grade and moved closer and closer to the witness. I felt a lot more than I thought on that short ride.

I took the second Central San Rafael exit and found my way to the motel Mr. Flogle had given as his address.

There was an empty parking slot marked VISITORS. I pulled the Dodge into place and stopped short enough to set the plastic daisy atop my radio antenna to bobbling, like one of those baseball figures with the wobbly heads.

The motel was medium upscale. It had two floors and was in the familiar horseshoe shape, with all the parking in the enclosed section. When I got out of my car, I noticed that a brand new dark blue Cadillac, with local license plates, had taken up the two parking places next to me by straddling the lines. *Old money.* Yep, I was in Marin County.

I climbed the stairs to the second floor and made my way

to the room number I'd scribbled in my notebook. It was number seven.

The door was ajar, and as I knocked a hearty voice called out my name. "Mr. Pentecost. Come right in."

I swung the door open and found myself facing three men. Two of them ignored me as I entered the room. The third man, and presumably the one who'd called my name, laughed.

"Sorry you had to come all this way for nothing," he said.

I looked at him closely. He was familiar and yet he wasn't. Then I remembered. *Time changes things.* The last time I'd seen him he'd been a teenager, drunken and bloody.

"Alec Pring," I said.

He'd put on about forty pounds, fairly well-hidden under the expensive tailored suit. He had jowls, and he was going bald.

"Arthur couldn't make it," he said, wearing a grin. "He won't be making it in the future. Arthur has decided to go away."

"You threatened him."

"Money doesn't have to threaten," he said.

"Then why the company?" I asked.

"They're for you. In case you don't listen to reason."

"I'm listening."

"Good." He nodded. "Much better than your father the night he showed up at the Country Club with that old bitch."

I took a step forward. The two other men regarded me with humor. They were ready.

"Your old man thought he could shame my poppa into giving him back the money. Can you imagine that?"

I couldn't.

"I say it was an accident. The law says it was an accident. And Arthur better say it was an accident. Hell, with that much money, he'll yell it was an accident."

I glared at his arrogance.

My anger made him grin even more. "So, Mr. Pentecost, I'm telling you what my poppa told your old man and that bitch. *Money talks and bullshit walks.* Do you want to walk away or do you want to crawl away? Makes no difference to me."

I turned and left the room with the sound of their laughter behind me.

It wasn't until I reached the Waldo Tunnel and headed down the grade towards the bridge that I began to think again. My thoughts were of the color lavender.

It was embarrassing to tell Marge about the meeting with Pring. There wasn't anything else I could have done but walk. But knowing it wasn't enough. Should I have taken a beating, possibly fatal, to make a point?

She sensed my distress. "Ward, there isn't anything you could have done."

"I know," I said.

"How about some lunch?" she asked.

The ham and Swiss cheese sandwich fed my body without feeding my mind. For that, I had something else in mind.

Marge had half a sandwich and we ate in silence, both occupied with our thoughts. Mine were dark and full of revenge. I'm certain that hers were about my mental well-being.

Afterward, I did not linger as usual. Instead, I took the cup of coffee into my office. I knew what I had to do. I closed the door behind me and withdrew *Septem* from the lower shelf.

The formulas in *Septem* were harder than the ones from *Numbers 1-6* I used on the prize Pring herd. They were longer and more complicated. For the event I was going to perform—the awesome event—it would not take just four pages but several times that, if I ever got the calculations completed. Right now I was in the most preliminary of preliminary steps. It would be days before I could begin to load the formulas into a spreadsheet and start the actual calculations. I clenched my jaw and continued. The familiar mug of dark roast coffee sat at the edge of the computer console. Was it the third or fourth tonight? I concluded that it didn't matter because tomorrow was just another vacation day. I pulled two weeks of my annual six just so that I would have the time to do this.

This was not something to be done at my leisure like the last spell. Haste was a factor, although it was strictly a personal condition. As long as a connection existed between me and the Prings—a physical connection—I felt dirty, unclean, soiled.

The only thing that directly physically connected me to them, and San Francisco to Marin County, was the bridge.

Now was the time I hinted at when I spoke to the deadly Mr. Joe Pucci, in my office, those many years ago. The Sicilian man, a friend of my father, offered to do something about Pring. I recalled the exact words I used. "It will be taken care of differently."

Now it would, if I could ever figure out the damned formulas. As soon as I thought that, one of the variables suddenly made sense in my head. It was going to be difficult but not impossible. I finished my cup of coffee. It was two o'clock in the morning. I would work for another hour and then try to sleep.

Now, at last, I was beginning to enter the final formulas into the spreadsheet. It was mystic-looking. The symbols, although entered in good old Times New Roman font, looked strikingly cabalistic.

The work progressed. I was entering the last few formulas. I would finish it tonight and run the results tomorrow.

An hour later with weary eyes, I shut down the operation and went to bed. Marge was still awake, and all thoughts of spreadsheets, formulas, and admonitions, disappeared utterly as she reached out to embrace me. Sleep could wait.

The next day, I ran the formulas flawlessly and printed the results. What I had were all the specifics needed to write out the spells. To the best of my knowledge, all the variables had been resolved. Now it was only necessary to write it in script form and to begin the casting.

There was a symmetry about it. There were seven steps to start with, repeated time after time. With each repetition the spell grew in strength until it was capable of a massive dislocation. It was what I wanted, the thing that would distance me from the Prings and their old money, from their vulgar, obscene tongues. It was a quarantine.

The rules were different this time. I actually read the Admonition to the Unwary, although I skipped the Admonition to the Impatient again when I was referred to it.

This was not a spell designed to perform one relatively simple thing, like the one I used in western Marin County. This one would take seven days in a row to cast, and I didn't have to be there physically. I would need a photograph of the structure with which to focus my energies and the vastly stronger energies I would be channeling.

Now I felt like what Aunt Chloe called me. *The most dangerous man on the planet.*

It was relatively easy to type out the spells. It merely took a little while. I made a special note to highlight the "return spell," which, after the first seven years, when the structure returned briefly, could keep it in place. It had a window of seven seconds in which to be cast. If I missed that one the next opening would be in forty-nine years, with the same number of seconds to work with. I didn't calculate after that, but it would be whatever the last opening was times seven—to infinity.

It was my intention to restore it after the first seven years. By then, the damage to Marin County would have been done.

Tomorrow, October 31st, I would begin. I scarcely noticed that it was Halloween.

∽⊗∾

The days went swiftly. The nights were the best I'd ever experienced. During that period, I achieved the dream of men throughout history. I was blessed with the vigor of a seventeen-year-old, combined with the wisdom of fifty-three years. I appreciated my wife as I never knew how to before. The feeling was reciprocated.

∽⊗∾

On Saturday, November 6th, I cast the final spell. I felt the power flow through me and then launch itself northward. The time was five fourteen in the afternoon. According to my homemade spellbook, it would be exactly twenty-four hours before the effect would take place.

That night was the best of all.

Sunday morning, I rose early, feeling relaxed and refreshed. I brewed myself a cup of dark roast with chicory and carried it into the office. Even before I'd begun to cast the spells, I'd decided upon these actions.

I took everything I'd ever printed on the subject of majik and ran the papers through the shredder. That included everything in my old briefcase. I erased all the spreadsheets and anything else that applied to the subject from the hard drive of my computer.

It was all clear now. There was absolutely nothing that could trace the event back to me.

Still basking in the afterglow of last night I sauntered out to the kitchen and joined Marge for breakfast. She had the same lazy, contented look about her that I once noted on Eileen Berry. We held hands across the table.

"There's a letter for you in the dining room," she said.

"When did it come?" I asked.

"Thursday afternoon. It was stuck in the pages of a catalog."

I got up from the table and went to get it. The white envelope bore the letterhead of the magazine that I'd graced with my story. So, I'd written my best for naught. Not today, I thought. This was not going to be a rejection day.

I went to the bedroom and opened the closet. My gray tweed jacket was hanging there and I deposited the letter in its inside pocket. It might make amusing reading after the event.

Then I tried to fill up the rest of the day. I stalked through the house all morning. In the early afternoon after I turned the television on and off for the twentieth time that day, Marge suggested I might want to go out for a while. When she suggests in that tone of voice, I usually take heed.

I did exactly what I wanted to do all day long, but hadn't admitted to myself. I drove out to the bridge. I could see the morbid anticipation in the act, and I was powerless to stop it. The Dodge guided itself out to the toll plaza, and kept on going across. I was a passenger in the driver's seat. I swear, I was driving and I was not driving. My eyes took in the *immensity* of the structure. The international orange towers seemed to brush the sky. The long deck leaped in a graceful arc across the Golden Gate. It was awesome.

At four o'clock in the afternoon, I pulled into one of the parking slots at the north end of the bridge. I reached into my jacket pocket and withdrew the letter I placed there earlier. It wasn't amusing at all.

It read:

Dear Mr. Pentecost,

Your story "The Girl Who Loved Basil Rathbone" has to be the best short story I have read this year, bar none. For your information, my wife is still crying over the ending, and I can't think of it without getting the sniffles. In the writing trade clever is easy, negative is easier and honesty is the hardest of all to write.

The honesty of "Rathbone" glows in the dark. I don't know anything about you, but please keep up the work.

Please sign the attached contract and return it. We pay upon publication.

Amos Markell

Editor

I was breathless as I reread the letter. It'd finally happened. So many years I'd been trying. I had to tell Marge! She alone would know what this meant to me. The tires flung gravel as I exited the parking lot and got in line for the underpass and the drive back to San Francisco.

What was I doing here anyhow? My stomach sank. I looked at the cars lined up in front of me, and it occurred to me that *people* would disappear with the bridge. Whoever was on the span when it happened would pay the price of my revenge. Of course, I'd already known that. But now, suddenly, the reality was driven home like spikes into flesh. What right did I have to do this? I'd justified it the way a drunk justifies one more drink. What had I done?

Then I was through the underpass and San Francisco bound.

The time was four ten PM. I wanted to get home. I wasn't going to watch the event. I wanted to climb into bed and pull the covers over my head in shame. I could not undo the spell. I'd spent seven days casting it. It was already a reality. The real world just hadn't yet caught up to it.

The Dodge's tires made the familiar *thrumming* as I crossed the expansion plates at the north tower. There was traffic in all six lanes, plus the sightseeing pedestrians on the westward walkway, with cyclists on rented bikes weaving carefully among them. The bridge loomed all around me, a true engineering marvel that was worth a lot of its hype. It *was* an impressive architectural feat. It had a glamour, and even a melancholy, that touched the heart, something perhaps like the Great Sphinx.

And, oh, what I was going to do to it ...

It was then that the sound muted, all the sound. No more traffic noises around me. No hissing of the wind through the partially open side window. Silence.

Why was the sky changing color? The blue was changing to lavender. I felt a rush of panic. And then another part of me laughed. It was that damned time sense, the one that'd been wrecked by the long ago alcoholic convulsion. I just couldn't think coherently about time. Certainly, those days of the year when the clocks got reset—"Spring forward, fall back"—were fairly harrowing for me.

Majik time is always standard time. "MST" I thought and laughed again.

The sky was filling with lavender. The international orange color of the bridge now began to look purple.

Daylight-saving time—which ended today, I suddenly realized—hadn't existed at the time the formulas were written. At standard time it was four fourteen, not *five* fourteen, yesterday when I cast the final spell. Twenty four hours ago!

In the cars alongside me, faces looked out in astonishment but not fear. They had no idea of what was coming. Certainly not the children in that school bus that passed me seconds ago, heading north.

The lavender was dropping lower. It was almost down to the roadway. All those people. Children, fathers and mothers, lovers, husbands—wives.

Out loud I said, "Oh, Marge I love y

—◦○◦—

FORTY-FOUR

NATHANAEL: The Majik of Sevens

I BEGAN TO LIVE THE DAY MY SON WAS BORN.

So it seems, at least. So my hindsight is making it, as it lumps the Bridge's reappearance/re-disappearance, the acceptance of Irene's and my novel by the publishers who contracted for it, and the birth of my child into one epic event.

So I will tell him, Curtis Harry Youngblood, one day, when his wandering curious blue eyes focus in comprehension of the world around him, when his tireless gurgling giggles turn into language. I will say, *Son, I began to live the day you were born.*

But for the moment, he is a five month old baby, and words are just part of the fascinating soundscape that surrounds him. There will be time enough to tell him later.

◦○◦

Suzette Lasome, Janeane's girlfriend, did not get a vote back when Janeane and I decided on the baby's name. The divorce was to be finalized before the birth. Nonetheless, Janeane and I discussed the hyphenation issue. Discussed it with marked civility and maturity, in fact. In the end I couldn't see putting our son through a mouthful like Young-blood-Pentecost or Pentecost-Youngblood for the rest of his life. Further, I felt Janeane's surname had a little less unwanted oomph than mine. We hatched the name Curtis together. Its shortened form, Curt, we both judged was aesthetically forceful without being gruff. Janeane left the middle name up to me, reserving only veto power. I chose Harry, after my grandfather on my mother's side.

Janeane said that sounded good.

The publishing house wouldn't go for the title under which I submitted the book, which was *Everyone Goes To Hell*, one of Irene's many discarded working titles. I don't yet know what name it will appear under, but I do know the novel will see print. The editor handling the project is pleased with this middle-aged continuation of Rosemary Parrish's romantic misadventures. He has said he particularly liked the elements of humor, which were "insightful and honest."

I have no idea how, in that final frantic chaotic month, I managed to put *humor* into a book that, for so long, had been so demoralizing, so disheartening, so demeaning an experience.

Sometimes, it seems, you just don't know where the words come from.

I have heard nothing from Irene I. Isis since the day I told her she was a lousy writer. I've programmed my phone not to accept calls from her Rhode Island number. I haven't missed her.

∽∞∾

Mom came out East for the birth, naturally. Curtis Harry Youngblood sucked air into his little lungs on April 13, arriving in the world a day ahead of schedule. Prior to that, I'd introduced Mom to my ex-wife and soon-to-be mother of our child. It wasn't as awkward as it sounds. However, Suzette managed to be unconscionably rude to Mom, referring to her as "the breeder's mother." (I'm "the breeder," for those not familiar with anti-heterosexual putdowns.) For her trouble, Suzette would have gotten my fist across her mouth had Janeane not intervened at that moment. Later, she apologized profusely for her partner's behavior.

Mom was the only one in our little circle with actual birthing and parenting experience. Janeane, whose own parents remained out of the picture, threw herself at Mom as if she were a life preserver. They got along very well.

So, astonishingly, did we. Janeane and I were all done being in love. We did not now become friends. But we set aside our resentments, and we cooperated. It was a simple thing to do. Our child was the priority.

∽∞∾

Two weeks before my son's birth, over four days' time, I wrote a short story entitled "The Music Behind the Wall." I wrote it in three-hour blocks, after which time I started having trouble concentrating. It was the first short fiction I'd attempted since high school.

In it, a forty year old single New England woman with a teenaged daughter enters, on a kind of forlorn whim, a mail-in contest to pick that year's upcoming Oscar winners. The woman, Joyce, hasn't gone to a movie in years. By a fluke, however, she gets every guess right and wins the grand prize of a dinner in New York with a tableful of renowned film critics. At the sumptuous hotel where the dinner takes place, she sits nervously while the critics try to entertain her with their vast knowledge of movies and witty repartee. Joyce finally breaks down, admitting how she won the contest. Her apologetic babbling shifts into a tearful lament over the terrible emotional gap that has opened between herself and her daughter in the years since her divorce from her husband. Now, Joyce grieves, she is unable even to coax one friendly word from her child. All she can do is work her job at the bank, cook dinner, do the laundry and other household chores and, when she lays down to another night of brittle, lonely sleep, to listen to her daughter's stereo and its ugly violent music on the other side of the common wall of their respective bedrooms. The assembled film critics, caught quite off-guard and touched by this divulgence, try to rally Joyce's spirits by sharing similar horror stories of their own children … stories which, for the most part, have believably happy endings. Joyce goes home with the first embers of hope she has felt in some long while.

I let the story sit for a day. Then I went back into it and removed every ornate adjective and adverb that wasn't absolutely crucial. There were quite a few. The plot, however, was perfectly straightforward and as unlike any of my overwrought adolescent attempts at fiction as was possible to be. The next day I submitted it.

When Curtis was three months old, I learned that my story had been accepted at the small press magazine to which I'd sent it. It would pay one cent per word, on publication of next year's spring issue. I would earn about forty dollars. The acceptance was conditional, though, on my willingness to strike the story's entire final paragraph. I balked, automatically. Then I reread the paragraph. It was a total break in voice from the rest of the piece. It was a summation, full of literary loop-the-loops, in which I instructed the reader how to feel about what he or she had just read. It was author's intrusion at its most grotesque.

I agreed to remove the paragraph and signed the simple contract I'd been sent.

It was the first professional fiction sale that would appear under my own name.

∽

I have lately talked to other divorcés who have had similar experiences with their exes—able to get along with them in an adult manner, without lingering rancor, at the instant their divorces went through. It's a curious syndrome. For all the hurt Janeane and I inflicted on each other, it now seems to have taken place in another lifetime.

When we settled the custody of Curtis, we behaved laudably. The lawyers both remarked on it.

∽

Four hours before Curtis' seven pound, two ounce self arrived in this world, Aunt Chloe appeared. She'd just flown in from Turkey, dumped her gear in a hotel room and come to the hospital. I didn't ask her how she knew which hospital.

I was very happy to see her. So was Mom. I watched with no little awe as, in the space of about three minutes, she disassembled Suzette's hostile attitude, charmed her, and got my ex-wife's lesbian lover to join wholeheartedly in the general truce.

Chloe waited outside the delivery room while she became a great-great aunt and Mom became a grandmother.

Mom wasn't upset about Janeane's and my decision regarding Curtis' surname. That the name of Pentecost was going to end with me was eclipsed by the simple fact of my child's new life.

Besides, Father was still a Pentecost.

Janeane was a trooper throughout the birth. After several minutes of joyful coddling, she passed Curtis to me. I held him, rocked him, welcomed him to the world. He fit perfectly in my arms. Then I passed him on to Suzette.

I received lots of congratulations, though some were a bit hesitant, considering my baby was being born to divorced parents. I didn't defend myself; I didn't try to justify anything. We don't choose what we're born into, but I was determined to give my son the very best of everything I could possibly manage.

Chloe's benefaction would certainly go a long way toward seeing to Curtis' comfort. I'd told Janeane all about the money. Following the birth, with sweat-plastered hair on her forehead and her eyes bright with fatigue, Janeane, meeting Chloe for the first time, passed our son to her and thanked her, simply and sincerely. Chloe gently hushed her.

Months back, when I was staying on for several weeks in San Francisco after the second incident with the Bridge, a thought occurred to me. I pressed Mom about it, and she finally admitted that, yes, Aunt Chloe had given her and Father a similar endowment when I was a baby. Chloe was the one, essentially, who paid for my college.

Curtis has blue eyes. Their color is startlingly clear.

Seven. In Latin, *septem*.

The Bridge was gone for seven years. It reappeared for seven seconds. But that is not the end of it.

Seven times seven is forty-nine.

The mathematics of majik is as obedient as the mathematics of what most of us agree is the real world.

I still have never missed a *Diamond* deadline, though when I have Curtis, I work at some very odd hours. Sometimes I'll set the car seat up on the desk, angle the computer screen and let him watch. He waggles his tiny limbs and makes excited noises. I explain that my book reviews aren't that thrilling, but he doesn't care.

Officially, he goes back and forth between me and Janeane for two weeks' custody at a time. We both give each other a lot of slack, though. It might be a lot of work taking care of Curtis, but it is no chore.

I surprised myself repeatedly the first few times I found myself alone with my son. I discovered I had no problems changing him or getting up in the middle of the night to his cries. I didn't feel put upon. However, when I'm out in public with him, I am occasionally annoyed by the attention he'll garner from strangers. I'm not jealous of it, but some people seem to assume he is an animatronic display of some sort, to be stared at, cooed to, patted. Once, in an elevator, I told a middle-aged woman who was being intrusively doting, "Lady, get your own goddamned kid."

Why was Father on the Bridge that day, at that particular minute of that specific hour? What was he doing driving that white Dodge back *into* San Francisco? More to the point: why did he use his unique foreknowledge to include himself among the Bridge's victims?

It was not punishment. It wasn't some pseudo-suicidal gesture. I put it together eventually and was quite satisfied with my deduction.

Father and his wrecked time sense. I will never reset my clocks again without thinking of that single shifted hour.

Curtis fell fast asleep in my arms on the couch one night. The tv was on and the remote out of reach, so I watched whatever came on. Thus I found myself sitting through an old black and white film version of a Sherlock Holmes story. Liberties were taken with Arthur Conan Doyle's original storyline, but the actor portraying Holmes was surprisingly convincing. He carried himself with a sinister melancholy, even as he operated without overt displays of emotion.

I was quite taken with the performance. It was the first time I could recall ever seeing Basil Rathbone.

Last month, when I contacted George Starks, who generously put me on to an agent he knew personally, I mentioned the Holmes movie. I told him I now understood why he'd never allowed his August Purity books—all of which I'd read by then—to be filmed. Who else but Rathbone could have played Purity, a transplanted Englishman who conducted himself and his cases with such exacting logic? Out of Rathbone's narrow face I'd seen August Purity's eyes staring.

The agent came back with a good offer from a publishing house. The spate of Bridge lit following the Golden Gate Bridge's initial disappearance had never really waned, but now such books are, predictably, hotter than ever. I wrote the collection's introduction, and the book will be rushed to the stands for Christmas. The introduction is brief and about Father, and nowhere in it do I mention that I too write. The publishers wanted an additional five thousand words of story text, so I picked out two more of Father's old shorts, though neither was of the same tolerable quality of the rest in the book.

Mom described a particular end of the world story, one with a young black girl for a protagonist that actually sounded quite intriguing, but I couldn't find it among the assortment of Manila envelopes I'd brought back with me to New York. So *The Toll: The Fiction of Ward Pentecost* will have to go to print without it.

The money will go to the estate of Ward Pentecost, which will eventually translate into Mom cutting me a check for a good chunk—if not all—of the payment and future royalties. She has taken a keen interest in the welfare and well-being of her grandson.

The ones who came off the Bridge almost a year ago do not speak of limbo or purgatory or the sorts of dreams some coma patients have. They tell no accounts of their seven year absences because there is nothing to tell. They have been *nowhere*, and that nowhere is painless, senseless, without time.

The very first drivers off both ends of the Bridge all experienced the same thing. They were cruising along, everything normal, when suddenly the air turned to lavender, all sounds turned to silence, and the traffic in front of them vanished. The passage of those seven intervening years didn't register at all.

Thirty-six people in twenty-five vehicles and twelve pedestrians and bicyclists made it off during those seven seconds. I have seen the SIT surveillance footage. In it, Ward's white Dodge is going about sixty miles an hour. It moved just over six hundred feet in those seven seconds, not enough to get it from the south tower to the toll plaza. That school bus, heading north, didn't make it off the span either.

Still, the world is grateful to have those forty-eight returned.

Next month is November. Another Memorial Society anniversary looming. It will no doubt be a record turnout this year. People will flood the Bridge site; boats will cram the Bay; people will even swarm the humble Marin County side of the vacant Golden Gate. At 4:14 PM there will be silence ... but this year it will be an expectant silence, a collectively held breath, one that will possibly even be shared worldwide.

Everyone will be waiting, wondering, watching.

Will the Bridge come back *again*?

It will. But not this year and not next year. Nor the year after that.

I won't attend this year's ceremony. Maybe when Curtis is two or three, I'll fly him out for it. He does, after all, have an array of relatives on the West Coast. He ought to meet his family.

Mom's decree to the family that no one exploit Ward's misfortune is still being faithfully observed. (I am the only one who ever transgressed, and Mom has absolved me.) It was only after that frenzied last visit, when everything changed for me, that I understood the full purpose of Mom's cloak of silence.

It preserved the dignity of Father's memory. Yes, it did that. It also prevented any ambitious media people or SIT agents from ever finding a thread they might pull ... one that might conceivably unravel the tangle of magic that has bound Ward Pentecost to the Golden Gate Bridge for nearly eight years now. Mom didn't tell the Scientific Investigation Team everything she knew about her husband. Like me, she'd known what to omit.

It is better that Father be remembered as just one more victim ... not, as Chloe has explained, as history's rarest genetic oddity. And not as one whose misguided intentions resulted in such grief.

In less than forty-nine years I will be seventy-six years old. No doubt, a great, great many things will happen to me during those years. I will experience unforeseeable events that will alter me in ways I can only imagine—and then only inexactly. But whatever and whoever else I may be at seventy-six, I will still be my father's son.

I will wrong my own son. It is inescapable. Even if I were to shut myself off from him utterly, right now, I would still do damage, in the shape of my absence. Humans harm one another. They do many other things, but they *do* harm each other.

Seven times seven is forty-nine. Forty-nine years is a long time, and perhaps the gatherers at the Bridge site will be thinner by then. Surely they will. Attention will wane. Interest will inevitably wither, at least a little. But when those forty-nine years have passed, on that distant November 7th, the world will gasp anew.

Seven times seven is forty-nine. Forty-nine seconds is a long time—longer certainly than seven seconds. A great many more vehicles will make it off the Bridge that day. Father will be among them. If my estimates are right, that busload of Novato schoolkids will finally be heading home too.

None of those who return will have chosen to have lost so many years, but they will all still have the remaining time which nature originally allotted for their existences. They can make of their lives what they will.

Seven times seven times seven is three hundred forty-three, and that is a *very* long time. I pity those final souls who must wait that many years to escape the Bridge. I lament those plodding pedestrians near the center of the span who will perhaps have to wait even longer.

If I don't live to see my seventy-sixth year, my son Curtis will be there. Mom has entrusted me with a letter she has written to her husband, which I have promised will be delivered. Ward Pentecost will not be met by strangers.

Meanwhile, the Golden Gate is empty again.

THE END

ABOUT THE AUTHORS

Victor Del Carlo was born March 30th, 1928, a child of the Great Depression. In his lifetime he has witnessed vast economic, social and technological changes. Things go so fast. He waits.

Eric Del Carlo, somewhat to his amazement, has seen his fiction appear in the pages of Asimov's Science Fiction and in novels published by Ace Books. He has reaped the benefit of a lifetime of shared ideas, inspirations, and analyses with his father.